# RIZZO'S WAR

LOU MANFREDO

# RIZZO'S WAR

MINOTAUR BOOKS
NEW YORK

C.1

RIZZO'S WAR. Copyright © 2009 by Lou Manfredo. All rights reserved. Printed in the United States of America. For information, address St. Martin's Press, 175 Fifth Avenue, New York, N.Y. 10010.

www.minotaurbooks.com

Library of Congress Cataloging-in-Publication Data

Manfredo, Lou.
  Rizzo's war / Lou Manfredo.—1st ed.
     p. cm.
  ISBN 978-0-312-53805-7
  1. Police—New York (State)—Fiction.  2. Brooklyn (New York, N.Y.)—Fiction.  I. Title.
  PS3613.A5368R59 2009
  813'.6—dc22

                                                                          2009012738

First Edition: October 2009

10  9  8  7  6  5  4  3  2  1

*To my wife, Joanne*

# ACKNOWLEDGMENTS

I would like to acknowledge the following people for the roles they have played in the creation of this novel:

Joanne, my wife, my soul mate, my teammate, for her relentless assistance and encouragement throughout the process of writing and editing this book.

Nicole, my daughter, for her pragmatic editorial assistance.

Otto Penzler for getting all this started and Michele Slung for her early interest and encouragement. They may never fully understand how much it means to me.

Nat Sobel, who undertook representation of my manuscript and then showed me how to turn it into a publishable novel.

Kelley Ragland and Matt Martz at St. Martin's Press for walking me through the process with great editorial skill and much charity.

Tim McLoughlin, extraordinary author and editor. Thanks for putting me in, coach. I swung for the fences.

To the following people for the years they spent telling me I could do this. Turns out they weren't quite as delusional as I suspected. Listed alphabetically, they are: Annette Kay, Bob Kay, Ron Matthias, Janice Meizoso, Frank Meizoso, Mary Noe, Barbara Schwartz, Len Schwartz, and my most recent cheerleaders, Bernadette and Vince Lombardi.

And, of course, my parents, especially my dad, who was the force behind the magical appearance of Hardy Boys books on the table beside my childhood bed.

*The more featureless and commonplace a crime is, the more difficult it is to bring home.*

—SHERLOCK HOLMES
"The Boscombe Valley Mystery"

# RIZZO'S WAR

# CHAPTER ONE

*September-October*

THE FEAR ENVELOPED HER, and yet, despite it, she found herself oddly detached, being from body, as she ran frantically from the stifling grip of the subway station out into the rainy, darkened street.

Her physiology now took full control, and her pupils dilated and gathered in the dim light to scan the streets, the storefronts, the randomly parked automobiles. Like a laser her vision locked on to him, indiscriminate in the distance. Her brain computed: one hundred yards away. Her legs received the computation and turned her body toward him, propelling her faster. How odd, she thought through the terror, as she watched herself from above. It was almost the flight of an inanimate object. So unlike that of a terrified young woman.

When her scream came at last, it struck her deeply and primordially, and she ran even faster with the sound of it. A microsecond later the scream reached his ears and she saw his head snap around toward her. The silver object at the crest of his hat glistened in the misty streetlight, and she felt her heart leap wildly in her chest.

Oh my God, she thought, a police officer, dear God, a police officer!

As he stepped from the curb and started toward her, she swooned and her being suddenly came slamming back into her body from above. Her knees weakened and she faltered, stumbled, and as consciousness left her she fell heavily down, sliding into the grit and slime of the wet, cracked asphalt.

\*  \*  \*

MIKE MCQUEEN sat behind the wheel of the dark gray Chevrolet Impala and listened to the hum of the idling motor. The intermittent slap-slap of the wipers and the soft sound of the rain falling on the sheet metal body were the only other sounds. The Motorola two-way on the seat beside him was silent. The smell of stale cigarettes permeated the car's interior. It was a slow September night, and he shivered against the dampness.

The green digital on the dash told him it was almost one a.m. He glanced across the seat and through the passenger window. He saw his partner, Joe Rizzo, pocketing his change and about to leave the all-night grocer. He held a brown bag in his left hand.

McQueen was a six-year veteran of the New York City Police Department, but on this night he felt like a first-day rookie. Six years as a uniformed officer first assigned to Manhattan's Greenwich Village, then, most recently, its Upper East Side. Sitting in the car, in the heart of the Italian-American ghetto that was Brooklyn's Bensonhurst neighborhood, he felt like an out-of-towner in a very alien environment.

He had been a detective, third grade, for all of three days, and this night was to be his first field exposure, a midnight-to-eight tour with a fourteen-year detective sergeant first grade, the coffee-buying Rizzo.

Six long years of a fine, solid career, active in felony arrests, not even one civilian complaint, medals, commendations, and a file full of glowing letters from grateful citizens, and all it had gotten him was a choice assignment to a desirable East Side precinct. Then one night he left his radio car to pee in an all-night diner, heard a commotion, looked down an alleyway, and just like that, third grade detective. The gold shield handed to him just three weeks later by the mayor himself.

If you've got to fall ass backwards into an arrest, fall into one where the lovely college roommate of the young daughter of the mayor of New York City is about to get raped by a nocturnal predator. Careerwise, it doesn't get any better than that.

McQueen was smiling at the memory when Rizzo dropped heavily into the passenger seat and slammed the door.

"Damn it," Rizzo said, shifting his large body in the seat. "Can they put some fuckin' springs in these seats already?"

He fished a container of coffee from the bag and passed it to

McQueen. They sat in silence as the B train suddenly roared by on the elevated tracks above this length of Eighty-sixth Street. McQueen watched the sparks fly from the third rail contacts and then sparkle and twirl in the rainy night air before flickering and dying away. Through the parallel slots of the overhead tracks, he watched as the twin red taillights of the last car vanished into the distance. The noise of the steel-on-steel wheels and a thousand rattling steel parts and I-beams reverberated in the train's wake. It made the deserted, rain-washed streets seem even more dismal. McQueen suddenly found himself missing Manhattan.

The grocery had been the scene of a robbery the week before, and Rizzo needed to ask the night man a few questions. McQueen wasn't quite sure if it was the coffee or the questions which had come as an afterthought. Although he had known Rizzo only two days, he suspected the older man to be somewhat less than an enthusiastic investigator.

"Let's head on back to the house," Rizzo said, referring to the Sixty-second Precinct station house, as he sipped his coffee and fished in his outer coat pocket for his Chesterfields. "I'll write up this interview and show you where to file it."

McQueen eased the car away from the curb. Rizzo insisted he drive, to get the lay of the neighborhood. McQueen felt disoriented and foolish: he wasn't even sure which way to the precinct.

Rizzo seemed to sense McQueen's discomfort. "Make a U-turn," he said, lighting the Chesterfield. "Head back up Eighty-sixth and make a left on Seventeenth Avenue." He drew on the cigarette and looked sideways at McQueen. He smiled before he spoke.

"What's the matter, kid? Missing the bright lights across the river already?"

McQueen shrugged. "I guess. I just need time, that's all."

He drove slowly through the light rain. Once off Eighty-sixth Street's commercial strip, they entered a residential area comprised of detached and semi-detached older, brick homes. Mostly two stories, the occasional three-story, some with small, neat gardens or lawns in front. Many had ornate, well-kept statues, some illuminated by flood lamps, of the Virgin Mary or Saint Anthony or Joseph. McQueen scanned the homes as he drove. The occasional window shone dimly with night-lights glowing from within. They appeared peaceful and warm, and he imagined the families inside, tucked into their beds, alarm clocks set and ready for the coming workday. Everyone safe, everything secure.

That's how it always seemed. But six years had taught him what was more likely going on in some of those houses. The drunken husbands coming home and beating their wives; the junkie sons and daughters; the sickly, lonely old; the forsaken parent found dead in an apartment after the stench of decomposition had reached a neighbor and someone had dialed 911.

The memories of an ex-patrol officer. As the radio crackled to life on the seat beside him, he listened with half an ear and wondered what his memories as an ex-detective would someday be.

"Six-Two unit one-seven, see the uniform C.I. Hospital ER. Assault victim, female. Copy, one-seven?"

Rizzo keyed the radio. "Copy, dispatch," he said.

"Alright, Mike. That call is ours. Straight up this way, turn left on Bay Eighth Street to the Belt Parkway. Go east a few exits and get off at Ocean Parkway. Coney Island Hospital is a block up from the Belt. Looks like it's gonna be a long night."

When they entered the hospital, it took some minutes to sort through the half dozen patrol officers milling around the emergency room. McQueen found the right cop, a tall, skinny kid of about twenty-three. He glanced down at the man's name tag.

"How you doing, Marino? I'm McQueen, Mike McQueen. Me and Rizzo are catching tonight. What'd ya got?"

The man pulled a thick leather note binder from his rear pocket. He flipped through and found his entry, turned it to face McQueen and held out a Bic pen.

"Can you scratch it for me, Detective? No sergeant here yet."

McQueen took the book and pen, and wrote the date, time, and CIHOSP ER across the bottom of the page, then scribbled his initials and shield number. He handed the book back to Marino.

"What'd ya got?" he asked again.

Marino cleared his throat. "I'm not the guy from the scene, that was Willis. He got off at midnight, so he turned it to us and went home. I just got some notes here. Female caucasian, Amy Taylor, twenty-six, single, lives at Eighteen-sixty Sixty-first Street. Coming off the subway at Sixty-second Street about eleven o'clock, twenty-three hundred, the station's got no clerk on duty after nine. She goes into one of them—what'd ya call it?—one-way turnstile things, the ones that'll only let you out, not in. Some guy jumps outta nowhere and grabs her."

At that point, Rizzo walked up. "Hey, Mike, are you okay with this for a while? My niece is a nurse here, I wanna go say hello, okay?"

Mike glanced at his partner. "Yeah, sure, okay, Joe, go ahead."

McQueen turned back to Marino. "Go on."

Marino dropped his eyes back to his notes.

"So this guy pins her in the revolving door and shoves a knife in her face. Tells her he's gonna cut her bad if she don't help him."

"Help him what?"

Marino shrugged. "Who the fuck knows? Guy's got the knife in one hand and his johnson in the other. He's trying to whack off on her. Never says another word to her, just presses the knife against her throat. Anyway, somehow he drops the weapon and she gets loose, starts to run away. The guy goes after her. She comes out of the station screaming. Willis is on a foot post doing a four-to-midnight, sees her running and screaming and goes over her way. She takes a fall, faints or something, bangs up her head and swells up her knee and breaks two fingers. They got her upstairs in a room, for observation on account of the head wound."

McQueen thought for a moment. "Did Willis see the guy?"

"No, never saw him."

"Any description from the girl?"

"I don't know, I never even seen her. When I got here she was already upstairs."

"Okay, stick around till your sergeant shows up and cuts you loose."

"Can't you, Detective?"

"Can't I what?"

"Cut me loose?"

McQueen frowned and pushed a hand through his hair. "I don't know. I think I can. Do me a favor, though, wait for the sarge, okay?"

Marino shook his head and turned his lips downward. "Yeah, sure, a favor. I'll go sniff some ether or something." He walked away, his head still shaking.

McQueen looked around the brightly lit emergency room. He noticed Rizzo down the hall, leaning against a wall, talking to a bleached blond nurse who seemed to be about Rizzo's age: fifty. McQueen walked over.

"Hey, Joe, you going to introduce me to your niece?"

Joe turned and looked at McQueen with a puzzled look, then smiled.

"Oh, no, no, turns out she's not working tonight. I'm just making a new friend here, is all."

"Well, we need to go talk to the victim, this Amy Taylor."

Rizzo frowned. "Is she black?"

"No, cop told me Caucasian. Why? What's the difference?"

"Kid, I know you're new here to Bensonhurst, so I'm gonna be patient. Anybody in this neighborhood named Amy Taylor is either black or some yuppie pain-in-the-ass moved here from Boston to be an artist or a dancer or a Broadway star, and she can't afford to live in Park Slope or Brooklyn Heights or across the river. This here neighborhood is all Italian, kid, everybody—cops, crooks, butchers, bakers, and candlestick makers. Except for you, of course. You're the exception. By the way, did I introduce you two? This is the morning shift head nurse, Rosalie Mazzarino. Rosalie, say hello to my boy-wonder partner, Mike Mick-fuckin'-Queen."

The woman smiled and held out a hand. "Nice to meet you, Mike. Don't believe anything this guy tells you. Making new friends! I've known Joe since he was your age and chasing every nurse in the place." She squinted at McQueen, then slipped a pair of glasses out from her hair and over her eyes. "How old are you—twelve?"

Mike laughed. "I'm twenty-eight."

She twisted her mouth up and nodded her head in an approving manner. "And a third grade detective already? I'm impressed."

Rizzo laughed. "Yeah, so was the mayor. This boy's a genuine hero with the alma mater gals."

"Okay, Joe, very good. Now, can we go see the victim?"

"You know, kid, I got a problem with that. I can tell you her whole story from right here. She's from Boston, she wants to be a star, and as soon as you lock up the guy raped her, she's gonna bring a complaint against you 'cause you showed no respect for the poor shit, a victim of society and all. Why don't *you* talk to her. I'll go see the doctor and get the rape kit and panties and we'll get out of here. The day tour can follow it up later this morning."

McQueen shook his head. "Wrong crime, partner. No rape, some kind of sexual assault or abuse or whatever."

"Go ahead, kid, talk to her. It'll be good experience for you. Me and Rosalie'll be in one of these linen closets when you get back. I did tell you she was the *head* nurse, right?"

McQueen walked away with her laughter in his ear. It was going to be a long night. Just as Joe had figured.

HE CHECKED the room number twice before entering. It was a small room with barely enough space for the two hospital beds it held. They were separated by a seriously despondent-looking curtain. The one nearest the door was empty, the mattress exposed. In the dim lighting, McQueen could see the foot of the second bed. The outline of someone's feet showed through the bedding. A faint and sterile yet vaguely unpleasant odor touched his nostrils. He waited a moment longer for his eyes to adjust to the low light, so soft after the harsh fluorescent glare of the hall. He glanced around for something to knock on to announce his presence. He settled on the foot board of the near bed and rapped gently on the cold metal.

"Hello?" he said softly. "Hello, Ms. Taylor?"

The covered feet stirred. He could hear the low rustle of linens. He raised his voice a bit when he spoke again.

"Ms. Taylor? I'm Detective McQueen, police. May I see you for a moment?"

A light, hidden by the curtain, switched on near the head of the bed. McQueen stood and waited.

"Ms. Taylor? Hello?"

The voice was sleepy, possibly sedated. It was a gentle and clear voice, yet it held a tension, an edginess. McQueen imagined that he had woken her and now the reality was hitting her. It had actually happened. No, it hadn't been a dream. He had seen it a thousand times: the burglarized, the beaten, the raped, robbed, shot, stabbed, pissed on. He had seen it.

"Detective? Did you say 'detective'? Hello? I can't see you."

He stepped farther into the room, slowly venturing passed the curtain. Slow and steady, don't move fast and remember to speak softly. Get her to relax, don't freak her out.

Her beauty struck him immediately. She sat, propped on two pillows, the sheet raised and folded over her breasts. Her arms lay beside her on the bed, palms down, straight out. She appeared to be clinging to the bed, steadying herself against some unseen, not possible force. Her skin was almost translucent, a soft glow emanating from it. Her wide-set eyes were liquid sapphire as they met and held his own. Her lips were full and round and sat perfectly under a narrow nose, her face framed with straight shoulder-length black hair. She wore no makeup, and an ugly purple-yellow bruise marked her left temple and part of her cheekbone. She was the most beautiful woman McQueen had ever seen.

After nearly three years of working the richest, most sophisticated square mile in the world, here, in this godforsaken corner of Brooklyn, he finds this woman. For a moment, he forgot why he had come.

"Yes? Can I help you?" she asked as he stood there.

He blinked himself back and cleared his throat. He glanced down to the blank page of his notepad, just to steal an instant more before having to speak.

"Yes, yes, Ms. Taylor. I'm Detective McQueen, Six-Two detective squad. I need a few minutes for some questions, if you don't mind."

She frowned, and he saw pain in her eyes. For an instant he thought his heart would break. He shook his head slightly. What the hell? What the hell was this?

"I've already spoken to two or three police officers. I've already told them what happened." Her eyes closed. "I'm very tired. My head hurts." As her eyes opened, they welled with tears. McQueen used all his willpower not to move to her, to cradle her head, to tell her it was okay, it was all over, he was there now.

"Yeah, yeah I know that," he said instead. "But my partner and I caught the case. We'll be handling it. I need a little more information. Just a few minutes. The sooner we get started, the better chance we have of catching this guy."

She seemed to think it over as she held his gaze. When she tried to

8

blink the tears away, they spilled down her cheeks. She made no effort to brush them away, but instead looked deeply into McQueen's eyes. Despite the steely toughness of their cold blue, she saw an empathy and warmth in his expression, and it brought her a reassuring comfort.

"Alright" was all she said.

McQueen felt his body relax, and he realized he had been holding himself so tightly that his back and shoulders ached. "May I sit down?" he asked softly.

"Yes, of course."

He slid the too-large-for-the-room chair to the far side of the bed and sat with his back to the windows. He heard rain rattling against the panes. The sound chilled him and made him shiver. He found himself hoping she hadn't noticed.

"I already know pretty much what happened. There's no need to go over it all, really. I just have a few questions, most of them formalities. Please don't read anything into it. I just need to know certain things. For the reports. And to help us find this guy. Okay?"

She squeezed her eyes closed again and more tears escaped. She nodded yes and reopened her eyes. He couldn't look away from them.

"This happened about eleven, eleven ten?"

"Yes, about."

"You had gotten off the train at the Sixty-second Street subway station?"

"Yes."

"Alone?"

"Yes."

"What train is that?"

"The N."

"Where were you going?"

"Home."

"Where were you coming from?"

"My art class in Manhattan."

McQueen looked up from his notes. Art class? Rizzo's inane preamble resounded in his mind. He squinted at her and said, "You're not originally from Boston, are you?"

For the first time she smiled slightly and McQueen found it

disproportionately endearing. "No, Connecticut. Do you think I sound like a Bostonian?"

He laughed. "No, no, not at all. Just something somebody said to me. Long story, pay no attention."

She smiled again, and he could see that the facial movement had caused her some pain. "A lot of you Brooklynites think anyone from out of town sounds like they come from Boston."

McQueen sat back in his chair and raised his eyebrows in mock indignation. " 'Brooklynite?' You think I sound like a Brooklynite?"

"Sure do."

"Well, Ms. Taylor, just so you know, I live in the city. Not Brooklyn." He kept his voice light, singsong.

"Isn't Brooklyn in the city?"

"Well, yeah, geographically. But the city is Manhattan. I was born on Long Island, but I've lived in the city for fifteen years."

"Alright then," she said, with a pitched nod of her head.

McQueen tapped his pen on his notepad and looked at the ugly bruise on her temple. He dropped his gaze to the splinted, bandaged broken fingers of her right hand.

"How are you doing? I know you took a bad fall and had a real bad scare. But how are you doing?"

She seemed to tremble briefly, and he regretted having asked. But she met his gaze with her answer.

"I'll be fine. Everything is superficial, except for the fingers, and they'll heal. I'll be fine."

He nodded to show he believed her and that, yes, of course, she was right, she would be fine. He wondered, though, if she really would be.

"Can you describe the assailant?"

"It happened very fast. I mean, it seemed to last for hours, but . . . but . . ."

McQueen leaned forward and spoke more softly so she would have to focus on the sound of his voice in order to hear, focus on hearing the words and not on the memory at hand.

"What was his race?"

"He was white."

"Was he taller than you?"

"Yes."

"How tall are you?"

"Five-eight."

"And him?"

She thought for a moment. "Five-nine or ten."

"His hair?"

"Black. Long. Very dirty." She looked down at the sheet and nervously picked at a loose thread. "It . . . it . . ."

McQueen leaned in closer, his knees against the side of the bed. He imagined what it would be like to touch her. "It what?" he asked gently.

She looked up sharply with the near panic of a frightened deer in her eyes. "It smelled," she whispered. "His hair was so dirty, I could smell it."

She began to sob. McQueen sat back in his chair and held his questioning for a moment. She needed time to compose herself.

And he needed to find this man. Badly.

"I WANT to keep this one."

McQueen started the engine and glanced down at his wristwatch as he spoke to Rizzo. It was three in the morning, and his eyes stung with the grit of someone who had been too long awake.

Rizzo shifted in the seat and adjusted his jacket. He settled in and turned to the younger detective.

"You what?" he asked absently.

"I want this one. I want to keep it. We can handle this case, Joe, and I want it."

Rizzo shook his head and frowned. "Doesn't work that way, kid. The morning shift catches and pokes around a little, does a rah-rah for the victim, and then turns the case to the day tour. You know that, that's the way it is. Let's get us back to the house, write up the reports, and grab a few zees. We'll pick up enough of our own work next day tour we pull. We don't need to grab something that isn't our problem. Okay?"

McQueen stared out the window into the falling rain on the darkened street. He didn't turn his head as he spoke.

"Joe, I'm telling you, I want this case. If you're in, fine. If not, I go to the squad boss tomorrow and ask for the case and a partner to go with it." Now he turned to face the older man and met his eyes. "Up to you, Joe. You tell me."

Rizzo turned away and spoke into the windshield before him. He let his eyes watch McQueen's watery reflection. "Pretty rough for a fuckin' guy with three days under his belt." He sighed and turned slowly before he spoke again.

"One of the cops in the ER told me this broad was a looker. So now I volunteer for extra work 'cause you got your head turned?"

McQueen shook his head. "Joe, it's not like that."

Rizzo smiled. "Mike, you're how old? Twenty-seven, twenty-eight? It's like that, alright, it's always like that."

"Not this time. And not me. It's wrong for you to say that, Joe."

At that, Rizzo laughed aloud. "Mike," he said through a lingering chuckle, "there ain't no wrong. And there ain't no right. There just *is*, that's all."

Now it was McQueen who laughed. "Who told you that, a guru?"

Rizzo fumbled through his jacket pockets and produced a battered and bent Chesterfield. "Sort of," he said as he lit it. "My grandfather told me that. You know where I was born?"

McQueen, puzzled by the question, shook his head. "How would I know? Brooklyn?"

"Omaha-fuckin'-Nebraska, that's where. My old man was a lifer in the Air Force stationed out there. When I was nine he died, so me and my mother and big sister came back to Brooklyn to live with my grandparents. My grandfather was a first grade detective working Chinatown back then. The first night we got there, I broke down, crying to him about how wrong it was, my old man dying and all, how it wasn't right and all like that. He got down on his knees and leaned right into my face. I still remember the smell of beer and garlic sauce on his breath. He leaned right in and said, 'Kid, nothing is wrong. And nothing is right. It just *is*.' I never forgot that. He was dead-on correct about that, I'll tell you."

McQueen drummed his fingers lightly on the wheel and scanned the mirrors. The street was empty. He pulled the Impala away from the curb and drove back toward the Belt Parkway. After they had entered the westbound lanes, Rizzo spoke again.

"Besides, Mike, this case won't even stay with the squad. Rapes go to sex crimes and get handled by the broads and the guys with master's degrees in fundamental and advanced bullshit. Can you imagine the bitch that Betty Friedan and Bella Abzug would pitch if they knew an insensitive prick like me was handling a rape?"

"Joe, both of those women are dead."

Rizzo nodded. "Whatever. You get my point."

"And I told you already, this isn't a rape. The guy grabbed her, threatened her with a blade, and was yanking on his own chain while he held her there. No rape. Abuse and assault, tops."

For the first time since they had worked together, McQueen thought he heard a shadow of interest in Rizzo's voice when the older man next spoke.

"Blade? Whackin' off? Did the guy come?"

McQueen glanced over at his partner. "What?" he asked.

"Did the guy bust a nut, or not?"

McQueen squinted through the windshield. Had he thought to ask her that? No. No, he hadn't. It simply hadn't occurred to him.

"Is that real important to this, Joe, or are you just making a case for your insensitive prick status?"

Rizzo laughed out loud, expelling a gray cloud of cigarette smoke in the process. McQueen reached for the power button and cracked his window.

"No, no, kid, really, official request. Did this asshole come?"

"I don't know. I didn't ask her. Why?"

Rizzo laughed again. "Didn't want to embarrass her on the first date, eh, Mike? Understandable, but totally unacceptable detective work."

"Is this going somewhere, Joe?"

Rizzo nodded and smiled. "Yeah, it's going toward granting your rude request that we keep this one. If I catch a case I can clear up quick I always keep it. See, about four, five years ago we had some schmuck running around the precinct grabbing girls and forcing them into doorways and alleyways. Used a knife. He'd hold them there and beat off till the thing started to look like a stick of chop meat. One victim said she stared at a bank clock across the street the whole time to sort of distract herself from the intimacy of the situation, and she said the guy was hammering himself for twenty-five minutes. But he could never get the job done. Psychological, probably. Kind of a major failure at his crime of choice. Never hurt no one, physically, but one of his victims was only thirteen. She must be popping Prozac by the handful now. We caught the guy. Not me, but some guys from the squad. Turned out to be a strung-out junkie shit bag we all knew. Thing is, junkies don't usually cross over into the sex stuff. No cash or H in it. This could be the same guy. He'd be long out by now. And except for the subway, it's his footprint. We can clear this one, Mike. You and me. I'm gonna make you look like a star, first case. The mayor will be so proud of himself for grabbing that gold shield for you, he'll probably make you the fuckin' commissioner!"

TWO DAYS later McQueen sat at his desk in the cramped detective squad room, gazing once again into the eyes of Amy Taylor. He cleared his voice before he spoke and noticed the bruise on her temple had subsided a bit and no attempt had been made to cover it with makeup.

"What I'd like to do is show you some photographs. I'd like you to take a look at some suspects and tell me if one of them is the perpetrator."

Her eyes smiled at him as she spoke. "I've talked to about five police officers in the last few days, and you're the first one to say 'perpetrator.' "

He felt himself flush a little. "Well," he said with a forced laugh, "it's a fairly appropriate word for what we're doing here."

"Yes, it is. It's just unsettling to actually hear it spoken. Does that make sense?"

He nodded. "I think I know what you mean."

"Good," she said with the pitched nod of her head that Mike suddenly realized he had been looking forward to seeing again. "I didn't mean it as an insult or anything. Do I look at the mug books now?"

This time McQueen's laugh was genuine. "No, those are your words now. We call it a photo array. I'll show you eight photos of men roughly matching the description you gave. You tell me if one of them is the right one."

"Alright then." She straightened herself in the chair and folded her hands in her lap. She cradled the broken right fingers in the long slender ones of her left hand. The gentleness made McQueen's head swim with, what? Grief? . . . pity? He didn't know.

When he came around to her side of the desk and spread the color photos before her, he knew immediately. She looked up at him, and the sapphires swam in tears yet again. She turned back to the photos and lightly touched one.

"Him" was all she said.

"YOU KNOW," Rizzo said, chewing on a hamburger as he spoke, "you can never overestimate the stupidity of these assholes."

It was just after nine on a Thursday night, and the two detectives sat in the Chevrolet eating their meals. The car stood backed into a slot at the rear of the Burger King's parking lot, nestled in the darkness between circles of glare from two lampposts. Three weeks had passed since the assault on Amy Taylor.

McQueen turned to his partner. "Which assholes we talking about here, Joe?" he asked. In the short time he had been working with Rizzo, McQueen had developed a grudging respect for the older man. What Rizzo appeared to lack in enthusiasm, he more than made up for in experience and an ironic, grizzled sort of street smarts. McQueen had already learned much from him, and knew he was about to learn more.

"Criminals," Rizzo continued. "Skells in general. This burglary call we just took reminded me of something. Old case I handled seven, eight years ago. Jewelry store got robbed, over on Thirteenth Avenue. Me and my partner, guy named Giacalone, go over there and see the victim. Old Sicilian lived in the neighborhood forever, salt of the earth type. So me and Giacalone, we go all out for this guy. We even called for the fingerprint team, we were right on it. So we look around, talk to the guy, get the description of the perp and the gun used. We tell the old guy to sit tight and wait for the fingerprint team to show up and we'll be in touch in a couple of days. Well, the old man is so grateful, he walks us out to the car. Just as we're about to pull away, the guy says, 'You know,' he says. 'You know the guy that robbed me cased the joint first.' Imagine that? 'Cased the joint.'—Musta watched a lot of TV, this old guy. So I say to him, 'What'd ya mean, cased the joint?' And he says, 'Yeah, two days ago the same guy came in to get his watch fixed. Left it with me and everything. Even filled out a receipt card with his name and address and phone number. Must have been just casing the place. Well, he sure fooled me.'"

Rizzo chuckled and bit into his burger. "So," he said through a full mouth, "old Giacalone puts the car back into park and he leans across me and says, 'You still got that receipt slip?' The old guy goes, 'Yeah, but it must be all phony. He was just trying to get a look around.' Well, me and Giacalone go back in and we get the slip. We cancel the print guys and drive out to Canarsie. And guess what? The asshole is home. We grab him and go get a warrant for the apartment. Gun, jewelry, and cash—bing-bang-boom. The guy cops to rob-three and does four to seven."

Rizzo smiled broadly at McQueen. "His girlfriend lived in the precinct and while he was visiting her, he figured he'd get his watch fixed. Then, when he sees what a mark the old guy is, he has an inspiration! See? Never overlook the obvious. Assholes."

"Yeah, well, it's a good thing," McQueen said. "I haven't run across too many geniuses working this job."

Rizzo laughed and crumpled the wrappings spread across his lap. "Amen," he said.

They sat in silence, Rizzo smoking, McQueen watching the people and cars moving around the parking lot.

"Hey, Joe," he said after a while. "Your theory about this neighborhood is a little bit off base. For a place supposed to be all Italian, I notice a lot of Asians around. Not to mention the Russians."

Rizzo waved a hand through his cigarette smoke. "Yeah, well, somebody's gotta wait the tables in the Chinese restaurants and drive car service. You still can't throw a rock without hitting a fuckin' guinea."

The Motorola crackled to life at McQueen's side. It was dispatch directing them to call the precinct. McQueen pulled the cell phone from his jacket pocket as Rizzo keyed the radio and gave a curt "ten-four."

McQueen called and the desk put him through to the squad. A detective named Borrelli came on the line. McQueen's eyes narrowed and, taking a pen from his shirt, he scribbled on the back of a newspaper. He closed the phone and turned to Rizzo.

"We've got him," he said softly.

Rizzo belched loudly. "Got who?"

McQueen leaned forward and started the engine. He switched on the headlights and pulled away. After three weeks in Bensonhurst, he no longer needed directions. He knew where he was going.

"Flain," he said. "Peter Flain."

Rizzo reached back, pulled on his shoulder belt and buckled up.

"Imagine that," he said with a faint grin. "And here we were, just a minute ago, talking about assholes. Imagine that."

MCQUEEN DROVE hard and quickly toward Eighteenth Avenue. Traffic was light, and he carefully jumped a red signal at Bay Parkway and turned left onto Seventy-fifth Street. He accelerated to Eighteenth Avenue and turned right.

As he drove, he reflected on the investigation that was now about to unfold.

It was Rizzo who had gotten it started when he recalled the prior crimes with the same pattern. He had asked around the precinct and someone remembered the name of the perp. Flain. Peter Flain.

The precinct computer had spit out his last-known address in the Bronx and the name of the parole officer assigned to the junkie ex-con. A call to the officer told them that Flain had been living in the Bronx for some years, serving out his parole without incident. He had been placed in a methadone program and was clean. Then, about three months ago, he disappeared. His parole officer checked around in the Bronx but Flain had simply vanished. The officer put a violation on Flain's parole and notified the state police, the New York Supreme Court, and NYPD headquarters. That's where it had ended as far as he was concerned.

McQueen had printed a color photo from the computer and assembled the photo array from which Amy had identified Flain. Flain had returned to the Sixty-second precinct.

Then Rizzo had really gone to work. He spent the better part of a four-to-midnight hitting every known junkie haunt in and around the precinct. He made it known he wanted Flain. He made it known he would not be happy with any bar, poolroom, candy store, or after-hours joint that would harbor Flain and fail to give him up with a phone call to the squad.

And tonight, that call had been made.

McQueen swung the Chevy into the curb, killing the lights as the car rolled to a slow stop. Three storefronts down, just off the corner of Sixty-ninth Street, the faded fluorescent of the Keyboard Bar shone in the night. He twisted the key to shut off the engine. As he reached for the door handle and was about to pull it open, he felt the firm, tight grasp of Rizzo's large hand on his right shoulder. He turned to face him.

Rizzo's face held no sign of emotion. When he spoke, it was in a low, conversational tone. McQueen had never heard the older man enunci-ate more clearly.

"Kid," Rizzo began, "I know you like this girl. And I know you took her out to dinner last week. Now, we both know you shouldn't even be working this collar since you saw the victim socially. I've been working with you for four weeks now, and you're a good cop. But this here is the first bit of real shit we have to do. So let me handle it. Don't be stupid. We pinch him, read him his rights, and off he goes." Rizzo paused, his dark brown eyes in McQueen's face.

"Right?" Rizzo asked.

McQueen nodded. "Just one thing, Joe."

Rizzo let his hand slide gently off McQueen's shoulder.

"What?" he asked.

"I'll process it. I'll walk him through central booking. I'll do the pa-perwork. Just do me one favor."

"What?" Rizzo repeated.

"I don't know any Brooklyn A.D.A.s. I need you to talk to the A.D.A. writing tonight. I want this to go hard. Two top counts, 'D' felonies. As-sault two and sexual abuse one. I don't want this prick copping to an 'A' misdemeanor assault or some bullshit 'E' felony. Okay?"

Rizzo smiled, and McQueen became aware of the tension that had been hidden in the older man's face only as he saw it melt away. "Sure, kid," he nodded. "I'll go down there myself and cash in a favor. No problem." He pushed his face in the direction of the bar and said, "Now let's go get him."

Rizzo entered first and walked directly to the bar. McQueen hung near the door, his back angled to the bare barroom wall. His eyes adjusted to the dimness of the large room as he scanned the half dozen drinkers scattered along its length. He noticed two empty barstools with drinks and money and cigarettes before them on the worn Formica surface. At least two people somewhere, but not visible. He glanced over at Joe Rizzo.

Rizzo stood silently, his forearms resting on the bar. The bartender, a man of about sixty, slowly walked toward him.

"Hello, Andrew," McQueen heard Rizzo say. "How the hell you been?"

McQueen watched as the two men, out of earshot of the others, whispered briefly to one another. He noticed the start of nervous stirrings as the drinkers came to realize that something was suddenly different here. He saw a small envelope drop to the floor at the feet of one man.

Rizzo stepped away from the bar and went back to McQueen.

He smiled. "This joint is so crooked, old Andrew over there would give up Jesus Christ Himself to keep me away from here." With a flick of his index finger, Rizzo indicated the men's room at the very rear in the left corner.

"Our boy's in there. Ain't feeling too chipper this evening, according to Andrew. Flain's back on the junk, hard. He's been sucking down Cokes all night. Andrew says he's been in there for twenty minutes."

McQueen looked at the distant door. "Must have nodded off."

Rizzo twisted his lips. "Or he read Andrew like a book and climbed out the fuckin' window. Let's go see."

Rizzo started toward the men's room, unbuttoning his coat with his left hand as he walked. McQueen suddenly became aware of the weight of the nine-millimeter Glock automatic belted to his own right hip. His groin broke into a sudden sweat as he realized he couldn't remember if he had chambered a round before leaving his apartment for work. He unbuttoned his coat and followed his partner.

The men's room was small. A urinal hung on the wall to their left, brimming with dark urine and blackened cigarette butts. A cracked mirror hung above a blue-green stained sink. The metallic rattle of a worn, useless ventilation fan clamored. The stench of disinfectant surrendered to vomit.

A single stall stood against the wall before them. The door was closed. Feet showed from beneath it.

McQueen reached for his Glock and watched as Rizzo slipped an ancient-looking Colt revolver from under his coat.

Rizzo leaned his weight back, a shoulder brushing against McQueen's chest, and heaved a heavy foot at the stress point of the stall door. He threw his weight behind it, and as the door flew inward, he stepped deftly aside, at the same time gently shoving McQueen the other way. The door crashed against the stall occupant and Rizzo rushed forward, holding the bouncing door back with one hand, pointing the Colt with the other.

Peter Flain sat motionless on the toilet. His pants and underwear lay crumpled around his ankles. His legs were spread wide, pale and varicose, and capped by bony knees. His head hung forward on his chest. He hadn't moved. McQueen noticed his greasy, black hair. Flain's dirty gray shirt was covered with brown, foamy, blood-streaked vomit. More blood, dark and thick, ran from his nostrils and pooled in the crook of his chin. His fists were clenched.

Rizzo leaned forward and, carefully avoiding the fluids, lay two fingers across the jugular.

He stood erect and holstered his gun. He turned to McQueen.

"*Morte,*" he said. "The prick died on us!"

McQueen looked away from Rizzo and back to Flain. He tried to fathom what he felt, but couldn't.

"Well," he said, just to hear his own voice.

Rizzo let the door swing closed on the sight of Flain. He turned to McQueen with sudden anger on his face. "You know what this means?" he said.

McQueen watched as the door swung slowly back open. He looked at Flain, but spoke to Rizzo.

"It means he's dead. It's over."

Rizzo shook his head angrily. "No, no that's not what it fuckin' means. It means no conviction. No guilty plea. It means 'Investigation abated by death.' That's what it means."

McQueen shook his head. "So?" he asked. "So what?"

Rizzo frowned and leaned back against the tiled wall. Some of the anger left him. "So what?" he said, now more sad than angry. "I'll tell you 'so what.' Without a conviction or a plea, we don't clear this case. We don't clear this case, we don't get credit for it. We don't clear this case, we did all this work for nothing. Fucker would have died tonight anyway, with or without us bustin' our asses to find him."

They stood in silence for a moment. Then, suddenly, Rizzo brightened. He turned to McQueen with a sly grin and spoke in a softer tone.

"Unless," he said, "unless we start to get smart."

In six years on the job, McQueen had been present in other places, at other times, with other cops, when one of them had said 'Unless . . .' with just such a grin. He felt his facial muscles begin to tighten.

"What, Joe? Unless what?"

"Unless when we got here, came in the john, this guy was still alive. In acute respiratory distress. Pukin' on himself. Scared, real scared, 'cause he knew this was the final overdose. And we, well, we tried to help, but we ain't doctors, right? So he knows he's gonna die and he says to us, 'I'm sorry.' And we say, 'What, Pete, sorry about what?' And he says, 'I'm sorry about that girl, that last pretty girl, in the subway. I shouldn'ta done that.' And I say to him, 'Done what, Pete, what'd you do?' And he says, 'I did like I did before, with the others, with the knife.' And then, just like that, he drops dead!"

McQueen wrinkled his forehead. "I'm not following this, Joe. How does that change anything?"

Rizzo leaned closer to McQueen. "It changes everything," he whispered, holding his thumb to his fingers and shaking his hand, palm up, at McQueen's face. "Don't you get it? It's a deathbed confession, rock-solid evidence, even admissible in court. Bang—case closed! And we're the ones who closed it. Don't you see? It's fuckin' beautiful."

McQueen looked back at the grotesque body of the dead junkie. He felt bile rising in his throat, and he swallowed it down.

He shook his head slowly, his eyes still on the corpse.

"Jesus, Joe," he said, the bile searing at his throat. "Jesus Christ, Joe, that's not right. We can't do that. That's just fucking wrong!"

Rizzo reddened, the anger suddenly coming back to him.

"Kid," he said, "don't make me say you owe me. Don't make me say it. I took this case on for you, remember?"

But it was not the way McQueen remembered it. He looked into the older man's eyes.

"Jesus, Joe," he said.

Rizzo shook his head. "Jesus got nothin' to do with it."

"It's wrong, Joe," McQueen said, even as his ears flushed red with the realization of what they were about to do. "It's just wrong."

Rizzo leaned in close, speaking more softly, directly into McQueen's ear, the sound of people approaching the men's room forcing an urgency into his voice. McQueen felt the warmth of Rizzo's breath touch him.

"I tole you this, kid. I already tole you this. There is no right. There is no wrong."

He turned and looked down at the hideous corpse.

"There just *is*."

# Chapter Two

RIZZO AND MCQUEEN LEFT THE SMALL COFFEE SHOP on Eighteenth Avenue and climbed into the Impala. Rizzo slipped the Motorola from his jacket pocket and glanced at his Timex: twelve-thirty p.m. He keyed the radio and spoke tersely.

"Dispatch, Six-Two one-seven," he said. "One-seven off meal, back in service."

He waited for the static laced "ten-four" response, then repocketed the radio.

"So," he said from the passenger side of the Impala, "I spoke to the boss last night."

McQueen glanced into his side-view mirror and angled the car into traffic. He drove at a leisurely pace, turning onto Eighty-sixth Street.

"Spoke to the boss about what?" he asked.

Rizzo dug out a Chesterfield and tapped it against his thumbnail. "About you," he said. "About us being partners. I told him it was okay with me if you were good with it. He said whatever we decided was fine with him."

McQueen shrugged. "Sure," he said. "I'm good with it."

Rizzo smiled and lit the cigarette. "Try to control your friggin' joy," he said with a chuckle.

McQueen glanced at the older cop. "No, Joe, really. It's okay with me. I'm happy about it."

Joe Rizzo nodded. "Well, you should be. I can show you how to do this job. And I need a new partner, so it's a win-win situation."

"Okay," McQueen said.

After a moment or two, Rizzo spoke again. McQueen could hear an edge of tension in his voice, a tone that was new to him.

"But before we jump the broom here, there's one thing you have to know. Something you should hear from me."

McQueen kept his own tone neutral as he responded.

"Alright, Joe. Shoot," he said.

"I've got an I.A. thing going on. Hangin' over my head. It's casting a little cloud, and you might get some shade time from it. It dates back a few months to when Morelli, that's my last partner, Johnny Morelli, got himself jammed up near the end. That's why he grabbed his pension and ran. Internal Affairs is still looking at him, and they can still nail him even while he's retired. But they can never touch his pension now that he started collecting it. So his wife will be okay even if they do dump on him."

McQueen slowed for a red traffic signal. He turned to face Joe.

"Jammed up with what? And what's it got to do with you?"

Rizzo nodded and dragged on the Chesterfield. "Those are some good questions, Mike. I figured you for a smart guy. Guess I was right." Rizzo sighed before speaking again. "I'll give you the *Reader's Digest* version. See, me and Johnny, we went through the Academy together. Then, after we'd been on the streets for a couple of years, we partnered up in the Eight-Three. Both of us were still in uniform. We worked together for about two years, then moved on. John got his gold shield same time I did, but he never got past detective third grade. I didn't understand it till we met up again four years ago at the Six-Two. He transferred in from Manhattan, and once I started workin' with him again, I realized why he was still only a third grade."

"Why? What happened?"

Rizzo shook his head. "It was booze, mostly. Gambling, too. When I first saw him at the Six-Two, I knew something had changed. It was in his eyes. It was like he was . . . I don't know . . . unplugged. Like his lights were out. He was walkin' and talkin' and breathin', but it was like he was dead. Just totally burned. And by then he had a rep following him. All of it rumor, innuendo, whatever, but enough to spook the guys in the squad. So I took him on. He became my partner. I nursed him along for four fuckin' years. He was as useless as tits on a bull, but I carried him. And he fucked up plenty, and I'd look the other way. He'd get himself all jammed up with the bookies and the shys and then he'd square it off with favors. Or, anyway, that's what the word was." Rizzo turned to face McQueen fully before speaking further. "'Course, I never actually saw anything out of bounds. If I had, I'da been obligated to turn him over."

The two cops held each other's gaze. A tapped car horn sounded behind them, and McQueen used the opportunity to look up at the light. It was green. Relieved to be free of Rizzo's hard brown eyes, he moved the Impala slowly forward.

"Okay, Joe," he said softly. "So what's the I.A. beef, and how do you figure into it?"

Rizzo took a final pull on his cigarette, then flicked it out the open window. He shifted in his seat and spoke to McQueen's profile.

"The word is," he said, "that about six, eight months ago Johnny was in real deep. Maybe thirty, forty grand to the books in Brooklyn. When they leaned on him, I guess he bit back. The story has it that when the local bookie couldn't handle it, he went up the ladder to the boss. Guy from right around here, Bensonhurst. Name's Louie Quattropa." Rizzo paused before going on. "Ever hear of him?"

McQueen nodded. "Who hasn't? Old time Mustache Pete type, runs the Brooklyn mob. Triggerman on the Joey Gallo hit about forty years ago, wasn't he?"

Rizzo nodded. "That's what they say, but he never got pinched for it. Anyway, once Quattropa gets involved, Johnny's fucked big-time, cop or no cop."

McQueen turned onto Bath Avenue and headed for the Sixty-second Precinct.

"So what happened?" he asked.

Rizzo sighed. "Well, that's what everybody is still tryin' to figure out. But what *seems* to have happened is this. After Quattropa steps in, it's starting to look grim for old Johnny-boy. But a month or so later, he seems like he's in the clear. He's not all twisted up, borrowing money, bouncin' checks, all fucked up. Instead, he seems miraculously debt-free. Starts hitting the booze a little harder, but other than that, he seems okay."

"And I.A. attributes this to what?" McQueen asks.

Rizzo shook his head sadly. When he spoke, McQueen heard an unsuccessfully concealed anguish in his tone.

"You ever hear of OCCB? Organized Crime Control Bureau? Works out of Manhattan?"

McQueen nodded. "Sure," he said.

"Well, it seems they had a mole in the Quattropa family. They had the guy by the balls on a heroin rap and squeezed him to wire up. They were maybe six, seven months from dropping a net on Louie."

McQueen felt his stomach knot. "And?" he asked.

Rizzo undid his shoulder belt as McQueen pulled the Impala into a slot at the front entrance of the precinct. He opened the door and placed one foot onto the asphalt. Turning, he spoke softly to his new partner.

"So one night the cops in the Seven-Six find the mole in an alley offa President Street. Four bullets in the head and a dead rat stuffed in his mouth." Rizzo paused. "Mustache Pete stuff," he said.

"And I.A. figures it was Morelli who fingered the guy to Quattropa?" McQueen asked.

Rizzo nodded and climbed out of the car. He closed the door and leaned in through the still-open window.

"Yeah, that's the theory. And I.A. thinks I can give 'em some lead, somethin' concrete, to work on John. So that's why they're breaking my balls."

McQueen exhaled deeply, then spoke.

"I gotta ask you, Joe. You understand that, right?"

Rizzo nodded. "Sure, kid. I'd do the same. But let me save you the trouble. The answer is 'no.' I don't know if Johnny set the guy up or not. Speakin' as a cop, I gotta say, it sure as hell looks that way. But I don't really know. And if he did arrange the setup, I had nothin' to do with it. I swear on my eyesight."

McQueen sat passively, then spoke in a low, somber tone.

"Would you tell me if you had, Joe?" he asked.

Rizzo let five long seconds pass before answering.

"No, kid, I guess I wouldn't," he said. Then he stood back from the car and walked slowly into the precinct.

SERGEANT WENDALL Tyler strode purposefully across the detective squad room and stopped at the cluttered desk of Joe Rizzo. Rizzo looked up into Tyler's deep ebony face and smiled.

"What's that in your hand, Wendall?" he asked. "Looks like you got a job for somebody."

The uniformed sergeant smiled and glanced around the squad room.

"Don't look like much choice, Joe. You and the kid are the only bulls here."

Rizzo reached out for the notepaper Tyler held out to him.

"What do we have here?" he asked, glancing at the address on the paper.

"Residential burglary, Joe," Tyler said.

Rizzo frowned. "Residential burglary? On Seventy-third Street?"

He glanced up at the clock on the squad room wall: Thirteen-zero-five. "At five after one in the afternoon, in broad daylight?"

Tyler shrugged. "Sector car caught it about twelve-thirty. I got a couple a units there now. So, you'll roll on this?"

Rizzo stood slowly. "Sure. Like you said, just me and Mike here."

Tyler grunted his thanks and walked away. McQueen, having seen the exchange, approached Rizzo.

"What's up, Joe?" he asked, glancing at the note in Rizzo's hand.

"Residential burglary, middle of the day on one of the quietest blocks in the precinct. I think I smell a junkie nephew that knew Aunt Concettina kept some cash stashed inside the family Bible. Let's go check it out."

Once again in the secure confines of the Impala, McQueen turned to his partner.

"One thing, Joe," he said.

"Yeah?" Rizzo asked.

"With Morelli. I can understand he was an old pal, old partner, Academy mate, all that. I've got a few guys like that myself. I'd help them out if they needed it. But with this Morelli, it just doesn't compute."

"What doesn't, kid?"

"You carrying this guy for four years, looking the other way, God knows how many times. You must have seen it coming, Joe. You had to see the bubble bursting someday. Yet you rode it out. Right to the end, crash and burn. I think you're smarter than that, Joe."

Rizzo laughed as Mike started the Impala and backed it out onto Bath Avenue. "Yeah," he said. "I'm a fuckin' genius, alright."

"So why, Joe? Why'd you hang in so long?"

Joe answered softly, his eyes growing dark. "You mean, why'd I hang so long unless I was a foul ball, too."

McQueen shook his head. "I didn't say that."

Rizzo nodded. "Yeah, sure you did. Just not out loud."

After a moment of silence, Rizzo continued.

"Okay, kid, one time and one time only. I hung in there because Morelli saved my ass once. Not on the job, not a cop thing. Something personal. Twenty years ago Johnny was a different guy. Straight-as-an-arrow stand-up guy. If it wasn't for him, I would have fucked up my life beyond belief. He saved it for me."

Rizzo turned full face to McQueen, who glanced briefly from the street to meet Rizzo's eyes.

"That's all I gotta say," Rizzo said. "Take it or leave it. I owed John Morelli. I still owe John Morelli."

Rizzo turned away and reached for his Chesterfields.

"That's all I gotta say about it," he said.

MCQUEEN TURNED the Impala slowly onto Seventy-third Street, squinting into the midday sun. He immediately sighted his destination: halfway down the street, on the right, two blue-and-white radio cars sat double-parked, their dome lights swirling and whirling red and white beacons. A tight group of neighbors stood before the house, their faces knotted and clenched in anger. One young woman, clutching an infant to her breast, stood slightly apart from the group, weeping gently. McQueen turned the car into the driveway, allowing it to straddle the street and sidewalk, carefully avoiding the eyes of the crying woman. He shut off the motor and reached for his notebook just as Rizzo spoke from the passenger seat.

"The outraged posse of neighbors," Joe said. "Always a pain in the ass."

McQueen glanced at his watch and noted the time as he climbed from the car: One-twenty p.m.

He and Rizzo strode past the small crowd and climbed the five front steps of the neat, two-family, detached brick home.

"The detectives," he heard a housewife say. The front storm door swung open before them, held from the inside by a uniformed officer. She looked at McQueen and Rizzo and rolled her eyes at them.

"This one really sucks, guys," was all she said.

McQueen entered the foyer and saw the two inner doors, one left, one right. The left door was open and led to a long hall.

The detectives followed the officer down the hallway. It was open on the left to a living room–dining room combination, and then continued on to the kitchen. The first two rooms appeared to have been ransacked.

Three more uniforms stood around the small kitchen table. They looked uncomfortable. When they saw the detectives enter, the three glanced in unison to the opposite side of the room.

McQueen followed their eyes to a dark blue blanket spread on the floor before the white refrigerator. The refrigerator purred gently, imposing an eerie sense of normalcy on the scene.

Something made a slight bulge at the center of the blanket.

Rizzo glanced at it and turned to the officers.

"Tell me," he said to a tall, red-faced cop of about forty named Bill Carlucci. Carlucci cleared his throat.

"Joe," he said, "we caught this burglary call about an hour ago. The guy that lives here is the landlord. He's eighty-five, lives alone. His daughter came by early this morning to pick him up. She lives out on Long Island. She takes him into the city for a doctor's appointment. Old guy had skin cancer. The tenants upstairs are a young married couple, they been at work all day, usually leave about seven-thirty, get home about six. The daughter and old guy came back home about noon, quarter after, like that. They find the place a mess. And that." He jutted his chin toward the blanket.

McQueen looked at the man. "What is it?"

The cop sighed and shifted his weight. "The old guy's dog. Scumbag who hit the place killed the dog. Butchered it up with a kitchen knife. It's a little mixed-breed mutt, weighs about fifteen pounds. Couldn'ta hurt a fly. Must've annoyed the guy, barking at him. The daughter told me it was a ballsy little thing. The old man is like totally destroyed. Got the dog about six years ago, right after his wife died. According to the daughter, it snapped him out of a pretty bad depression, gave him back his will to live after he lost his wife. He's in the bedroom layin' down. His daughter is with him and we got a call out to the family doctor. Guy said he'd come over since the old man refused an ambulance."

The cop shifted on his feet again. He looked embarrassed as he spoke.

"Joe," he said, "Joe, I know it *sounds* like bullshit, but this here is a real fuckin' tragedy."

Rizzo looked into the man's eyes and nodded slightly. He glanced at McQueen before crossing the room. He squatted down and gently lifted the blanket. The small, brown and white dog lay beneath it, its eyes open, a small bit of pink tongue pushed out between clenched teeth. Multiple stab wounds bloodied and mangled its flesh. A shiny sliver of intestine protruded from one wound.

McQueen crossed the room and stood beside the squatting Rizzo. He looked down, and then away from the sad little body.

Rizzo tossed the blanket back over the dog and stood up slowly.

He faced his partner.

McQueen looked with concealed surprise into the glistening eyes of Joe Rizzo. Rizzo blinked hard, twice, and the glisten vanished. When he spoke, it was in a voice McQueen had not heard before.

"This guy," he said in his strange new voice, "this guy done this, he made a serious fuckin' mistake when he killed that animal."

Rizzo crossed the room to the red-faced officer.

"Bill," he said, his voice now once again familiar but tense to McQueen's ear. "How long you been a cop? Fifteen years, maybe? Yet you roll up on a burglary and you figure it's okay to let two civilians go into the bedroom? The bedroom, the first place a burglar heads for, the first place we could maybe grab some good prints? You let them in there to contaminate the scene? The daughter probably straightened out the whole fuckin' room already."

Bill frowned and squinted at Rizzo. "Prints? You think the print guys are gonna roll on an isolated residential burglary some junkie asshole pulled off?"

Rizzo turned from the man and spoke with his back to him.

"Oh, I'll get the prints alright. On this one, I'll get the prints. Where's the knife? Did he leave it?"

This time the female cop answered. "Yeah, it's in the sink. Right there."

McQueen stepped to the worn white porcelain sink. The knife was the only object it held: eight inches of bloody steel with a black handle, a smudged fingerprint of drying blood visible on the black plastic.

"Guy didn't wear gloves, Joe," he said. "You want prints, they can find some."

Rizzo grunted in satisfaction. "I'm gonna call the print guys and cash in a favor. You wait for the doctor to get here, then go talk to the daughter. She'll know more about what's been stolen than the old man. Especially her mother's old jewelry. Get a detailed list. Find out if they got a junkie nephew or asshole cousin or brother-in-law runnin' around the family coulda done this. If not, maybe a neighbor or a friend or anybody knew the house was empty this morning. I'll make my call."

Later that afternoon, McQueen listened while Joe spoke to the first grade detective from the Crime Scene Unit who had arrived to dust for fingerprints. The three men stood alone in the now empty kitchen. Teenaged neighbors had carried the dog out for burial in the small backyard. The old man slept, sedated by the family doctor, the daughter sat quietly by her father's side, her eyes still producing tears. The uniformed officers had helped with questioning some neighbors, and then left.

"Joe, you must be crazy pulling me offa two homicides to dust for this shit. If the boss knew about this I'd be up in Harlem dustin' chicken bones by Saturday night."

Rizzo lit a Chesterfield and blew some smoke at the man. "Yeah, Ronnie, you already told me how important you are. Just don't forget how you got your gold shield in the first place. You should kiss my fuckin' ring when I ask you for something, you ingrate."

The man flushed slightly. "Joe, whata ya want from me? I catch the big stuff, not this kinda crap. Who has time for this?"

Rizzo laughed. "Did I forget to tell you? This here *is* big stuff. We figure this for Jack-the-fuckin'-Ripper. Didn't you hear? He ain't carving up hookers in London no more: his new M.O. is knocking over houses in Bensonhurst. He gave himself away with the hatchet job on the dog."

McQueen glanced at his watch. "Joe," he said, "it's getting late. I'm going to talk to the woman again."

Joe smiled and spoke to Ronnie. "My partner, he's got a hot date tonight with Miss New Haven, so all of a sudden, he's in a hurry to do some work." McQueen left the room and walked down the hallway to the bedroom.

Pausing at the doorway, he could see the reflection of the scene through the mirror on the far wall. The old man, frail and slight, sleeping restlessly on his back, his daughter seated beside him, leaning inward from a harsh-looking, straight-backed chair.

He tapped gently on the door frame.

She turned at the sound and smiled weakly when she saw him.

"Oh," she said, wiping her eyes with a crumpled tissue. "Oh."

Mary DiPaola was fifty-one years old, the youngest of his three children. Her two brothers lived out of state, one a Navy admiral and the other a computer engineer in California. She lived with her husband and one of her children on the exclusive north shore of Long Island. Some of this McQueen had gotten from cooperative neighbors when he had canvassed them. Other than pedigree and circumstantial information, he hadn't learned much. No one had seen or heard anything with regard to the break-in.

"I need to speak to you," he said.

She glanced at her father. "I'd rather not leave him," she said.

McQueen nodded. "I understand. He's heavily sedated. He can't hear us, we can talk right here."

She thought about it a moment. "Alright. If you think it'll be okay and won't disturb him. He's had a terrible shock."

McQueen entered the room and accepted the invitation to sit opposite her in a chair the twin of her own. It felt as severe as it had looked, and he shifted his weight seeking the least uncomfortable position.

He glanced through his two pages of notes.

"Okay," he said. "When we spoke before you gave me most of what

I need. I just want to double check it and ask a few more questions. Okay?"

She nodded. "Yes."

McQueen cleared his throat. "So, you get here about eight this morning, pick up your dad, drive into the city. That was St. Vincent's Medical Center, right? On Seventh Avenue?"

"Yes."

"You see the doctor, then come back to Brooklyn. Stop at the Acme, pick up a few things for your dad, then come home. You see the front door broken open, find the two rooms ransacked, call nine-one-one from your cell, and then your dad insists on looking for the dog."

She nodded. "The other police officers, especially the woman, told me how we should never have gone in, the burglar may still have been inside, but my dad didn't see Spike. Spike was the dog's name. He was such a cute, harmless little bundle of fur that my dad named him Spike. He said it was so the other dogs wouldn't beat him up, he'd have a tough name." She began to cry again, then smiled sadly at McQueen. "Can you imagine?"

McQueen returned the smile. "Yes, ma'am. I can imagine."

She dabbed at her eyes. "My father was a longshoreman for forty-two years. He raised three children in this house and educated each of us. He took my mother to Italy twice, just because he knew she wanted to go. He had no interest, just liked to travel in the States. He won a silver star and purple heart in the war and never told us how he got them. My mom had to tell us. He saved eight soldiers' lives and shot the hell out of an enemy gun position. Had his left pinky shot off and didn't even realize it till later on. He's a tough, good, kind man. But the death of that dog is going to kill him. You watch, it'll be just like when my mom died all over again. He loved that dog with all the love he couldn't give my mother anymore. Does that make any sense to you? Do you understand what I mean?"

McQueen shifted in his seat. "Yes," he said softly. "I know exactly what you mean. And it makes perfect sense, really, it does. I'm very sorry about all this. All I can do is try and find this guy. Put him away for the burglary. You can get your dad another dog. Maybe it'll help."

She frowned and wrinkled her brow. "Or maybe it won't."

McQueen looked into her deep, dark eyes. Their intensity forced honesty into him.

"Or maybe it won't," he repeated softly.

They sat in sad silence for a moment. McQueen cleared his throat.

"Okay," he said, too gruffly even for his own ears. "Let's see. Is there anyone you can think of, a friend's son, a neighbor, family member, anyone who knew the house would be empty this morning and who might be capable of doing this? Anyone with, say, a drug problem or gambling debts or anything like that?"

She sat back in her chair and stared at him. "You think someone we know, someone who knows *us,* could have done this? Do you really think that? That is really terrifying."

McQueen shrugged. "I don't think anything. I don't not think anything. I'm open, that's how you work these things. Anything is possible. Maybe not probable, but possible. Think about it. Wasn't your father usually home most of the time? When he did go out, where'd he go? To the corner store? To walk the dog? How long would he be gone? Now today he's out for three or four hours, and what happens? Someone breaks in and burglarizes the place. We ran a computer check on the stats: there hasn't been a residential burglary in this sector for two years. It just looks like it could be a targeted situation. We need to check that aspect out. That's all I'm saying, Mrs. DiPaola."

McQueen saw the tension drop from her shoulders. She shook her head slightly.

"Of course," she said with a tired smile. "Of course, you're right."

She furrowed her brow. "Honestly, though, I can't think of anyone. Certainly no one in our family. We've been very lucky that way, blessed actually. There are no drug problems, no one arrested, nothing like that. And the neighbors, they all seem fine. Those two boys taking care of Spike, great kids. They help my dad out a lot. They're always there for him."

McQueen nodded and took up his pad and pen. "What would their names be?" he asked.

She frowned at him and seemed about to say something, but then appeared to think twice. Her tired smile reappeared. "The taller one is Jamesy Bruno, he lives next door at thirteen-thirty. The younger one is Petey Mazzilli. He lives across the street at thirteen-fifty-one."

McQueen nodded. "How old are they?"

"Jamesy just turned sixteen and I believe Petey is fourteen."

McQueen jotted down their names, addresses, and ages and scribbled in the margin, "check juvenile/family court."

When he looked up again, tears were now streaming down her face. She saw the surprised look in his eyes.

"You just don't know," she said, her voice cracking. "You can't know. This house is all he had left of his life with his wife and children. He refuses to leave it. He loved it here. I've tried to get him to come with me. I have an enormous house, he'd have his own apartment. But he won't leave. He told me once that if he left here, he would be leaving my mother's spirit all alone, and he could never do that. He loved this house; he's lived here for over forty-five years. Now every time he walks in, he'll picture that mess in the living room and that poor, beautiful little dog grotesquely murdered in the very kitchen my mother loved. It'll just never be the same for him. Can you see that? Do you understand what this will be like for him? He can never leave here, but it will never be the same again. This will kill him, I'm telling you, this will kill him."

McQueen watched sadly as she sobbed. He glanced at the old man, lying drugged in a furtive sleep beside them. He cleared his throat before he spoke again. "I have a list and description of everything you say is missing. If it's recovered, it will all be returned to your dad."

When she spoke again, it was in a strange, eerily familiar voice. McQueen shivered slightly as he realized where he had heard that voice before.

"I'm not an evil or mean person," he heard her say. "I don't wish bad on anyone. But when you find the man who did this, I hope you kill him. I hope he forces you to shoot him. I hope he *dies.*"

McQueen sat back in his seat. The voice he had heard was an exact match to Rizzo's when the detective had looked up from the dead dog.

Despite the closeness and warmth of the room, the voices echoing in his head made him shudder with a sharp, sudden chill.

LATER THAT night, McQueen sat gazing into the mesmerizing blue of Amy Taylor's eyes. They were nestled at a quiet corner table near the front window of Romano's Ristorante, a very old, established family-owned and operated restaurant just off the corner of Seventy-second Street on the main commercial artery of Thirteenth Avenue.

McQueen, not fully familiar with the local restaurants, had taken Joe Rizzo's enthusiastic recommendation for Romano's with some misgivings. The place was situated just inside the northwest boundary line of the Sixty-second Precinct, and police department policy was clear: stay out of bars, restaurants, and most other public establishments in your precinct when off duty. The opportunity, or appearance of opportunity, for corruption was too pronounced. But Rizzo had been insistent.

"It's a great place to eat," he had said. "Best clams oreganato in the whole city, and the veal is fantastic. And the pasta. Just don't let Miss White Bread pour any ketchup on it. Besides, this ain't Manhattan with all the bosses running around. That 'stay out of the precinct' stuff, nobody worries about that around here. Me and my wife eat there every week, no problem."

Despite the assurance, Mike had his doubts and, as he listened to Amy speak, began to regret the choice.

"So," she said, sipping at her martini. "How are you, Mike?"

He thought fleetingly of Spike, with his small pink tongue protruding. He shook his head slightly to clear the sight away and dropped his gaze to the caramel-colored liquid of his straight-up Manhattan.

"I'm okay, I guess," he said, raising his eyes back to her face. "How about you?"

She offered a weak smile, and he pretended to accept it.

"Fine," she said, and her eyes looked away.

It was not unexpected, and suddenly McQueen wished he were somewhere else. Things had changed between them.

Their relationship had been going well, the exciting, dizzying new days of mutual attraction, a perceived affection, the dawning, perhaps, of something special.

And so, two evenings before, they had fallen into bed, Mike's heart bursting with love and desire and his body responsive and strong in anticipation. But it had not gone well, and they both knew it; both now felt its presence at the table between them.

Mike's police experience had taught him that victims of sexual crimes often carried with them harsh reminders. He had hoped it wouldn't be the case with Amy, but now realized it was. She had been awkward, distracted, almost afraid. It had been a perfunctory, sterile encounter, resembling more a dance rehearsal than a session of lovemaking. It had reminded him of his first frightening, mysterious, and unsatisfying sexual experience, the strongest memory being his fervent desire for it to be over with, so he could escape back into the beckoning summer night.

McQueen sipped his drink. It was icy cold and smooth, and the alcohol soothed him. He sat back slightly in his seat and looked across at the sad, beautiful face of Amy Taylor.

"We should probably discuss it," he said, a melancholy smile touching his lips.

"Why don't we eat first, Mike? It'll keep that long."

Now they smiled at one another, their first genuine smiles of the evening, and Mike realized that despite the awkwardness, despite the lack of connection, their night of lovemaking had been an intimate one, a touching one. Perhaps in some way more so than a successful physical encounter would have been.

Just in a different and somber and final way.

"Okay," he said, his voice as light as he could make it. "Small talk it is. Let's see . . . how's this? How was your day?"

Amy laughed and reached out, touching him gently on his cheek. "There you go," she said. "We can do this. My day was fine, how was yours?"

"Just another day on the job," he said.

She sipped at her drink before speaking. "I've heard police refer to their careers as 'the job.' Do you see being a police detective as merely a job? Don't you see it as a career?"

Mike pondered it for a long moment before answering.

"That's a good question. I'm not sure I have an answer. You know, a lot of the guys I've worked with over the years, Joe, for instance—especially Joe—they always wanted to be cops. Joe never even considered anything else. He joined the Army right out of high school with the understanding that they would make him an M.P. Then, when he got out, he went to the police department almost immediately. He doesn't know anything else. I just sort of fell into it. I never saw myself as a nine-to-five kind of guy, and I was young and looking for some excitement. I took the test for the cops while I was still in college, very casually, almost on a lark. I don't know, it just sort of happened."

"Well," she said, "I think it's noble. If you do it correctly, and I believe you do, it can be a very noble thing."

His mind's eye, often a troubling companion to him, visualized her assailant, Peter Flain, slumped spread-legged on the toilet, his chest covered in bloody vomit. He remembered the "deathbed confession" Rizzo had concocted.

"Yeah," he said, the sadness of his smile going undetected by Amy, "noble."

She nodded and reached for a bread stick. "Truly," she said.

Mike considered her words. "You know," he said, as he watched her bite gently into the bread stick and raise a hand to guard against the crumbs, "Joe said something very similar to me the other day."

Amy gave an exaggerated sigh, but her eyes were smiling at him as she spoke. "Why do I always feel like Joe is sitting right beside me whenever I'm out with you?"

Mike laughed. "I'm sorry. Really. But I do spend a lot of time with the guy."

"I know. It's just that, well, he frightens me a little. But go on, what did he say? You can tell me."

"What he said was, over the years he'd met a lot of guys on this job, mostly Irish guys, he claims, that view it as more of a calling than a job *or* a career. Like being a priest or a minister or a rabbi. That's pretty much how he sees it himself. A calling. He joked about it, said it was just like being a priest but without the altar boys, but I could see he meant it. He said there's a purity to it. That's the word he used, 'purity.' It's really a passion with him. I've got to tell you, though, I don't fully understand it. I may not be sure how I feel about it, but I don't think I would describe being a cop with words like 'calling' or 'purity.'"

Amy seemed to think it over as the waiter returned with a smile and a casual word. He placed an appetizer of sliced fresh mozzarella and tomato before her and another of sizzling baked clams before Mike. When he had left, she spoke again.

"Is Joe a good detective? Is he good at what he does?"

Mike squeezed some lemon over his clams as he answered.

"Amy, this guy is one of the best. He amazes me just about every tour we pull. He's got a deep bag full of tricks from years of experience, but lots of guys have that. He has something more, something unique. Instinct, I guess. A feel for which direction to go in, where to look first. In the beginning, I figured it was just lucky guesses, but it's definitely more than that. He's way over the law of averages for lucky guesses. It's instinct and gut feeling. He's like some kind of savant sometimes, but please, promise me you'll never tell him I said that. I just don't understand why he's still at precinct squad level. He should be homicide or some prestige outfit, maybe citywide Major Case Squad. Something."

Amy cut a neat square of cheese and topped it with a slice of tomato. She sampled it and raised her eyebrows at Mike.

"My God, this is delicious. I don't know what kind of detective Joe is, but he's an excellent judge of restaurants."

As the meal progressed, they fell into an easy sort of rhythm, a pressure having been lifted. Both now knew this would be their last evening together, and all that remained were the appropriate words and the soft, chaste kiss good-bye. Amy felt responsible for the breakup and defensively turned the conversation to McQueen's own ambitions, hoping to ease him along less painfully.

He responded to her. He told her how he had originally intended to use civil service examinations to advance himself, since he lacked the political connections and powerful friends within the department required to move up through influence. In fact, he was currently on the list for sergeant and could be reached as early as the following year. But his lucky break in getting the mayor's bump up to detective had changed his thinking.

"If I can do a good job and not make waves, catch someone's eye, maybe I can go back across the river into a special unit. Policy and Planning, maybe, or Community Affairs. Possibly teach at the Academy. There are lots of places to be other than out on the street."

The meal played its rituals out, and when the espresso was placed before them, the time was at hand. The specter that sat with them was not that of Joe Rizzo, as Amy had joked, but something worse. Something unavoidable. Something unchangeable.

Mike smiled around the espresso cup and spoke before he sipped.

"So," he said gently. "Who's going to say 'It's not you, it's me' first?"

Amy returned the smile but her eyes were heavy. Once again, as in the confines of her hospital room, Mike saw her deep sapphire eyes moisten.

"Oh, Mike, believe me. It's not you. You're a wonderful guy, my knight in shining armor. But . . . it's just that . . . the other night. The other night. When we . . . when we made love. It came out so wrong. Oh, we got through it, and you were gentle and wonderful and patient. But all I could see, all I could feel, was that horrid man in that dirty, claustrophobic subway turnstile. It was terrifying. And you're too much a part of that, too much a reminder. I can never . . . probably never . . . get past that. And it's just too unfair to you. Can you understand that?"

McQueen downed his espresso in a single gulp and turned for the waiter. Catching the man's eye, he signaled for the check.

"Of course I can," he said gently. "But you have to promise me something. Just one thing."

"Of course, Mike, anything," she said, tears in her tone.

"Let it be my loss. Just mine. Move past it, get through it. When you meet someone else, get beyond it. Don't let that junkie ruin your life. It's just not worth it. Promise me. My loss only. Okay?"

Amy reached across the table and laid a gentle hand over his. "Of course, Mike. Of course I promise. And thank you for understanding."

With that, the waiter appeared and placed the check discreetly before McQueen. Thankful for the normality of the act, he freed his hand from Amy's and fingered the check. He found himself frowning at it and, in a further retreat from this painful moment, quickly ran the math through his mind. He looked up and, again catching the waiter's eye, beckoned him back to the table.

"Shall I take that, sir?" the man inquired innocently, a slight Italian accent tugging at the end of his words.

"Not just yet. I think there's a mistake here."

The waiter frowned with great concern and leaned inward. He read the check McQueen held, then pursed his lips.

"No, sir," he said with great dignity. "I don't believe there is a mistake. Here," he continued pointing to the green guest check. "Here, the lady had the chicken francaise. You, sir, had the veal marsala. And there is the bottle of Bolla pinot grigio. No, sir, I believe the check is in order."

McQueen's frown deepened. He glanced at Amy. Through her sadness, she looked quietly confused. McQueen lowered his voice and spoke again.

"What about the appetizers? The cheese and the clams? The two cocktails? The espressos?"

The waiter wrinkled his brow.

"Forgive me, sir, but I have no memory of serving those items you mention. And Mrs. Romano, she personally double checks each order as it goes in and out of the kitchen, as well as each guest check before it is presented. Surely she would have noticed such a large oversight. No, sir, Mrs. Romano will have no more memory of these items than I myself. Now, if you'll excuse me, there is no hurry. Whenever you are ready."

With that, he strode with great purpose to service a nearby table.

McQueen looked up from the check into the now surprisingly amused eyes of Amy. He saw the wine shining impishly in the sea of their blue.

Damn that Rizzo, McQueen thought.

THE FOLLOWING afternoon, McQueen sat quietly in the passenger seat of the Impala gazing over the flat green waters of the Narrows, that lower portion of New York Harbor that runs like a river between the boroughs of Brooklyn and Staten Island. The Impala was nosed in under the shadow of the Verrazano Bridge, a steady hum of east-west traffic from the Belt Parkway behind them, the bridge traffic sounds droning from above.

He watched as a young mother pushed a baby stroller on the paved walkway along the far edge of the wide expanse of grass that lay just in front of the car. The sun reflecting off the water behind her gave the woman an almost ethereal appearance. The warmth of the late November day was unusual, and it seemed to enhance McQueen's introspection.

His thoughts, never far from Amy since he had awoken that morning, now settled on her and their brief, tender relationship. As he watched the young mother disappear around the bend of the walkway, he admitted to himself for the first time that he had loved Amy Taylor. Still loved her.

But she was gone now. And there would be no getting her back.

Rizzo sat behind the wheel of the car, scribbling notes for the report he would type up later that day. They had just come from a job at Our Lady of Guadalupe Roman Catholic Church on Fifteenth Avenue. The parish priest had called to report a theft from the poor box. He was required to report it to the police department in order to put a claim in with the insurance company. Rizzo would file his report, call the priest with a complaint number, and never consider the matter again. Neither the detectives nor the priest harbored any illusions of the thief ever being found.

"Probably one of the altar boys," Rizzo had remarked with a grin after they had left the rectory.

"So," Rizzo said, looking up from his writing. "How'd the date go last night?"

McQueen turned to face his partner. A sad smile came to his lips as he replied.

"Like the maiden voyage of the *Titanic,* I guess," he said, a sadness in his tone, despite himself.

Rizzo dropped his eyes from the young cop's face and turned back to his notes.

"That's too bad," he said casually. "I figured you liked her quite a bit."

McQueen hesitated before speaking. Although still new in his friendship with Rizzo, McQueen sensed something in the older man, something more than was first apparent. And despite his usually private nature, McQueen suddenly felt the need to talk.

"It was more than that. I think, maybe, I may have been in love with her."

Rizzo stopped writing and casually slipped his pen into a breast pocket. He fumbled through his jacket and produced a Chesterfield, lighting it and blowing smoke out the open driver-side window before speaking.

"So," he asked, his voice soft. "What went wrong?"

McQueen told him. When he mentioned the reason Amy had given, the bitter image of Flain and the assault so vividly tied to McQueen's presence in her life, he saw Rizzo's eyes flicker with recognition and sadness.

"Yeah, well, you gotta figure that would be there," he said. "You been seein' her, what?, about two months now? The fact it took so long for her to go to bed with you shoulda tipped you she was having problems with it." After a moment, he added, "But who knows? Maybe she can get past it in time. You never know with that kinda thing. Give her awhile, then maybe call her."

McQueen shook his head. "No. I saw it in her eyes. We're done. It's over."

Rizzo sighed and dragged on his Chesterfield. Then, smoke hazing around his mouth, he spoke.

"You know, Mike, I hate moments like this. Makes me feel like an old man. But, I gotta tell you, I've been around for a few years. And I been married for over twenty-five. I went to high school with Jennifer. When I went into the Army, she went off to college. When I got back home, she was just starting to teach school. We kind of picked up where we had left off in high school and next thing you know, we're married. Fairy tale, right? Well, you want to know the truth? Looking back, you want me to tell you the truth? You figure you were in love with this girl from Connecticut, right? Well, you wanna know when me and Jen fell in love? Real, honest-to-God lasting love? After my third daughter was born and I was the only one working. A Brooklyn patrolman, I could barely put the mortgage payment together let alone keep everybody in Pampers and formula. That's when we fell in love. That, kid, is what love really is."

He took a last drag on his cigarette and tossed it out the window.

"Now," he continued, "I don't mean no offense, so don't get all pissed off. But what you had with Amy was what I had with half a dozen girls over the years. You had half a hard-on and half an infatuation. Keep that in mind, and you'll get through this a whole lot easier. You talk to me about love after you've been married to someone for a few years. Trust me on this, Mike. Keep it in perspective and you'll lose a lot less sleep."

McQueen shook his head. "I don't know, Joe," he said softly. "I hear what you're saying, but this . . . this was different. Do you believe in love at first sight?"

Rizzo laughed. "No," he said.

McQueen smiled. "Yeah. Me neither. But that first time I saw her, in the hospital, the day she got attacked, I felt *something*, Joe, something strong. And once we started dating, I got a handle on it, started to understand what it was."

Rizzo reached for another cigarette, lighting it as he spoke.

"And what was that, Mike?" he asked.

"Well," McQueen responded with a shrug. "It's hard to put into words, but . . . Amy was different from any of the women I've met since I became a cop. It was like when I was at NYU and I met girls from all over the country, from overseas even. They were interesting, intelligent, educated . . . sophisticated is the word, I guess."

Rizzo expelled smoke. "So?" he asked.

Again McQueen shrugged. "I don't know, exactly, but . . . when I was with her, it was like the road not taken, you know? Like if I hadn't become a cop, if I'd become some corporate wheel somewhere. I probably would've married someone just like Amy, capitalized on living in the city, led a completely different kinda life. Different from a cop's life." His eyes implored Rizzo to understand. "That's what Amy gave me, Joe."

After a moment, McQueen said, without humor, "I know it sounds stupid. But I can't help that. It's how I feel. Losing Amy feels like . . . I don't know, a world closing down for me—permanently. It's dumb, I know, but what can I tell you? I fell in love with her."

Rizzo examined the burning tip of his Chesterfield, then raised his gaze to meet the sad eyes of his young partner. He sighed before speaking.

"Mike," he said gently, "you did fall in love, I guess. You fell in love with *something*." He smiled before continuing. "But . . . and this here is the important part: whatever you fell in love with wasn't necessarily *her*. You might wanna consider that."

After a brief moment, Rizzo reached out a hand and laid it gently on McQueen's shoulder.

"End of lecture," he said. "Hell, with that face of yours you'll find a new girlfriend in no time. If it wasn't you was an Irishman, I'd let you go out with one of my daughters. An Irishman *and* a cop, that is."

Despite himself and his heavy heart, McQueen laughed out loud. "I'll keep all that in mind," he said, his mood lightening as he spoke.

"That is, of course, if I don't wind up in jail for some on-the-arm-clams and a couple of drinks. No wonder you have I.A.D. riding you. I should have known you were sending me to . . ."

Rizzo waved a hand at him and turned back to his notes, a smile deepening in his face. "If that was even remotely possible, me and half the precinct'd be scratchin' our nuts in Sing-Sing. Even those I.A. pricks aren't interested in it."

McQueen finished the sandwich he had been picking at and crumpled the wrapper, dropping it over the seat onto the rear floor to be dealt with later. The radio between them crackled to life.

A female dispatcher's voice, in a clipped, singsong cadence sounded, "Six-Two squad one-seven, ten-one the squad. Copy?"

They were being directed to telephone the detective squad back at the precinct. Rizzo looked up from his notepad and glanced over at McQueen.

"Handle that, Mike, I'm almost finished here."

McQueen picked up the radio and keyed the send button. "Ten-four, dispatch, one-seven copies."

An inaudible squawk back told McQueen he had been heard. He reached for his cell phone and punched in the number.

"Mike, that you?"

"Yeah, who is this?"

"Bobby Dee. How you guys doing out there?"

"Good, Bobby, getting ready to come back in. What's up?"

"We just got a call from Ronnie Torres over at C.S.U. He got a hit on some prints Joe's breaking his balls about. He's faxing it over. Coming through now, I can see it. Tell Joe for me, okay?"

McQueen smiled. "Do me a favor, Bobby, take a look at it. Is it on that Simione burglary yesterday?"

"Hold on, Mike."

Rizzo had stopped writing at the mention of the burglary. He sat silently watching his partner's profile.

The detective came back on the line. "Mike? Yeah, it's the case of the great doggie mass-a-cree. Tell Joe to go get the prick."

McQueen smiled. "I'll do that, Bobby, thanks. Just toss the report on Joe's desk, we'll be there in twenty minutes."

"Take your time, Mike, it ain't going nowhere." The line clicked dead in McQueen's ear.

"Tell me," Joe said.

"Your pal Torres had a hit, he faxed the info over to the house. It's there now."

Rizzo smiled. "That's good. Let's go take a look."

MCQUEEN GLANCED around at Rizzo's desk and frowned. "How do you find anything in all this mess, Joe? You've got newspapers from three weeks ago here. Most of this stuff is now officially garbage."

Rizzo dropped heavily into his chair and smiled up at McQueen. "Kid, I know where everything is. Besides, look around. The whole place looks like this. Your desk is the only neat thing here and that's 'cause you're—whata ya call it?—anal. You got an anal personality with a desk like yours. The other day I seen you dusting it, for Christ's sake. If it weren't for me vouching for you, half the squad'd figure you for a queer, you're so neat. They all know you worked the Village in uniform for a couple a years. Pretty boy like you musta got a few offers from the ar-*tists* down there."

McQueen shook his head and sat down opposite Joe at the small desk. "Never mind. Forget I said anything, you and the other Neanderthals."

Rizzo laughed. "We got a mick or two and Schoenfeld's a Jew, but I don't think we got any Neander-whatever-the fucks."

He sat in silence while Rizzo read the fax report from C.S.U. He saw Joe frown and reach for the phone. McQueen noticed the slight eye tic his partner exhibited when he was upset or unhappy about something. McQueen held his silence and waited.

"Eddie?" Joe said into the phone. "Joe Rizzo, Six-Two in Brooklyn. How you doing? Yeah, yeah, me too. Glad you're okay. Listen, we got a rash in common. Guy named Anthony Donzi. You know the name? Hey, Eddie, hold on, my partner's here, I'm putting you on speaker, okay? Go ahead."

McQueen leaned in toward the black phone as Joe gently replaced the receiver.

"Joe?" he heard through the speaker. "Can you hear me alright?"

"Yeah, Eddie, what about Donzi? You ran a print on him two months ago and got a hit. You ever find him?"

"No. Last-known address was out in Queens. Hadn't lived there in two or three months. I had some friends from the One-Twelve poke around for a while, but it looks like the guy left the borough."

Joe frowned at the phone. "What'd you need him for in Manhattan?"

They heard the detective named Eddie sigh. "Son of a bitch goes into one of those First Avenue pickup bars down by the hospital, winds up beating some nurse half to death. Broke up her face pretty bad. Problem is, she's some cousin or in-law or some shit to the chief of thoracic surgery. He's all over the phone with the politicians and I get calls from two inspectors and the chief of detectives himself. I got brass all over my ass, and guess what? I can't find the guy. Everybody knows we lifted a perfect palm and four fingers off the hood of the car he was pounding her on, we got his name, address, the whole nine yards. Made me look like a real asshole when I couldn't find the guy."

Joe rubbed his eyes wearily. "Guy disappears, he disappears. But they never understand that, do they? Well, he's turned up now. Two days ago, in my friggin' precinct. Killed a dog and hit a house, broad daylight."

Eddie's voice was tight when he spoke again. "Sounds like him, the sadistic prick. You got a lead on him?"

Rizzo blew air through his lips. "Why I'm calling you, buddy. I see on the run sheet you made the same requisition two months ago, I figured *you* could help *me*."

"Sorry, Joe. I struck out. I got his rap sheet here somewhere if you want it. I can fax it over, save you some time."

"Okay, Eddie, send it now. Thanks. If I get a noose on the guy, I'll call you. You share the collar. Get the humps off your back."

"I'd owe you for that, Joe, big-time. I'll fax it right now."

Joe broke the connection and turned to Mike.

"This is not good. The guy seems to have gone underground."

McQueen shrugged. "Maybe this guy Eddie's not the sharpest knife in the drawer. Maybe we can do better."

Rizzo smiled. "Yeah, well, some squad guys couldn't find the Pope in a whorehouse, but not Eddie Giambrone, he's pretty good."

McQueen reached across the desk and slapped Joe on the shoulder. "Pretty good? Well, maybe he's pretty good, but he's not *us*, partner. Remember me? I'm the anal guy. We'll find him."

Joe glanced at the clock high on the wall opposite his desk before speaking. "Yeah," he said absently. "But for now, it's quittin' time. Sign out and go home. I'm going to talk to the boss and clear our morning. We're eight-to-four tomorrow, right?"

"Yes."

Joe nodded. "Okay, then. I need to call a friend of mine, set it all up. I'll see you tomorrow."

McQueen stood and stretched his back muscles. "Set what up?" he asked.

Rizzo dismissed McQueen with a backward wave of his hand. "I'll tell you all about it tomorrow. Get going, see you in the morning."

McQueen shrugged and turned to leave. Suddenly he missed Amy acutely and toyed with the idea of calling her. Maybe even driving over to her place and dropping in.

But then he remembered her words.

He couldn't compete with the ghost of a dead junkie. He left the squad room and headed for home.

JOE RIZZO sat at the kitchen table, sipping his beer, his wife, Jennifer, opposite him.

"So, honey," she said, raising a coffee cup to her lips. "How was your day?"

Rizzo shrugged. "The usual. Just another day in paradise. How 'bout you?"

"Not too bad. The kids are beginning to settle in, getting used to the new school year. I think I've got a good group this term. We'll see."

Joe nodded absently. "Well," he said. "I told McQueen. I told him yesterday, about the I.A. thing."

Jennifer's eyes clouded. "Oh," she said. After a moment, she continued. "Are you going to partner with him? Permanently?"

Rizzo nodded. "As permanent as anything is on this job, yeah."

"He was okay with it? The Internal Affairs thing?"

He shrugged. "Seemed to be. He's not sure if he believes I'm clean, though. Can't blame him for that."

Now her eyes blazed anger. "No," she said sharply. "You certainly can't blame him for that. Why you allowed that man, that damned Morelli, to manipulate and use you all those years is—"

Rizzo held up a hand, palm outward, and smiled gently. "Please, Jen, I know, I know. I've heard this a thousand times."

Jennifer shook her head angrily. "Don't dismiss me, Joe, I'm not one of your skell suspects. Friendship and loyalty are fine, but Morelli turned out to be worthy of neither from you. Not to the extreme you went, that's for sure."

Joe smiled again at his wife. He sighed. In addition to Jennifer's dark beauty and tall, lean body, from their first meeting as teenagers Rizzo had been strongly drawn to her feisty independence and strong sense of self. It had often been difficult to deal with on a day-to-day marital basis, but Joe somehow managed—mostly by recognizing the wisdom of her words, even when they stirred an unsettling discomfort in him.

"I know, Jen," he said with a shrug. "You're probably right. But what's done is done, okay? I don't want to rehash it again."

Jennifer shook her head and compressed her lips. When she spoke, her tone was formal.

"Fine, Joe," she said. "But don't dismiss me. It pisses me off."

Joe smiled sadly. "Whatever you say, sweetheart. Whatever you say."

# Chapter Three

*December*

THE FOLLOWING MORNING, McQueen and Rizzo met in the squad room. Rizzo had cleared three hours for field investigation purposes, during which time they would not be required to respond to any new crime scenes unless an absolute priority arose. They left the precinct house and Rizzo drove directly to a diner on Fourth Avenue.

"So," McQueen said when they were seated in a rear booth sipping at coffee. "What's the big deal plan you've got for us this morning?"

Rizzo shifted in the cramped seat and buttered some toast.

"We're going to see a friend of mine down at the State Supreme Court on Adams Street. He's a court clerk, works in the criminal term clerk's office on the tenth floor. He has computer access to the state 'crims' system. I want him to run our boy Donzi through. See what we got."

McQueen frowned. "Why can't you just call him and do it by phone?"

Rizzo smiled across the small table, answering as he stuffed eggs and toast into his mouth.

"Well, kid, it's tough to look for something over the phone when you don't know what you're looking for. See, this 'crims' thing, it goes beyond the guy's rap sheet. The sheet tells us crimes, arrests, convictions, dispositions, jail time, stuff like that. 'Crims' is the state court's setup. Tells us more. Gives us names. Victims, judge assigned, defense lawyer, D.A. that prosecuted. Names. We see the same name two, three times, we can figure maybe they know something about this guy, something

51

personal that don't show up on a computer screen or printout. It gives us somebody to talk to."

McQueen shook his head slightly. "About what, Joe? What do we talk to them about?"

"It's simple. You saw Donzi's rap sheet. Guy grew up in Queens, got locked up six times out there. Twice for burglary. Then he's got three more arrests, all three in Manhattan, two assaults, one receiving stolen property. Then there's that open assault on the nurse that Giambrone struck out on, also in Manhattan. See what I'm sayin' yet?"

McQueen thought for a moment before answering.

"No priors in Brooklyn. Guy's a newcomer."

Rizzo's smile radiated across the table. "Bingo. He's a fuckin' immigrant, like you. See how smart our idiot Republican mayor was to bump you up? He knew you had great potential."

"So we're looking for some tie to Brooklyn. Hopefully come up with an address where he might be."

"Exactly correct. It would explain why the squad in Queens that Eddie called in couldn't find him. Donzi may have resituated his professional operations to sunny Bensonhurst."

They ate in silence for a moment longer before McQueen spoke again.

"You know, Joe, I have to tell you, you surprise me every day. Remember the first case we caught together? Amy's assault? I figured you for some kind of slacker looking to avoid work, not get involved too much. But I was wrong. Take this, for instance, this dead dog burglary case. You seem pretty gung-ho for it, like with most of the cases."

"Yeah," Joe said, chewing his bacon. "I'm a fuckin' enigma, alright."

McQueen laughed. "For a guy uses a good Republican word like 'enigma,' you were pretty hard on our beloved mayor. I have to admit, I figured *you* for a right-wing Republican, Joe. Don't tell me you're a candy-ass Democrat?"

"Mike, remember my grandfather? Guy I told you about, raised me from when I was nine? Well, very early on in our relationship he sat me down and told me, 'Kid,' he said, 'kid, you want to just keep things simple and always remember three things: you're a Roman Catholic, a Mets fan, and a Democrat. In that order.' I remember thinkin' how I wasn't even sure what a friggin' Democrat was, so I asked him what the difference was, what was a Democrat, what was a Republican. You know what he said?"

"No, Joe, I guess I don't."

Joe laughed. "He said, 'Kid, that's exactly what I mean. Don't be asking a whole lot of questions, complicating every goddamned thing till you don't know which way is up. Just keep it simple: you're a Roman Catholic, a Met fan, and a goddamned Democrat. Period.'"

They ate in silence for a while. When Joe spoke, his voice had lost some of its usual irony, a subtle seriousness now permeating his tone.

"As for that thing with Amy, that first case of ours, let me say this. I knew then, like I know now, you were pissed about that. Especially since you figured at the time I thought it was a more serious crime. I thought it was a rape case. Well, not that I need to, but I'll explain it to you, 'cause I like you, you're a good cop, a good guy." He smiled into McQueen's eyes. "Hell, kid, you're my partner, so I'll explain it. It's something you already know, you just don't *know* you know it. Remember when you were in uniform? You'd roll up on some disaster, some murder or rape or whatever? What'd ya do? You secured the scene, grabbed hold of any witnesses, and called the boss. When the detectives got there, you turned it over to them and went back to looking for the best deal on donuts. Why? 'Cause there was nothing else you could do, that's why. It was out of your hands. You can't share in all the pain all the time, it's not humanly possible. You work a case, okay, that's different. Some of the stench will stick to you, some of the pain will be yours. But it's different, because it's *your* case. You *can* do something, like now, with this poor old guy and his broken old heart on account of Spike getting whacked. Maybe we can find this guy, this Donzi, lock him up, send him upstate. Let him think about what he did to that dog while he's getting raped in the shower.

"You see, Mike, I didn't think we'd be involved in the investigation of Amy's case. And I've got my policy: don't share the pain if you can't help. You've gotta minimize what you carry around from all the wreckage, otherwise you turn into something not much different from the skells we hunt down. You turn into some bitter old drunk smacking the wife around 'cause she overcooked the pasta."

McQueen nodded, realizing that Joe had been right: he *had* known all this. He just never knew he had known it.

McQueen frowned as he spoke to Rizzo. "But that's not what you said, Joe. At the time, I mean. Remember? You said you didn't want the case because you didn't want extra work. You only changed your mind when you remembered that old case and that maybe it was the same perp. You figured we'd close the new case quickly and pad the stats. Remember?"

Joe nodded, no offense on his face or in his mind.

"Sure I remember. Back then, you were a stranger to me, just some kid I may or may not be working with again. But now, now it's different. Now you're my partner, so I'll tell you this: you wanted to go to the squad boss and ask for Amy's case, remember? He'd figure you had a motive for that, a reason. He'd figure what I figured: you wanted to get to know her better, catch the guy, maybe impress her a little. He'd probably have given you the case, and that, my friend, is a favor you owe him. You should avoid asking for favors unless it's absolutely necessary. *Do* favors, don't ask for them. That way, when you need something, people owe *you*, you don't owe them. Back with Amy's case, I said whatever I said because it didn't matter at the time. Now, you're my partner. It's different. Now we tell each other the truth. In the middle of all the lies we swim around in, we at least tell each other the truth."

McQueen reflected for a moment before saying, "Yeah, Joe, the way of the world—lies and favors. It kind of sucks sometimes, doesn't it."

Now Rizzo laughed, and when he spoke again, the old ironic wise-guy tone was back in his voice.

"Well, hang on, kid, because things are going to get a lot better. The women are coming on strong. Every day they grab a little more of the power, a little more of the world. It's not much, not yet, but it's definitely coming. And once the broads are in charge, you watch the difference. The men got to run things for the first few thousand years, and an argument can be made that they couldn't have fucked it up any worse than they did. But don't worry, 'cause here come the women."

McQueen sat back in his seat in not-completely-mock surprise.

"Joe, say it ain't so, buddy. A Democrat, okay, I can deal with that. But a feminist, too? Are you sure you're even a real cop?"

"Don't worry, Mike, I ain't wearing panties under these Kmart chinos, relax. But I'll tell you this. You ever hear of an old broad named Golda Meir? Ring any bells?"

"Yeah, I know the name. Prime minister or premier or whatever of Israel. Long time ago, I think way back in the sixties."

"Yeah, that's her. Tough old lady, bet she iced a few rag-heads in her day. But she once said something that I'll never forget. Something that no man, not Winston Churchill, not Eisenhower, not Anwar Sadat, no man in her position could've even thought to say. She said, 'The fighting between the Arabs and the Jews will stop when the Arabs learn to love their children more than they hate us.' See what I mean? That's the way a woman thinks. When they're running things, the wars will stop. Stop cold. Because women see warfare as nothing more than killing one another's children, which, by the way, is just what it is. But men, they're okay with that. You kill mine, I kill yours, let's see who's got the biggest dick. But the women, they're too smart for that. You watch, Mike. It's comin'."

They finished their meal in relative silence and returned to the gray Impala. Rizzo took the wheel and swung a wide U-turn across the four lanes of Fourth Avenue, pointing the hood northbound toward the heart of the borough, the downtown area. The morning rush hour was thick, and Rizzo tapped the steering hub judiciously, sounding the car's siren in short, assertive "wup-wups" to help them weave through the traffic.

When they arrived at the squat, city-block-long concrete hulk of a building that housed the Kings County State Supreme Court, Rizzo parked in the No Standing Zone on Adams Street and tossed the NYPD Official Business parking plaque on the dashboard. They nodded a greeting to the court officer assigned to the outside security post and entered the lower lobby. They sidestepped the magnetometers by displaying their badges to one of the officers manning it and walked through the hallway. McQueen followed Joe to the elevators, and they rode in silence to the tenth floor.

With their badges draped around their necks, they entered the clerk's office and stepped behind the information counter into the heart of the long, brightly illuminated room. Rizzo glanced around and spotted the man he was looking for. They walked to the rear of the room to a wide, neatly kept wooden desk. A man of about forty sat behind it, his gold clerk's shield displayed from the breast pocket of his open-collared sport shirt.

"Hello, Tim, how are you?" Joe said.

The man looked up from behind the desk through wire-rimmed glasses and rose to shake Joe's hand.

"Hey, Joe, I didn't see you come in. How are you?"

They shook and McQueen was introduced.

"Mike McQueen, my new partner. This here is Tim O'Connor. He's a boss up here, nothing he can't get done when you need somethin'."

O'Connor, a former court officer and now supervising court clerk, shook off Joe's comment casually.

"Yeah, and it's rocket science. Only a genius could get this stuff done."

The three of them sat. A Dell computer occupied the side of O'Connor's desk.

O'Connor listened as Rizzo explained what he needed and why. When Joe had finished, O'Connor frowned.

"Sounds like one of your long shots to me, Joe, but what the hell, it doesn't cost anything to try. Let's see what we get."

The clerk took the rap sheet from Rizzo's hands and scanned it with a quick, experienced eye. He keyed up the computer and punched in the digits of Donzi's NYSID number. They watched the screen and waited.

Twenty minutes later, they returned to the Impala. Rizzo pulled the car away from the curb, cleared the end of the service road, and swung a U-turn in front of the Marriott Hotel on the east side of Adams Street, opposite the courthouse. He drove toward the Brooklyn Bridge and the lower Manhattan headquarters of the New York County district attorney.

The assistant district attorney whose small, cluttered office they found themselves in was a local celebrity of sorts.

Darrel Jordan had been born and raised in a middle-class African-American neighborhood of Queens, New York. He had been the star of his high school basketball team, and in his senior year the college recruiters had come calling. His father was a graduate of Queens's St. John's University and so Darrel's choice had been an easy one.

After leading St. John's to two division championships, Jordan had gone as a fifth-round draft selection to the NBA and the Detroit Pistons. A Rookie of the Year trophy and two MVP years were followed by a devastating knee injury that sent him back to Queens and the campus of St. John's. But this time it was St. John's law school. Although his undergraduate years had been on a full athletic scholarship, Jordan had been a serious student who actually earned his B.A. degree in history, with a strong minor in public administration. Now, with a pocketful of NBA cash, he pursued and earned his law degree.

The celebrity-conscious Manhattan D.A.'s office eagerly recruited him, and he had now been there for almost eight years. It was common knowledge that when he satisfied the minimum requirement of ten years as an active member of the New York Bar, a judgeship on the New York County Supreme Court would be his for the asking.

As they sat in his office, McQueen found himself in the unfamiliar but satisfying position of at last having one up on Rizzo: the A.D.A. was an old acquaintance of Mike's. They had worked together on more than a few occasions when McQueen was a patrol officer in Manhattan. Jordan prepared and prosecuted cases that arose from arrests McQueen had made. They had spent many long hours together, with Jordan preparing the young officer for his courtroom testimony.

After they had caught up on one another's lives, Jordan leaned across the desk and spoke directly to Rizzo.

"You can't imagine how happy I was to get that call from you today. This guy Donzi, he made my skin crawl. Anything I can do to help put him away, just ask. I've tried this guy twice. Sent him away for three years the first time, but he got an acquittal on me the second time out. Goddamned jury bought his bullshit alibi hook, line, and sinker, and he walked right out the front door."

Rizzo shrugged. "It happens. Especially in Manhattan with all these bubble-brained liberal yuppies who learned from the movies that the guy on trial is always innocent, no matter how much evidence says he's guilty." Rizzo's face tightened as though he had just swallowed something very evil.

"You remember that old Henry Fonda film, *Twelve Angry Men?* That movie got more murderers acquitted than F. Lee Bailey and Johnny Cochran combined."

McQueen smiled into Jordan's face. "Joe's a Democrat, Dar, can you tell? He's a feminist, too."

Jordan laughed and raised his hands, palms out, toward the pair. "Don't get me involved in any domestic disputes here, gentlemen. If a fight were to break out, what with me being the only gentleman of color in the room, the cops will surely lock my ass up and give you two medals. Just tell me how I can be of help."

"It's like this, Darrel," Joe said. "We learned from 'crims' that you tried this asshole twice and they were both long trials. You lived, ate, and drank this guy for a lot of days. You must have some trial notes, a thick file, a bunch of stuff that potentially may help us. I'm looking for a tie-in to Brooklyn. Bensonhurst, specifically, but anyplace in Brooklyn. This guy didn't just pluck an address out of a phone book and then drive in from Queens or grab a subway from the city. This was just a two-bit residential burglary, he grabbed some cash and a few old rings and jewelry, some silverware and electronics. He didn't even bother to hit the upstairs apartment. This was a pocket change job, a target of opportunity, something a junkie would do to score a bag or two. But Donzi's no junkie. He just needed a few bucks, so he hit a convenient mark. He was in the neighborhood, so he thought he'd drop in, you see? If he was living in Queens, or over here, he'da hit a house nearby. What I need to know is this: Why was he in my precinct? What brought him there?"

Joe sat back in his seat. "Any ideas?"

Jordan looked at Rizzo, then at Mike, then back to Rizzo.

"This is about an isolated house burglary? That's what this is?" He shook his head and turned down his mouth. "You boys in Brooklyn got a lot of time on your hands, I see. Unless . . ." Now he smiled at them and shook his head slowly. "How good-looking *is* the lady of this burglarized house? Or is she a relative of yours? Aunt Millie, maybe? It doesn't matter to me, you understand, but I am a little bit curious."

McQueen answered for them. "It's not like that, Darrel," he said. "This is totally legit. The guy that got hit was eighty-five years old, lived for his little mutt of a dog. Donzi carved the dog up and left it in the kitchen for the guy to find. The old man is just blown away. It really pissed Joe off. Me too, I guess. It's that simple."

Jordan looked from one to the other and then nodded slowly. "Okay," he said. "If you say that's the reason, so okay."

"That's the reason," Rizzo said.

Jordan sighed. "Well, you're right about the notes and files, there's a ton of it. Two big folders, if I remember. I used part of the first folder at the second trial, thought it might have something that would help me. It didn't. Maybe it'll be luckier for you guys. I'll have them pulled and sent over to the Six-Two by tomorrow."

"Thanks," McQueen said.

"What about your own memory? Anything come to mind?" Rizzo asked.

Jordan shook his head sadly. "No, I've been going over it as we spoke and I can't recall any ties to Brooklyn. But hey, I try thirty cases a year. There could very well be something, and I'm just not remembering. If there is, it should be in the files. I hope you can read my handwriting."

Rizzo smiled and stood to leave. He extended his hand across the desk and shook Jordan's hand.

"I hope it's better than your fuckin' jump shot used to be," he said.

BOTH RIZZO and McQueen were off duty for the next two days, and when they returned to the squad room at four p.m. on Sunday afternoon, they found two thick trial folders waiting for them. As a security precaution, someone had removed them from their Federal Express jackets, examined them, time-clocked them as received, and then stacked them on Rizzo's desk.

"Perfect timing," Rizzo said. "Sundays are always slow in this precinct. Instead of watching one of those stupid-ass stock car races, you can read through one of these files."

McQueen punched at Rizzo's arm. "They're not stupid, and anyway, the season ended last week."

"Thank God" was Joe's only reply.

McQueen took the top folder, the one representing the most recent Donzi trial and acquittal, and crossed the room to his own desk. He dropped it on the corner and checked his messages. He spent an hour making calls on some of the various cases he and Joe were carrying.

Sunday was always a good time to find people at home, and Rizzo had told him that if you were going to speak to people over the phone about police matters, it was generally better to do it when you could reach them at home.

"No one wants to explain to you how Junior threw Granny down the steps last night while their coworkers are sitting right next to them listening. Makes for an embarrassing coffee break."

When he hung up the phone, he turned back to the file.

An hour later, McQueen's tired eyes narrowed and he squinted at Darrel Jordan's scribbled trial notes. He turned the page sideways and lowered his head closer to it. With a faint smile, he flipped back through the file and rechecked a prior entry. Satisfied, he pulled the two loose-leaf sheets free from their binder and crossed the room.

"Joe, I've got something," he said.

Rizzo looked up with watery eyes. "I hope so," he said, reaching for a cigarette. " 'Cause all I've got is a goddamned headache."

"You can't smoke in the squad room, Joe," Mike said, glancing at the Chesterfield. "It's bad enough in the car."

"Oh, screw it, who's here? Just us, and you don't mind."

"Ever hear about secondhand smoke, Joe? You're killing me with it."

Rizzo laughed. "Yeah, that's it. Secondhand smoke. Or maybe I'm just stinkin' up your fancy shirt."

Mike raised a hand in surrender. "Never mind, Joe. Smoke. Kill us both."

Rizzo laughed, but put the Chesterfield down, unlit. "What'd you find?"

McQueen laid the two pages of handwritten trial notes before Joe. The first was numbered at the top in black ink, "8," the second in the same ink, "13."

"It's lucky thirteen, Joe. I think."

Rizzo squinted down at the pages, following McQueen's pointing finger to page eight.

In the right-hand margin, in Jordan's difficult scrawl, Rizzo read, "Girl in second row, right side. Second day she's here, smiled at D. Ask D.I.—who is she?"

Rizzo looked up. "D.I.," he said. "That would be the detective-investigator assigned to assist Jordan at the trial."

McQueen nodded. "Darrel wrote a note to remind himself to ask the D.I. to check out this woman who showed up at court. Now look over here, page thirteen."

Rizzo followed the finger. Halfway down the page, scribbled in an offhand, inconsequential way, Jordan had noted the results of the D.I.'s efforts.

"D.I. says girlfriend of D.—name Geanna Fago, lives in Brooklyn."

Rizzo looked up with a burn of glee in his eyes.

"Mike," he said, "if we struck out with this, the only idea I had left was to go to the Department of Corrections' computers and try to find an ex-cellmate of Donzi's that maybe now was in a pinch and could use us to help him out, quid pro quo. But that was gonna be even more of a long shot than this."

McQueen laughed. "A.D.A.s and cellmates. Talk about strange bed-fellows."

Rizzo laughed back. "Imagine that? An A.D.A. and a cellmate, the same kind of whore, far as we're concerned."

"Yeah, but Joe, if they're whores, what does that make us?"

Joe nodded and reached again for the Chesterfield. "Pimps, my boy, flaming, royal, fuckin' pimps!"

They laughed and looked back down at page thirteen.

Geanna Fago, Brooklyn.

TUESDAY NIGHT they sat in the Impala. The darkness of Seventy-sixth Street enveloped the car. It was a cold, moonless night in early December and the weather had turned seasonal. It was very cold inside the car. Rizzo had forewarned his young partner.

"Wear long johns under your street clothes. Two pairs of heavy socks and warm shoes or boots. Bring gloves and a hat, if you've got one."

"Joe," Mike had said, "we're not going to Alaska. It's thirty degrees outside, not thirty below zero."

Rizzo had nodded. "Right. And you sit in a car for a few hours without moving, you freeze your ass off. Believe me. This ain't your blue-and-white radio car, you got the motor running all night and the heater going. This is a residential block on a weeknight. You run a motor parked in front of somebody's house, everybody's looking out the window to see what's up. They'll be calling the cops on *us*. Listen to me. Dress warm."

Now, by nine o'clock, the wisdom of Rizzo's words were no longer lost on the young detective. Despite his compromised clothing, McQueen felt chilled to the bone, shivering visibly every so often.

"See?" Rizzo would say at each and every shiver.

By nine-fifteen McQueen was squirming in his seat and preparing himself to prove Rizzo right on yet another point. Rizzo noticed the squirm and smiled as he made it easy for his partner.

"You about ready for a Snapple bottle, kid?" he asked casually.

Despite himself, Mike laughed aloud. "Yeah, you old hump. Where are they?"

"Right where they should be. On the floor in the back. I hope you got good aim, 'cause piss on the carpet really stinks after a few days. Believe me."

They had shut down the interior lights, so Mike went to the backseat and picked up one of the empty Snapple bottles Joe had brought along. The wide expanse of the bottle neck seemed right. He arranged himself precisely and urinated into the bottle.

When Joe heard it, he turned slightly in his seat and said casually over his shoulder, "Bet it ain't so amusin' now, huh? I'm not so funny now, right, bringing along those bottles?"

McQueen emptied his bladder, cursing the two cups of coffee he had drunk before leaving the squad room that evening. When he finished, he gingerly replaced the twist-on cap, tightly. He found himself unconsciously warming his hands against the now tepid glass of the bottle.

"What'll I do with it?" he asked Joe.

"Hold on to it. Tomorrow we'll slip it back into the soda case, next to the apple juice."

McQueen ignored Joe's chuckles and braced the bottle on the floor, against the rear seat.

They sat in silence, each watching the darkened front porch of the two-family home, fifty yards before them across the street. Nothing stirred. The cold street was deserted. McQueen idly watched a nearby home's window as it flickered and danced with shifting light patterns from a television screen, dull gray rays counterpointing the reds and greens and sparkling whites of the Christmas decorations most houses displayed. He glanced at Rizzo's profile and noticed how the man's gaze rarely left the car's side-view mirror or the house where Geanna Fago lived. It had been a long day for Rizzo. Despite their scheduled start time of four p.m., he had arrived at Fago's house by noon. Earlier that morning, he had learned, through a contact at the phone company, that a line was currently active for a Geanna Fago at the address they now watched. It was a two-family home located only four blocks from the scene of the burglary. Rizzo had gone to the house to interview the elderly landlord that afternoon. Yes, Fago lived upstairs. No, she wasn't home right then, she was at work. Yes, a man did spend a lot of time there. In fact, the landlord suspected the man had been living there full-time for the past two or three weeks. What was his name? The landlord didn't know, but he had heard Fago call him "Tony" a couple of times. The man did not like either of them, Rizzo discerned.

Rizzo produced the color mug shot of Anthony Donzi. Yes, the landlord said, that's the guy. No, he wasn't there right now. He had left a few hours ago. He'd probably be back that night. Usually came in about six or seven o'clock.

Rizzo called McQueen and had gotten him to come in early as well. By three o'clock they were back at 360 Adams Street, the Supreme Court building, waiting for a judge to read their affidavits. The judge placed them under oath, questioned them, and then signed an arrest warrant for Anthony Donzi, for one count of burglary and one count of animal cruelty at the Simione residence the week before. Then he signed a search warrant for Geanna's apartment.

Here they sat, Donzi's picture taped to the dashboard before them, the arrest and search warrants tucked inside the breast pocket of Rizzo's overcoat. McQueen glanced at his Timex.

"You're sure this landlord didn't drop a coin on us? Sure he's legit?"

Rizzo rubbed his eyes. "Positive. Salt-of-the-earth type, retired fireman. He's not too fond of Geanna, and he hates Donzi. Don't worry, they'll show. Maybe they went out for dinner or a few drinks, whatever.

They'll show. If they don't, we come back tomorrow. They ain't going nowhere. Relax."

With that, a car passed them on the one-way street. As it reached the house, brake lights glared, and the car veered sharply left and into the driveway. Mike had run a DMV on Fago and Donzi that afternoon: it was her dark red Escort. A man was driving.

The landlord didn't own a car and had told Rizzo that he allowed Geanna to park in the driveway for a forty-dollar-a-month surcharge on her rent. Rizzo grunted with satisfaction as he saw Donzi step out from the driver's side. Geanna exited the opposite side, and together they climbed the front steps. Rizzo and McQueen watched as she unlocked the front door and entered the house.

"Seems a little unsteady on his feet, old Tony does," Rizzo murmured. "Must be a little drunk. Maybe he'll be looking for a fight and I can crack his fuckin' skull for him."

McQueen picked up the Motorola from the seat and gently keyed the send button.

"Dispatch, one-seven, Six-Two notifying for backup at the location, k?"

"Ten-four, one-seven, will advise Six-Two backup at the location, k?"

"Copy, dispatch, ten-four." He went off the air and tucked the radio into his belt. Surprisingly, he found he had to urinate again.

"Now we wait," he heard Joe say, more to himself than to McQueen.

And so they sat in the now strangely comforting darkness of the car and waited. McQueen glanced at the suddenly stony profile of Rizzo and decided not to speak. Instead, he found himself reflecting on the impressive reach the older detective commanded.

All the complex arrangements had been made with two simple phone calls by the senior detective. After securing the arrest and search warrants, they had returned to the squad room. McQueen had sat passively opposite Rizzo at the maddeningly cluttered desk. He waited as Joe first called the commanding officer of the Brooklyn Emergency Services Unit and then the chief of Central Dispatch Operations.

"I'm going down to see Pete," Rizzo said as he hung up the phone. "Wait here a minute."

"Pete," McQueen knew, was Sergeant Peter Hansen, the supervising officer of the precinct-level communications unit. Rizzo was gone for less than twenty minutes, and when he returned he dropped into his chair with a broad smile.

"We're all set," he reported. "Here's the deal. Tonight we go sit on Geanna's little love nest and wait for her to come home from work. Then we wait some more for Donzi to show up. Once they're both tucked inside for the night, we radio dispatch, identify ourselves, and tell them to send the cavalry. Dispatch will notify the Six-Two communications desk and they'll call in E.S.U., which I've got on standby. Then they'll send the sector car out to assist. Everything official, by the book. Friend of mine at E.S.U. promised me four guys with a battering ram. Counting us and the sector car, that's eight bodies. We bust in the door, shove the arrest warrant down Donzi's throat, the search warrant up Geanna's ass, and that'll be that. Only one more call I gotta make."

And with that call, Joe's reach in the department was made clear to McQueen. The young cop recalled the ease with which Rizzo had arranged for the fingerprint team on the Simione burglary, the way the courthouse doors had swung open wide for him and half a dozen other examples. Rizzo truly understood, perhaps even better than he himself realized, the exquisite power of the favor, the special treatment, the subtle weight of a due-on-demand obligation.

McQueen had watched and listened and learned as Rizzo placed the call to Detective Eddie Giambrone, across the river in the squad room of the Twenty-third Precinct.

"Eddie?" Joe said. "Joe Rizzo here. I was hoping to catch you at your desk and not have to bother you at home. You up for a little night work this evening?"

"Tonight, Joe? I'm leaving at six. It's my son's birthday, I promised him I'd be home tonight. Why? What's up?"

"It's that Donzi thing. We've got a strong lead on him for tonight. We may get him."

McQueen heard Giambrone's grunt come through the speakerphone.

"Damn," he said. "That's great, Joe. I'll call and cancel and be there, just tell me where and when."

Rizzo chuckled and looked up at McQueen, winking.

"No, Eddie, don't do that, go to your kid's birthday. This is short no-tice, anyway; it couldn't be helped. But it's okay. If we get lucky and col-lar this joker tonight, this is what we can do. I'll use my teenage partner as the arresting detective. His arrest report will carry me and you as the investigating detectives. We'll book Donzi and run him through arraign-ments on the Brooklyn burglary only. Then tomorrow, or whenever, you rearrest him in custody on your Manhattan assault. You go down as the arresting on it with me and you as the investigating."

Rizzo paused there before speaking again. "Sound okay to you, buddy?"

Now it was Giambrone who paused. When he did reply, McQueen could hear the gratitude in his tone.

"That sounds very generous of you, Joe. Really. I appreciate it. I'll owe you for this, Joe, big-time."

Joe's laugh was genuine as he replied. "You bet you will, pal. Some-day, and that day may never come, I may call upon you for a service. But . . . until then . . . consider this a gift on your son's birthday."

Now it was Giambrone's turn to laugh. "Where have I heard that one before, Don Rizzo? It sounds real familiar."

"Who knows?" Joe said with a shrug and a second wink at McQueen. "People have been stealing my lines for years. Maybe you heard it in a movie somewheres."

And so now, as they sat in the Impala, McQueen felt himself smiling in the darkness at the memory.

"Joe," he said, breaking the heavy silence in the frigid air, "you are really something."

Rizzo turned to him with a puzzled look. "What?" he asked.

"With that Giambrone thing. The guy gets to go to his son's birth-day party without a care in the world. You grab Donzi, give Giambrone half the credit, plus let him take the arrest for the Manhattan assault. Not many guys would do that."

Rizzo smiled and spoke with his eyes still on the house. "Yeah, well, my stats still look good, and now I got another guy in Manhattan owes me. You get screwed a little, but it's a win-win situation for both of us."

"I see that, Joe. You're some cop, a regular Batman."

Now Rizzo laughed and faced Mike before speaking. "Kid, I'd watch who I said that to if I was you, 'cause if I'm Batman, that's gotta make you the heterosexually challenged Robin, the Boy Wonder."

With that, a blue-and-white radio car pulled alongside them in near silence, its headlights dark. Rizzo opened the driver's window of the Impala and waited as the passenger window of the blue-and-white slid silently down.

"Hello, Tommy," he said to the baby-faced uniformed cop. "How you doin' this evening?"

"Good, Joe. Pretty quiet. They told us you might need the sector car tonight. You got a warrant, something like that?"

"That's right. This is what I need you to do. Roll around the block and go up to Fourteenth Avenue. Wait there on the corner for the E.S.U. guys. Key the radio twice when they show up, hold them there, and then we'll drive up and go over things. We don't want our man glancing out a window and seeing all this activity."

Tommy, the young cop in the radio car, nodded and hit the up button on his window.

"Okay, Joe," he said as the window closed and the car slid slowly away.

Within ten minutes, the Motorola sounded sharply from where it was tucked at McQueen's waist. Two distinct clicks, followed by silence. Rizzo reached forward and fired the engine. "Let's go," he said.

They rode past the house to the corner. Rizzo made a sharp left, drove quickly along the avenue, and then another left at Seventy-seventh Street. He sped the length of the block, jumped the stop sign, and made a third left onto Fourteenth Avenue. At the corner of Seventy-sixth Street, the blue-and-white sector car stood idling at the fire hydrant, a black Emergency Service Unit panel van double-parked alongside. As Rizzo swung in behind the van, its doors opened and four imposing officers climbed out, their dark, paramilitary E.S.U. uniforms melding into the cold blackness of the night air.

Rizzo and McQueen exited the car and met the officers on the sidewalk. The two uniformed sector cops joined them.

Introductions were made. The E.S.U. supervisor, a tall, burly black sergeant, was an old acquaintance of Rizzo's. The name tag on his outer jacket said "Simmond."

"Jake, thanks for coming," Rizzo said to him.

"My pleasure, Pisan," Jake responded, his voice surprisingly delicate-sounding coming from his broad face and imposing mass. "What you got for us this evenin'?"

"Arrest and search warrant. Guy named Donzi. Anthony Donzi. It's a 140.25 Penal Law and a 353.A of the Agriculture and Markets Law."

Jake's eyes narrowed as he reached out for the arrest warrant Rizzo offered him. "A burglar? You got the cavalry out here for a burglar? What's the matter, your grandmother off tonight, couldn't help you out?"

Rizzo laughed. "Just a little insurance, that's all. You ladies will be back to the mah-jongg game by eleven o'clock."

Simmond scanned the arrest warrant as he spoke. "And what the goddamn is a three whatever-whatever of the agricultural shit-kicker law? I never even heard of it."

"Agriculture and Markets Law. A 353.A is aggravated cruelty to animals. You can do two years for it."

Simmond shook his head and handed the warrant back to Rizzo. "Don't even want to hear about that, Joe. Sorry I asked. I got a feeling when I write my memoirs I'll be leaving tonight out of 'em."

"Here's the deal," Joe said, slipping the warrant back into his coat and taking out the search warrant. "We got a search warrant, too—all legit and legal. The landlord is cooperating, gave me a key to the front door of the house. We unlock it and go in. Up the stairs to the apartment door. It's a 'no-knock,' so you guys break it and we go in. Probably two people in the four-room apartment, Donzi and a woman, Geanna Fago. He's thirty-one, six feet even, about one-ninety. She's twenty-eight, five-six, one-forty."

"Weapons?" Simmond asked.

"Don't know, probably not, but if anything, maybe a knife."

"Let me see the search warrant," Simmond said.

"Right here," Rizzo replied, waving it in front of his shoulder. As he began to put it back into his coat, Simmond reached out a large, neatly manicured hand and stopped him.

"Let me see that, Joe," he said firmly.

Rizzo paused and frowned at the man. "You think I'm jerking you off, Jake? Is that what you think?"

Simmond laughed. "Your hand's too damn small to be jerkin' me off, white boy. I just need to check the address, that's all. I like to make sure I've got the right door. We bust down a door at the wrong address and granny chokes to death on her dentures, I'm on Eyewitness News tomorrow. 'Affirmative Action Negro Screws Up—film at eleven.' I don't need that."

Rizzo passed the warrant to Simmond. They spoke while the sergeant read.

"Donzi may not be a pushover," Rizzo said. "He's got a couple of assaults in Queens and a few in Manhattan. Likes to use his hands."

Simmond grunted and handed the warrant back to Rizzo, the address committed to his memory. "Well, is that so? Hey, McSorley, you hear that? This guy we're gonna grab likes to fight. He's a tough guy."

They all looked to the E.S.U. officer named McSorley. The man stood six-four, weighed two hundred and forty-five pounds. There was not an ounce of visible fat. Despite his body armor and bulky E.S.U. outer jacket, the power of his chest and arms was very evident. He was hatless despite the cold, and his shaved head glimmered in the scant glow of a distant streetlight. His ears stood sharply out from his skull and were almost translucent. When he was spoken to, he smiled at his sergeant. One upper front tooth was missing.

"Mongo like tough guy," he said in a monotone. "Mongo like fight."

Rizzo glanced at McQueen and then spoke to Simmond.

"Maybe we'll let him deal with Donzi," he said.

Simmond chuckled. "Just keep your hands away from his mouth" was all he said.

"One more thing," Rizzo said. "I want everyone to hear this. This is my collar, me and my partner's. But for tonight, Jake is running the show. We all look to him to make the calls. Everyone clear?"

They all nodded. Rizzo looked satisfied and turned to Simmond. "Okay, boss. What now?"

Jake Simmond reached up and tugged the brim of his baseball cap style hat lower on his brow.

"Okay," he said, his voice less delicate than before, "we all roll to the house in our own vehicles. The van first. Joe, you next, then the blue-and-white behind. Does this house have a driveway?"

Rizzo answered. "Yeah, the perp's car is in it. Red Escort."

Simmond nodded. "I'll block it in with the van. You guys double-park but leave the street clear for traffic. Me and McSorley will go in and up first—let me have the front-door key—we'll take the upstairs door and go in and cover. My other two guys will cover the rear of the house. You and Mike and the uniforms run through, take the girl out and make sure you get McSorley's attention when you locate Donzi."

He glanced around. "Ready?"

Everyone nodded and moved to their respective vehicles. They followed the black van and watched as it swerved sharply to the rear of the red Ford, blocking it tightly into the driveway. The four E.S.U. cops jumped from the van and Simmond and McSorley were at the front door of the house before Rizzo and McQueen had fully cleared their own car. The other two E.S.U. cops ran toward the house rear. As Simmond unlocked and pushed the door wide, six men rushed into the front foyer. They took the long staircase silently, two at a time. McQueen watched as Simmond and McSorley swung the short, heavy battering ram violently against the door, just above the cheaply plated doorknob. The door flew inward and they rushed after it.

The screams Geanna let out were piercing. She stood opposite the men in the small kitchen, her back to the darkened window behind her. She threw a hand across her mouth, her other arm up and across her bare breasts. Her white panties glared in the overwhelming light from the huge fluorescents above them. The uniformed sector car officers rushed to her and spun her sharply around and up against the purring brown refrigerator. Shouts and threats and instructions clashed in the air from all sides as she was handcuffed and pushed to the floor. McQueen saw Rizzo, Colt drawn and held high, rush through the hallway shouting orders. He followed the older man into the semi-darkened bedroom and saw Donzi, half dressed and disheveled, trying to reach a rear window and its prized fire escape. As Rizzo ran around the bed that separated them, McQueen leaped across it and threw his body at Donzi. He crashed squarely into the man's back and drove him solidly into the thick, heavy plaster and lathe wall. Rizzo heard a dull thud as Donzi's head slammed the surface. McQueen landed on his feet, gained his balance, and lifted his hands toward Donzi. But the fight was over. The blow had weakened Donzi's legs, and the man swooned and stumbled and fell to the worn, musty-smelling carpet. McSorley suddenly appeared, pushing with surprising agility past Rizzo and roughly cuffing the dazed Donzi. He rolled the man facedown onto the carpet and placed a heavy booted foot behind Donzi's head, pressing slightly on the back of his neck to discourage any further movement or resistance. He looked first at Joe and then to Mike.

"Mongo disappointed" was all he said.

Rizzo holstered his weapon and looked at McQueen, standing beside the giant McSorley and the prostrate Donzi.

"Jesus," he said to McQueen with a small smile tugging at the corners of his mouth. "You really *are* Robin, the Boy Wonder."

"YOU GUYS got some fuckin' nerve breaking in here like this," Geanna Fago said bitterly. She sat at her kitchen table, rear cuffed, a bathrobe draped over her and secured across her bare breasts. Rizzo sat at the same table, filling in the bottom of the search warrant and smoking a Chesterfield. He looked up at her and very deliberately flicked some ashes onto her kitchen floor.

"Now, Geanna," he said, "is that any way for a nice girl like you to talk to the police? Especially after we got off to such a great start and all, what with you doing your 'Girls-Gone-Wild' interpretation."

Her face darkened and she spit her words at him.

"I'm gonna sue all you fuckers."

Rizzo shook his head gently. "Geanna, Geanna, let's be reasonable, okay? I showed you the warrant. We found two antique rings that match the description of the stolen property. We found two silver pieces that match, too, not to mention that coke you had out in plain sight in the bedroom. Your lover boy is under arrest and so are you. Even the shyster lawyers in Brooklyn wouldn't take this case, honey, so why don't you just shut the fuck up? I'm starting to like you even less than your asshole boyfriend, and I pretty much hate him."

She frowned at him and actually seemed to snort, almost like a horse, but she remained silent. Rizzo smiled at her with satisfaction and turned back to his paperwork.

McSorley had uncuffed Donzi and watched silently as the man

dressed for his trip to central booking. He then recuffed him and sat him in a chair in the small living room.

McQueen and Rizzo had done a semi-thorough search of the apartment and had located some of the items stolen in the Simione burglary. Rizzo had ignored Donzi until after the found items were recorded on the warrant. Then he had walked over to the man and stood over him, a cigarette burning in his hands.

"My name is Rizzo. Sergeant Rizzo. You're under arrest for Penal Law violation 140.25, burglary in the second degree, and aggravated cruelty to animals, a charge punishable by up to two years. You're looking at fifteen max on the burg-two. Plus there's an open assault in Manhattan. That, with your rap sheet, makes you a predicate felon. This time, Donzi, you're going away forever. You have the right to remain silent. You have the right to have an attorney and to have the attorney present during all questioning. If you can't afford an attorney, one will be provided at no cost to you. If you waive your rights, anything you say can be used against you in court. You understand? Good. Now, just shut up, 'cause I got so much evidence on you, a confession would be a waste of my time."

And with that, he had walked away and not so much as looked at Donzi for the remainder of the night.

"Alright, Mike," Rizzo said as they huddled together in the foyer just outside the apartment door. "Take Bonnie and Clyde down to 120 Schermerhorn Street and book them. I'll give the apartment a thorough search and take whatever we have down to Gold Street and log it with the property clerk. Then I'll call Giambrone and tell him we got Donzi. Make sure you tell the A.D.A. writing tonight to put a 'hold' in with the Department of Corrections pending rearrest on the New York case. Tomorrow, I'll call Simione's daughter and let her know this is over with and how to get her stuff back from the property clerk. I called the precinct, they're sending a female cop over to help tuck Geanna's tits back in. Take the cop with you in her car and let her help with the paperwork down at Schermerhorn Street. When you get there, ask for Bill Cosentino. He's the night shift supervisor, an old friend of mine. He'll get you out quicker if you tell him it's for me. Remember, Sergeant Cosentino."

"Okay, Joe. Thanks. I'll see you tomorrow."

"Yeah, kid, tomorrow."

Mike turned to leave. He felt a hand on his arm and turned to face Joe.

"And kid," Joe said, his voice tired but gentle. "You did good tonight. Everybody did good."

They smiled at each other, then Rizzo turned away and went back into the apartment.

IT WAS close to midnight when Rizzo swung the Impala into a parking slot at the Sixty-second Precinct. He gathered up his paperwork and climbed from the car. Twenty more minutes, he figured, and he'd be heading for home. He locked the Chevy and turned toward the precinct.

"Hello, Joe," a man said from the shadows to Rizzo's left. "How're you doing tonight?" Rizzo turned to the voice. As he did so, the man stepped slowly from the shadows. Rizzo frowned at him.

"Why, if it ain't Detective Sergeant Ralph DeMayo," Rizzo said with a tight smile. "Out kinda late, aren't you? Not padding the overtime I hope."

The man laughed and shook a cigarette loose from its pack, offering it to Joe. Joe took it and reached for his own lighter.

"No, not at all. Just finishing up a night tour. You know—like a real cop."

Rizzo lit his cigarette and held the lighter out to DeMayo. They smoked silently for a moment.

"So," DeMayo said at last. "You wanna talk here or inside? Up to you, Joe."

Rizzo blew smoke at the man's chest. "Well, actually, Ralph, I don't want to talk at all."

DeMayo smiled and leaned against the Impala's front fender.

"Okay, Joe, here will be fine. Let's chat."

Rizzo shook his head. "You I.A. guys go out of your way to be pricks. That's the problem, you know. Nobody holds your job against you. Just the way you choose to do it."

"Yeah, well, I'll bring it up at the next division meeting. But for now, let's talk."

Rizzo leaned his back against the car. "Informal, sort of? Like with no D.E.A. lawyer present? Like that? A little chat between old pals?"

DeMayo smiled around his cigarette. "Yeah, like that," he said. "You're not a target of the investigation, Joe. Just a possible collaborating witness. So no lawyer necessary. The target is your old goomba, Johnny Morelli. We know that, you know that, he knows that. So relax."

"I guess I've got your word of honor on that, eh, Ralph?"

"You bet."

Rizzo laughed. "Well, then, let's talk. But make it quick. I've been workin' since this morning. I'm tired. Say what you came to say and then beat it."

DeMayo dropped his smoke to the street and ground it out under the sole of his shoe. He raised his eyes to meet Joe's.

"You want it quick?" he asked, his voice hinting at malice. "Okay, buddy. Quick it is. For four years you worked with that piece o' shit, Morelli. Four years while he went from one jam to another, drunk every day, on duty, off duty—it didn't matter to him. And when the jams got too tight, he bought his way out with favors and accommodations and muscle and influence, all at the expense of the job. All at the expense of every good cop out there breaking their humps to keep the lid on this city."

Rizzo shook his head angrily and hissed his answer. "This is old news, DeMayo. And you can't prove any of it. We've had this conversation a half dozen times. Say something new or get lost. I'm sick of looking at you."

DeMayo smiled coldly. "Okay, Joe. How's this for new? For those four years you partnered with him, he was useless to you. Wasn't worth a damn as a cop. Yet for three of those years, you guys led Brooklyn in cleared cases. Pretty fuckin' remarkable, don't you think?"

"And that tells you what?" Rizzo asked with cold eyes.

"It tells me you're a pretty smart guy, Joe. You cleared those cases on your own, with no help from that shit bag. It tells me you can see things, understand things, read people. Yet I'm to believe you can't help us nail Morelli for leaking that OCCB mole to Quattropa? With that, you saw nothing, understood nothing, read nothing? Went right over your head, it did."

"So I'm not as smart as you think, I guess," Joe said.

DeMayo shook his head. "Wrong, Joe. Here's what I—what we at

I.A.D.—think. We think you *can* help us, Joe. We think you know something about Morelli's IOUs and what happened to them. And understand this, Joe: none of us can quite figure out why a straight cop would turn a blind eye to Morelli time after time. Why a straight cop with seniority would even work with him in the first place. Because you were old buddies? What are we, twelve-year-olds playing blood brother in the tree house? No, Joe. It's starting to look like cash here, pal. Maybe we need to start poking around your finances. Talk to the wife, maybe your mother and sister, maybe we *should* be targeting you, Joe. Then you can have your D.E.A. union lawyer. Get your dues' worth."

"Is that what tonight is, Ralph? Threat night?"

DeMayo pulled a second cigarette and lit it. "No, Joe. Let's call it imagination night. See, it's getting harder and harder for me to imagine you're clean. Maybe Morelli and his mob pals *were* paying your bills. Maybe you even helped him get the info on the OCCB plant. Maybe you're as guilty of accessory to murder as he is. Yeah, Joe, it's getting hard for my tired little imagination to picture you clean."

They stood facing each other for a few moments, DeMayo smoking casually, Rizzo seething silently, before DeMayo spoke again.

"Enhance my imagination, Joe," he said softly. "Give me somethin' solid. Something I can use against Morelli. You give me that, and I think my imagination will kick in real strong. So strong, in fact, it'll convince me you're clean. So strong, I'd be able to write 'confidential cooperating witness' on your jacket and file it away forever. Maybe even get you a Commissioner's Commendation. That would dot the Is and cross the Ts and you'd be out of it."

Rizzo remained silent. DeMayo slipped car keys from his pants pocket and turned to leave.

"Think it over, Joe. We'll talk again. Soon."

He walked back into the shadows and out of Rizzo's sight. A moment later, Joe heard a car start. He turned, paperwork in hand, and entered the Sixty-second Precinct building.

# CHAPTER FOUR

## *December-January*

IN THE DAYS FOLLOWING THE DONZI ARREST, December had turned bitterly cold. The streets of Bensonhurst were swept with a cold, wet sleet that quickly hardened to sheets of treacherous ice. The sector cars patrolled slowly, their studded winter tires scarring and churning the city's black ice as they rolled from auto accidents to slip-and-falls to aided cases.

Crime turned inward with the cold. The purse snatchings and street corner assaults, the vandalisms and disorderly conducts morphed into acts of domestic violence, commercial burglary, and barroom brawls. Generally, the detective squad caseload diminished as the influx of new crimes dropped with the temperature, allowing the twelve detectives of the Sixty-second Precinct to rework their older cases, clearing them slowly like stout, mature trees in a dark, foreboding forestry.

Joe Rizzo, with his fourteen years as a detective and twenty-six as a New York City cop, used seniority to secure holiday leave at Christmastime. McQueen, the junior man, worked the dismal, dark hours of the Christmas eve shift, but thanks to Detectives Schoenfeld and Ginsberg, he had Christmas Day off.

McQueen had found himself somewhat surprised to realize he was looking forward to the holiday more now than in recent years. Without being able to articulate exactly how or why, he was nonetheless aware that it was his broken relationship with Amy that was partially responsible. His feelings of Christmas warmth and nostalgia were strong, and he was anxious to spend the day nestled among family and familiar traditions.

He would travel to his sister's house in Albertson, New York, the small, upscale Long Island suburb where she lived with her husband and two children. His parents were in for Christmas, staying with him in the city, and they would all be together for the holiday.

McQueen's sister, ten years his senior, was a thirty-eight-year-old civics professor at Hofstra University. Her husband, a man McQueen looked to as more a favorite uncle than brother-in-law, was a commodities trader on Manhattan's Wall Street. Between them, they had a considerable income and lived a comfortable, privileged life.

McQueen's parents had retired five years earlier and moved from the canyons of Manhattan to the rural beauty of Virginia. Elizabeth McQueen had always been an intelligent, ambitious, and fiercely independent woman. She had met her equal in McQueen's father, Edward, when they were both young, passionate union organizers for the Eastern New York State territorial office of the AFL-CIO. Together they had risen to the union's loftiest heights, gaining national influence and power in labor. Once retired and resettled in Virginia, it hadn't been long before Elizabeth had taken up the cause of local labor issues in her new role as elder statesperson.

When his parents retreated to Virginia, they left Mike to live in their mortgage-free two-bedroom Manhattan co-op, the sole condition being that he take responsibility for the rather steep monthly maintenance charge. He and his sister were told that upon the death of their parents, the co-op would be left to both heirs, to be shared equally.

The irony of his current living conditions had never been lost on young McQueen. Indeed, on his police salary, he would barely be able to afford a monthly parking garage, let alone the price of a co-op in the area of Manhattan known as Gramercy Park.

Indeed, it had been only extremely good fortune that delivered the property to the McQueen family in the first place. When his sister had, at age twenty-three, left the family home on Long Island to start out on her own, McQueen's parents sold their house and moved to what was then a two-bedroom rental apartment. When the building converted to co-op status shortly afterward, his parents had used some of the profit from the

Long Island sale and, together with an extremely generous stipend from the union, purchased the apartment at a manageable insider price. After some years, that price had grown far and away out of any of their reach, including that of his affluent sister and brother-in-law.

And so, as the holiday arrived, McQueen found himself in a reflective mood. Despite his sadness at losing Amy, he was able to appreciate his good fortunes and face the coming new year with a reserved sense of optimism.

Any sense of melancholy touching at him, he attributed to the breakup. What else, after all, did he have to be sad about?

Nothing that he could see.

TWO DAYS after Christmas, McQueen sat at a small corner table in a Tribeca bistro called Bubby's. His black Mazda stood just off Hudson Street on North Moore in a no parking zone, the battered NYPD plaque on the dash, its multicolored hologram reflecting the last of the day's dying light. He sipped at his drink and looked across the table into the ebony face of Priscilla Jackson, the thirty-year-old police officer he had partnered with during his last twenty-four months in uniform. She scowled into her vodka and shook her head sadly as she spoke.

"Can you imagine this, Mike?" she said. "Finally, after all these years, I hook up with a woman who is totally cool with being gay, completely *out*, squared away with her family, and then I run into *this* bullshit. You have any *idea* how pissed I am?"

He smiled at her. "Oh, I think I might have some idea, Cil. Believe me."

She swallowed some vodka and screwed up her face as she responded.

"Picture it, Mike. Christmas eve. I'm sitting in their living room, we're all making small-talk chitchat, picking at hors d'oeuvres and sipping that crappy honky eggnog. Very civilized, and I'm thinking, 'How fine is this, Mama and Papa all cool with the black lesbian their baby white girl hooked up with.' Then, out of the blue, Mama leans across the coffee table and says to me, 'So, dear, are you giving any thought to your future career plans?' And me, little Miss Naive-Ass, I say, 'Oh, sure. I'm on the list for sergeant.'

"Well, Mama's jaw just about hits the tabletop, and she forgets all her rich liberal manners and says, 'Sergeant? You mean, it is your intention to continue to work as a *policeman*?' "

Mike's laugh caught some alcohol in his throat, and he broke into a racking cough. Priscilla folded her arms across her chest and sat back in her chair, her scowl deepening.

"This is funny to you?"

Mike waved a hand at her while he regained his voice.

"No, no, Cil, really. It's just . . . just . . . police*man*? She actually said that?"

Cil reached for her drink. Despite herself, her face gradually relaxed into a small smile. For countless times since he had first met her, Mike thought to himself how very beautiful she was.

"Word, Mike," she said, holding her right hand up, palm outward. "Imagine that? Fancy East Side do-gooder turned into a tight-ass, redneck bitch right before my eyes."

Mike stirred absently at his drink with an extended finger.

"Funny you brought all this up. I've got sort of a similar situation going on myself. The first case I worked with the squad, I met a girl, Amy Taylor. Remember? I mentioned her to you before."

Cil's smile broadened. "Not the first hookup you made through the job, as I recall."

"Yeah, but this one was different. I think I was in love with this one."

She leaned across the table and ran her fingers gently across Mike's cheek. "Judging by the look on your face and the word 'was,' I'm gonna guess there's trouble in paradise. Am I right?"

Mike smiled sadly into her dark eyes. "You could say that," he said. "She broke it off about two months ago. We're done."

Priscilla shook her head in mock disbelief. "*She* dumped *you*?" she asked. "That don't sound like the way it works with you, partner. Ain't you first out the door, usually?"

Mike took a slow sip of his drink. "Not this time," he said.

Priscilla smiled at him. "They say the first cut's the deepest, Mike. I guess now you know."

"Yeah, I guess."

Priscilla leaned closer to him and spoke softly.

"What happened, Mike? Can we figure a way to make it better?"

McQueen sighed and patted her hand. "Not this time, sweetheart. Not this time."

After he finished filling her in on the details, she frowned and sat back in her chair.

"That sucks," she said. "Big-time."

She rubbed at her jaw and blew air through her lips before speaking again.

"You know, Mike, life is funny. You never know with this stuff. Look at me and Karen. She tells me her parents have known she was gay since high school, no problem. She tells her mother about me being black, and the old lady tells her that she, herself, dated a black guy in college. So again, no problem. I figure—bingo!—at last, I don't have to deal with the bigotry bullshit. And then what happens? I go and run smack into a cop-bigot! So, like I say, life's funny. You never can figure it. Maybe this chick will get over it, see you for who you are, not some flashback to the bogey-man in the subway."

She shook her hair and pulled at her vodka.

"Listen to me, you never know. You get home some night and she's on your machine. 'Mikey, baby, I miss you so much! I'm sorry. Call me!' "

McQueen shook his head and smiled. "I got as much chance of that happening as I have with you, Cil: zero. Believe me."

They drank slowly and continued to vent to one another, and as they spoke, Mike thought back to their blue-and-white sector car and the many long hours they had spent together talking, getting to know one another, exploring each other's backgrounds, so different from the other. It was during those long talks that Mike had first fully realized how privileged his own youth had been.

Priscilla Jackson was the third of five children born to a single mother amid the rubble of the South Bronx. Through sheer strength of charac-ter, she had dodged each pitfall pockmarking her environment and had managed to graduate high school and go on to an associate's degree at Bronx Community College. From the chaos of her daily existence, she had sought sanctuary in the discipline and regimentation of the police department. When finally she had found the strength to announce her sexuality to her tired, beaten-down mother, it had culminated in shock and rage and near violence. It was the last time she had ever seen the woman who had birthed her.

When McQueen had first been assigned from Greenwich Village's Sixth Precinct to the East Side's Nineteenth, he and Cil had worked together on an intermittent basis. After his years in the Village, with its almost carnival-like atmosphere, he had experienced a certain amount of culture shock with the transition. Cil, with two years already logged in the silk-stocking Nineteenth, proved herself an able and patient guide. She had found Mike's obvious and genuine indifference to her sexual orientation refreshing and impressive. Eventually, they asked to be partnered and had ridden together until his promotion to detective.

"Of all the nights to call in sick," she had moaned when Mike's solo arrest of the would-be rapist had led to his being awarded a gold shield.

After his transfer to Brooklyn, they had seen and spoken to each other periodically and had remained good friends. On this evening, as they exchanged Christmas presents and caught up with one another's lives, both found the friendship mutually therapeutic.

As their evening together drew to a close, Mike shared a final confidence with his ex-partner.

"It's an Internal Affairs thing Joe Rizzo is caught up in," he said.

After hearing him out, Cil sat back and waved for the waiter.

"Well, that calls for another drink, Mike," she said with a smile. "One more for the road."

When their second drinks arrived, she leaned in against the table and spoke in low tones, her dark eyes intense.

"I've got a friend, old partner of mine, went over to I.A. years ago. It was his path to a gold shield, so he took it. He once told me that they like it when a young clean cop gets partnered with a guy they're looking at. They figure the young guy will kind of keep a check on things and if he ever does see something that looks wrong, he'd come forward with it. Plus, they know a young guy would be easier to squeeze if it came down to that—giving the other guy up. Guess it makes sense in their world."

She sat back and sipped at her drink. "Just watch your ass, Mike," she said. "Keep your eyes open, and if Rizzo *is* wrong, don't fall on any grenades. Give him up and move on."

McQueen shook his head. "I've got a strong feeling he's okay, Cil. Maybe he turned his head a few times with the drinking and the fuck-ups, but nothing as heavy as a mob setup. He's an old-fashioned guy and he has some kind of strong sense of obligation to Morelli, something from the old days. He says it's not job-related, but who knows?"

"Well," Cil said, "just keep those baby blues wide open, Partner. Don't get slicked is all I'm sayin'."

He nodded. "I don't intend to. See, the thing is, I like Joe, I think he's a good guy and a friggin' great cop. I want to work with him, at least for a while. I'm kinda stuck with him now, anyway. I agreed to work with him just before he told me about this I.A. thing. Then, when he mentioned it, I didn't want to back out. But I'm not sure what I would have done if I'd known in advance."

Cil shrugged. "Well, just go with it. Play it by ear, one day at a time. If it starts to look like maybe he was in on that gangster shit or maybe covered it up or whatever, you can walk away. Meantime, you learn from the guy."

Mike drank his Manhattan. "Yeah," he said, "I guess. I'd just feel better if I knew where Joe's sense of obligation to that guy came from. I think it would help me evaluate things better."

"I.A. can get rough, Mike. If they start to play hardball with Rizzo, you'll know it. He'll show the signs."

"Yeah, well, every once in a while he seems a little distracted, maybe stressed. He gets quiet. You know."

She nodded. "Yeah, Mike. I know." After a moment, she spoke again. "Don't be surprised if they stop in to see you. I.A. I mean. If they do, hear them out. Don't get all macho'd up. Hear them out."

"Okay, Cil," Mike said with a sad smile, "that sounds like good advice."

Cil's return smile was bright. "Bet your ass it is, bro. I'm the source for good shit. You know that."

When at last they were parting, Cil leaned over and kissed him gently on the cheek.

"You get past that girl, Mike. Nobody better than you."

He kissed her back and smiled into her deep brown eyes. "Or you," he said.

As he walked to his car, he heard her shout out his name. He turned into the cold wind that blew down the length of North Moore Street from the Hudson River. They were now a half block apart.

"Remember," she shouted through cupped hands. "If you ever do need a best *man*, I'm available!"

McQueen drove north and then east through the cold streets of Manhattan. He found open curb space at Twentieth Street just off First Avenue and parked the Mazda. Climbing out, he glanced up at the parking regulations posted on the red and white sign next to the car: "No Parking—Trucks Loading and Unloading Only." With his NYPD Official Business plaque on the dash, Mike locked the doors and crossed diagonally to the massive residential building housing his co-op apartment.

He entered the warmth of the lobby and strode across the black marble floor toward the elevators.

He noticed the neatly attired security guard look up from his desk as he approached.

"Hello, Mike," the man said, his face beaming with a broad smile. "How you doing?"

Mike smiled back. He knew the man to be a retired police officer supplementing his pension with steady night tours at the lobby desk. Mike was very much aware that the casualness of the man's tone was reserved only for him: the other residents—bankers and lawyers, doctors and a minor celebrity or two—would receive more formal greetings.

"I'm good, Hal. Real good. How are you?"

"I'm okay, thanks. Oh, your parents left about twenty minutes ago. Your dad wanted me to tell you they'd be home late, not to worry. They were going out with some friends."

Mike nodded. "Thanks."

Hal nodded, comfortable with the young cop with whom he shared a common ground. "No problem," he said. "How much longer they in town?"

Mike punched at the elevator button. The doors slid silently open, and the soft lighting and gentle Muzak beckoned him to enter.

"Couple more days. They want to get home for New Year's eve. Must have a big hoedown going on back in Hootersville."

Hal laughed and waved a dismissive hand as he turned back to his paperback. Mike stepped into the elevator, pressing the button for the twelfth floor.

When he reached the apartment, he found his mail, no doubt courtesy of his mother, stacked neatly on the small, round foyer table. He glanced through it and decided to leave it there. He removed his heavy outer coat and hung it on the antique coatrack.

The sound of his phone ringing led him into the bedroom. He sat on the edge of the bed and, without glancing at the caller ID, answered the phone.

"Hello?" he said absently.

"Hello, this is Detective Sergeant Ralph DeMayo. I'd like to speak to Michael McQueen, please."

Mike felt a cool emptiness in the pit of his stomach. He cleared his throat before answering.

"This is McQueen," he said tightly.

"Hello, Mike," the voice said. "Sorry to call so late. I tried reaching you earlier but there was no answer. You got a minute?"

"Who is this?" Mike asked. "What's this about?"

"I'm Ralph DeMayo, Internal Affairs Division, One Police Plaza."

Mike kept his voice neutral. "What can I do for you?" he asked.

"Well, you know we're looking at your partner? Joe Rizzo?"

"Yeah. I heard."

"Well," DeMayo continued, "I thought you should know. That's why I called, to make sure."

"So, okay," Mike said. "Now you know that I know."

"Right," DeMayo said casually, "that's taken care of. You got a pen and paper handy, Mike?"

"Why?"

"Just want you to jot down my number, that's all. In case you need to call me sometime."

"Why would I need to call you?" Mike asked, a tightness creeping into his voice despite himself.

He heard DeMayo's chuckle come through the line. "Well, I guess I don't know, Mike. But you never can tell. Just in case. Maybe after you and Rizzo work together for a while and you get all buddy-buddy, maybe you'll have something to tell me."

Mike hesitated. Some seconds passed before he spoke again.

"Give me the number," he said softly.

After he did, DeMayo's voice grew lighter. "Have a nice night, Detective," he said. "Hope to talk to you again sometime."

The line clicked dead in Mike's ear.

He hung up and stood slowly. He undid his belt and slipped the sleek Glock nine millimeter free, then placed it, still holstered, under his mattress near the head of the bed. Finally he undressed and pulled on worn sweatpants, dropping heavily onto the edge of the bed.

He had wanted to be a lawyer, he remembered. That first year at NYU before declaring a major, he had wanted to study law. He rubbed at his eyes, heavy from the alcohol he had consumed earlier, and tried to recall exactly when, and under what circumstances, he had changed his mind. But he hadn't, he realized. Not consciously, anyway. His mind had simply changed itself. He finished his four years of college, took his degree, and then, one day, the notice had come in the mail.

They had reached his name on the civil service list for police officer. They were calling him in for a medical screening.

And suddenly Mike had felt a heavy weight lifting from his shoulders, a weight he hadn't been aware existed until it was blessedly gone.

No suits, no ties, no subway rides at eight-thirty, coffee at nine, meeting at ten-fifteen. Instead, dark city nights, rain-swept weekends, sunrises and sunsets, excitement, some danger—an adventure.

"Your father's blue-collar genes," Edward McQueen said with a smile when he heard of his son's plans. "The PBA is a hell of a good labor union."

His mother had concealed her disappointment well, and a less loving and respectful eye than Mike's own would probably have missed it. But he hadn't missed it. He knew it was there.

Along with something else. Fear.

But they gave him their full support, and he had gone ahead and done it. And it had worked out pretty well.

But that was almost seven years ago. Now Mike lay back flat on the bed, staring at the gently illuminated ceiling.

He wasn't quite sure how it was working out now. Not sure at all.

He closed his eyes and pushed the thoughts and doubts from his mind, letting the alcohol in his blood seek sleep for him.

As the thoughts slowly misted and floated away, Amy's sad, beautiful face materialized gently to replace them.

He opened his eyes and sat up slowly, willing her away. As he realized she may periodically appear to him in his quiet hours, he also realized, with a cruel and absolute finality, that she was gone.

Gone forever.

Mike allowed his body to slowly lie back down, and as he drifted into a fretful sleep, he wished her well.

# CHAPTER FIVE

*March-April*

THE WINTER RAN ITS COURSE HARSHLY, punishing the city with dismally cold days and frantic, swirling snowstorms. The officers of the Six-Two found themselves spending many an overnight at the precinct house, watching television and sleeping between shifts, the snows too deep and the ice too treacherous for them to wend their way home to Staten Island or Nassau or Suffolk.

By mid-March, the citizens as well as the cops of the precinct wore the haggard, ashen faces of a winter-weary people, tired of the cold, tired of the bleakness of the cityscape, tired of the slipping and sliding, the fender-benders, the shoveling and sore backs. Their shoulders carried the perpetual slump of the challenger of constant cold winter winds, and their skin had become dried out, itchy, brittle to the touch. Each gray day that dawned brought silent, stoic skyward glances and soft, resigned sighs.

"Worst winter I ever seen in Brooklyn," Joe said to McQueen one midnight as they stood at the squad room window, watching as the swirling snow obliterated Bath Avenue once again.

And then, one morning, it was all over. March 20 dawned yellow with sun. The stubborn masses of dirty, frozen snow that seemed to cling to every curb, every corner, every patch of grass or soil had softened on that day. In a week, they were gone, and the balmy breezes sweeping the streets chased the air's cold bite from the nostrils and erased the last shadows of the dissipating dark gray clouds.

It was just such a morning when McQueen walked into the squad room at seven-fifty and signed in on the duty board. He went to his desk, bade farewell to the two morning shift detectives as they left for the day, and sat to sip his coffee and pick at his bagel.

McQueen scanned his e-mail as he ate, then checked his messages. A known car thief they were after had been arrested in the neighboring Sixtieth Precinct. A housewife, reported missing by her husband the week before, had turned up in Atlantic City, New Jersey: her boyfriend's cousin, a divorce attorney, had just served papers on the bewildered husband. A raid on a Manhattan pawnshop had produced three items related to a Six-Two commercial burglary from back in February. Mike jotted down some notes and turned back to his coffee. He saw Rizzo walk in and waved him a greeting. Joe smiled back and said, "Hiya, kid," and went to his own desk.

At nine o'clock, the squad room door opened and the day tour supervisor of patrol, a tall, lanky Irishman, walked in. Mike was standing next to Rizzo's desk, talking to his partner, when the uniformed officer approached them.

"Hello, Joe," he said, glancing and nodding a greeting in an offhand manner to McQueen.

"Why, it's my favorite lieutenant, Francis McLoughlin. What can I do for you, Frank? I gotta tell you, though, I don't have any beer in my desk drawer. Sorry."

The lieutenant did not appear amused. "That's good, Joe. Let me see, I'm Irish, it's nine in the morning, so I must want a beer. Is that it? Is that the joke? Did I get it right?"

Joe chuckled and McLoughlin turned to McQueen and said, "Mike, it's a wonder you haven't shot this dago yet. You must have the patience of a parish priest."

"So, Frank, what brings you up all those stairs to the squad? What can we do for you?" Rizzo asked.

The lieutenant leaned his buttocks on the side of Joe's desk and folded his arms against his chest before speaking.

"Joe, we got a shooting. Over on Bay Twenty-third Street in Bath Beach. Few more blocks south and it woulda been the Six-O's problem."

Rizzo frowned up at the man. "What kinda shooting? Mob thing?"

McLoughlin shook his head. "No. Looks like a break-in got nasty. I don't have all the details yet, I'm about to go over there. I got three sector cars and a sergeant there now."

"What's the status of the victim?" Joe asked.

"Dead."

Rizzo ran a hand through his slightly thinning brown hair. "You call in Brooklyn South yet?"

He was referring to the Brooklyn South Homicide Squad, which held responsibility for murder investigations in a half dozen Brooklyn precincts, the Six-Two included.

"I did that, yes, of course. But Joe, spring is in the air and they got a heavy body count from the weekend and two more last night. They want you guys to handle it, at least initially. I called D'Antonio at home and he said to give it to you, you're senior detective sergeant working. Rossi and Schoenfeld are in the field, I called them in to assist. They said they'd meet you at the location in about an hour."

Vincent D'Antonio was the fifty-three-year-old detective lieutenant who ran the detective squad at the Sixty-second Precinct.

Rizzo rose silently and stretched out his back muscles. He looked over at McQueen. "You up for some blood and guts, Mike?"

McQueen shrugged. "Whatever," he said, turning to go get his jacket.

"Here's the address," McLoughlin said, handing Rizzo a yellow Post-it. "I'll see you over there." He turned and left the room.

Twenty minutes later, Mike pulled the gray Impala to a stop in front of the two-story brick home of the address McLoughlin had given them. He double-parked behind one of the five police cars scattered before the house. Two of the cars had dome lights swirling, the regimented metallic clicking of their drive gears sounding a depressing counterpoint to the musical chirping of springtime robins perched in the trees that lined the neat, quiet, narrow block of single-family homes.

The two detectives approached the house, eyed silently by the small weekday morning crowd gathered there—mostly older, retired men and women and young mothers clutching at outer street garments thrown hastily over bedclothing. Rizzo and McQueen climbed the steps up to the broad, open, stone-covered porch. The small garden plots bordering the steps had not yet begun to bloom, but their statues of Mary and Jesus were clean and well maintained. The front door stood slightly ajar, a full color bust of Jesus, imposed over a Sacred Heart, hanging from it in greeting. McQueen pushed the door fully open, and they entered.

The shooting had taken place in the upstairs apartment, a large, six-room dwelling that encompassed the entire second floor of the house. The inside staircase led to an entry door that opened into the simple kitchen. Rizzo saw McLoughlin standing among a tight circle of uniformed officers.

He spread his hands wide in front of his chest and said, "First on the scene. Tell me."

Two young uniforms stepped forward. The older of the two, a twenty-six-year-old Hispanic male, cleared his voice.

"We caught the initial call, Detective. This is our sector."

Joe looked at the cop and smiled. He could hear the disappointment in the young man's voice and found himself instantly liking him. The cop was sad that someone in his sector had been shot on *his* watch. It somehow seemed a failure on his part. Rizzo remembered the feeling. He knew it would not survive the young cop's entire career, but instead wall itself away in some secret corner of his psyche, and disappear from his tone and mannerisms.

"Tell me," Joe repeated, keeping his voice soft.

The cop looked down to the notepad clipped into the inside cover of his bulky summons book. He scanned it, flipped a page, scanned some more, then raised his eyes to speak to Joe. He checked his notes sporadically as he spoke.

"We were on our way back to the precinct, seven forty-five. We were midnight to eight. We get a call, shots at this location, citizen down, ambulance on the way. We got here just before they did. The guy that lives downstairs, he owns the house. Lives here with his wife. Guy is sixty-one, wife is sixty. The victim lives up here alone, he's the landlord's older brother, sixty-six. They're basically immigrants, even though they came here from Italy over thirty years ago. They all speak Italian to each other, they got statues and saints all over the place—you know the drill."

Rizzo nodded, yes, he knew the drill. There were nested enclaves within the enclave of Bensonhurst itself: along certain stretches of Eighteenth Avenue, English simply was not required. A person could shop, see a doctor or dentist, rent an apartment or even buy a house without knowing or speaking a single word other than Italian in either the Sicilian or Neapolitan dialect. Over recent years, there may have been a slight shrinking of the borders of the inner enclaves, but only slight.

"Go on," he said to the cop, whose name tag read "Silva."

"Well, we get here and the guy and his wife are out on the porch. They tell us they went out to the market around seven. They picked up some fruit and some cheese for breakfast and came back home. They put the car around back in the detached garage, and just as the guy's closing the garage door, he hears a shot—from inside the house, upstairs. He tells his wife to call the cops from a neighbor's house, and he goes in the back door. He runs through the downstairs apartment into the front foyer and up the steps to his brother's place, and he finds the guy dead."

"Where?"

Silva indicated with a leftward tilt of his head. "In the bathroom."

Rizzo turned to Mike. "You bring gloves?"

McQueen nodded, producing two pairs of latex gloves from the pocket of his sport coat. He gave one to Joe and, as he followed Rizzo down the corridor leading off the kitchen, he pulled the other pair onto his hands.

The house was at least seventy years old, probably older. The bathroom, although obviously well maintained, looked original, with intricate one-inch black and pink ceramic floor tiles and matching four-inch pinkish-purple wall tiles edged in black. The tub rested against the far wall opposite the door, a separate built-in shower stall located on the near wall to the left of the entrance. The smooth pink porcelain of the tub was immaculate, and it glistened in the light from the fluorescent above the small sink on the far left wall.

Rizzo stood in the doorway, scanning the scene. He only glanced at the body, which lay fully clothed in the bathtub. After a moment, he stepped fully into the room. McQueen walked in behind him and focused his attention on the built-in hamper on the right wall, allowing only his peripheral vision to include the corpse in his sight. The scent of blood was in the air.

Rizzo turned to his left and opened the shower curtain slightly. The separate shower stall was done in darker pink tiles. They also glistened as though new. On the floor of the shower, three litter boxes sat neatly aligned. Each held an unspoiled flat expanse of sand-colored cat litter.

"I guess this guy has cats," Joe said.

McLoughlin, standing in the foyer just outside the room, answered. "Three of 'em. They been running from under one piece of furniture to another since the cops got here. Every time somebody gets near one, it takes off. They don't like people much, it seems."

Joe released the shower curtain and went to the tub. He knelt beside it and, without turning, beckoned for McQueen to come closer. Mike felt himself flushing and knew he had somehow annoyed Joe by hanging back. He moved to the tub and squatted down. Rizzo turned to face him and their eyes met.

Joe smiled at him. "Relax a little, kid," he said, just barely loud enough for Mike to hear him. Then Rizzo turned to the corpse.

The body was fully dressed in street clothes. Nicely creased black pants, a clean, freshly ironed shirt. Black gold-toed socks.

Joe glanced down to the floor near the foot of the bathtub. A pair of black wingtip shoes, brightly polished, were perfectly placed there.

The man's head was to Joe's left. It was tilted to the left and leaning against the tile wall. A small black and purple bruise, centered by a smaller dark hole, appeared just under the temple. A gray-black spattering haloed the wound site.

Joe pointed to the spatter. "Powder burn. Gun was real close," he said, presumably to Mike, but seemingly more to himself.

The tile wall behind the head was coated with a violent splash of red and gray matter, a fine sprinkling of white bone splinters adhering to it. Both arms were fully inside the tub, splayed across the front of the body. A slight fecal odor nudged at the blood scent. About a quarter inch of blood pooled at the center bottom of the tub.

Rizzo reached a gloved hand into the tub and lifted first one, then the other of the arms, examining the hands carefully.

"No bruises, no cuts," he said in the same low tones. "Probably no struggle." He gently replaced the arms onto the body, looking down at the neatly cut, filed and buffed fingernails. He reached in and took hold of the pant material on first one, then the other leg, lifting each, looking underneath them. He looked behind the small of the back and moved the body slightly to see behind its left side. Then Rizzo slowly stood from the tub. McQueen rose with him.

"Let's get started," he said.

Rizzo turned to face McLoughlin, who now joined them in the small bathroom.

"What do you need, Joe?" the lieutenant asked.

"You going to hold the morning tour over, Frank?" he asked.

McLoughlin nodded. "I already told the eight guys here I'd author-ize the overtime. Plus, Rossi and Schoenfeld got here, they're down-stairs. They've started to canvass the neighbors."

Rizzo nodded. "Good. Get the uniforms to look for any sign of forced entry. All the doors, all the windows, upstairs, basement, every-where. And have them walk up and down the whole street. I want the plate number of every car parked out there, and up on Bath and Benson Avenues, near the corners. While they're at it, let 'em look in the bushes and under the cars. In the garbage pails, too. We need that gun."

"Alright, Joe. I'll take care of it. I'll call the house, get a couple more guys over here from the day shift to help out. Anything you want me to handle personally?"

"Yeah, Frank, if the gun don't turn up, call the Department of Envi-ronmental Protection. Bureau of Water and Sewer Operations, it's out in Queens someplace. Tell them we may need a search on the sewers. They need twenty-four hours' notice, then they can send a crew out here to check the storm sewers for the piece."

"Okay, Joe, I'll take care of that. Anything else?"

"If you can, do a permit search for everybody who lives in the house. I doubt if you'll get a hit for a pistol permit, but you never know. Did you call in for a forensic team?"

"Yeah. They're backed up. Probably get here late this afternoon."

Joe smiled a tired smile. "Business is booming, alright. Well, we need somebody to check out that tub. It looks like the bullet cleared the skull and took some bone out the left side of the head. But it didn't penetrate the tile wall. Might not've even hit it, who knows? But that bullet is probably somewhere in the tub, under the blood. I checked all around;

it didn't ricochet and land out in the room somewhere. We could really use that bullet."

McLoughlin nodded and turned away, reaching for his cell phone as he walked.

"Mike," Rizzo said after a few minutes. "Go get Silva for me, okay? I'm gonna look around a little more."

Rizzo departed the bathroom and turned left at the hallway, walking its length to the rear of the apartment. He glanced into what would normally serve as a second bedroom, its paneled door hanging wide open. The immaculate parquet floor shone in the morning sunlight streaming through the room's two windows. There was not a single item in the empty room, not even a picture on any of the walls.

When he reached the very end of the hall, Joe entered the master bedroom.

Ten minutes later, he left the room. Slowly, he walked back through the kitchen. He looked into the sink. The gleaming white porcelain reflected Rizzo's image. It held no dirty dishes. The drain rack next to it was also empty. No dinner dishes, no breakfast dishes. Rizzo crossed the room and opened the refrigerator. It was well stocked. Each shelf contained at least a few items. Rizzo smiled at them: just as he had found in the bedroom, everything was arranged in neat, orderly rows, in size place, labels facing outward. He reached in and removed the bottle of ketchup. Unscrewing the cap, he examined the neck of the bottle opening. Clean. No residual ketchup. He turned the cap over in his hand. The inside was also clean, not a trace of ketchup. He replaced the cap and put the bottle back, closing the refrigerator door.

McQueen reentered the apartment with Silva following closely behind him. He had found the young officer walking the block, copying down plate numbers and looking for the gun.

"Silva," Joe said. "Did the brother mention if the front door of the house was open? You know, when he ran through his apartment and into the front foyer to go upstairs, did he say if the front door of the house was open?"

"No. No he didn't mention it."

"Did you or your partner ask him?"

The young cop looked uncomfortable. His eyes dropped away from

Joe's for an instant. When he regained his composure, he looked Joe in the eye.

"No. We didn't think of it."

Joe nodded. "Okay, thanks. Where's the guy now?"

"In his apartment. He's real upset."

Rizzo smiled and glanced at Mike.

"Yeah, I bet he is," he said.

"SOMETHING IS very wrong here, Mike," Rizzo said, drawing on his Chesterfield and blowing smoke out the passenger window. "This don't add up."

McQueen sat behind the wheel of the Impala, still double-parked in front of the house. He watched as the ambulance that had initially responded pulled away. The EMT on board had declared the victim dead. The body would wait for an official pronouncement from the medical examiner and remain in the bathtub. There was no further need for an ambulance.

Before Mike could answer, the rear door of the Impala swung open and Detective First Grade Morris Schoenfeld climbed in, dropping heavily into the seat. He immediately began to fan the air in front of him.

"But damn it, Joe," he said. "Still with those goddamned cigarettes?"

Rizzo laughed and flicked the nearly gone butt out onto the sidewalk.

"Yeah, Mo, it's good to see you, too. Whatda ya got?"

Schoenfeld shifted in his seat and looked down at his notes as he spoke.

"No one outside when the shot went off. First anyone knew something had happened was when the radio cars started to light up the block. Except for a Mrs. Cottone, lives next door. The landlady ran to her place to call the cops. Then the landlord made a second call saying somebody shot his brother."

Joe scratched at his forehead. "What about the gossip?"

"Well," Schoenfeld went on, "there is *that*. Seems like the victim was a class-A nut. Sweet guy, but a real screwball. Would only go outside on odd-numbered days. Would only walk one way on the block: toward Bath

Avenue. If he needed to go up to Benson Avenue, he'd come out, walk toward Bath, then go all around the block. A few people told me the same kind of shit, he wouldn't step on cracks in the sidewalk, always carried an umbrella no matter what the weather, stuff like that. Obsessive-compulsive type. But they say he was a nice, gentle guy, wouldn't hurt a fly and kept to himself, a real loner."

McQueen asked, "What about the brother? How'd they get along?"

Schoenfeld sighed. "It ain't going to be that easy, Mike. We can take a look at the brother, but I doubt it. All the neighbors me and Nick talked to said the same thing: these two guys loved each other."

Now Joe spoke. "Where is Nick?" he asked, referring to Nick Rossi, Schoenfeld's partner.

Morris smiled. "Oh, there's a thirty-year-old divorcée lives in the house down there on the right. Nick just remembered a coupla more questions he had for her."

Rizzo grunted but sat in silence. After a while, Schoenfeld spoke.

"Is Brooklyn South gonna take this?"

Rizzo shrugged. "I doubt it, but I don't know. Anyway, there might not be anything to take."

"What do you mean?" Schoenfeld asked.

Rizzo turned half in his seat and winked at the man. "I got a theory," he said, tapping at his temple with a forefinger.

Schoenfeld reached for the door handle. "Yeah, you got a theory and the other guinea has a hard-on. You work on your theory, I'm gonna go grab Rossi out of that broad's house before he makes one of his unfortunate emotional commitments. I'd hate to see him with another broken heart."

With that, he left. McQueen turned to Joe.

"So," he asked. "What's the theory?"

Joe smiled. "Suicide," he said.

Mike looked at him, expecting a laugh. But none came. He saw that Rizzo was serious.

"Suicide?" he asked. "Joe, they searched the whole block, they can't find a gun. Even assuming the guy blew his brains out, got up and ran to the window and threw the gun out, jumped back into the tub and died, they would have found the gun."

"Murder just doesn't add up, Mike."

McQueen shook his head. "I think *suicide* doesn't add up, Joe."

"Mike, you heard McLoughlin. He talked to the landlord, this guy, Natale Catanzaro, he spent his whole life taking care of his brother. The older one, Vincente, he never held a job, never could work, he was too screwy. Natale, he took care of him back in Italy, got him over here and then took care of him some more. Gave him a place to live, food on his table, and a family around him. These are religious people, Mike. You see these statues all over the place, the Jesus on the door. I saw Natale's living room, there's a friggin' altar in there. You commit suicide, the Catholic Church won't give you a funeral mass. Won't even let the casket sit at the altar. You commit suicide, you're in big trouble with the Church. You think Natale would allow that to happen to his big brother? After a lifetime of looking out for him, you think he's gonna let him down now?"

McQueen pondered it. "So you figure the guy climbed into the tub, blew his brains out, and then his kid brother finds him, grabs the gun, calls the cops, and says it's murder?"

"Bingo," Joe said, reaching for another Chesterfield.

"Based on what, Joe? A guess?"

"No, not just a guess. You saw the apartment. This guy's a bachelor all his life and my mother's kitchen isn't as clean as his, and she's half a nut herself. You saw his closet—the shirts all lined up: blue shirt, blue hanger, white shirt, white hanger. The guy cleans the inside of his ketchup cap, for Christ sake."

"And that's it? You get suicide and cover-up from that?"

Joe shook his head and lit the Chesterfield. "No, of course not. I get suicide from the shoes, mostly."

McQueen frowned. "The shoes? The ones on the shelf in his closet? The ones all lined up?"

"No, not those. I mean the shoes outside the tub. Remember how the guy was dressed? He's up at seven in the morning, no job to go to, nothing to do all day except line up the turds in the litter boxes. Then he puts on his neatly pressed pants, irons a shirt, polishes his shoes, and decides to kill himself. Ever roll up on a suicide by gunshot when you were in uniform, Mike?"

McQueen flashed back to the small basement apartment, Greenwich Village, four years ago.

"One," he said.

"Where'd you find the guy?"

McQueen's mind re-created the image: living room. On the sofa.

"Let me tell you," Rizzo said before Mike could respond. "In his bed. Or on his sofa, or big, comfortable easy chair. Right?"

"The sofa."

Rizzo nodded. "That's where they do it. Or down in their basement workshop or out in the garage. Someplace they feel safe, comfortable, peaceful. They look for some security to give them that last little bit of strength so they can pull the trigger and get real comfortable, real peaceful, forever. That's the plan."

McQueen looked puzzled. "So how does your theory fit in here with the tub? The guy was a cleanliness freak, so he was comfortable and secure in the *bathtub*?"

Joe smiled and blew cigarette smoke into the dash.

"No. He was a cleanliness freak so he did it where he'd make the least amount of mess. Now Natale just has to hose down the wall, pour some bleach into the tub, run the water, and five minutes later he could rent the place out. No muss, no fuss. Nobody shoots themselves in the tub, Mike, except for our man Vincente. And while we're on the subject, who comes into somebody's house, puts them in the tub, and shoots them? Think about it."

Mike did think about it. "Wouldn't a guy like this leave a suicide note? Tell his brother where the checkbook is, where the keys to the apartment are, when to ditch the milk in the fridge, stuff like that? We went over the place pretty thoroughly, I didn't see any note."

Joe responded. "You're absolutely right. Guy like this would leave a note, probably with a photocopy or two. So when Natale grabbed the gun, he grabbed the note. And don't forget about the shoes, Mike. The shoes."

McQueen shook his head. "*What* goddamned shoes, Joe?"

Rizzo laughed. "*The* shoes. The ones by the tub. Don't you see it yet? If somebody did decide to whack this guy in the friggin' tub, they would have just told him to get in and then shot him. But Vincente put himself into that tub. And he figured when the bullet tore through his brains, his body might jerk around a little. So what does he do? He takes off his shoes, lines 'em up outside the tub, nice and neat, and climbs in."

"Why, Joe? Why? What does that even mean?"

"It means he didn't want to scuff up the nice shiny porcelain, maybe even chip it, that's what it means. The blood and gore you can wash away. Black scuff marks, on the other hand, you got to rub at those. And chips would be a disaster. Only an inconsiderate slob could do something like that, but not our boy Vincente."

McQueen thought it over. As much as he found himself wanting it not to make sense, he did see the logic in it.

"So that was it, Joe? The shoes tipped you to this?"

"Well, not at first. The litter boxes were what first got me thinking. What single guy living alone with three cats has clean litter boxes? I started to think that since the place was so clean, the whole bathroom all shiny, that he cleaned everything just before he shot himself. So when we got here the place wouldn't be a mess. But after I saw his bedroom, that's when I took another look at the shoes. This guy had cuff links lined up in his jewelry box so perfectly he must have used a ruler."

They sat in silence for a while. Then Mike spoke.

"What now? How you going to play it?"

Rizzo shrugged. "It's probably a slam dunk. I get the M.E. to run some tests on Vincente. That'll show if he fired a gun recently. Angle of entry should help, too. You shoot a guy who's down in a tub, entry will be from above. Guy shoots himself, it's an upward or near level entry. We can go forensic on this, but I'd like to try and let Natale off the hook. If we have to spend a lot of tax dollars on this thing, the D.A. is going to want obstruction charges, maybe even a promoting a suicide count against the guy. I've avoided talkin' to him until I had this figured out. It may come down to who scares him more, the cops or the Church. Maybe I can get him to fess up and hand over the gun and the note, if there is one. We'll see. Otherwise, we sit on him and get a warrant for the house. I'll go talk to him now. Come on, those blue eyes and pale skin of yours should rattle him pretty good. Probably remind him of the mick immigration officer that robbed him when he first got off the boat."

★ ★ ★

THE NEAT, sun-splashed living room, located at the very front of the house, had three leaded stained-glass windows that opened out over the front porch and street. McQueen, Rizzo, and McLoughlin sat together on the long couch, a mahogany coffee table before them, Natale Catanzaro to their right in a formal, pleated chair.

Natale was a small man, five-six, with the weathered, leathery face of an out-of-doors worker. His hands were callused and strong, and despite his age, Catanzaro still worked part-time as a laborer for a local construction firm. His eyes, although saddened by the day's tragedy, were bright and alert. And as he looked from the face of one cop and into another, a distrust began to nudge at his expression.

Rizzo, by unspoken understanding, would take the lead in the interview.

"Mr. Catanzaro," he said, leaning casually forward, elbows on knees, fingertips touching, "I'm sorry we need to do this. I hope you understand."

Catanzaro held Joe's eyes as he answered.

"*Si*," he said. Then, with a small shake of his head, "I'm sorry. I meant to say, 'Yes.'" Despite over thirty years living in Brooklyn, his voice still held a strong Italian accent, and he made no attempt to lessen it.

Rizzo smiled.

"*Non c'e' bisogno di chiedere scusa amico mio. Amo sentire la lingua italiana, anche se solo una parola.*"

The man let some seconds pass in silence before answering.

"*Bene. Ma per i nostri amici americani parliamo in inglese.*"

"Of course, we'll speak in English." Rizzo smiled first at McQueen to his right, then at McLoughlin to his left. "I was just tellin' him how I love to hear the Italian language spoken. But he suggests we stick to English so you two *Americanas* can understand."

McQueen smiled his response. McLoughlin scowled his. "Whatever you want, Joe," the lieutenant said.

"*I* want you to find the man who murdered my brother," Catanzaro interjected. "I want him to be punished. My brother was a good, gentle man. This should not have happened."

Rizzo nodded. "No, it should not have happened. But it did." He reached into his jacket pocket and took out a notebook. Opening it, with his eyes downward and scanning his notes, he spoke to Catanzaro.

"What makes you think it was a man? Did you see him?"

Catanzaro's face, Rizzo noted as he lifted his gaze, showed no emotion.

"No. I did not see anyone. But a murder like this, only a man could do. Don't you agree?"

Rizzo smiled once more. "I wish I could. But the truth is, anyone could have done it, man or woman. Right now I see five possibilities. One: somebody broke into the house and killed Vincente for whatever reason. But, you know, we had five guys search around, and they can't find any sign of forced entry. And you told Officer Silva you had locked the house up last night before going to bed, then left through the back door this morning and locked it behind you. You were very certain about that, Silva said."

"He's right. I am positive."

Joe nodded. "That brings us to the second possibility: Vincente let the killer into the house. That would mean he knew him or her, or else someone conned him into letting them in. But from what Detectives Rossi and Schoenfeld told me, that's not likely because Vincente never answered the door, not even for a neighbor. If you weren't home, the door just didn't get answered. Is that correct?"

"Yes. Vincente is . . . was . . . he was shy. He didn't like to get involved with people."

"Okay then. Next possibility: someone who has a key let themselves in. A friend. A neighbor. Maybe a family member."

Catanzaro's eyes flared slightly, and his voice was hard when he answered.

"There are no murderers in this family, Detective Rizzo. My son is a vice president of Johnson and Johnson, and my daughter is a doctor at Mount Sinai Hospital. There are artists and teachers in our family, but there are no murderers."

"I didn't mean any offense," Rizzo said, raising his right hand to shoulder level. "I'm just running it all down for you."

The man seemed to ponder that for a moment, and they all saw his face relax slightly as he spoke again.

"I understand," he said.

Joe smiled. "That's interesting. About your daughter, I mean. My oldest girl is at Cornell Medical School. She has two years to go."

Now Catanzaro relaxed more fully and, for the first time, smiled. McQueen was envious of the perfectly set, pearly white teeth of the older man.

"You have my sympathy, Mr. Rizzo. For the tuition, I mean."

Rizzo laughed. "I just thank God my wife works," he said.

They sat in silence for a moment, then Catanzaro spoke.

"There is no one else with a key to this house. Only my family, and I have explained that to you."

Nodding, Rizzo glanced back to his notes. "Okay," he said. "Fourth possibility."

Catanzaro sat passively. Rizzo held his gaze. The man did not look away. Rizzo waited for a question to come from Catanzaro. When, after ten long seconds had passed and none had come, Rizzo spoke again. He kept his voice low.

"Vincente was killed by someone who lives here."

Catanzaro did not respond but still held Rizzo's gaze.

"Who lives here, Mr. Catanzaro? You, your wife . . . anyone else?"

Catanzaro echoed Rizzo's flat tone. "No," he said.

Rizzo sat back on the couch. He shook his head slightly and glanced at McQueen, his eyebrows arching slightly.

"Well," he said, again facing Catanzaro, "I gotta tell you, something you told the uniformed officers just doesn't make sense to me. Assuming they got it straight, of course. And assuming I got it right from them."

Now it was Catanzaro who leaned forward in his seat, his powerful hands dangling between his open knees.

"Please do not assume, Senore Rizzo. Make your accusation. If you are evil and ignorant enough to imagine such a thing, then be honest enough to say it. Don't worry, you are safe: I cannot murder you as well. You have your policeman friends all over my home."

Joe raised both hands, palms outward. "I'm making no accusation, Senore Catanzaro." He slowly lowered his hands and gave a tight smile. "But be assured, sir, if one needs to be made, I'll have all the honesty you require."

They sat in silence for a moment, and Catanzaro's gaze turned slowly to a glare. McLoughlin cleared his throat and spoke for the first time since the introductions.

"Alright, gentlemen. No one likes this. Let's just get on with it and get it done. Joe, do you have a point to make here?"

Rizzo nodded, his eyes not leaving Catanzaro's.

"When you came home, you put the car in the garage, then closed the garage doors. Right?"

"Yes."

"Your wife was with you, in the driveway out back?"

"Yes."

Rizzo shook his head. "See, here's the first part I don't understand. It's seven in the morning, you're in your own driveway and you hear what you believe is a shot. From upstairs. Right away, you tell your wife, 'Go call the cops, get an ambulance.' "

Catanzaro frowned. "And that is odd to you? What should I have done?"

"Well, I don't know. Most people hear a sound like that they just keep listening. They say, 'What was that?' Then they listen some more. If they don't hear anything else, they forget about it. Believe me, I've been out to more than a few shootings. One shot, no call. Two or three shots, twenty calls. But you, right away, you knew it was a shot. Not a backfire, not somebody dropped something, not a firecracker—a shot. Yet you told Silva there's no gun in the house, and we checked: no one here has a pistol permit. Someone who keeps a gun in the house, they come home, they hear a noise like that, they might immediately think 'gunshot.' But you say there is no gun in the house. Still, you not only knew it was a shot, but you knew that it came from upstairs. Where your brother was. And that bathroom, it's way up near the front of the house. And judging from the exit wound, I'd say it was a relatively small-bore gun. Not very loud, not really. So, you barely heard a noise, instantly identified it as a shot, determined the location, and got the wheels turning to get some help. That's pretty remarkable, Mr. Catanzaro, I gotta tell you." Now Joe paused, smiling slightly. "You know, just to be honest and all."

Catanzaro looked first to McLoughlin's face, then McQueen's. He could read nothing in either.

"Is there more?" he asked.

"Well," Joe continued, "you said you thought there might be an intruder in the house, someone firing a gun, and so what do you do? You go running right in. That's pretty heroic of you."

Catanzaro's smile was without mirth. "Or foolish," he said.

Rizzo nodded. "Yes. Or foolish. But you did run right in. Right through your apartment, right past the still closed front door of the house and right up the stairs. Right to Vincente."

"And from all this, I see that you think I killed my brother. Is that what you have decided? That I killed my older brother, like a savage animal, and that my wife assisted me?"

Rizzo didn't answer. Catanzaro looked from one cop's face to the other. They were stoic and unyielding. Catanzaro sighed before speaking.

"It must be very sad to live your lives. To have such thoughts occur to you all the time. It must make it difficult for you to love anyone."

The silence now, at least to McQueen, became so uncomfortable that, despite not being sure he should, he decided to speak, just to hear the sound and to break the scream of the stillness.

"You said five possibilities, Joe. I think you only covered four so far."

Rizzo smiled and glanced at Mike. "That's right," he said, and turned back to Catanzaro. "You want to hear the fifth possibility, sir?" he asked, his voice suddenly more gentle.

For the first time, Catanzaro looked away from Rizzo, turning his eyes to the small altar at the far end of the room. A statue of the Blessed Virgin, her hands clasped over her heart, eyes downcast, stood framed by two votive candles that flickered and danced in memory of Vincente.

"No," he said, a hoarseness in his voice.

Rizzo stood slowly and crossed the room to the altar. He produced the scarred Zippo from his pants pocket and sparked it to life. Slowly, he lit a third votive: as it first flared and then steadied to a stable glow, he made the sign of the cross and stood silently for a moment. Then he crossed the room to the far corner, diagonal to Catanzaro. Sitting heavily in the high-back chair, he spoke across the room.

"Suicide, Natale," he said softly. "Your brother committed suicide."

"No!" Catanzaro said sharply, looking to Rizzo with anger. "No! He was killed. Slaughtered like the innocent lamb he was."

Rizzo shook his head. "No, he wasn't. You knew it was a shot you heard because you knew there was a gun in the house, an illegal gun you and half the people in Brooklyn keep for protection. You knew it came from upstairs because that's where your brother was. You knew that somehow Vincente must have found the gun, even though you had it hidden away somewhere. You knew he found it and used it. You knew right away. Maybe he'd been depressed lately, maybe he even said something to you. I don't know. What I *do* know is that you sent your wife to call nine-one-one, and you ran into the house to try and help him. And when you found him and he was dead, you still tried to help him. You took the gun, you took the letter he left, and you hid them. They're in this house somewhere right now. I can get a search warrant, and we can sit here while your home is torn apart until we find it. And then, Natale, I'll have to lock you up for obstruction. The D.A., maybe he'll want to add a promoting suicide charge. That's an 'E' felony, by the way. Hell, who knows, he might even want a manslaughter count against you, I can't say."

Catanzaro suddenly jumped to his feet. McQueen felt his stomach begin to knot and instinctively positioned his feet on the deep carpeting for possible quick action.

But the man made no movement toward Joe. Instead he said sharply and simply, "No! No suicide! *Omicidio!*"

Now Rizzo stood deliberately and slowly crossed the room, placing a gentle hand on Catanzaro's arm. As he did so, the last reserve of composure left the man. His shoulders slumped with a dead weight, and his eyes pooled with tears.

"*Non e' una disgrazia per Lei, Signore,*" Joe said in soft tones indicating there was no disgrace to Natale. "*Nessuna disgrazia.*"

The man sobbed as he answered. "*Si, e' una disgrazia. Per la mia famiglia. Per la Chiesa. Per Dio stesso.*"

Rizzo shook his head, no, no, there was no disgrace to his family or his Church: certainly none to God.

"*Lui trovera' la pace solo quando Lei mi dira' la verita',*" Joe said. "The truth, Natale. He can only rest in peace if you tell me the truth."

Natale Catanzaro, a strong man seasoned by sixty-one years of life's cruelties, sighed. He sat back down, Joe's hand sliding gently from his arm.

"*Sì*," he said softly. "The truth. I will tell you the truth."

RIZZO, ALONG with McLoughlin, left for the precinct, where they would take a formal statement from Natale and Katarina Catanzaro. McQueen had stayed behind to wait for the medical examiner. He had carefully placed the Ruger thirty-two-caliber revolver, now tucked safely into a clear plastic evidence bag, onto the floor in exactly the same spot that Natale had found it. He also held a photocopy, made earlier by Detective Rossi at the corner drugstore, of the short, neatly written suicide note Vincente had left for his brother. The original had gone, also in an evidence bag, back to the precinct with Rizzo.

The forensic team arrived at the same time as the medical examiner, both fresh from the scene of a double homicide in Coney Island. Photographs and measurements were taken, the body officially pronounced dead and finally removed to Kings County Hospital morgue for autopsy. The spent bullet was found, as Joe had imagined it would be, submerged in the blood at the bottom of the tub. It, too, was bagged, and now rested in the pocket of McQueen's sport coat.

When at last they had left, McQueen and a uniformed officer sealed off the room with yellow crime scene tape, then went down to their vehicles. Mike returned to the precinct to voucher the gun and bullet and prepare his own supplemental DD-5 report to add to the one Rizzo had already completed before leaving for the night. When he was finally finished at eight-fifteen p.m., he was physically and mentally drained.

It had been a very long day, and Mike was glad it was over. He wished his night promised some bright pleasure to counterpoint the seemingly endless darkness of the day, now, finally, behind him.

But there was no bright promise. Only an elegant, empty apartment.

He left the precinct for the black Mazda and drove slowly home.

# CHAPTER SIX

*June*

"WHAT TIME IS MIKE COMING for dinner tonight, Dad?" Carol Rizzo asked as the waitress placed breakfast down before her.

It was early Saturday morning, and Joe Rizzo gazed across the small dinner table and smiled into the large brown eyes of his youngest daughter, her nineteenth birthday just a few months away.

"I told him about seven," he answered, nodding a thank-you to the waitress as she moved away. "Plenty of time for you to doll yourself up. Just remember what I told you: no dating cops."

His smile broadened as he reached for his toast. "You just can't trust most of 'em," he said.

He expected a smile in return and was surprised to notice a flicker of discomfort pass over her face. Carol was the third of Rizzo's daughters, and he had learned a lot about raising girls over the years. Between his parental experience and his cop's instinct, he knew he was sitting with a young lady who had something to say. One of the things he had learned was that honesty, although not necessarily the best policy, was more often than not the lesser evil when dealing with one's offspring.

"So," he said, his voice easy and light. "Let's see what we have here. It's eight-thirty on a Saturday morning and you're up, dressed, and out with the old man for breakfast—on your summer break from college, no less. Plus, you got that look on your face."

Carol's brow furrowed and her eyes dropped to her suddenly attention-craved eggs.

"Look?" she asked. "What look?"

Rizzo laughed. "Oh, I don't know. Maybe that 'Why's the sky blue, Daddy?' look. You know, that 'Why does Grandma have a mustache?' look. That look."

This time it was Carol who laughed. "Oh, God, remember that?" she said raising her eyes back to his face. "At the dinner table, Christmas eve, no less? In front of the whole family. How old was I?"

Joe chuckled. "Four, I think. It was the first Christmas eve I wasn't workin' since you'd been born. Grandma Falco gave me a look that burned out my retinas. Like *I* had said it instead of you."

They ate in silence for a few moments, remembering. Then Carol spoke, her voice more somber.

"Am I that transparent, Dad? How do you really know I have something to tell you?"

Rizzo shrugged. "It's been awhile since you went to breakfast with me, honey. Lunch, yeah, but breakfast? You're a teenager. They don't do breakfast. Not before noon, anyway."

Their eyes met across the table.

"Look, honey," Joe said, putting down his fork and smiling with kind eyes at the child who had suddenly turned into a grown woman. "Don't let me have to figure this out. Just tell me. Whatever it is, you know I'm on your side. We'll handle it. It can't be that bad."

A puzzled look crossed Carol's face. Then, slowly, recognition began to enter her eyes, and she twisted up her lips and dipped two fingers into her water glass. Flicking water at Rizzo's somber, set face, she stuck her tongue out and raspberried him.

"Is that what you think, Daddy, I have something to tell you, so right away I'm pregnant? Is that what you think?"

Rizzo smiled and brushed water off his cheek. "Honey, I've got three daughters and a wife: I gave up domestic thinking years ago. I'm just sayin', whatever it is, tell me. I promise, I can help."

Carol tapped her fingers on the tabletop and allowed herself to cool off. Then she raised her right hand and said in an exaggerated, mock Italian accented voice, "I'mma swear I'mma no gonna havea no baby and I'mma nicea girl."

Rizzo laughed and retrieved his utensils, then said, "*Basta che non fuma.* 'As long as you don't smoke.'"

Now Carol laughed and her anger, at worst brief and fleeting, was fully gone. She felt the easy, comfortable security her father always seemed to instill in her, and she leaned in toward him and spoke.

"I absolutely, positively hate college. It's like locking myself into an asylum full of reality-disconnect lunatics endlessly debating the nature of the debate and never getting to the heart of anything. Everything is gray: nothing is ever black or white, good or evil, right or wrong. Blah-blah-blah. I tried it for one whole year. I'm done with it. I want to quit."

Rizzo sipped at his coffee. "That's it? That's what this is?"

Carol nodded and leaned back into her seat. "Oh, and I'm addicted to heroin and killed two of our neighbors and stole their money. You know, to buy drugs."

He laughed. "Okay, okay. I'm sorry for whatever it is you thought I thought, okay? Forgiven?"

She nodded. "Reluctantly," she said.

"Well, I'll take it."

They ate in silence for a moment or two. Then Joe spoke.

"Look, honey. You know my 'options' speech? You've heard it?"

"Dozens of times, Daddy. Dozens."

He nodded. "Yeah, well, it's one of my better ones. There's no need to go over it again. Let's just apply it here. You get a degree, then you have options: go on to graduate school, or start any career you want, or get married, whatever. You don't get a degree, you cut out some options. The more options you have, the easier life is. Period. Undeniably correct. You can look it up. Google it, even."

She nodded, her shoulder-length brown hair bobbing about her pretty, round face. Rizzo noticed the intensity in her eyes and wondered, "Where have all these years gone to? When did this child become a woman?"

"I have a plan, Daddy. I know what I want."

Rizzo smiled. "That's great, honey. But tell me, does getting a degree cancel out the plan? How could it hurt? Maybe next year, sophomore year, will be different, better. You take more electives in the second year, stuff you're interested in, less of the required courses. You should talk to your sister, talk to Jessica. Once she started to focus on that art history stuff she loves, college became fascinating to her. It still is, and she'll be a senior next year already. Besides . . ."

Carol held up a hand, palm out, in front of him.

"I want to be a cop," she said softly. "Like you."

Rizzo put his utensils down and sat back in his seat. He shook his head slowly and looked into her determined, wholesome, sincere face.

He smiled sadly and sighed.

"Couldn't you just be pregnant instead?" he said, and wondered if he was joking.

THE BAR was housed in a battered, nineteenth-century redbrick building on a weary, littered street on Manhattan's Lower East Side. The recent influx of young professionals and their gentrifying ways had not yet visited this particular block.

Joe Rizzo parked his Camry at a broken meter and tossed his NYPD plaque onto the dashboard. He crossed diagonally to the bar and went in. In contrast to the bright afternoon sun, the barroom stood in semi-darkness, an odor of alcohol and dankness hanging in the air.

Rizzo scanned the room, his eyes narrowing as he found his man. Slowly, he crossed the room to the rear corner and slid a scarred wooden chair back from the table. He sat heavily.

The lone man at the table, a bottle of Fleischmann's vodka and a rock glass before him, looked up at Rizzo.

"Hello, Joe," the man said with a slight slur and a bitter, crooked smile. "Whatdya know?"

Rizzo looked into the bloodshot, lifeless eyes in the bloated face. He shook his head slightly as he spoke.

"Hello, Johnny," he said. "You look like shit."

John Morelli laughed. He seemed genuinely amused by Rizzo's remark. He leaned to his right and waved a hand at the thin, elderly man serving as bartender.

"Hey, Sammy," he called out. "Bring another glass and some ice over here, will ya?"

Rizzo twisted in his seat and made eye contact with the man.

"Cancel that, Sammy," he said coldly. He turned back to Morelli.

"You seem okay with drinkin' alone, Johnny. I'll pass," he said.

Morelli shrugged and raised his glass in a toast to Rizzo. "Whatever you say, partner. You was always the boss, anyway. Whatever you say."

They sat in silence, Morelli sipping absently at his drink, Rizzo stony and cold, his mind swimming with memories and regrets.

"It's partly my fault, Johnny," he said at last, a sad softness in his voice.

Morelli lowered his glass and leaned forward, focusing slowly on the man before him. "You going liberal on me, Joe? Wringin' your hands and guilty as hell? Do me a favor, keep it to yourself. My stomach churns enough, I don't need to hear this bullshit from you. Okay?"

Rizzo sat back in his seat and remembered the man he used to know. The man whose body was now inhabited by this twisted, pitiful drunkard. He shook his head as he spoke.

"Alright, Johnny. No problem."

Morelli drained his glass and reached for the bottle. He poured four fingers into it and swirled it around the glass, then lifted it slowly. He took a long drink and placed it down again. Then he raised his watery eyes to meet Rizzo's.

"You think I set that rat up to get whacked, don't you, Joe?" he asked in a low, somber tone. "You think I got The Chink to wipe my tab for it, don't you?"

Morelli referred to Louie Quattropa by his nickname, Louie The Chink.

"Don't you?" he repeated, leaning forward and speaking more forcefully.

Rizzo nodded. "Yeah, Johnny, sometimes I guess I do," he said.

Morelli nodded. "So, okay," he said. "So what's the fuckin' problem then? Walk away and forget about it. You're a cop. You're good at walkin' away and forgettin'. It comes with the job."

Rizzo reached out and laid a gentle hand on Morelli's.

"Did you, John?" he asked softly. "Did you set that guy up?"

Morelli held Rizzo's gaze as he answered.

"Fuck you, Joe," he said in a barely discernible hiss. "Take your I.A.D. wire and get the fuck out of my sight."

Rizzo removed his hand from Morelli's. He stood slowly and reached for his wallet.

"I'm sorry, John. I thought, all those years, I thought I was helping you somehow. But I wasn't. I see that now. I was just what the counselors call an 'enabler.' I helped you, alright. Helped you right into that fuckin' bottle. I thought I was protecting you, nursing you along toward the pension. But I was really doing the opposite. I was helping you go right down the shit-hole."

Rizzo pulled two twenty dollar bills from his wallet and dropped them onto the scarred tabletop. Before turning to leave, he leaned his weight onto his arms, palms down on the table. With his face just inches from Morelli's, he spoke in a soft, flat whisper.

"I'm sorry, John. I hope you can forgive me. I can never repay you for what you did for me. But you're dead now. Dead to me. Dead to yourself."

Rizzo stood and looked down into the flat, lifeless eyes.

"I might as well finish the job, Johnny. Take those twenties. The rest of the day is on me. Me and Jennifer."

He turned and left the bar. It was getting late, and his new partner would be at the house for dinner in a few hours.

It was time to move on.

LATER THAT afternoon, Rizzo sat at his kitchen table and looked into the angry eyes of his wife, Jennifer Rizzo. A pile of fresh string beans sat between them as they methodically snapped off the ends of each bean, tossing the plump bodies into a stainless-steel colander. The evening's activity, a family dinner party hosting Rizzo's young partner, had taken a backseat to a more pressing family affair.

"But Joe," Jennifer said, her dark brown eyes flaring in the well-lit kitchen, "of all things, a *cop*? Just as we're reaching a point where soon you'll retire, the worrying can start all over again? This can't be happening."

Rizzo reached out for a fresh handful of beans.

"Nothing is actually happening yet, hon," he said. "We left it off that she would stay in Stony Brook. She wanted to transfer to John Jay for an associate's degree in criminal justice. I told her two years full-time college credit would qualify her for the job, and she'd only lose credits if she transferred. She's going to stay in Stony Brook for now. Besides, what was I supposed to do? We've spent the last twenty-four years telling our daughters they could be anything they wanted to be, go anywhere they wanted to go. Remember? If a boy could do it, a girl could do it. Remember?"

Jen's eyes softened and she smiled sadly. "Except pee standing up," she said.

Rizzo wrinkled up his brow.

"Excuse me?" he said.

Now Jen laughed, and the sound of it pleased Joe. "As I recall," she said, "on Marie's twelfth birthday, one of us told her exactly that. And it wasn't me."

Rizzo pursed his lips as he remembered. "Whatever," he said. "The point is, with Carol, we need to focus on keeping her in school. Forget about tryin' to talk her out of going on the cops. We'll fight that battle another day. The next test for the job isn't until the fall. A lot can change between now and then. For now, we just need to keep her in Stony Brook."

Jen shook her head. "I don't know, Joe, you know these kids. When they make up their minds they're as focused as you are. Marie with medicine, Jessica with her art. What makes you think Carol will be different?"

Rizzo scratched at his head and frowned. "I don't know," he said, a soft sadness in his voice. "But I'll be damned if I let her go on this job. It's changed too much, it's different from when I was her age. We keep her in school, then, when the time comes, if she still wants to be a gangbuster, I know a couple of guys over in the city. FBI guys. They owe me a favor or two. And another guy over in Newark, with Customs. If I have to, I'll get them to hook her into the feds. It's a whole lot safer and cleaner than NYPD. Look at this mess I've got with the Morelli thing. Can you imagine Carol dealing with this?"

"FBI?" Jen said. "With all this terrorist stuff going on? Joe, I don't want her doing that either."

Joe raised a calming hand. "I know," he said. "Believe me, I know. I don't want her involved in any of this any more than you do. But, if worse came to worst and we couldn't change her mind, that would be the way to go: the lesser of two evils. Trust me on this, Jen. We don't want her on the streets for NYPD. The lesser of two evils, if necessary, that's all I'm saying."

Jennifer sighed and rose to carry the now full colander to the sink for rinsing. "Should we tell her, Joe? About Internal Affairs? Maybe if she sees that even a smart, honest cop like you can get all jammed up, maybe she'll . . ."

Joe smiled up at his wife, his eyes kind, the sadness out of his tone. "Relax, Jen, we'll handle it. Even if she takes the test in the fall, it'll be at least a year after that before they canvass her for the job. Let's just keep her in school and sit tight. Then we'll see."

Standing before him, the colander clenched tightly before her, the tension in her face stabbed at him.

"I can't do it again, Joe," Jennifer said softly. "I can't lie in bed at two in the morning and wonder what my young, rookie cop is doing. I did it with my husband. I did it with my nephew. I won't do it with my daughter."

Rizzo nodded. "I know," he said. "I know."

She started toward the sink, then paused and looked back over her shoulder to Joe's determined, set face.

"I'm glad we agree here, Joe," she said. "I know your love-hate relationship with that job of yours is mostly love. I'm glad we agree here."

Rizzo thought he heard a question in her tone.

The determined look on his face hardened. His eyes narrowed as he spoke.

"Do you know what she said to me?" he asked, his voice flat.

Jennifer turned fully to face him, placing the colander on the table. She had heard that flat tone before.

"What?" she asked softly.

"She said she didn't like college because nothing there is right or wrong, black or white—everything is gray."

Rizzo reached into his pants pocket and pulled out a crumpled pack of Chesterfields. He stood slowly, fishing his Zippo from a second pocket.

"Sound familiar?" he asked. "If my baby becomes a cop, she'll find out there is no right. She'll see there is no wrong. She'll see there just *is*."

He turned and walked to the side door, the cigarette in his mouth. He spoke without turning.

"Two generations of Rizzos living with that are enough. There isn't going to be a third. And it's not because she's a female. I'd feel the same with a son."

He opened the door and walked out, closing it silently behind him.

# CHAPTER SEVEN

JOE RIZZO PULLED HIS CAMRY into the driveway of the neat, two-story brick house he had called home for more than twenty years. Stopping just short of the detached garage's closed doors and turning off the engine, he glanced at his wristwatch. It was eight-twenty a.m., Sunday morning, June third. He smiled as he climbed out of the car and into the warm morning stillness of the tree-lined Brooklyn neighborhood of Bay Ridge. The scent of freshly brewed coffee wafted through the air. Regardless of the tour he had worked, Jennifer, unless working herself, greeted him with a time-appropriate beverage or meal. One advantage of living in a precinct that bordered the Six-Two was the short commute home. Jennifer knew that unless he had called to tell her different, he would be home fifteen to twenty minutes after signing out and leaving the squad room.

Joe entered the rear door and walked through the small pantry into the not-much-larger kitchen. The room was clean and uncluttered and showed no signs of the previous night's elaborate dinner party. Jennifer, clad in cut-off pajamas, her dark brown tresses piled atop her head and secured with a large white hair clip, turned from the stove and smiled her greeting.

"Hello, Jen," he said, crossing to her and kissing her offered cheek. "Coffee smells good."

"Sit down, I'll pour you a cup. How'd your night go?"

Rizzo had worked a long, mostly slow midnight-to-eight overtime tour at the squad room, partnering with the only detective in the Six-Two senior to himself, Billy Calabrese.

"Good. Pretty quiet. I managed to grab about three hours' sleep, so I'm wide awake. I worked with Billy. He crossed another day off his calendar."

"When's he retiring?" Jennifer asked.

"Three more weeks. That's one party I guess I'll have to go to. Billy broke me in when I started over at the Seven-Six. We go back a long way."

Jennifer sighed. "I wish it were you getting out, Joe. Enough is enough. Remember the original plan? Do twenty years and get out? We're way over the limit. I wish we could walk away from it all. The whole mess."

Joe laughed. "Yeah, well, I didn't figure on my firstborn deciding to go to medical school. We should've just married her off straight outta high school, like your cousin Rose did with her daughters."

Jennifer laughed. "Well, don't give up hope. Maybe one of the other two will elope. Then we'll save tuition *and* a big wedding bill."

Joe looked around. "Where are the princesses, anyway? Still asleep?"

With that, the oldest Rizzo girl, Marie, walked into the small kitchen and smiled at her father. She wore cut-off jeans and a loose-fitting NYPD T-shirt, her black hair pulled straight back and secured with a blue ribbon. Even without makeup, her dark beauty struck Rizzo as it always did, as if he had never seen her before. He smiled at her as she spoke.

"Hi, Daddy," she said. "Home already? Did you have fun oppressing the masses and violating minority rights?"

"Sure did, sweetheart. Me and my partner came across this homeless Hindu-Muslim-AIDS victim-Asian-man of color-Puerto Rican, and we got to burn down his teepee."

Marie crossed to him and kissed the top of his head. "That's nice, Daddy. I'm glad you had a good time. And that partner, would that be the young good-looking guy who was here for dinner last night? The one Mom seems to be in love with?"

"Lust, dear," Jennifer corrected with a smile as she brought Joe his coffee. "Not love, lust. I only love your father."

Joe shook his head and sipped at the coffee. "There has to be a law somewhere about how a man's wife can talk when he's sitting right in front of her." He sighed. "And as for my young partner, no, I didn't work with Mike. Last night was an extra tour I pulled to help pay your tuition. So a little appreciation would be nice."

Marie smiled. "Thank you, Daddy," she said sweetly. "I'm sorry I wasn't here last night. Carol and Jessica gave Mike two thumbs-up."

"Well," Joe said with a laugh. "All three of you can just forget about him. What have I been telling you ever since you went to the junior prom with that Tommy Brennan character? They'll be no Irish sons-in-law in the Rizzo home."

Marie stiffened her back and bowed her head formally to Joe. "Ah, yes, Papa-san," she said. "Me remember now."

Rizzo sighed. "Everybody's got an act," he said.

The two women sat down and joined Rizzo for a light breakfast. Marie was home for the next three weeks, after which time she would return to Cornell Medical School for her summer lab courses. They continued catching up on one another's lives as they ate. The two younger Rizzo girls, Carol and twenty-one-year-old Jessica, were still asleep upstairs.

"You know," Joe said, "I met a guy not too long ago who had a daughter that's a doctor. She's over at Mount Sinai in the city."

Marie broke off a piece of buttered toast and handed it to her father, anticipating his need. "That's a pretty good hospital," she said. "Where did you meet him?"

Joe thought of Natale Catanzaro, sitting tightly on his stiff chair, one floor below his brother's corpse.

"Through the job. Guy came in one night to make a complaint about some noisy kids hanging out by his house. We got to talking and he told me about his daughter. He was really proud of her, you could tell." Joe looked into the deep dark eyes of his oldest daughter. He smiled at them. They were her mother's eyes. "Almost half as proud as I am of you," he said.

She smiled back but raised her eyebrows with her reply. "Well," she said, "let's hope I can stick it out and actually graduate."

Joe shrugged. "You'll do your best, honey, like you always do. That'll be more than good enough, don't worry."

They continued to eat for a while in silence. Joe's thoughts once again turned to the Catanzaros. He wondered how they were doing in the aftermath of the suicide. The medical examiner had issued a preliminary finding of death by suicide, and the D.A. indicated to Joe that he had no problem looking the other way on the initial attempt by Natale to cover things up. Once the suicide was officially declared, the entire matter would simply fade away.

Those thoughts brought another case and another man, Dominick Simione, to Joe's mind. Simione had experienced a pragmatic Sicilian comfort the day Rizzo had stopped by to tell him about Anthony Donzi's arrest. Now he made a mental note to tell Mike that he had called Simione's daughter, Mrs. DiPaola, to see how the man was getting on, and the news had been relatively good. Although the old man still grieved for his slaughtered Spike, the family had gotten him a puppy, also a mixed breed. This one he named Luna, and the new dog seemed to be helping. Simione's grandson was home from college for the summer and moved into the Brooklyn house, and was spending a good deal of time with his grandfather. The neighbors visited often, and the two youngsters who had buried Spike pooled their pocket money and purchased a small marble headstone for his grave. They had placed it there with great solemnity, and the parish priest offered a blessing for them all at the gravesite. Joe now made a second mental note to call the Brooklyn and Manhattan D.A. offices to see how the plea bargain was shaping up with the various charges Donzi faced. Geanna Fago had spent four nights in jail and then paid a five-hundred-dollar fine for her guilty plea to possession of cocaine. Rizzo knew that the best Donzi could hope for, under ideal circumstances, would be ten to fifteen years on a guilty plea to all charges.

All in all, the best possible outcome. It was all a cop could ever expect, and Joe took quiet comfort and modest pride in it.

Now he washed those thoughts from his mind and turned to face the day with his family.

"Finish your breakfast, then go upstairs and wake up Heckle and Jeckle," he said to Marie. "If we get started showering, shaving, powdering, combing, and makeupping, we just may be able to make the eleven o'clock mass at Regina Pacis."

* * *

LATER IN the day, with pasta and roast chicken swelling in his stomach, Joe lay, half asleep, on the plush leather La-Z-Boy double recliner nestled in the den where the thirty-two-inch color Sony held dominance. He watched through heavily lidded eyes as the Mets held on to a very tenuous two-run lead going into the ninth inning at Pittsburgh. He was only vaguely aware of a phone ringing as he dropped fully into sleep. A moment later, his wife's gentle hand on his shoulder awakened him.

"Honey?" he heard her say softly, the cordless phone held in her hand, the mouthpiece pressed into her side. "Joe? It's the boss, D'Antonio. He says it's important."

Although of southern Italian heritage, D'Antonio had a shock of thick, full blond hair, piercing blue eyes, and the ruddy complexion of a Scotch-Irishmen. Because of his overall appearance, he was referred to as The Swede by his detectives, albeit not within his earshot. It was almost unheard of for a Six-Two squad detective to get a call from The Swede at home: Joe found himself instantly alert at hearing it was D'Antonio.

As he took the phone from Jennifer, she hesitated, and their eyes met. Joe sat passively in silence. Jennifer sighed, then, without speaking, turned and left the den, closing the door gently behind her.

Joe lifted the phone to his ear.

"Hello, Boss," he said. "Is New York under attack again?"

The deep, clear enunciation of the lieutenant's voice reached through the earpiece to Rizzo.

"No, Joe, nothing that dramatic. I'm sorry to bother you at home, it couldn't be helped."

"No problem, Loo. Tell me."

"You're on for a midnight tonight, right?"

"Yeah, me and McQueen.

"Yes, well, that's why I needed to catch you at home. Get ahold of McQueen, cancel the midnight. I want you both in tomorrow morning, eight, eight-thirty. My office."

Joe sighed. "Whatever it is, we didn't do it, Vince. Enter a 'not guilty' for both of us."

D'Antonio laughed. "No, no, nothing like that. I got a call today from

Police Plaza. A community affairs inspector, guy by the name of Manning. Do you know him?"

Joe thought a moment. "No. I don't think so."

"Well," D'Antonio said, distaste in his tone, "he's a big-time kiss-ass political scumbag. Lately, the last year or so, he's been stroking a guy from out your way, Bill Daily. Know the name?"

"Yeah, sure," Joe replied. "He's a councilman from Bay Ridge, lives a few blocks from me. He also runs the local Democratic club. Thinks he's a real big shot. His old man was a state senator for the district for thirty years. A Republican. The son went over to the Dems because the field was less crowded over there, what with Bay Ridge bein' pretty straight Republican. He got lucky a few years ago and got elected. Now it's like he's the Pope. And you know, people around here don't change things too quick. Once you get in, you're in."

"You ever meet the guy?"

"No."

"Well, you will. Tomorrow. You and Mike have an appointment with him, at his house. Him and his wife, ten a.m."

Joe frowned into the mouthpiece. "And why would that be, Vince?"

"It's his daughter. She took off about three weeks ago. She's done it before, very troubled kid. Diagnosed bipolar when she was fourteen."

"Bipolar?" Joe asked. "Manic-depressive?"

"Yes."

"What does this have to do with me and Mike?"

"It's like this, Joe. The kid called up Mommy. It was her nineteenth birthday, and she was way down, depressed as hell. The old lady thought the kid sounded suicidal. She panicked and called a friend of hers in the mayor's office. The friend told Daily, he got crazy, had a blowout with the wife. He wants all this kept quiet, he's got an election coming up and he's trying to sell himself and his family like a *Leave It to Beaver* bullshit fairy tale. That doesn't leave a lot of room for screwy teenage daughters running around loose doing God knows what."

Joe shook his head. "Nineteen. Nineteen and sick, and all this asshole cares about is his election. My Carol turns nineteen in a couple a months and I worry she may stub her toe on a desk at college."

He heard D'Antonio sigh through the line. "I know. I was just saying the same thing to my wife. But what are you going to do? That's the way these guys think."

Joe paused for a moment. "Again, though, Boss, I gotta ask: What does this have to do with me and Mike? If the kid went missing, she lives in the Six-Eight, it's their jurisdiction, they cover Bay Ridge. How are we involved here?"

"Joe," D'Antonio said, a forcefulness working into his voice. "We're involved, all of us, because the mayor's office told the Plaza and the Plaza told us. You come in tomorrow, eight, eight-thirty, and I'll lay it all out for you. You and Mike are off the wheel, you make your own hours—days, nights, whatever it takes. I got a blank overtime check in my pocket for this one, you can pay some tuition. It can work out okay, Joe. Meet me halfway on this one."

Joe blew air gently through his nostrils, loudly enough for The Swede to hear. "Yeah, sure, Loo. Whatever you say. It all sounds real legit so far."

"In the morning, Joe. Save it for the morning."

The line went dead. Joe dropped the phone onto the seat of Jennifer's half of the recliner. He sighed and stood up slowly, trying to remember where he had left his address book.

He needed McQueen's home number. He had never really memorized it.


MIKE MCQUEEN had just returned home when the shrill ringing of his telephone sounded. He walked through the apartment and answered it on the fourth ring.

"Hello?" he said.

Joe Rizzo's voice, clear and distinctive, sounded in his ear.

"Hello, Mike, hope I'm not interrupting anything."

"Not at all, Joe. I just walked in. Caught a movie with a couple of friends. What's up? Anything wrong?"

"No, kid, right as rain. But don't ruin your night. We're off midnights. The Swede wants us in at eight tomorrow morning for a special assignment. Some politician's kid went missing and we're supposed to find her. Very hush-hush, the guy's got an image to protect."

Mike frowned into the mouthpiece.

"Does this sound okay to you, Joe? I mean—"

Joe cut him off. "I know what you mean, Mike. And no, it doesn't sound okay to me. But The Swede has his balls between the Plaza and what's okay, so guess what? He's goin' with the Plaza. But it's not a big deal. We'll work it all out tomorrow. Take the night off and I'll meet you at the squad at eight. We'll get the whole story then and decide how to play it. We're off the wheel and The Swede more or less told me we can write our own paychecks till we settle this. It'll be okay."

"I hope so. I'm too new at this to be getting involved with some political bullshit."

Joe laughed. "Yeah, so I gathered from your buddy-buddy adventure with the mayor."

"That was different, Joe. That was just dumb luck. This . . . this could be trouble. Especially with us walking on eggshells with that Morelli thing. We don't need to go stepping on our dicks right now."

"No way. I'll handle it. Let's hear The Swede out and then we can make a decision. It'll all work out. Trust me, I won't let us get hurt."

"Alright, Joe. Tomorrow, eight a.m."

"Take care, kid, see you then. Have a good night."

McQueen hung up the phone. He had planned on a short nap before the drive to Brooklyn and a midnight tour. Now the balance of the evening lay empty before him.

"IT'S LIKE this, guys," D'Antonio said. He was seated behind the large desk in the squad commander's office, Rizzo and McQueen opposite him in two hard, straight-backed wooden chairs. "This councilman, Bill Daily, he needs to get his daughter back. She's off her medication and doing God only knows what. He's worried about her, and he wants her back, ASAP."

Rizzo frowned. "Last I heard, Boss, the department had an outfit all set up for just such a situation. It's called the Missing Persons Squad. Works outta Manhattan. Why not go to them?"

The Swede shook his head. "No good, Joe. We have to avoid regular channels on this one. You know the newspeople have access to the special squads; it's all public information. They see this kid went missing and Daily's political enemies use it against him, and his friends use it to get him sympathy votes. It becomes a media circus. And besides, confidentially, the guy is not all that fond of the kid, and I gather the feeling is very mutual. She's been a political liability and an embarrassment. There've been a few incidents where the Six-Eight patrol units had to get involved. That's why he wants it out of the precinct of jurisdiction. There's too much history there, and he figures it's more likely to get out. Somebody in the Six-Eight passing tips to a reporter, whatever. The Plaza came to me and said, 'Use your best man on this.' So, okay, that's you, Joe. You're my best man."

Rizzo laughed without humor. "Well, that just makes me feel warm all over, Boss. But let me ask you this: Where's the crime? The kid is nineteen and hates her old man and she moved out. Even if we find her, what do we do? Arrest her for being a crappy daughter? She can tell us to fuck off and there isn't a thing we can do about it. There's no crime here, Vince. This guy Daily is using the department as his own private detective agency, and I'm not sure why. Something goes wrong here, it's my ass, mine and Mike's. Let me take a wild guess here: You don't want us to submit DD-fives on this, right? No 'Investigation Follow-ups' on this one, correct?"

D'Antonio compressed his lips and let air escape from his nostrils before answering. McQueen saw that the man was just as uncomfortable with this as Rizzo was.

"The guy can't use a private eye on this. God knows where this kid is and what she's doing. He can't have that kind of info being raffled off. It's political suicide. He knows the cops won't blackmail him. Maybe pinch him for a favor or two, but that's the price of doing business."

Joe blew air through his lips. "You didn't answer me, Boss. No DD-fives on this, nothing on paper, correct?"

"That's right, Joe. You report directly to me. Orally."

Rizzo nodded. "No paper. So if me and Mike get stuck holding the bag on this, we've got nothing to back us up."

D'Antonio leaned across the desk. "Except me," he said, his eyes and voice hard.

Rizzo smiled and shook his head. "Vince, you know I love you. But this is political. You won't be able to help us, even if you try, and believe me, I know you'll try. If I didn't think you would, I'da walked out of here already."

D'Antonio leaned back in his seat. He tapped nervously on his desk with a pencil and shifted his gaze from Rizzo to McQueen.

"Mike," he said. "You haven't said one word. What do *you* think about this?"

Mike shrugged. "Whatever Joe decides, I'll go with him."

D'Antonio nodded. "I can respect that," he said. "But you should consider this: you guys handle this, do it right, and you got people at the Plaza, people at the city council, and people with the mayor himself who owe you. A young detective can cash those tickets in *big*-time. Just something you might think about. And Joe, tell me something. How do you figure a grateful councilman and some top brass at the Plaza on your bandwagon can hurt? Especially now. You know. All things considered."

They sat in uncomfortable silence for a while, D'Antonio's implication not lost on either detective.

Finally, Rizzo spoke.

"Vince, you know this guy? Do you *really* know this Daily?"

D'Antonio shook his head. "I know the name. I know he's a wheel in city politics. But no, I don't know him personally."

Rizzo produced a Chesterfield and dug out his lighter. He put the cigarette between his lips and struck the Zippo. Just before touching flame to tobacco, he looked across at D'Antonio and smiled.

"You don't mind me smoking here, do you, Boss? I mean, since we're bendin' the rules and all?"

D'Antonio's face tightened with anger, and his fair skin began to flush. He said nothing as Joe touched flame to cigarette. Reaching across the desk, Joe picked up a paper-clip holder and emptied its contents, positioning it for use as an ashtray. Then he spoke to his supervisor.

"I'll make you a deal, Vince. We'll do this for you. But for you, not Daily, not the mayor, nobody but you. In return, I write my own paycheck. Mike's, too. Also, you get Daily to go down to the courthouse, talk to one of his ass-kisser judge friends down there. Let him get a mental hygiene warrant for the kid. She's off her meds, unwilling to go for help, and she's a danger to herself or others. She qualifies for one. The judge can do it in chambers, it's all confidential. They can even fill the papers out themselves, don't even need a court clerk there. Mental hygiene warrants aren't computerized, so there'll be no leaks, no publicity. Then he hands me the warrant. That gives me the legal authority to look for her and take her into custody if we find her. The catchment hospital on a warrant for Bay Ridge is either King's County or Coney Island, but if Daily gets the okay from a private hospital and the judge endorses the warrant accordingly, I can take her straight to anyplace that agrees to accept her. The councilman can use his influence at a private mental hospital, they can even Jane Doe her if he wants to. That way there's no media involvement. The kid can get treated and that'll be the end of it."

D'Antonio thought it over. He frowned as he began to speak again. "If I remember correctly, don't you have to bring her back to the judge when you execute a mental hygiene warrant? Doesn't he have to give her a hearing, with a court-appointed lawyer, and then decide whether or not she goes to a hospital?"

For the first time, Mike spoke without having been spoken to first.

"I think that's right, Joe," he said. "I remember that from when I was studying for the sergeant's exam."

Rizzo expelled Chesterfield smoke as he answered. "Absolutely, Mike. But the law also says we can EDP her if, in our judgment, she needs to go straight to the hospital for her own safety. Then, technically, we wouldn't have actually executed the warrant. It stays active for the balance of the initial thirty days it's good for. In the meantime, the hospital can hold her and treat her as long as two psychiatrists sign off on it."

Rizzo had referred to a provision of the mental hygiene law that allowed a police officer to deal with an emotionally disturbed person on an emergency basis. Patrol officers did it frequently, although it was a rare occurrence for a detective.

"And it's all legal and aboveboard," Mike said, nodding.

"Bingo," Joe answered with a smile. "And yet sleazy enough that even this prick Daily would like it."

D'Antonio spoke up as he fanned the air in front of him to clear the cloud of cigarette smoke. "We don't know the guy's a prick, Joe."

Rizzo laughed. "Oh, we don't? Didn't you tell me yesterday that he's more concerned about his election than his kid's welfare?"

"Concerned, I said, not *more* concerned."

"Oh, sure, Boss, you know, you're gettin' good at this, maybe you could write some speeches for him. You know like, 'it depends on what the meaning of *is* is.' Stuff like that."

Now the anger in D'Antonio surfaced.

"Damn it, Joe," he said harshly, "knock this shit off. What am I supposed to do? I got brass calling me every five minutes. Daily lit up the Plaza—they even got a call from the governor's office. They picked our precinct 'cause it's next door to the Six-Eight and we're familiar with the turf. Plus, we're off the beaten path, no one knows we're alive over here. It's the perfect way to get it done and keep it quiet. Cut me some slack here, Joe. I'm on the spot."

Rizzo reached across and ground out his cigarette in the paperclip holder.

"Yeah, Vince. That's why you get to wear those pretty gold bars on your shoulders when you suit up for a funeral. You're supposed to be on the spot."

A few moments passed before D'Antonio spoke.

"I can probably sell the mental hygiene idea. And I can cover your overtime bill. Anything else?"

Rizzo nodded. "You post us openly on the duty board as 'special assignment.' We're not only off the wheel, but we don't catch any new crimes. We've got three or four cases we're working now that need attention. Assign them to somebody else, somebody good, and you follow up, make sure they stay on top of it. If they do clear anything, me and Mike get included in the stat breakdown."

D'Antonio nodded. "Done. Anything else?"

Rizzo looked over at Mike. "You need anything, Mike? Want me to send him out for coffee and maybe some breakfast?"

McQueen sat silently. D'Antonio spoke softly.

"Fuck you, Joe," he said.

Rizzo stood slowly, the meeting over. He smiled as he leaned across D'Antonio's desk and spoke into the man's eyes.

"Boss," he said, his voice low and threatening, "you wanna work in a whorehouse, every once in a while somebody's gonna pay to piss on you. Get used to it."

With that, he turned and began to walk out. At the same time, McQueen rose slowly from his seat and looked silently at the lieutenant. D'Antonio met Mike's gaze and smiled weakly.

"Don't say anything, Mike," he said softly. "The son of a bitch has a point, and he wouldn't be Rizzo if he didn't feel compelled to make it."

McQueen turned and followed his partner out into the squad room.

# CHAPTER EIGHT

"LET ME TELL YOU about this guy Daily," Joe said as they climbed into the gray Impala. "Just so you get who we're dealing with here."

"So you know him," Mike said.

Joe shook his head. "No. Never had the dubious pleasure. But he's kind of a local celebrity in Bay Ridge, and I do live there. From what I hear, I gotta tell you, this whole thing smells bad."

"How so?"

"Well, this kid, his daughter, it's not like she's a junkie or a hooker or some left-wing radical nut. She's not even a lesbian, which could be a real problem for a Bay Ridge politician. No. The kid's sick, she's got a legitimate mental illness. And this guy Daily's the master of spin: makes old Bill Clinton look like Harry Truman by comparison."

"So what? I'm not following you, Joe."

"It's like this. Daily is bending over backwards to keep it all hush-hush. You'd think he'd just go the other way, spin it to his advantage. 'Look at me,' he can say, 'my baby is sick and I'm trying to help her. In fact, I'm such a great guy, I'm trying to help all the psychiatrically challenged kids out there. That's why I've introduced city council bullshit bill number two million and two that'll get the federal government to outlaw mental disease, thus doing away with it forever and curing all our sick children. But my lowlife Republican adversary won't help us because he sucks and gets richer from mental illness, the bastard. So vote for me and we'll be free!' You know, the usual crap. No opponent of his would dare to even bring it up. And what voter is gonna hold it against a guy because his kid is sick? It just doesn't compute."

"So what's the reason?" Mike asked.

Joe shrugged. "Damned if I know. But I bet we'll find out. And when we do, we may have to renegotiate our deal with The Swede. We'll see."

McQueen hesitated before speaking again.

"What do you think, Joe?" he began tentatively. "Can this Daily help out with I.A.? On the Morelli thing? Get them off your back a little?"

Rizzo shrugged. "I don't know. Maybe. I.A.D. isn't any different from the other specialized units in the department—it's just as stacked with politically ambitious pricks." Here Rizzo smiled before continuing. "Ralph DeMayo being one of them, I might add."

McQueen shook his head. "Figures," he said.

Rizzo's smile faded as he saw tension enter his young partner's eyes.

"Has he called you again?" Joe asked softly. "Reached out any-more?"

McQueen again shook his head. "No," he answered. "Just that one time."

Rizzo nodded. "Well, he will. Believe me. When he does, just answer his questions, the truth, the whole truth, and nothin' but the fuckin' truth."

A tight smile now formed on Mike's lips. "Easy enough," he said, "since I've got nothing to say to him of any value." He glanced over at Joe. "And that's fine with me, Joe."

Rizzo laughed. "Don't worry that pretty little head of yours, Mike. I ain't gonna confess to you."

McQueen blew some air through his lips. "Because there's nothing *to* confess, right?" he asked.

"Absolutely. The only thing I'm guilty of is lettin' Morelli make me into a class-A horse's ass."

McQueen nodded. "Okay," he said.

After a few moments, Rizzo spoke again. His tone was reflective and soft, and McQueen got the impression the older cop was merely think-ing out loud.

"Besides," he began, "I.A.D. won't push too hard on this Morelli thing. They know that even if they do nail him somehow, he can only lead them to some underling of Quattropa's, some foot soldier one step above a street mugger. Assuming Morelli's even guilty, that is, and can lead them anywhere. If they nail him, that soldier goes into the river the next day, and the cops hit a dead end. No, I.A.D. is just stirring the pot a little. OCCB wants Quattropa. He's the real target. They grab him, they can always backtrack it to Morelli. Quattropa then says Morelli turned the mole over to some family associate, and he had the guy whacked on his own. Quattropa says he didn't know anything about it. He gives up some names, they drop a charge or two against him."

Rizzo turned in his seat now and spoke more directly to Mike. "You see, kid, it's a one-way street: Quattropa can lead to Morelli, but Morelli can't lead to Quattropa. It becomes a question of which fish they wanna fry more, Quattropa or Morelli."

Rizzo dug out a Chesterfield and lit it before continuing.

"I'm bettin' on Quattropa," he said.

With over an hour until their ten o'clock meeting with Mr. and Mrs. Daily, they decided to go to Joe's favorite diner on Fourth Avenue. Once seated, McQueen moved the conversation to lighter topics.

"You know, Joe," Mike said, sipping coffee across the table from Rizzo, "I was talking to some friends about you and I mentioned what a good detective you are. But I've gotta tell you, I couldn't explain why you were still at precinct squad level. You've got the smarts, the stats, the *balls,* everything, yet you're still at the Six-Two. I have to say, Joe, I don't get it."

Joe smiled as he replied. "Kid," he said, a twinkle in his dark eyes, "I get two calls a year from Jimmy Santori, the boss over at Brooklyn South. He begs me to jump over to homicide and work for him. He figures I'm his ticket to bigger and better things once I get his clearance rate up. And I turn him down every time."

"Can I ask why, Joe? Is it the blood and guts?"

This time Joe laughed his reply. "No, kid, if it ain't *my* blood or *my* guts, I got no problem with that. But you know, every once in a blue moon Muffy might kill Buffy over Faw-tha's stock portfolio, but usually it's just two knuckleheads in a bar fighting over the last cheese doodle. Who needs that? Most murders nobody cares about. And when John Q.

Public is leafing through the papers and sees some hip-hop drive-by or mob rubout or he-say she-say stabbin', he shakes his head and turns the page. He can't relate to it. No, that stuff doesn't scare folks much."

Mike thought for a moment. "You're probably right," he said.

Joe nodded as the waitress placed their breakfast before them.

"Thank you, dear," he said as she smiled and walked away. "I *am* right," he continued. "What scares people, especially in the Six-Two, is when they hear of a burglary or a mugging or God forbid a rapist runnin' loose. Then they get scared because when they hear about something like that, they worry about their kids, their wives, their husbands, or their old parents. That's what scares people, and that's what I—what *we*—do. The little crimes have the biggest effect on most of the people. It's like a cancer eating away at the quality of their lives. Me and you, we're their chemotherapy. We fight the cancer, keep it at bay. We may never win, not completely, but we're all these people got. So the harder we fight, the more they live in peace. There's no special squad anywhere does more than that, Mike. So I'm happy right where I am. Me and my family live in Brooklyn, my mother's right here. So every asshole I lock up is one less can hurt them. What else should I wanna do?"

Mike chewed his scrambled eggs and thought a moment.

"I understand what you mean," he said.

Rizzo nodded. "'Course you do. Not just the glamour boys in P.D. are important. When you think about it, they mostly serve the big shots and the insurance companies. The really horrible crimes are the day-to-day stuff, the undramatic stuff you never see on TV or in the movies. The kinda stuff we catch. Like with your ex, and that shithead Flain, may he rot in hell. You never see some Hollywood actor starring in a movie about that. But how happy is everybody that Flain's gone? How much better off is everyone with Donzi gone? It doesn't get more important than that."

They continued eating in silence, each with his own thoughts. After a while, Mike asked a question.

"Joe, you started telling me what you know about Daily. Want to finish?"

Joe nodded. "Yeah, but I'll give you the *Reader's Digest* condensed version. Daily comes from an old Bay Ridge family—the Irish equiva-

136

lent to the WASPs came over here on the *Mayflower*. His old man was a
state senator from the Ridge, Republican like most Bay Ridge politicians. He was a pretty good guy, and he got a lot of respect. Even the
Italians voted for him. The Democrats *always* ran an Italian against him
just to try and steal the seat. So the old man tried to get junior into politics, brought him to the clubhouse, introduced him around, sent him to
some fancy law school down south. Even had him puttin' up posters
and answering phones during campaigns, you know, like a regular person. But the kicker was Daily Jr. was such a hard-on, so abrasive, that
despite his old man, he couldn't get anywhere. So what does he do? He
jumps ship, joins the Democrats. And they were very glad to have him;
it was a slap at the old man and the controlling Republicans. They musta
promised the kid something, probably a judgeship. As part of the deal,
he ran against the local Republican councilman. Guy was about eighty,
held the seat about forty years. The idea was junior would run, embarrass his father and the GOP on behalf of the Dems, and then, after he
lost, they'd pay him off with some patronage job. Don't forget, the
Democrats own Brooklyn—lock, stock, and barrel. A Republican can't
get arrested anywhere outside Bay Ridge, Marine Park, or Dyker Heights.

"So, anyway, Daily had a brother, a younger brother. Guy went on
the cops straight out of college, just like you did. But unlike you, this kid
was the son of a state senator and local political leader. So after three
years inside at some desk job, they make him a detective at Major Case.
Imagine that? Kid couldn't find his own dick with both hands, but they
got him workin' Major Case.

"So one night the kid comes home to Bay Ridge and double-parks
outside a grocery store on Fifth Avenue. He goes in to get some milk
and cold cuts and walks straight into an armed robbery in progress. He
forgets he's an asshole and thinks he's a real cop, so he tries to take down
the perp, and ten seconds later, he's got two rounds in him—one right
through the jugular. He's dead before he hits the ground.

"Well, the old man, like I say, was an okay guy. He takes it real hard.
Winds up stepping down from the state senate the next year and moving to Florida. And then six months later, *he* dies.

"Only in this case, the apple did fall pretty far from the tree. Daily
was three weeks away from the election when his brother was killed, so

all of a sudden he becomes Mister Law and Order, gun-control guy. He starts all his speeches with a teary eulogy for his dearly departed brother and how it's time to take the streets of Bay Ridge back from the gun-wielding thugs. Never mind that it's got the lowest violent crime rate in the city and his brother was the first cop killed in Bay Ridge since 1941. But our boy Bill, he didn't let the facts interfere with his campaign, and guess what? He wins the fuckin' seat! Takes it right out of the hands of the Republicans who held it since Jesus registered to vote. So after he got reelected a couple of years later and showed he had a lock on the seat, the local Dems just about canonized him. Nowadays, from what I hear, he's the power behind the Kings County Democratic chairman, one of the most powerful county chairs in the state, if not the whole northeast. The actual chairman is just some black businessman figurehead the bosses put in to show how progressive and open-minded they are, but it's Daily who's really running the county. So that's why the Plaza jumped when he called. That's who we're dealin' with here. I hope you got some asbestos jockey shorts in that sharp wardrobe of yours, 'cause you may be needing them."

THE STATELY home on Colonial Road had fourteen rooms and a detached three-car garage which, at the dawning of the twentieth century, had served as a carriage house. Apple and pear trees grew in the large rear yard amid manicured gardens and a lush lawn. The wraparound front porch with its white nautical-style railing held delicate, exquisitely detailed wrought-iron outdoor furniture from a bygone era of hoop skirts and parasols, knickers and buggies. A towering, majestic oak tree ruled the front yard, casting morning coolness across the facade of the house.

McQueen swung the Impala slowly onto the narrow, circular driveway and pulled around the oak to twin iron and brass hitching posts that had stood at the entryway for over a hundred years. He shut down the motor and turned to face Rizzo.

"Joe," he said, "if I didn't know for a fact that I was still in Brooklyn, I wouldn't believe it. We're less than, what?, a mile from your house?"

Joe chuckled. "Well, in distance, my place is seven avenues southeast of here; in salary, it's about three hundred grand a year from here. Approximately, of course."

They climbed out of the car onto the flawless cobblestone drive. Mike glanced at the Chevy: he hoped it didn't have any leaks. Staining this driveway would be like spraying graffiti on a museum piece.

They climbed the front steps and Rizzo leaned on the teak and copper doorbell. Three resonant, musical chimes sounded from deep within the house. A moment later, a blurry white figure of a woman approached them, her features ghosted by the thick, frosted glass of the front door.

The housekeeper looked without expression at the blue and gold of Rizzo's detective badge as he held it up to the glass. He saw her eyes move to the identification card next to it in the leather case. She studied the photo, and then raised her eyes to scan his features.

Satisfied, she opened the door and led them into a large room at the front of the house, which she referred to as the parlor. There, they took seats in antique, wine-colored crushed-velvet chairs. When the woman left them, McQueen's eyes met Rizzo's.

"How much do you think a councilman makes, Joe?" he asked in low tones.

Rizzo smiled broadly. "Not this much, kid, not this much."

William Daily was just under six feet tall, tanned, with silver-gray hair, despite being only forty-five years old. He stood erect and confident in the doorway of the parlor, looking first at McQueen, then at Rizzo. McQueen found himself standing under the gaze: Rizzo remained seated, crossing his legs and smiling at the man.

"Councilman?" he said. "I'm Detective Sergeant Rizzo, Joseph Rizzo. I'm the best man in the Six-Two, just like you asked for."

Daily stood still in the doorway. McQueen saw irritation flicker briefly in the not-unhandsome face. But it vanished quickly, and the man smiled broadly, exposing pearly white but chillingly caninelike teeth. He crossed the room in long, fast strides and extended a hand to the still seated Rizzo.

"It's a pleasure to meet you, Detective. Good of you to come."

Joe stood slowly and shook the man's hand. He nodded toward McQueen. "My partner, Mike McQueen."

Daily crossed the room to Mike and shook his hand. "Thanks for coming, Detective. Maybe we can get this nightmare over with and get my Rosanne the help she needs.

Mike nodded. "Yes, sir. That's the plan."

The three men left the room, Rizzo and McQueen following Daily's lead to a large, sunlit den, also on the ground floor. A broad, old-fashioned-style bay window looked out into the rear gardens. Daily sat behind a massive mahogany desk in front of the window, the two detectives across from him in bull's blood–colored leather armchairs.

Daily led them in small talk for a few moments, telling them his wife would join them upon their request. During the course of the conversation, the councilman learned from Joe how Mike had come to be promoted to detective.

"The mayor is a good man," Daily said. "I've tried to convince him to switch party affiliations, but he's adamant. Despite his clearly progressive vision for our city, he still believes that he's a Republican. But let's not go there—I don't know either of you gentlemen's political affiliations."

McQueen smiled inanely, but remained silent, while Joe laughed out loud.

"I'm an anarchist," he said. They then turned to the business at hand.

"My daughter is sick, gentlemen. Sick. And her mental illness is just like any other disease, no different from cancer or diabetes or hypertension. Some people get it, and some people don't. Unfortunately, Rosanne's got it. It's called bipolar disorder. Are you familiar with the term?"

"We are," Joe said.

"Good. But what you must realize is there still remains a stigma attached to this illness in some minds. If Rosanne did, in fact, have diabetes, no one would dream of trying to capitalize on it. But politics, being what it is, and people, being what they are, my opponents would indeed try to use this against me. Thus, these rather Machiavellian measures to ensure some discretion. I am hoping to have your empathy."

Rizzo leaned forward in his seat and spoke softly. His tone made Mike, already uneasy with Joe's general demeanor, even more uncomfortable.

"Look," Rizzo said. "I'm here to find your daughter. Period. I don't really give a damn about the rest of it. The kid is missing and, I been told, off her medication. That's not good. So let's just keep our eye on the ball here, okay? If I have to walk on eggshells around you and your wife and the politics, this ain't gonna work out. Why don't I be the cop and you be the citizen, and let's see what we can do."

Daily's face iced over for a barely discernible microsecond. Sitting back in his chair, he reached across the desk to a heavy, wooden humidor. He removed a cigar and turned the box to face the detectives, then slid it silently across the highly polished desk.

"If this has been an example of your walking on eggs, Joe—may I call you Joe?—I'd hate to see your less diplomatic side."

Joe smiled and reached out, taking a cigar and sniffing at it delicately.

"Well, Bill—may I call you Bill?—I've only got one side. And thank God my wife seems to love it."

They lit their cigars and smoked silently for a few moments. Mike leaned to his left, as far from the smoke as possible. The councilman took note and reached a hand under his desk. Mike heard an electric motor begin a low hum from somewhere in the room.

"A smoke-eater," Daily said to him by way of explanation. "I go to great lengths to avoid the 'smoke-filled room' cliché when I meet here on political matters."

A few moments later, Rizzo turned back to business.

"I'll need your cooperation on this. Have you ever heard of a mental hygiene warrant?"

Daily shook his head. "I hadn't, actually. But Lieutenant D'Antonio called earlier and explained it to me. I had just gotten off the phone with a State Supreme Court judge I'm acquainted with when you arrived. I'm going down to the courthouse this afternoon, and I'll have the warrant by late day."

"Good," Joe said, nodding. "It pays to have acquaintances. We also need a complete list of your daughter's friends—names, addresses, phone numbers, and nature of relationships. For instance, best friend, schoolmate, casual friend, friend of a friend, college roommate, whatever. Also any boyfriends you may know of. Was your daughter being treated by a psychiatrist?"

"Yes."

"We'll need that information as well. And I want your permission and your wife's permission, in writing, for us to search Rosanne's room. If we remove anything, we'll give you a receipt."

Daily nodded. "That all sounds reasonable."

"Good. We need a recent photo, close-up, in color. I have to know about any hobbies, pastimes, sports stuff, anything like that she enjoys. The names of any teachers at her school she talked about or admired or whatever. I need her cell phone and credit card history and numbers and prescription medication information. Does she own a car?"

"Yes. It's out in the garage. It has been since the day she disappeared."

Joe nodded. "Disable it," he said. "Get a mechanic out here to pull the distributor. Is the car in her name?"

"Yes, it was her high school graduation gift. Last year."

"Well, assuming she's still local somewhere, which might be a big assumption, we don't want her sneaking back home some night and takin' the car to get farther away with. And if it's in her name, she can take it and sell it, if she's low on cash. Disable it."

"I will. Today."

"Alright," Joe said, jotting a note on his pad.

"Is there anything else?" the councilman asked.

Rizzo looked up from his notes and smiled coolly at Daily. "Oh, yeah. There's plenty. But for now, I'd like that written permission to search her room. And we need to talk to your wife. Can you call her in, please?"

Daily rose from his seat, placing the cigar down into a crystal ashtray. "I'll go get her. Please excuse me."

McQueen followed the man with his eyes. When he cleared the doorway, Mike leaned over to his right and spoke softly to his partner.

"Joe," he said, "if we don't find the girl, this guy is going to take great pleasure in nailing your ass to the wall."

Rizzo smiled broadly around the butt of his cigar, puffing great clouds of smoke.

"Yours, too, buddy," he said matter-of-factly. "Yours, too."

LATER, AS the two detectives searched through the upstairs bedroom of the missing girl, they spoke in low tones.

"How smart was it to be a wise-ass with this guy, Joe?" Mike asked. "If we find this kid and you want to tap Daily for some grease at I.A., it could come back to bite you."

Rizzo shrugged. "Fuck him," he said. "Guys like him don't do favors 'cause they like you. They don't *not* do favors because they don't like you. It's just business to them. Don't worry about it."

McQueen shook his head but remained silent, scanning the room casually.

"It bothers me that she left the car," Rizzo said. "What teenager takes off and leaves a brand-new car sittin' in the garage? I sure as hell wouldn't have."

McQueen, turning from the walk-in closet he had just opened, said, "Maybe she didn't need it. Maybe she left with someone. A boyfriend, or some neighborhood kid who's just as well off as she is and has a brand-new car, too."

Rizzo nodded, sliding a desk drawer open as he replied. "Could be. She called and spoke to her mother on Saturday, so we know she's not stuffed down a sewer somewhere. At least not as of Saturday anyway."

McQueen scanned the messy shelves in the closet.

"What'd you think of the mother, Joe?"

Rizzo shrugged. "Hard to say. She might have been sedated. She seemed intimidated by Daily, don't you think? Like she was afraid to talk too much, afraid she might say the wrong thing."

"Wrong thing about what?" McQueen asked.

That brought another shrug from Rizzo. "I don't know. But that's the feeling I got. And Mike, I got closer to her than you did. It's barely eleven in the morning and I smelled booze on her."

McQueen turned to face his partner. "Booze on her breath? Really?"

"Couldn't say if it was on her breath or not. It could have been oozing from her pores. That would mean a real bender last night. It's a shame, she looks like she could be a classy dame."

"Well," Mike said, "maybe it's just the stress. It's got to be tough having a young daughter missing, especially one with problems like this kid."

Mike continued searching the closet. He eyed the numerous shoe boxes strewn across the floor. They all appeared open and uncovered, some with two shoes, some with one, some with mixed pairs. One box in particular caught his eye. It was nestled in the rear corner, almost obscured by the many scattered objects around it. And this box was different from the rest: this one was closed, its top pulled and tied with a red ribbon. Mike stepped through the clutter and bent down to the box. Its weight told him there was something other than shoes inside.

"Hey, Joe," he called softly after opening the box. "Take a look at this."

Rizzo crossed the plush, sea green carpet to his partner. He looked at the object Mike held.

"Well, well," he said with a tight smile. "The infamous teenage-girl diary. Each one of my daughters had one. They struck fear into my heart, I'll tell you that. I wouldn't touch them with a ten-foot pole. Some things a father just doesn't need to know."

Rizzo took the thick, black, leather-bound book from Mike and dropped down heavily onto the bed.

He flipped the diary casually to the last written page and looked at the date.

"Last entry was a couple a months ago," he said, then gestured to Mike to take a seat next to him. "Come on," he said. "Let's take a quick look, see if it's worth taking with us. There pretty much has to be *something* in here that can help us."

After twenty minutes of scanning the pages, which were written in the consistent black ink of a roller ball pen, their eyes met.

"My God," Rizzo said, his head shaking slowly, side to side. "This is one fucked-up little princess."

McQueen felt a cold, empty knot in his stomach. The anguished, black-hued prose that comprised half the pages had read to him almost like a physical assault: he felt a gnarling, nervous flutter in his chest. The other half of the pages, interspersed with chilling randomness throughout, were written in a florid, broad-stroked hand, contrasting as day from night, with the depressive, pain-drenched ramblings. This wild writing sang with acute glee and boundless energy, full of ambitions and dreams and improbable schemes and rallying cries of cheer and childlike exuberance.

McQueen stood and walked to the window. He looked out at the equally regal houses that surrounded the Daily home. His eyes dropped to the yard behind the house, its fruit trees and gardens tossing colors into the morning's bright sunlight. He turned back to face Rizzo.

"Talk about a gilded cage," he said.

Rizzo nodded silently, still flipping through the diary.

"Listen to this, Mike," he said as he began to read a passage. "'*I'm lost in a pool of semen, drowning in it, fucking and sucking my way to hell.*

*And I can't stop. I won't stop. It doesn't matter, anyway. I hate these stupid boys and their stupid dicks. I hate them!'"* Rizzo looked into Mike's eyes. "You know why I read you that entry?" he asked.

McQueen felt his facial muscles begin to tighten. "No, Joe, I don't. But do me a favor, okay? No jokes. This isn't funny."

Rizzo smiled sadly. "No shit, Mike. I got three daughters. It's a whole fuckin' lot less funny to me than it can ever be to you. I read that page because the next page is torn out. Here, look, you can see the remnants down in the inner spine of the book."

Mike crossed the room and followed Joe's finger to the fold of the diary. He saw the slight, ragged end of the missing page.

McQueen nodded. "What's your point, Joe?"

Rizzo scratched at his temple. McQueen noticed the slight nervous eye tic begin to blink in his partner's eye.

"I'm not sure. But doesn't it strike you as bein' odd that this kid writes, in graphic terms, about screwing around and then decides to tear the next page out? What the hell was on there? Who was she afraid would see it? Her mother or father? She wasn't concerned about the fuckin' and suckin' coming up at the dinner table, so what the hell *was* she worried about? There's drug references in here, too—marijuana and cocaine. But apparently she wasn't worried about anyone seeing that either. And the stuff about the shoplifting and riding in a stolen car. Why would she leave all that in, then tear something out? And that's where the diary ends. All of a sudden, she stops writing in it. She was still home until three weeks ago but stopped her diary months ago after she tears out the last entry."

McQueen thought for a moment. "She's sick, Joe. Who knows why she does something? Maybe she just lost interest."

Rizzo shrugged. "Maybe," Joe said.

"Maybe when she ran off," McQueen continued, "she figured someone might look in the diary for clues to help find her. Just like we're doing. So she tore that page out."

Rizzo pondered it, then shook his head. "So why not just ditch the whole book? Or take it with you, don't leave it at all."

McQueen sat on the bed next to Joe and took the diary from him. As he began to leaf through it, he found that even now, with the contents already known to him, it chilled him and upset him. He closed the book, putting it down. After a moment, he spoke.

"Do you think Daily has seen this?" he asked.

Rizzo stood slowly and took the book from his partner. He shook his head.

"Doubtful. If he knew it was here and he's all worried about his family image, he'd've tossed it or hid it away somewhere. No, I'd say he doesn't know it exists."

Rizzo slipped the diary into his inside jacket pocket. Smiling, he said, "We'll just forget to include this on the receipt we give them. I don't want a tug-of-war with the old man over this. And I wanna read it through carefully. Okay?"

Mike shrugged. "Whatever you say, Joe."

A knock sounded on the closed bedroom door. They turned in unison to look at it.

"Come on in, Councilman," Rizzo said, just loudly enough to be heard on the far side of the door. "We were just talkin' about you."

ONCE BACK in the sanctuary of the Impala, they resumed their speculations in secure privacy.

"So," Mike said, "what do you figure, Joe? I'm thinking some kind of sexual abuse thing. Daily himself, or maybe one of his big-shot political pals that he's obligated to cover up for. She writes it in her diary, then thinks twice about it and tears it out. Then she drops the diary completely and a few months later, she runs off."

Rizzo nodded. "Yeah, it's possible. A guy like Daily would have to cover up for just about anybody, he couldn't risk the negative press. Yeah, it's possible, I guess. It sure would explain a lot. The hush-hush on this, the mother all tight-lipped and intimidated, the missing page. I don't know, though . . ."

McQueen glanced over as he drove, speaking to Rizzo's profile.

"Something bothering you about it?" he asked.

Joe nodded and faced Mike. "Yeah, it's too simple. Plus, we got nothing but a hunch, and let's face it, that's based mostly on neither of us having much use for Daily. Don't get me wrong, it could fly. But it's a real long shot, at best. Let's not get so focused on it. We'll try to develop it and see where it goes. And even if it's true, it doesn't give us any help finding the girl."

Mike nodded and turned his eyes back to the traffic as he wove the Chevrolet through the cool, shaded streets of this upscale section of Bay Ridge.

"Okay, Joe. But I hope you're right about Daily not knowing about the diary. We don't need him accusing us of stealing it."

Rizzo laughed. "That's nothing to worry about. We forgot, that's all. We didn't steal nothing."

"So what's next?"

Joe sighed and dug a Chesterfield from his sport coat. "I've got a friend, a personal friend, not through the job. He's a lawyer who does mostly civil stuff, medical malpractice and products liability, things like that. He and his partner have a firm over on Vesey Street in Manhattan. I'm gonna call him tonight. I figure we'll do our DD-fives on this, just like we would to document any investigation we worked. But since D'Antonio doesn't want us to file any, I'll fax them over to the office on Vesey, to my friend Lenny. The fax will show date and time, and he can hold on to them in the capacity of our attorney. That way, if this ever gets weird on us, and the political hacks come after our heads, we've got a file to show what we did, why we did it, when we did it, and how we did it. It'll be bet- ter than nothing if push comes to shove."

McQueen frowned. "Will this guy Lenny go for it? I mean, if he's a lawyer, he may not want to piss off some connected politician like Daily who could maybe make some calls and hurt him."

Rizzo laughed. "Well, I'll find out tonight when I call him. But Lenny usually has more balls than brains, and he's got a lot of brains, so that means a lot of balls. I don't think it'll be a problem."

They drove in silence for a while, entering the area of Bay Ridge where Rizzo lived. The houses, though much smaller and less stately than Daily's, were no less well kept or attractive. Rizzo noted it with silent pride as he watched the blocks flow past the Impala's windows.

"We got a lot to do today, Mike," he said. "All in-house stuff, no field- work. When we get back to the squad, we'll look through this box of stuff we took, the notebooks and yearbook and the rest of it. I'll read the whole diary. Then we'll get on the phone. I have to tell the medical examiner's office to put us on the 'Jane Doe' notification list. Any white teenage girls wash up on the beach somewhere, we need to know about it. I'll get us a regional notification, too, through the state police. Then we gotta call every drugstore chain in Brooklyn and all the independents the Dailys have used in the past. If the girl fills a prescription for her Depakote, they'll call us. And we have to set up appointments for tomorrow, first with her shrink, then her sister, then the local kids she hung with, especially that Morgan kid. The one that took her to the prom. It sounded like their relationship was pretty serious at one point. He might know something."

"Alright, Joe," McQueen said as he negotiated a stop sign. "Sounds like a plan."

Joe nodded. "Also, there's a priest runs a shelter down on Smith Street in Red Hook. Takes in runaway kids, druggies, head cases, abused, whatever. Last I heard, the guy was still in business. We'll stop by and talk to him, see if he's seen her, give him a heads-up to call us if she should show."

"We're meeting the sister near NYU, right?" McQueen asked.

Rizzo nodded and blew smoke out the window. "Yeah, your alma mater. You can bond with each other while you sing the school song, maybe she'll give up her kid sister for you."

McQueen laughed. "Spit in my face more likely. The faculty at NYU makes sure the student body has a proper disdain for the fascist cops sent by the industrialists to stifle their pursuit of latte."

Rizzo chuckled. "A little bitter, I see. Well, you know what? Fuck 'em. When some cretin is shovin' a switchblade up Professor Dickweed's ass, you watch how fast he starts looking for a cop."

When they arrived at the precinct, Rizzo slid the cardboard box containing Ms. Rosanne Daily's belongings from the rear seat, and they climbed the cracked stone steps into the building. For the next four hours they worked together, mostly without conversation, carefully picking their way through the sad fragmented facts of the young girl's life, then methodically working the telephones.

When at last they were done, McQueen went into the grimy toilet and splashed cold water onto his face, meeting his own eyes in the discolored mirror above the sink.

"Michael, my friend," he said softly to his reflection, "this is no way for you to be spending your childhood."

# CHAPTER NINE

## *July*

MIDMORNING THE FOLLOWING DAY, the detectives sped north on the East River Drive toward the Lenox Hill office of Dr. Raymond Rogers. Earlier, Rizzo had stopped at the Daily household and taken possession of the newly issued mental hygiene warrant for Rosanne Daily. The housekeeper had silently handed it to him at the front door.

"Is Mr. Daily in?" Joe had asked.

"No, sir," she had replied.

"May I speak to Mrs. Daily, then?"

The woman stared at him with blank eyes. "Mrs. Daily is indisposed and cannot be disturbed. Mr. Daily was quite clear: I was to give you this envelope and wish you a pleasant day."

Now, as Rizzo exited the highway and pushed the Impala through Manhattan's crosstown traffic, he smiled grimly.

"You remember that old TV show, *The Addams Family*?" he asked.

Mike said, "I've seen the reruns once or twice on late-night cable. Why?"

"Why? Are you kiddin'? These Daily characters should do a remake; they'd be naturals."

They parked in a No Standing zone on East Seventy-first Street and entered the commercial-residential building where Dr. Rogers had his practice. Once inside, the detectives did a quick, informal appraisal of their surroundings and came to the same conclusion, expressed by Rizzo.

"This guy doesn't come cheap," he said.

Rogers was fifty years old, tall and slim with finely etched facial features and small, pale hands. His thinning hair was combed straight back, accentuating the narrowness of his face. He ushered them into a semi-dark, elegantly simple room where the scent of leather and maple wafted in the cool air. They sat in individual chairs in a loosely formed semicircle.

"How may I assist you, Officers?" the doctor asked, his voice level and deeper-sounding than one would expect from his appearance.

"Well," Rizzo said, taking out a pad and searching for his pen, "as I told you on the phone, Rosanne Daily has been missing for a while. Her parents, of course, are very worried. Especially after that phone call last Saturday. Mrs. Daily says the girl sounded suicidal."

The doctor smiled tightly. "Laypeople, particularly parents, are very quick to suggest suicidal impulses. In fact, such impulses are quite rare."

Both Rizzo and McQueen had fleeting visions of Vincente dance past them.

"How about in this case? With Rosanne?" Mike asked.

"Unlikely. Rosanne, as I assume you have learned already, is more inclined toward self-abasement when she goes untreated. How long has it been since she medicated?"

"Nobody knows," Rizzo said.

The man shook his head sadly. "That's unfortunate. But, again, I must ask, how may I assist you?"

"Tell us something we can use to find her. Where do you think she would go? Who does she trust? Is there some problem, some specific problem she's running from?"

The man smiled sadly. "I am bound by confidentiality, gentlemen. I'm certain you are both aware of that."

Joe leaned forward in his seat and spoke slowly.

"Yeah. We know that. I'm not asking you to violate her privacy, just tell me where you think she might go under the circumstances. You know what we're trying to do here. We can get her into Gracie Square for all the treatment she needs. But first we've got to find her."

The doctor looked from one detective to the other. He was subtly impressed with the uniformity of their expressions and assumed that, despite the youth of the taller one, they had worked together for a good many years.

"I can only confirm information if you already know it. Ask your questions accordingly."

Rizzo nodded. "Okay, Doc, it's a deal. We know her father pays your fee. No insurance is utilized."

"Correct."

"We know you were treating her for about three years, with varying degrees of success. We know she's bipolar and supposed to be on fifteen hundred milligrams of Depakote a day."

"Also correct."

"We know she stopped coming to see you about a month ago. We don't know why."

"Nor do I."

"But that's accurate? A month ago?"

"Yes."

"We know she didn't get along with her father, and we know she didn't like him much."

The doctor's brow furled as he answered. "We're getting into a gray area here, Sergeant."

Rizzo pressed the point.

"You said you could confirm what I already knew. I know she and her father did not get along. I have that on good information. Is that information correct?"

With some reluctance, Rogers nodded his answer.

"Yes."

"And she didn't like him much."

"Correct."

Rizzo leaned forward, his voice lowering as he spoke.

"Why?" he asked.

The doctor smiled. "Don't insult my integrity, Sergeant Rizzo, and I won't show you the door."

Rizzo sat back heavily in his seat. The fingers of his right hand drummed lightly on his thigh. He took a few breaths before proceeding.

"There are a few entries in her diary about someone she refers to as 'FC.' Do you know who that is?"

Dr. Rogers seemed to hesitate. His brow furrowed as he answered.

"What sort of references?" he asked.

"Oh," Rizzo said casually, "just stuff like, 'saw FC today,' or 'stopped in to see FC,' stuff like that."

Rogers shook his head. "No," he said. "I'm afraid I don't know the reference."

"Are you sure?" Rizzo pressed. "You seemed to hesitate there, Doc."

Rogers frowned. "I am quite positive. I was thinking, that's all."

"Besides the disease, besides the bipolar, was something going on in her life, something new and different and bad, or old and familiar and bad? Something she may have decided she needed to run away from?"

The doctor frowned. "How would that be of help to you in locating her? It seems irrelevant why she ran, but rather, to where she ran. Irrelevant for your purposes, I mean."

Rizzo responded civilly but forcefully. "Let me decide what's relevant to what I need to do here, Doctor, okay?"

"Certainly, Sergeant Rizzo. And I will decide what is appropriate for us to discuss about my patient."

Rizzo's head cocked as he looked sternly at the man. The doctor returned his look without emotion.

McQueen cleared his throat and spoke. "Look, Doctor, why don't we keep this very simple, very open? We're not the least bit interested in getting into this young lady's psyche. We just need to find her. Is there anything, any fact at all that you can think of, that might help us do that? Surely you want her found. She needs help, you more than anyone know that."

The doctor looked at the earnest young policeman and sighed.

"Detective McQueen, if there was anything I felt could be of use to you, I would surely provide it. I've been going over this since your call yesterday afternoon. I've replayed the tapes of our most recent sessions; I've gone through all my notes. I even asked my appointment secretary if perhaps Rosanne had mentioned something to her, someplace where she felt she could be happy. You see, that's all Rosanne ever wanted, was to be happy. She has no idea what true happiness is; all she knows is a progressively more crippling depression and the exhausting, false high of a chemical rush that torments her no less brutally than the depression itself."

The doctor paused here and dropped his eyes to the floor. When he raised them again, they were rimmed with pain.

"It was my responsibility, gentlemen, to ease that torment." He paused again and looked from one to the other of the policemen.

"To date, I have failed miserably. If you find her, I'll get one more chance, one last chance to help her. I want her found, gentlemen, perhaps more than anyone—with the exception of her mother. Find her, Detectives. Unfortunately, you must do it without my assistance, because I have nothing more to offer you."

"WELL," MIKE said bitterly as he took the NYPD-Official Business placard from the dash of the Impala and tossed it into the glove box, "that went great."

Rizzo smiled and fired the engine. "Relax, Mike. We knew it was a long shot and probably a waste of time. The guy was holding back, but I believe him when he says he'd give us something if he thought it would help. At least we found out the guy's legit. If we do find her, we'll be putting her in good hands."

"I guess," Mike said. "Did you notice the doctor said the only one who wants her found more than he does is her mother? Not her *parents,* her mother. Did that strike you as being odd?"

Joe nodded. "You bet it did. I mean, it could have just been an expression, something you say automatically, but I didn't get that impression. The old man is payin' the tab, but it's the mother the doctor figures is concerned. Dr. Rogers must know just how much this guy resents Rosanne and how much the kid really hates him."

"Well, let's go see what the sister has to say," Mike said.

Rizzo glanced at the digital on the dash. "We've got plenty of time before we have to meet her. NYU is in the Village, let's go down there and grab something to eat. You can take me to one of the old haunts from your radio car days. If we don't see DeMayo hiding behind a lamppost, we can eat for free."

"IMAGINE THIS," Rizzo said, dragging on a Chesterfield and then blowing smoke out the open driver-side window. "We have to meet this kid in the street, like we're a couple of drug dealers?"

They sat in the Impala, parked at a fire hydrant on East Ninth Street just east of Fifth Avenue. McQueen glanced at his wristwatch.

"She's late, supposed to be here five minutes ago."

Rizzo squinted through the cigarette smoke. He watched as a tall, young woman made her way slowly through the pedestrian traffic on the sidewalk. She wore cut-off jeans and a battered Yankees T-shirt. A blue Yankees cap sat on her head, her sandy brown ponytail bouncing and swaying behind her as she approached.

"There she is," Rizzo said. "Yankees shirt and cap, just like she told us."

McQueen chuckled. "You've heard that old bartender axiom, Joe? Never talk politics or religion with the customers? Make like a bartender with this girl, but add one more topic: baseball. You start with that Mets line of yours and she may walk out on us."

Joe grumbled his reply. "Yeah, yeah, friggin' pain in the ass Yankees fans got no sense of humor."

Lynn Daily, twenty-two years old and a political science major at New York University, recognized the gray Impala, two somber-looking men seated inside, for what it was: an unmarked police car. As she neared the car, the younger man in the passenger seat made eye contact with her. She smiled at him, noting his good looks and the broad shoulders beneath the plain blue sports jacket he wore. She angled toward the car, and the man opened a small black leather shield case, holding it just below the top of the car door. She saw the shiny blue and gold, noted the number, "1862," and read the word "Detective."

"Ms. Daily?" he asked.

She widened her smile and stepped to the rear door of the car, opening it as she answered.

"Yes, that's me," she said, climbing in and slamming the door closed behind her. "And you are . . . ?"

"McQueen, Ms. Daily, Mike McQueen."

Rizzo turned in his seat and smiled at the woman. "And I'm Joe Rizzo, miss. We spoke on the phone."

"Yes, I remember your voice. It's very distinctive. Nice to meet you both." She extended a hand across the seat back, and they all shook. McQueen noticed that the girl carried her father's mannerisms but closely resembled her mother in physical appearance. She was very attractive and refined, with an easy manner. He found himself liking her despite this being their first brief meeting.

"I'm sorry about the secrecy, guys," she said. "I just didn't want to meet at school and have to explain to anyone why I was talking to the police. This just seemed more, I don't know, practical."

"It's not a problem, Miss Daily," Rizzo said with a grin. "We wouldn't want to embarrass you. This shouldn't take very long. Would you like to get some coffee somewhere, or would you rather talk here?"

She thought it over for a moment.

"Here will be fine. How can I help you?"

"First of all, Ms. Daily," Mike began, speaking over his left shoulder to the woman, "whatever we do ask you, please don't take it personally or read anything into it. We just have to cover certain standard bases, that's all. To help find your sister."

She smiled. "You have nice eyes, Detective. Very beautiful. You know, it's genetically unusual for someone with brown hair to have blue eyes. Did you know that?"

Mike returned the smile. "Someone did mention that to me once. I think it was my mom."

"Ms. Daily," Joe said, his tone light, "was that your way of telling us to relax, you won't mind a few personal questions?"

She laughed. "No, that was my way of flirting with your partner, but okay, I get it." She raised her right hand and crossed her heart with the fingers of her left. "I do solemnly swear I will not behave like the little rich bitch with the big-shot father that you probably had me pegged for, amen."

McQueen nodded as he answered. "Thank you," he said.

"When did you last see your sister, Ms. Daily?" Joe asked.

She thought for a moment. "I didn't go home when classes ended. I'm staying at the dorm to work as a teaching assistant at the summer Head Start program. I guess I was last home about two, two and a half months ago. I saw her then."

"Are you two close?" Joe asked, leading the questioning while Mike sat silently, observing.

She shrugged. "We were once. I love Rosanne very much, I really do. But it hasn't been easy. She's been having problems—behavioral, mental, whatever—for most of her life. At one time we both attended the same high school. She was two years behind me. If you guys remember high school, you know it can be rough, probably more so for a girl than a boy. Well, it didn't make it any easier for me being known as 'Rosanne the Plumber's' big sister. All the silly little pimply faced boys thought, 'Hey, I bet it runs in the family.' Try dealing with *that* every day. I guess that was the beginning of our growing apart. She was just too wild, and, I hate to say it, too crazy. Can you sympathize with that, or do you think I'm some kind of monster?"

Rizzo shook his head, Mike smiled when she glanced at him.

"I think I understand, Miss Daily," Joe said.

"Please, call me Lynn."

"I think I understand, Lynn." Rizzo paused and rubbed an index finger across his jaw. "Was that really her nickname at school? Plumber?"

"Yes. Very sweet, isn't it? Some joker figured, 'She keeps everybody's pipes clean, so she's a plumber.'"

"I'm sorry," Mike said. "Young kids can be cruel."

"Everyone can be cruel, Detective. Young kids can be cruel, but honest."

Joe responded. "We read your sister's diary. We know she had problems. What we're looking for is information as to where she may have gone. Some friend, maybe. A boyfriend, whatever. Do you have any ideas? Your parents couldn't give us much."

Now, for the first time, her face seemed to cloud over. Despite the deliberate attempt she had been making to keep things as light as circumstances allowed, now, when she spoke again, the detectives heard a new, more somber tone in her voice.

"My sister had a diary?" she asked.

Rizzo nodded. "Yes. We had your parents' permission, written permission, to search her room and examine whatever we found. We found the diary. She had it hidden pretty well, but we found it."

She looked from one to the other before speaking. "Was my father home? At the time, I mean? Does he know she kept a diary?"

"Yes, he was, Ms. Daily," Mike said. "And no, he isn't aware of it. As far as we know, anyway. Why? Is that significant?"

She shook her head and her casual smile came back to her mouth, but Mike noted that it did not reach into her eyes.

"No, no. I just thought, you know, when she ran off, you'd think she would have taken the diary with her. I'm sure she wouldn't want our parents to see it. No girl would, certainly not one with Roe's history."

Rizzo kept his face neutral as he replied. "I see," he said.

"There's a mention in the diary of someone she calls 'FC.' She refers to 'FC' as 'him' a couple of times. Do you know of any male 'FCs' in her life?"

Lynn thought for a moment. She appeared genuinely puzzled by the reference.

"We have an uncle, my mother's brother," she said after a moment or two. "Uncle Frank, Frank Christiansen. But he lives in Minnesota. I haven't seen him in two or three years. Neither has Rosanne, as far as I know."

Rizzo shook his head. "Can't be him. She seems to have just dropped in on the guy from time to time. But she never gives any details."

Lynn frowned. "God knows what that's about. Her record with men is not a positive one."

A moment or two of silence passed before Joe continued.

"Did anything happen lately to cause her to run off? Something unusual or particularly upsetting to her or your parents?"

"Not that I'm aware of," she answered.

"All things considered, how did Roe get along with your parents? Any particular ongoing problems?"

Lynn Daily laughed. "You're joking, right? My father is a public figure and his youngest daughter is running around whoring herself one minute, then locking herself in a dark closet crying hysterically the next. Of course there were problems! They were at each other's throats constantly."

Joe laughed. "I tell people all the time I'm a detective, Lynn, but I don't ever say I'm a very bright one. I leave that stuff up to Mike here. You know, he's an NYU graduate. Majored in impressing all the coeds with his pretty blue eyes. That's why he wound up a cop: his grades weren't so pretty."

She turned to Mike with wide eyes. "Really? You're a grad?"

Now it was Mike who raised his right hand and crossed his heart. They spent the next few minutes discussing the educational advantages offered by one of the nation's foremost universities. They found they had some professors in common and laughed at the shared experience of weathering the same idiosyncrasies and personality quirks of the academic lions who roamed the halls of the school.

When Joe thought the conversation had served its purpose and re-relaxed the woman, he went back to his questioning.

"How do you and your dad get along, Lynn?" he asked gently.

She shrugged. "Fine. My father always favored me. I was his little Miss Goody-Goody. I was good for his career. Same as now, I'm an asset. NYU student, volunteer mentor to the underprivileged, the perfect campaign poster."

Now it was Mike who spoke.

"You sound resentful," he said.

She laughed. "No, not really. Just realistic. My dad is not an emotional man. He's not all warm and cuddly. He provides very well for our family. And in return, he asks us to play our roles with dignity. It helps him get elected. I've dealt with it as long as I can remember, and it's just business as usual." She smiled deeply into Mike's eyes. "I'm a well-adjusted, upwardly mobile happy camper. Life could be worse, believe me."

Rizzo let a few moments pass. When Lynn offered nothing further, he continued his questioning.

"Did Rosanne have a boyfriend that you know of?"

"No, not really. She had one once, a nice neighborhood kid—John Morgan. He lived down the street on Ridge Boulevard. They went to Roe's prom together, but even John, as naive as he was, knew it wasn't going to last. His parents almost had a stroke when they found out he was going with Rosanne. Her reputation tended to precede her with parents, if you know what I mean. After the prom, they kind of went their separate ways. He went off to Villanova, and she stayed in the neighborhood."

"Did she have friends? I mean like a group of kids she hung out with regularly?"

Daily nodded. "Sure. A bunch of white-trash losers that hung out on Fifth Avenue. A pathetic little dive of a bar called McDougal's. Last I heard, they were still serving alcohol to underage kids there." She smiled, then spoke with obvious sarcasm. "Funny how everyone in the neighborhood seems to know that, except for the patrol cops in the Sixty-eighth Precinct. How do you suppose that can be possible?"

She looked from one to the other. Mike kept his face passive and remained silent. Rizzo smiled broadly.

"I guess they must all be Mets fans in the Six-Eight. But about your sister, we know she used some drugs—grass and coke—but would you say she had a problem? A habit? Or was it just recreational?"

"Absolutely recreational," she answered, her tone and demeanor back to normal. "If anything, she had an alcohol problem. Gin, mostly. I've seen her drink it straight from the bottle like it was soda. Whenever she would swing into a phase, she'd start to drink. If there was a drug or two around, fine, she'd have some. But it was the booze she sought out. You should check the hospitals for alcohol-related admissions. If she's on a real tear without my parents to rope her in, God knows what could happen to her."

"Tell me about when you last saw her. When was it? Two and a half months ago? Back around the beginning of April?"

She nodded. "Yes, that's exactly when it was. We had a nice talk, actually. She was on her meds, seeing her doctor, Mom was keeping her pretty busy. She seemed okay, for *her*. Come to think of it, though, she did mention something about some guy she had met. And she was all excited because he had a motorcycle and the warm weather was coming. Roe figured she'd get to ride with him a lot. Just in case she wasn't in enough danger from her illness, she had to develop a strong fondness for motorcycles—those big, loud, horrible Harley things usually driven by some miscreant baboon. Just what Roe needed." She shook her head, a sad smile on her face. "Maybe he's the mysterious 'FC'?"

"Do you know anything about the guy?" Mike asked. "Where he lived, or worked, anything like that?"

The smile left her lips. "No," she said softly. "Wouldn't it be nice if I did? Maybe she's with him right now. My mother said she left without her car. I always wondered about that because she really loves that car. She told me once it made her feel normal, just like the other little rich girls: graduate high school, get a car, go to college, have a career, get married, have children, get divorced, and grow old. That's how she put it. She told me that of all those things, the only ones she would ever be able to accomplish were high school and getting that car. It was very sad."

Mike dropped his gaze from her face when he saw her eyes begin to well with tears. He heard her clear her throat and speak again.

"She's my baby sister," she said softly. "Please, find her."

Rizzo spoke in low, even tones. "Lynn," he said, "I promise you we're going to try. We're going to try our best."

Lynn Daily looked into the dark brown pools of Rizzo's eyes, and McQueen, now watching her carefully, saw a yearning trust tentatively enter her eyes. With tears beginning to flow, she smiled weakly at them both.

"Thank you," she said.

They sat in silence for a few moments and then she spoke again.

"When you find her, what will you do? I mean, you can't arrest her, not just for being missing. What are you going to do?"

"We've got that all worked out, Lynn," Mike said.

When she heard his words, her eyes suddenly hardened. Her voice had a sharp edge when she spoke.

"You don't have any authority to take her home," she said. "You're not simply two errand boys for my father, are you? What exactly do you have 'all worked out,' Detective McQueen? Dragging her back home?"

Rizzo and McQueen exchanged fleeting eye contact as Rizzo answered for them.

"Not a chance, Lynn," he said gently. "But would it be a problem if we *did* bring her home? What would the problem be?"

She looked from one to the other, and now a slight panic entered her eyes. She seemed at a loss, her mouth silently forming as if to speak, but no words coming forth.

McQueen leaned forward toward her.

"What, Lynn? Tell us. What's the problem?"

She shook her head. "There is no problem," she said softly. "She just needs help. Get her some help. Get her to Dr. Rogers."

McQueen leaned back away from her. He looked at Rizzo.

"That's the plan, Lynn," Rizzo said, reaching out a hand and patting her shoulder gently. "That's the plan."

★　★　★

LATER, THE two detectives sat in a small espresso shop on Christopher Street in the West Village. The Impala sat out front, late-day sunlight reflecting from its gray fenders.

Their interview with Lynn Daily had taken more than an hour. Rizzo now leafed silently through his notes as he sipped at his coffee. Mike, too, sat in silence, his cappuccino growing cold before him on the small marble table. He reflected on Lynn Daily's words and demeanor and the conclusions he had drawn from them.

It was clear that Lynn suffered deep feelings of guilt in connection with her younger sister. Perhaps, Mike reasoned, age and distance had combined to ease those memories of the difficult position Lynn had been placed in by the actions of Rosanne. As a young adolescent growing up, it could not have been easy for Lynn, and perhaps she had often been short or harsh with Rosanne. It was possible that Lynn wished she had handled things differently, with a maturity and insight that she now possessed, but could not possibly have mastered five or six years earlier. If, in fact, she was feeling guilty over her previous relationship with Rosanne, she was being unfair to herself, and unrealistic.

McQueen believed that Lynn knew something, something that she had not been able to bring herself to tell them, and he suspected that her guilt stemmed from that untold something. And when she suddenly feared they were merely hired guns bought and paid for by her father to hijack Rosanne, she had nearly panicked. It had become clear to them that Lynn feared her father, and even more so, feared him on behalf of her younger sister. Mike had seen her turn suddenly from an articulate, intelligent young woman in charge of her life and her surroundings into a scared, insecure young girl who sees monsters under her bed. It unsettled him. He knew it held significance, but neither he nor Rizzo had been able to draw anything further from her. She had only truly relaxed again when shown the mental hygiene warrant and told how it would allow them to civilly detain Rosanne and either deliver her to a sitting Supreme Court judge or, if they thought necessary, take her directly to Gracie Square Hospital's psychiatric emergency room where Dr. Rogers would be paged at whatever hour of whatever day to come care for Rosanne immediately.

"Did you notice how, when we told her we're supposed to take

Rosanne to the judge first, Lynn almost passed out?" Mike said to Rizzo.

Joe nodded. "Yeah, I saw that. And then I saw the relief in her face when we told her our plan was to go straight to the hospital with the kid."

"Yeah, I caught that, too. She must figure the old man has the judge in his pocket."

Rizzo sipped his coffee and fingered an unlit cigarette. "She's probably right, too. When I first picked up the warrant at Daily's this morning I called over to the courthouse, spoke to my friend down there. Remember Tim? The court clerk helped us out with finding Donzi?"

"Sure."

"Well, Tim told me they have a whole separate court part set up in the civil term to handle these mental hygiene matters. But guess what? Our boy Daily never went there, never got the warrant from the judge who's supposed to issue them. No, he got it from another guy, a guy named Banyan."

McQueen frowned. "Is that legal?" he asked.

Joe nodded. "Tight as a drum legal. Any judge in a county trial term court can issue a mental hygiene warrant. Daily went outside channels and I'm guessin' this guy Banyan is a friend of his, or somebody he owns, and the guy sitting in the mental hygiene part isn't."

"That may or may not mean anything," Mike said. "He could have gone to Banyan to save time or avoid publicity or whatever."

"Sure," Joe agreed, "or it could be something else, some other reason. We don't know."

"Well, Joe, I'll tell you this: I'm becoming more and more convinced this guy Daily was abusing his daughter or covering for someone who did. There's little doubt in my mind. I could see it on Lynn's face."

Joe shrugged. "Mike," he said gently, "you saw *something* on her face. You don't know what. Neither do I. It's still too early to get set on something, something you might try to defend later, even if it starts to look like it's going bad. You got to keep an open mind. Do I *think* Lynn seemed to feel guilt about something, something that maybe she knew and wasn't telling us? Yes, I do. Do I *think* there's something wrong with the old man here, something tied to Rosanne runnin' off? Yeah, I'm leaning that way, too. But what are the reasons for her guilt, and how does Daily play into it, specifically? I have no friggin' idea, kid, and neither do you. Don't lock yourself in. The abuse thing looks possible. But we can't say it, not yet. Keep your mind open, Mike, or something else, something that looks even better than the abuse angle, will fly right by you. You'll miss it. And maybe make me miss it, too. Stay with me on this, Mike, I know what I'm talkin' about."

Mike nodded. "Okay, Joe. But something is very fucked up here."

Rizzo laughed and popped the still unlit Chesterfield into his mouth.

"Mike, if it ain't fucked up, why would we be involved with it? It's what we do: we're the un-fucker-uppers."

Mike smiled and shook his head. "Point made, Partner. Point made."

Rizzo stood up slowly and dropped some bills onto the tabletop.

"Good," he said. "I won't harp on it. Let's get back to Brooklyn before I start picking out mauve socks to go with my teal sweater. I've had my fill of the Village for today. Let's go see that runaway priest over in Red Hook, then call it a day. I figure we bill The Swede for about five hours overtime today, Mike. That sound right to you?"

"Joe," Mike said, standing slowly and taking a last sip of cappuccino, "a great man once told me, 'There is no right, and there is no wrong. There just *is*.'"

# CHAPTER TEN

FATHER ATTILIO JOVINO HAD COME to the priesthood later in life than most. An infantry soldier of the Vietnam War, he had first seen the face of God in the explosive discharge from a Remington Combat shotgun he wielded in a steamy jungle battle that had proved to be his last. While at the Army base hospital in Germany recovering from wounds suffered in that last fight, he had asked for and received a visit from the chaplain. From there, his course had been a long but clear one, and he had sailed it well.

So very many years later, he found himself in this small, cluttered office at the rear of the storefront sanctuary that he ran. The Non-Combat Zone was known throughout Brooklyn and beyond as a haven for the mistreated, disenfranchised, addicted, or ailing children of a modern society. Father Tillio turned away no one, and he had successfully browbeaten, strong-armed, extorted, and begged enough money from the church and city, the state and even federal government to provide first-class social, medical, and psychiatric help for countless teenagers during his fifteen years running the shelter.

Now, he gazed across his desk at an all too familiar sight: two policemen, fidgeting nervously in front of the huge crucifix that hung on the wall above and behind him. He smiled at them as he began to speak.

"I don't believe I've ever seen either of you two gentlemen here before," he said. "Am I correct?"

"That's right, Father. We've never been here," Rizzo answered.

"Well then, I must tell you my policy. First, before I even speak to you, it is requested that each of you make a donation to the shelter. If you insist, I will accept a check, although my experience with policemen's checks has not been particularly positive. I am, however, equipped to accept MasterCard, Visa, or, if you are gentlemen of means, American Express."

"I don't think you can charge to talk to us, Father," Joe said pleasantly. "We're cops, here on official business, not reporters looking for a fluff piece for the Sunday magazine."

Father Tillio smiled benignly. "Secondly," he said, ignoring Rizzo's remark entirely, "I do not give up any children. You can tell me the charge, you can tell me the name of the child you are looking for, and then you can leave. If the child is here, I will talk to him or her, contact Legal Aide, and then perhaps the child will surrender to the appropriate precinct. Now, before we begin, may I suggest fifteen dollars each? A very modest donation, Detectives. Sign yourselves out an hour later tonight and your overtime will more than cover it."

Rizzo laughed. "Wouldn't that be stealing, Father? You know, as in, 'Thou shalt not . . .' Like that?"

"I'll grant you a special dispensation, Detective. Let's make it twenty dollars each and I'll include you in my nightly prayers for, shall we say, one week?"

McQueen reached for his wallet. "Stop talking, Joe, or I won't be able to afford this."

"Do you mind if I smoke, Father?" Rizzo asked while reaching for his own wallet.

"Not if you'll offer me a cigarette, sir, so I may join you," the priest replied, drawing a receipt book from his desk drawer and producing a battered ashtray at the same time.

Twenty minutes later, they were escorted out onto the dismal stretch of Smith Street that housed the Non-Combat Zone. Father Tillio shook his head sadly.

"I'm truly sorry I wasn't able to help you, Joe," he said. "But if the girl should turn up, I'll call you. I have both your cell numbers. I will show her picture around also. Sometimes it's like a network these kids develop. Maybe we'll get lucky. With God's help, of course."

"Of course," Joe said. "You be careful around here, Father. That collar won't protect you on *this* street. But I guess you know that already."

"Don't worry about me, Joe. Our friends at the Seventy-sixth Precinct take good care of me. And I can kick the butts of half these street thugs without any help. Besides, the neighborhood is improving. Gentrification is finally reaching us. They even opened up a bookstore not very far from here."

Rizzo looked around at the battered, littered street. "Forgive me, Father, but a dump is a dump is a dump."

Jovino nodded and smiled as he spoke. "Have you ever been camping, Joe?" he asked as they reached the Impala.

Rizzo shook his head. "No, can't say that I have, Father. Why?"

"Well, you know, people always tell you they've camped under the stars. Or they've been out to the country or the lake or the mountains, and they slept under the stars. Well, Joe, I sleep right here, right here on Smith Street in Red Hook, Brooklyn, New York. And you know what?"

He looked from one to the other. Joe raised his eyebrows and shrugged, Mike shook his head.

"I sleep under those very same stars. Every night. They're right up there, same as in the mountains. I just can't see them. But they're there, Joe. Just like God. Right here on Smith Street, billions of beautiful stars and one beautiful God."

The priest shook their hands. "Find this poor child, Detectives. Find her and let the doctors use God's grace to help her. Do that, and God will smile on you. You just won't be able to see Him doing it.

"Not yet, that is."

AT SEVEN-THIRTY the next evening, Rizzo and McQueen found themselves standing at the worn, battered bar in the dimly lit McDougal's Tavern on Fifth Avenue in Bay Ridge. They took seats at the corner bar on backless stools and eyed the bartender as he nervously approached them.

"This guy has visions of his liquor license flyin' out the door," Rizzo said with a smile before the man came within earshot.

"What can I get you guys?" the bartender asked with a tight smile, his lifeless, watery brown eyes shifting from detective to detective.

Rizzo allowed his own smile to broaden as he replied. "Well, buddy, I'll have a bottle of Heineken, no glass. Mike, how 'bout you?"

"Nothing for me," McQueen said.

Joe nodded. "So you get off cheap, buddy," he said to the bartender. "One beer on the house and we appreciate your generosity."

When he returned with the beer, he placed it before Joe and leaned against the inner bar.

"You guys are *cops,* right?" he asked.

"You bet," Joe said, taking a pull from the beer bottle. "Want us to flash some tin and scare off the Mouseketeers back there?"

The man glanced over his shoulder to the rear barroom. A group of eight young people, seemingly under the legal drinking age of twenty-one, were gathered around four small booths that surrounded a pool table and jukebox, talking loudly and drinking beer.

He turned back to face Rizzo. "You guys new to the Six-Eight? I haven't seen you around before."

"What makes you think we're from the Six-Eight?" McQueen asked.

The man reddened. "Well . . . I just figured. You know. This here is the Sixty-eight Precinct you're in. So I just figured."

Rizzo placed the green beer bottle down on the bar top. He leaned in closer to the man and spoke softly, their faces only inches apart.

"Here's what you gotta figure, buddy. You gotta figure, 'How can I get these two nice cops out of here before they fuck up my liquor license?' That's what you got to figure. Not to mention jeopardizing any little deal you cut for yourself with the Six-Eight patrol unit. We won't even mention that."

The bartender looked from face to face, and then sighed. "What do you need, guys? I'm not looking to bust your balls, believe me. What'd ya need?"

Rizzo sat back on his barstool and drank some beer. He glanced over at McQueen.

"Tell the man, Mike. Tell him what we need."

McQueen produced a color photo of Rosanne Daily from the inner pocket of his sport coat. He laid it on the bar before the man.

"What's your name?" he asked.

"Sean," the man answered.

"Well, Sean, take a look. Do you know her?"

He picked up the photo and scanned it. Then he raised his eyes to Rizzo. "I cooperate, and you leave. Is that the deal?"

Rizzo answered softly. "You talkin' to me, Sean? It was my partner here who asked you the question."

Sean turned his eyes to McQueen.

"Answer me, Sean. Do you know her?"

The man thought for a moment, dropping his eyes back to the photo. He sighed again before responding.

"Yeah, I know her. Comes in here couple 'a times a week with the rest of those assholes." He jerked his head toward the rear of the bar-room. "What'd she do?"

"When did you see her last?" Mike asked.

He shrugged. "I don't know. Now that you mention it, it's been a while. Maybe a month or so."

"You have any idea where she is?"

He laughed. "How would I know? I don't know where any of these kids, I mean people, are when they ain't here. All I know about this kid is she was half a nut, drunk most times I saw her. Very loud and always stepping out into the alley with half the guys here. The old-timers here, they called her Sally from the Alley. You figure out why."

"Is that what you *thought* her name was? Sally?"

The man frowned. "No, it was Rosalie or Rosemary, something like that. Sally was just what the old-timers called her. 'Cause it rhymed with 'alley,' I guess."

"Any of the clientele in here nicknamed 'FC'?" Mike asked.

"Not that I know of."

"How about initials? Any FCs?"

The barman shrugged. "You kiddin'? How would I know that? Maybe yes, maybe no—I don't know."

McQueen took the photo and slipped it back into his pocket.

"So what you're telling us here, Sean, is you can't help us. Is that what you're saying? You can't help us?"

Now Rizzo spoke. "I gotta tell you, Sean, that's what I'm hearin', too."

The man spread his arms and said weakly, "Give me a break, guys. I don't even know what you want. Help you with what? I told you I recognize the kid, but she ain't been around for a while. I know squat about her, other than what I tol' you already. Look, go ask them in the back. They know her pretty well, believe me. Go ask them, be my guest. I'll get you another beer while you're at it, guy. Be my pleasure. I'm trying to do right here."

The three men examined one another for a moment, then McQueen spoke.

"Well, what do you think, Joe? Is this guy legit?"

Rizzo dug out and lit a cigarette, then placed the pack on the bar, under the sign that read "No Smoking Allowed." He pondered Mike's question for a moment, then answered with a tight, cold smile.

"No, Mike. I think he's full of shit. Know what tipped me off? The 'alley' business. See how he told us the kids in the back were grabbing some head offa Rosanne and, what'd he call them?, the old-timers? They were gettin' some, too. Everybody was getting some. Everybody but Sean. See, Sean here is a real stand-up guy. Just ask him, he'll tell you. He's a stand-up guy, and he's telling us everything he knows. Right, Sean? You've told us everything, right?"

Sean's face tightened. He wiped at the bar top in front of them with a cotton dishrag. When he spoke again, it was in a lower tone. He seemed resigned to some unpleasant, inevitably bad ending to this unexpected visit from the two detectives.

"You believe what you want, I ain't saying no more about it. The only thing I can remember about this kid is something just came to me, just now popped into my head."

"And what would that be, Sean?" Mike asked.

"One night, around ten, ten-thirty, I was leaving for the night. She had been here, suckin' down gin for a few hours. She musta left a few minutes before me, I don't know. When I went out to get in my car, I seen her on a bike. A motorcycle. A big, noisy, old-fashioned-looking thing, not like those Jap racing bikes. She was hanging on to the back of some guy looked like a fuckin' caveman. I remember thinkin', 'This kid is going to hell in a handbasket.' She was like that—just a wild, crazy kid. But, hey, what could I do about it? I'm just a bartender, I can't help her."

He looked from one cop to the other. "That's it. That's all I know. You guys want to close me down, break my balls, I can't stop you. Do what you gotta do."

Rizzo dragged on the cigarette and tapped his fingers on the bar top, thinking it all over. Then he dropped the butt into the beer bottle and listened to it hiss itself out.

He sighed and turned to Mike.

"That's it, Mike. He's done. I don't think you can get anything else out of him, he's told us what he knows."

"You know, Joe, that's the second motorcycle reference we've had," Mike said.

"Yeah," Joe replied, turning back to Sean. "Her sister told us she was into bikes. Tell me about the bike, Sean. Anything at all you can remember."

Sean thought for a moment. "Well, I wasn't really looking at it, you know? I mean I heard the bike, glanced at it and saw her on the back. Then I went home."

"You said the guy looked like a caveman," Mike said. "What else did you notice?"

"Well," Sean answered, scratching at his head. "The bike looked black, real shiny, with a lot of chrome on the engine and long, straight chrome exhaust pipes, two of 'em, both on one side. I think it was a Harley-Davidson. The asshole drivin' it almost ran me over as I was tryin' to cross the street."

"Any plate number?" Mike asked.

Now Sean laughed. "Yeah, right. Don't you wish."

Rizzo spoke now. "What about the guy? Anything about him? Was he carrying colors?"

"Colors? You mean, like gang stuff?"

Rizzo nodded. "Yeah, like that. Was he a Hell's Angel, some club name on his jacket?"

The man thought for a moment. "Well, he did have a leather jacket with all kinds of shit on it. Could have had some name on the back, but that's where she was, sitting behind him with her arms wrapped around his stomach. Fat fuck he was, too."

Mike asked, "What about the stuff on his jacket? What was it?"

Sean shook his head. "I don't know, the usual shit, Nazi stuff, skulls—those guys are all the same. I did notice one thing, though. Looked weird, you know, out of place."

"What was that?"

"On his shoulder I think, the shoulder of his jacket. There was a symbol thing, you know, like a logo."

"What, Sean? What was it?" Mike asked, impatience creeping into his tone.

"I'm not sure. I must have seen it wrong, couldn't a been what I thought, unless the guy is in some sissy-ass motorcycle gang, if there is such a thing."

Now Joe leaned in and spoke with even more impatience than his partner had.

"Sean," he said, "just tell us, for Christ's sake, just spit it out."

Sean looked from one to the other. "A wooden shoe, okay? I think it was one of those wooden shoes, like they got in Holland."

Mike and Joe glanced at each other, then back to Sean.

"Yeah, a wooden shoe," the man repeated. "With wings on it. You know, like a logo or something."

"YES," JOHN Morgan said, "she was spending time with some motorcycle guy."

It was the following day, and the two detectives were interviewing the prom date and former boyfriend of Rosanne Daily. They found him working in the cluttered storeroom of a small bookshop on Third Avenue called A Novel Idea. After completing his freshman year at college, John was now home for the summer.

Joe looked into the young, eager face of the boy. He seemed very glad to hear that the detectives were searching for Rosanne. The night before the detectives had gotten little information from the surly, unpleasant group that was gathered at the rear of McDougal's. If anything, there had been an attempt to mislead the detectives, the result of a mistaken sense of loyalty to their perceived fellow misfit, Sally from the Alley.

But Morgan was different, a good kid from a nice family. He had met Rosanne through that very family. His mother had long been friends with Mrs. Daily, although the friendship had not fully survived John's involvement with Rosanne.

"My mom did everything she could to get me to stop seeing Roe," he had told them. "I finally realized she was right, and I ended it. Roe's mother was pretty upset. I guess she thought I could help Roe somehow. You know, calm her down a little, maybe straighten her out."

"Could you?" Mike had asked gently.

John Morgan had smiled sadly. "No. No way. It was way over my head."

Rizzo smiled at the boy and continued the questioning.

"John," he asked, "do you know who this motorcycle guy was? Did you ever hear his name?"

The boy shook his head. "No. I would only get to speak to Roe when I ran into her, you know, mostly by the house. I live just down the block from her. Once we split up, that was it. She kind of hated me for a while. I still feel bad about that."

"Did you ever see the guy?" Rizzo asked.

"No, not really. One time, though, I guess Roe's parents were away or just out, and I saw a big, black Harley in their driveway. But I never actually saw the guy."

They spoke for twenty minutes, and the detectives, despite John's cooperation, had again learned next to nothing. The boy had no idea where Rosanne could be. He only wished he did; his concern for her was genuine.

"I hope you can find her," he said, as they shook hands to part.

"We'll try," Mike answered. "You call us if you hear anything."

They had a similar outcome when they visited the grand, sweeping manor on Shore Road that was home to Judith Hansen, the young woman who was once Rosanne's closest childhood friend. Judith had not seen nor heard from her in well over a year.

"I'm sorry," she said, a sweet sadness in her voice. "I wish I could help. Whatever you learn, and whatever you hear about Rosanne, try to remember this: she's really a very nice person, very kind and caring and generous. She's just sick. It's not her fault; it's that horrid illness. Please don't judge her. Just find her and get her some help. It sickens me to think of where she might be, and under what circumstances. Please, find her."

And so they had left the elegant home and driven off into the streets of Brooklyn to try and do just that.

Find her.

# CHAPTER ELEVEN

MCQUEEN CLOSED THE DOOR behind him, tossing his car keys onto the small table in the foyer. He glanced at his wristwatch. He had more than enough time to shower, dress, and meet his former college roommate for dinner and drinks. He was looking forward to an evening of rehashing the good times from his student days. As he headed for the bedroom, the flashing red message light on his answering machine caught his eye. He ambled over and pressed the play button.

"Hello, Detective McQueen," he heard an unfamiliar voice say in crisp, well-enunciated tones. "Inspector Manning here, David Manning. I'm at the Plaza, Community Affairs, Citywide Liaison. My number is 212-555-8768. Give me a call when you get this message. I'm following your progress on the missing persons case you're handling. Call me, please. Thanks."

McQueen frowned. It was only three in the afternoon, so he assumed he could reach Manning now. He picked up the receiver and dialed.

"Good of you to call back, Mike," Manning said. "I know how hard you've been working on this business we're all caught up in. Lieutenant D'Antonio has been keeping me advised."

"Yes, sir," Mike answered.

"Mike, I only called to thank you. On behalf of the mayor as well as myself. I know how hard you'll keep working, and I'm sure we'll have a good result."

"Yes, sir. We'll do our best."

"I know that, Mike, I do know that. And I'm sure you're fully aware of the sensitive nature of this whole situation. A real family tragedy, I'm sure you realize that. Best to keep it all out of the political arena. Let's just find this girl. Keep focused. Once you do, you can just walk away from the whole thing and let the family and the doctors handle it."

"Yes, sir. That's the plan."

"Good, good. And Mike, let me be very clear and very frank here: if this all goes smoothly, if everyone is happy at the end, no one is going to forget this. Certainly not I, but I assure you, the mayor and his people, not to mention the parents, no one will forget this. For a young man such as yourself, just starting out in the Detective Division, their memory can be a formidable profit for a job discreetly done. And your partner, Sergeant Rizzo, with his experience and reputation, can enjoy some lofty years when he chooses to retire. And a cop with his years on the job always has some little situation or problem he has to deal with. Not many of those I can't straighten out, I must say. You see my point here, Mike. Regardless of either of your plans for the future, this whole thing can be quite beneficial."

"Yes, sir."

"Well, Mike, I've got to jump off now. Please tell Rizzo what I said; I may not get a chance to call him directly. And give him my best. Tell him I said, 'Go get 'em!' Just one old cop to another."

"Yes, sir. I'll tell him. I'm sure he'll understand."

"Good. I'm sure he will. Take care, Mike, I'm looking forward to meeting you at some point. Who knows, maybe we'll even be working together at the Plaza in the future. Good-bye."

The phone went dead. Mike dropped into a chair next to the phone. He thought about what had just happened.

Like Manning, McQueen knew Rizzo would understand. He would discuss it with Joe tomorrow.

For tonight, it was old friends and old memories, and he wasn't going to allow himself to think about anything else.

THE SMALL coffee shop on Reid Avenue was located in the heart of the black Brooklyn neighborhood known as Bedford-Stuyvesant. McQueen and Rizzo sat together at a small table in the rear, their breakfast before them. Rizzo glanced around at the other customers. They seemed to be oblivious to the casually dressed white visitors.

"Years ago," Rizzo said as he buttered his toast, "two white boys in here would be gettin' looks to kill. Especially two white guys they made for cops. Nowadays, nobody seems to mind."

"Isn't that a good thing?" McQueen asked.

"Bet your ass it is," Rizzo said, pushing the toast into his mouth. "It'll be an even better thing when two black guys who *aren't* cops can eat in Bensonhurst and not draw any stares. We're still a couple of years away from that. But it's coming."

They ate in silence for a few moments, and then McQueen spoke.

"So, Joe, I got a phone call yesterday."

Rizzo looked up from his plate. "Oh?" he said. "DeMayo again?"

Mike shook his head. "No. Not DeMayo. Inspector Manning, from the Plaza."

Rizzo frowned. "Manning? Ain't that the guy D'Antonio told us was kissin' up to Daily?"

McQueen nodded. "The very same."

A tight smile crossed Joe's lips. "Tell me," he said.

When Mike finished reporting the conversation, he sipped at his coffee and asked, "So, Joe. What do you think it means?"

Rizzo laughed. "Come on, Mike, you may be a new detective, but you been around life and the department for long enough. You know damn well what it means."

Mike smiled. "Yeah, I guess. But I wanted your take on it."

"Sure," Joe said pleasantly. "Here it is: they want us to find this kid, get her to the hospital, then walk away and forget about it. I recently had a formerly great man tell me cops were good at that. Walkin' away and forgettin', I mean. I guess maybe he was on to something."

"And?" Mike pressed.

"And, whatever we see, if we stumble across any skeletons in a closet somewhere, we ignore it. Then we get the payoff: you go to some suit-and-tie manicure job at the Plaza, and I get DeMayo off my ass. Plus, I get my paycheck padded for a year or so to jack up my final salary when I retire. I collect five or ten grand a year extra in my pension the rest of my life, Daily's secrets stay safe, and everybody's happy."

McQueen chewed his toast. "So Daily bit?" he said.

Rizzo smiled broadly. "Like a fuckin' largemouth bass. He musta had Manning punch us into the computer and see what they could do for us. They saw your record and education and figured you for a pretty boy Plaza decoration. Then they saw DeMayo was on my back and—bingo—problem solved. Their problem, that is. I wouldn't be surprised if Manning sized up DeMayo as a climber who'd be very happy to play ball."

"So Daily definitely has something to hide?" McQueen asked.

Rizzo shook his head. "There ain't no definites in this racket, kid. It could just be Daily wants to light a fire under us so we find Rosanne. So he can get reelected. Or maybe he's afraid we'll find out something else. Something he wants kept quiet.

"Either way, if we play it right, we'll come out better than we went in."

Mike shook his head slowly. "I knew this guy was molesting this kid, Joe. I knew it from the start."

Rizzo smiled around his coffee cup as he replied.

"Mike, with all due respect, you didn't know it then, and you still don't know it. I told you, don't wall yourself off with some half-assed theory that starts to look good. Keep an open mind."

"Then *what*, Joe? What is it? You know it's something. It's gotta be something."

Rizzo watched as a tall, very pretty black female entered the coffee shop, slipping sunglasses off her face. Her eyes met his, then she glanced toward Mike, sitting with his back to the door.

"Oh, yeah, Mike. That it is. Something. Could even be what you're thinking. But it could also just be some political bullshit. You know, keep the black sheep out of the papers. We'll see. And now," Rizzo said, dabbing his mouth with a napkin and standing slowly, "I think we have a guest."

Priscilla Jackson greeted Mike with a broad smile as he also stood, turning to face her.

"Hello, Partner," she said, and they exchanged kisses. She pulled a chair over from an empty table and positioned it, then faced Rizzo across the table.

"And you must be the incredible Joe Rizzo who Mike has forgotten me for." She extended her hand and they shook. "Did Mike tell you I'm a dyke?"

Rizzo laughed. "Really?" he said. "That's funny, we were just talkin' about wooden shoes the other day, and now I meet a dam."

Cil frowned. "A *dam*? What does that mean?"

Rizzo smiled at her. "Well, a dyke is a dam in Holland, ain't it?"

A moment passed, and now it was Priscilla who smiled.

"Okay, Joe, I get it. You're cool, and I'm sorry. It's just that, you know, with cops your age, I gotta be a little aggressive sometimes or they start getting witty, if you know what I mean."

Joe nodded. "I do, and apology accepted. Let's sit down."

They made small talk and Priscilla ordered breakfast. When the waitress had refilled their coffee cups and moved away, Mike turned to his ex-partner.

"Cil, we could have easily done this over the phone, but it was a good excuse to see you again, and I wanted you to meet Joe. I hope you don't mind."

She shrugged and sipped her coffee. "I live three blocks from here, Mike, you know that. And I have to eat, so it's no big deal. Really. I'm glad to see you and meet your new partner. So, what's up?"

"Cil, Joe and I are working on a missing persons case. A kid, nineteen-year-old daughter of a local politician. It's kind of being done on the Q.T. because the guy has an election coming up in November, which is why we'd rather not go through the Intelligence Division with this."

She nodded. "Okay. What can I do for you?"

"Mike mentioned you used to ride, Priscilla," Joe said. "Motorcycles, I mean."

She nodded again. "Yeah, I rode from when I was just a kid. I stopped last year when I hit thirty because I figured if I took a bad fall, I might not bounce so well anymore. But I've still got the bike; it's in my garage. Maybe someday I'll fire it up again."

Joe shook his head. "Leave it where it is. Don't push your luck."

"Cil," Mike said. "I know you were mostly an independent, but you did ride with some clubs around here in Brooklyn, right?"

"Yeah, I did. I rode with the Black Bitches when I was young and stupid, then later with the Cheetahs. When I came on the job, I rode with the Blue Knights for a while. You know, the cop club, all cops and law enforcement people. But what's this got to do with your missing princess?"

"Priscilla, you ever hear of a club that rides under a shoulder patch of a wooden shoe with wings? Ring any bells?"

Priscilla sat back in her seat and rolled her large dark eyes at the two men.

"Good-fuckin'-lord," she said. "If your gal is with them, her ass is in big trouble."

Rizzo's eyes lit up with the answer. Mike leaned closer to her and laid a gentle hand on her arm.

"Cil, you know them? You know who they are?"

She bobbed her head slowly. "I can't believe *you* don't know, Joe," she said to Rizzo. "Mikey boy here, he's new to the borough, but you, Joe, you've never crossed paths with The Dutchmen?"

Rizzo shook his head. "Never even heard a them. Tell me."

"They ride out of Coney Island. Got a house over on Twenty-fourth or Twenty-fifth Street off Neptune Avenue. They all live there together, like some fucked-up version of an old hippie commune. They're badasses, guys, real badasses. The one that founded The Dutchmen about twenty years ago is some lunatic from Holland. Zegling somethin' or other. To get initiated into his gang, you've got to cut your earlobe off, or rather, he does it for you. With a scalpel, I heard. They got a guy in the gang used to be an Army medic. He sews them up after the lobe comes off. If you get promoted to captain, they cut the other one off. This guy from Holland, he figures it's clever: you know, Dutchmen, Vincent van Gogh, cut your ear off. Get it?"

Mike sat back in his seat. "Wow," he said.

Priscilla looked across the table at Joe. He waited until the newly arrived waitress laid Priscilla's breakfast before her, then replied with a grin.

"Well," he said cheerfully. "I'm impressed. I never figured these guys to have any class. At least these monkeys have to learn something about van Gogh."

They sat in silence for a while, then Priscilla spoke.

"Mike," she said, "if you go see these guys, at a minimum take the

Six-Oh sector car with you. They don't like strange cops coming around, I remember that. They're just pirates and misfits, guys so screwed up, even the other psychos won't ride with them. There are a half dozen bad outlaw biker gangs in this city, running drugs and guns and extortion rings, and they all pay up to the Angels in Manhattan, over in the East Village. But The Dutchmen worked out a deal with them; word is they pay just half the going rate. Don't get me wrong, if it came down to a war there'd be a lot of dead Dutchmen and not just with their earlobes cut off, their balls, too. But the Angels know it wouldn't be an easy ride, so they compromised. I gotta tell you gentlemen something. The word 'compromise' wasn't in the Hell's Angels dictionary until they ran across The Dutchmen."

Rizzo and McQueen exchanged looks. Rizzo shook his head and smiled sadly. "I think I'm too old for this shit, and Mike here is too pretty. You have any suggestions, Priscilla?"

She thought for a moment, then spoke. "Try to work it through the Six-Oh. Get an audience with the leader, the Dutch guy. Have a sit-down, maybe with the precinct gang liaison officer along for the ride. He must have built some kind of relationship with them. If that doesn't work, call me. I can put you into the leader of the Angels. Guy they call Papa Man. He's got a woman helps him run the operation. Word is she's bi, but lately, last couple of years, she's been exclusive with him. They call her Mama Man. These people are all a little fucked up."

"You think?" Rizzo said, raising his eyebrows, a wide grin on his face. "They seem pretty kosher so far."

Priscilla shook her head, her pretty facial features now set in a grim clench.

"Joe," she said steadily, "I know your type, bro. That wise-ass eye-talian attitude of yours might do you right in Bensonhurst, but it won't cut it with these guys. It's like I told Mike when he came up to the East Side from the Village: it's a whole different latitude. You better be ready to get real with these dudes."

Joe raised his hands in mock surrender. "Okay," he said, still smiling. "Whatever you say. You're the expert when it comes to the bikers."

Priscilla nodded and smiled back, her face relaxing a bit.

"That's the truth, Joe, believe it."

They sat in silence for a few moments, finishing their meals. Then Priscilla spoke up.

"Guys," she said, "the more I think about this, the more I know you won't get anywhere on your own with The Dutchmen. I doubt if the Six-Oh gang officer can even get you in the door. You may have to go in hard, with E.S.U. and a squad of uniforms, just bust the place and see if the princess is there."

Rizzo shook his head. "Can't do that," he said. "The only paper we're holding is a mental hygiene warrant. We can't storm the place on that. There's no indication of any crime here, Priscilla, just a screwed-up runaway kid. We'll have to play it through the local precinct."

Priscilla frowned. "It won't work, Joe. If she's there, and they don't want to give her up, they'll stonewall you and the Six-Oh and tell you what you can do with your civil warrant."

"Then what, Cil?" Mike asked, frustration surrounding his tone. "If the kid is with these animals, she's in deep shit, believe me. From what we've been told, she's in a tailspin. We may not have a lot of time here."

Joe rubbed at his eyes with the thumb and index finger of his left hand.

"He's right, Priscilla. We have to act fast," he said, dropping his hand and looking at her.

She sighed. "Look," she said. "I told you I could get you in to see Papa Man over in the East Village. If anybody can get you an audience with The Surgeon, it's the Angels. I think that's the way to go with this."

"The Surgeon?" Mike asked.

Priscilla nodded. "Yeah, that's what they call the guy who runs The Dutchmen. Because of the earlobe thing . . . since he's the one who does the cutting at the initiations. He's known to bikers as either The Surgeon or Chirurg, which I think means surgeon in Dutch."

"You seem to know a lot about this, Priscilla," Joe commented.

She nodded. "Yeah, more than I care to. Years ago, when I rode with the Cheetahs, one of the guys was married to Papa Man's sister. Back then, I was still in the process of sorting through the straight-gay-straight-gay thing, and I went with the guy's main man for a time. We'd hang out with the Angels, and a couple of times The Surgeon and a few Dutchmen showed up, and I just happened to be there."

She looked from one to the other, a small smile on her face.

"My misspent youth," she said, a sadness prying into her voice.

Joe laughed. "Hey, Cil," he said, waving for the check. "Me and two of my friends robbed a car once, when we were all in high school. Shit happens. It's called, 'growing up in the big city.'"

Mike looked at them, his face without expression.

"I once took violin lessons," he said.

Now Rizzo and Priscilla burst into laughter.

"Damn, Mike," she said. "I know we're confessing heavy shit, but some things you got to keep to yourself, boy. That's just too freaky!"

When the check came, Rizzo took it and waved it at Priscilla.

"You can thank the good Lieutenant D'Antonio for the meal. We've been eatin' off him for the past week or so."

"Set it up, Cil," Mike said. "Get us a sit-down with this Papa Man character. Whenever and wherever he wants, just make it soon. This kid is probably with The Dutchmen. We need to get her back."

She nodded. "Okay, Partner, I'll run over to see the Cheetahs today. Maybe in two or three days we'll have something set."

"What's it going to cost us?" Rizzo asked.

She shrugged. "Something, for sure. Papa Man may want a favor, The Dutchmen will have their hands out. I'll get it by the Cheetahs for free. They owe me a couple of good turns."

Joe nodded. "Thanks, Cil, Mike told me you were a good cop. When this is all over with, maybe we can square it with you."

Priscilla shrugged. "No need. What goes around, comes around."

Rizzo rose and dropped bills onto the tabletop.

"Amen," he said. "Amen."

# CHAPTER TWELVE

IN THE DAYS FOLLOWING THEIR MEETING with Priscilla, Mike and Joe traversed the streets of Brooklyn in their continuing search for Rosanne Daily. As they waited to hear of any progress made in arranging a meeting with the Hell's Angels, they chased other leads culled from the teenager's spinster aunt and the Daily's live-in maid and the alcoholic custodian of her former high school. Despite all efforts, the only promising discovery remained the winged wooden shoe emblem of The Dutchmen and the black Harley Rosanne had last been seen riding off on.

On this particular day, McQueen had spent the morning interviewing some of Rosanne's ex-classmates, then met with Rizzo at the diner on Fourth Avenue to compare notes. Rizzo had successfully managed to isolate some of the young drinkers from McDougal's Tavern and attempted to gather additional leads on Rosanne's involvement with the motorcyclist and her possible whereabouts.

Both detectives found it implausible that Rosanne's friends had no knowledge of or information on The Dutchman she was involved with. Rizzo could not decide if they were stonewalling him or truly had nothing to add. Neither detective had learned anything new, so Rizzo decided they would call it a day and start fresh in the morning.

McQueen met with Priscilla in a cop watering hole one block from the Nineteenth Precinct where she had just finished a day tour. Over an early dinner of bar food and beer, they discussed the case.

"How's the search going, Mike?" Priscilla asked as they sat at the scarred wooden bar and began to eat. "Any closer to finding the princess?"

Mike shrugged. "No, not really. That lead to the biker gang is all we really have. And a nickname we can't run down. If you can set us up with the Angels, who knows? We may get lucky and find her."

Priscilla smiled at him and winked. "I ever let you down before, Mike? I'll get it done ASAP. You watch."

They ate in silence for a while, then Priscilla spoke again.

"I really wish you didn't have to deal with those motherfucker Dutchmen, though. They're dangerous skells. You need to watch yourself. And keep that wise-ass Rizzo on a leash, or he'll get your skull busted for you."

He winked at her. "You bet. But believe me, we're not in any danger. It'll all be very cut-and-dried, just a series of business dealings. We give them this, they give us that. You know. It's not like in the movies, Cil, no car chases, no shootouts."

She shook her head. "These dudes are a different kind of danger, Mike. Can you and Joe kick some ass? Sure you can. But these motherfuckers are evil. The Dutchmen don't see shit like we do. They twist up life and chew on it, then they spit it in your eye. They look to hurt just 'cause it feels good. To deal with them, you gotta connect with them, and then you better watch your soul. It ain't your ass I'm worried about, lover, it's your fuckin' soul."

Mike nodded and poked at his food with a fork. "I know, sweetheart, I know," he said, looking up and smiling sadly. "That's why I think, sometimes, this job really blows, you know? Like, what's the point of all this? You lock up one scumbag, there's twenty more to take his place." He took a long pull on his beer and turned to look into her deep, dark eyes.

"What's the point of even finding this kid, Cil? So they can pump her full of medication and give her a teddy bear to sleep with? Maybe she's better off wherever the fuck she is."

Mike shook his head. "I mean, I'm going to try to find her, of course, it's what we have to do. But in general. I don't see the point in a lot of what I do. I'm not saying I'm unhappy being a cop, not exactly. Just . . . I don't know . . . unsure. That's the word: unsure. I'm not certain I see myself doing this for the rest of my working life."

"Well," Priscilla said, a smile on her lips, "you lookin' for a point, start lookin' at life. What's the point of *that*? Damned if I know, but I ain't rushin' out to die, not just yet. You do what you can to help out, and then you move on. Let God sort out the details."

McQueen flagged the bartender with two raised fingers. He watched the man draw fresh beers for him and Priscilla.

"See?" Mike said as the man placed the steins before them. "Now that's a job with a fuckin' point."

Priscilla shook her head and reached for her beer. When she spoke, anger touched at her eyes. "This is why I got so few white friends. Here you are with a full stomach, a good paycheck, a fat pension comin' to you, and you're bitchin' about 'what's the point?' You all uncertain about it? Go sell insurance. Or shoes. See the point of that."

McQueen smiled. "I forgot how it never pays to piss you off, Cil," he said.

Despite herself, Priscilla laughed. "Damn right," she said.

They sat in silence for a while, each in their own thoughts. McQueen realized his feelings of uncertainty, his lack of purpose, were nothing new. They had begun to nag at him some time ago. The focus and sense of simplicity he had seen in Rizzo had somehow highlighted his own career doubts. Although McQueen didn't quite understand it, he knew it to be true.

After a few moments, Priscilla spoke again. Her tone was softer, reflective, and McQueen found himself taken by it.

"I ever tell you why I came on the job, Mike?" she asked.

"No, not really," he answered.

"When I was growing up, I lived in a terrible, fucked-up environment. My mother had problems with men and booze and it wasn't a very good time for me. Well, when I was about ten years old, there was this black beat cop walked my street in the Bronx. I remember he was tall with bushy hair and he had a big old gray mustache. His name was Ted. He always had a good word for me, used to give me candy, and when it was my birthday or the end of the school year or some other special day, he'd take me to the corner ice cream parlor and treat me to a sundae." She laughed. "Looking back, I figure the guy was getting the ice cream on the arm. But he was always neat, clean-looking, soft-spoken. I used to pretend he was my father. It went on for a couple of years."

Priscilla shook her head slowly. "I never knew who my father was. My mama probably didn't either." She laughed again. "Hell, maybe that cop *was* my old man."

McQueen looked into her now sad eyes. "Whatever happened to him?" he asked.

Priscilla took a drink of beer and ran a hand across her mouth. "I don't know. One day," she said, her tone now flat, "he was just gone. I never saw him again. He must have retired or gotten transferred. I made a half-assed try at tracking him down after I graduated from the Academy, but never did.

"But that guy, he really made a difference," she continued. "He showed me I could mean something to somebody. He showed me one big old black man could be something, too, something special. I never forgot that."

Mike nodded. "I guess not," he said.

Then Priscilla nodded, smiling. "You go work for Merrill-Lynch, Partner. See what kind of difference you make there. You see what I'm saying?"

He smiled. "Yeah, maybe. I guess. I don't know. But I do know this: if I stay with the department, I want to move up. I understand Joe's point of view about the little crimes being important and the local people needing us. And I understand what you're saying, too. That works well for both of you, but I need more than that. I want to move up, get back across the river, get into the Plaza."

"Well," Priscilla said as she drained her beer stein. "You need a hook to do that. And I'll bet my sweet little black ass that if you save this honcho's daughter, besides doing a righteous thing, you might just get that hook, my honey. Know what I'm saying?"

Mike poked at his french fries, then reached for his beer.

"Well," he said, "I don't know. But I guess we'll find out."

He turned to face her.

"And," he continued, "maybe soon. You get us that sit-down, Cil, and then we'll see."

# CHAPTER THIRTEEN

RIZZO AND MCQUEEN WALKED OUT of the Sixty-second Precinct and climbed into the gray Impala, McQueen behind the wheel. It was ten-thirty on an early summer Wednesday night, warm rain falling steadily.

"Well," Rizzo said as he belted himself into the car, "here goes nothin'."

McQueen started the engine and spoke as he adjusted the rear- and side-view mirrors.

"It's got to be better than the last few days. I'm so tired of spinning our wheels and chasing shadows, looking for other answers. We have the answer: she's with The Dutchmen. All we need to do is get in there and grab her."

Joe nodded. "Yeah, I guess. That's probably true. But the rest of it, all the stuff we've been doing the last couple of days, had to be done. Couldn't be avoided to handle this right."

They were both referring to the long, tedious, fruitless hours they had spent interviewing and reinterviewing family members, friends, neighbors, and former teachers of the missing girl, then tracking and running down the few leads they had received. It had taken them nowhere: the only road that had ever held any promise at all led straight to The Dutchmen. Tonight's work would, they hoped, put them on that road with the guarantee of clear passage, that guarantee courtesy of the New York City chapter of the Hell's Angels.

As he pondered it, Rizzo shook his head. "Talk about strange bedfellows," he said with a humorless smile. "A couple of Six-Two detectives and the Hell's-friggin'-Angels."

They rode in silence, each with his own thoughts, rain beating against the car in tinny counterpoint to the solid slapping sound of the windshield wipers. McQueen found himself fighting a sudden melancholy. He was just about to switch on the car's FM radio, when the Motorola handset on the seat near Rizzo began to click rhythmically. Three clicks, a pause, three clicks, another pause, then three last clicks.

Rizzo sighed and glanced at the digital on the dash.

"The old man must be closing up a little early tonight," he said. "I guess the sector car is busy on a job."

McQueen slowed for a traffic signal, the reflected red of the light glaring watery in the windshield's wet field of vision.

"What?" he asked.

Joe smiled. "That clicking. It's kind of a code. Remember those free clams you were getting all frantic about? The ones they gave you at Romano's Restaurant? Well, kid, the check just arrived. Drive over there, Thirteenth and Seventy-second Street."

McQueen had been a cop long enough not to ask any more questions. He frowned and shook his head slightly. "It figures," he said grimly.

When he rolled up on the restaurant, a double-parked white Buick sat out front, a man behind the wheel, its motor purring softly, hazard lights flashing in the darkness. The restaurant appeared to be closed.

"What now?" Mike asked.

Joe shrugged. "Nothing. Old man Romano comes out, gets into the Buick with a bagful a cash from the night's receipts. We follow him and his son to the bank on Seventy-fifth Street, they toss the bag in the night-deposit box, toot their horn 'thanks,' and we go our separate ways. Takes about three minutes, the whole deal. The sector car usually handles it, but when they get busy, they click for any units in the area that might be available." Joe looked at Mike in the dark interior of the Impala. "We were available."

Mike watched silently as Romano stepped out of the restaurant, locked the front door, and waved them a greeting. Once inside the Buick, McQueen followed him to the bank. When they were done, he pointed the car back toward the Gowanus Expressway and Manhattan and turned briefly to Joe.

"How smart was that, Joe?" he asked curtly. "I.A.D. breathing down your neck and you still working old contracts?"

Rizzo chuckled. "Relax, kid. I've got one eye on our mirrors every second. If I.A.D. could work a good tail, they'd be out doin' real police work. There's nobody watchin' us. Besides, I.A.D. investigations go on for years: they don't spend a lot of consecutive time on most cases. I can't be all paranoid for the rest of my career."

"It's not paranoia, Joe, if someone's really out to get you."

Rizzo let out a full laugh. "Good point, but, you know, they may not be out to get me. They might just wanna put the fear of Jesus into me so I'll give up Morelli. Which, by the way, I would've done on day one if I could've proven he set the murder up. But free clams and following an old man to the bank, that ain't nothin'. You know that."

"I guess that's one of those things that isn't right, isn't wrong . . . just *is*, right, Joe?"

Joe nodded and reached for his cigarettes. "Exactly," he said. "Nothin' illegal about it. The guy is a citizen and he's afraid to go three blocks at night with a bag full a cash in his hands. So he calls the cops, and we help him out—protect him. That's our job. If the guy appreciates it, offers some thanks, what's the problem?"

McQueen shook his head. "If you're not seeing it, I can't show it to you."

"Mike," Joe said patiently. "We're cops. We don't do 'right' and we don't do 'wrong.' We do 'legal' and 'illegal.' What we just did, that falls in between, that's the gray area. It's a judgment call. Don't lose any hair over it, okay?"

After a moment, Joe spoke again.

"You know, Mike, people are people. They're always going to do certain things—like smoke or drink or gamble or even go to prostitutes. All of those things were once, or still are, illegal. But things change. Prohibition came and went. Gambling? My old man got locked up the first month I was born for being in a poker game in back of a bar. Now you can do it anyplace, plus go to Off-Track Betting or Atlantic City or Las Vegas Night at the church fund-raiser, buy a Lotto ticket from the state . . . whatever. See, it all changes—right, wrong, legal, illegal—most of that stuff can't be regulated 'cause it's human nature. If you tell somebody it's illegal to drink or smoke or gamble or go to a cathouse, next thing you know there's some guy banging on a pulpit someplace telling you it's illegal to be gay or read some book or see some movie.

"That's why being a cop is so simple. If the good citizens tell us something is illegal, we lock people up for it. If they tell us it's okay, then it's okay. If it's illegal, you can't do it, period. If it's legal, you can. When you get into that gray area, you decide for yourself. But 'right,' 'wrong'? What is that? It's wrong to kill someone, right?"

"Yes," Mike answered.

"Well, suppose the guy raped your daughter? You walked in on it, saw him doing it. You blow the guy away, cold-blood. Is that wrong? I don't know. Could be wrong, could be right—hell, it just *is*. But I'll tell you something: it's totally illegal, and I'd have to lock you up for it. I might also give you a pat on the back, but I'd lock you up.

"That thing with old man Romano, was that legal? Is it right? Is it wrong? I don't know. It just *is*, Mike, that's all."

McQueen shook his head. "That's a cop-out, Joe. It's just a cop-out."

Joe smiled. "Well, kid, that's what makes it so interesting. You think it's a cop-out, but you did it anyway. You going to report it to anybody, Mike? DeMayo maybe?"

He shook once more. "Of course not, Joe. You know that."

Rizzo smiled. "I rest my case."

McQueen leaned forward and switched on the car's radio. They drove to the city with little further conversation, the classic rock station they had agreed on playing softly.

PRISCILLA JACKSON glanced at the wall clock above the front desk of the Nineteenth Precinct and turned to the sergeant seated beside her.

"Time for me to get into my civvies," she said to him.

He spoke without raising eyes from his paperwork.

"Okay, Jackson. You comin' back to the house later?"

She stood and began to walk away, toward the stairs leading to the small, cramped, second-floor female locker room.

"Nope," she said over her shoulder. "When I'm done with the detectives, I'm going home."

He nodded. "Okay. Be careful."

Priscilla had been scheduled for a four-to-midnight tour on patrol, but a call from the Six-Two detective squad commander, Vince D'Antonio, had freed her for temporary assignment to the Detective Division.

Tonight, she would once again team up with her old partner, Mike McQueen.

As she changed out of her dark blue patrol uniform, she reflected on the young cop she had ridden with for two years.

Priscilla had recognized early in their relationship the refreshing lack of pretense and superficiality in her new partner. Without ever verbalizing it or even alluding to it, Mike had made it obvious that her sexual preference was of no concern or significance to him. Although reluctant to ever admit it, Priscilla preferred working with a male partner, but finding a suitable one had always been difficult. She found herself constantly having to make allowances for their macho posturing and lack of empathy for the citizens they came in contact with, be they victims or perpetrators.

But with Mike, it had been different. He was a unique combination: a smart, educated man who also commanded a tough, street-smart attitude instilling in Priscilla a cold comfort: he would handle himself well and was capable of covering her back even in the worst of situations. And although his deep blue eyes could grow icy and hard, he never lost his humanity or concern for those they served. When circumstances so dictated, Mike could be coldhearted and was not a cop to be pressed or fooled with. Yet he carried with him a sensitivity and gentleness that Priscilla found herself sometimes having to work hard to try and equal.

Priscilla had always enjoyed those occasional long, slow nights together, usually during the harsh winter months, where their conversations were not limited to sports and women and the evil nature of mankind, as with most male partners, or to the never-ending man trouble and child-care issues of female partners. No, with Mike it had been different. Music, movies, cars—even art and theater—had been discussed. They had even reflected on the more philosophical nature of life, each from their varied backgrounds and viewpoints, and Priscilla knew they had both broadened and grown as a result.

She missed him. And as she finished lacing her sneakers and adjusting her black leather ankle holster, she smiled as she realized that Mike's strong, confident good looks and aura of danger hadn't been hard to deal with either. He had attracted good-looking young women like a magnet.

Priscilla closed and secured her locker. As she left the room and made her way to the front entrance of the precinct, she wondered how Mike was faring with his new partner. Joe Rizzo seemed so different from Mike; not just older, different. She wondered if Rizzo's problem with Internal Affairs was in some way contributing to Mike's gnawing unease and dissatisfaction with his career. She had always known Mike to be mildly unhappy somehow, but no more or less than any other cop she knew. On their last few meetings, though, it appeared more pronounced. It had almost intruded on their time together.

She remembered Mike telling her of a chance encounter he recently had with some old war veteran, victim to a burglary. The man had apparently sensed Mike's melancholy and asked about it.

"This guy lived a long time, Cil," Mike had told her. "He's seen a lot, knows a lot. He saw something in me, just like that. It's more than just losing Amy. I just wish I knew what the hell it is."

She had shrugged. "A lot of those old war dudes are half nuts, Mike," she said with a casualness she hadn't really felt. "They come from a different time. A bad time. Repressed as hell—couldn't ask for help, couldn't cry—all fucked up. They kept everything inside. He sees you showing your concern and feelings for him, so he figures you got a problem, a weakness. He's puttin' his cross on your back, that's all. I'd not let it ruin my nights, you know?"

Mike had smiled sadly. "Yeah, okay, Mommy, I know how special I am."

Priscilla had laughed. "You call me 'Mommy' again, I'll give you something to be unhappy about, boy."

Now, as she waited for the gray Impala, she hoped it would pass. She already had enough confused people in her life. She'd hate to see Mike become another one.

When Rizzo and McQueen arrived at the East Side precinct, they saw Priscilla waiting under the eave out front, shielded from the rain, dressed in civilian clothing. They pulled to the curb and Rizzo hit the lock release for the rear passenger door.

Cil ran through the rain and scrambled into the backseat of the Impala.

"Okay, guys," she said. "Let's do it. St. Mark's Place, between First and Second Avenue. I just got off the phone: Papa Man is there and awaiting our arrival."

"Thanks again, Cil," Mike said over his right shoulder. "I'm sorry you had to get dragged along."

She shrugged. "The only way the Angels would agree. My man at The Cheetah's told them I was good people, but he couldn't vouch for you guys. I'll vouch to Papa for you, then all the little niceties are tied up. It's no problem, I'm glad to help."

McQueen had little trouble finding the building once he turned onto St. Marks Place. Two thirds of the way down the street, on their left, stood a tenement surrounded by nearly forty motorcycles. Some were covered against the rain, others exposed, some on the street, others up on the sidewalks, their high handlebars and chromed engines and pipes glistening under the streetlights.

He angled the car into the curb in front of a fire hydrant and shut the engine. Joe reached for the Motorola and turned it off, slipping its thin body into the inner pocket of his sport coat.

"I hope you remembered to oil up that fancy Glock of yours, Partner," he said with a grin. "This place looks a little like Dodge City to me."

McQueen laughed. "Do you have that flintlock you call a sidearm on you?"

"My Colt? I sure do. Any gun you can carry for twenty-six years and never have to fire, that's a goddamned good gun. A guy keeps a gun *that* good."

Priscilla sounded up from the rear seat.

"Gentlemen, please," she said. "Put the testosterone back in your scrotums. There will be no trouble tonight. We came under The Cheetah's banner, we ain't kicking the door down. You'll see: these guys are very classy, in their own way, of course. They're like old-time Mafioso, or Hollywood's idea of old-time Mafioso. Relax. And Joe, just think before you try to be funny. Subtle irony may be lost on these guys, and it'll be tough trying to get a motorcycle boot out of your ass."

Rizzo laughed. "Okay, Cil. I get it. I'm Henry Kissinger tonight."

"Well," she said, opening the car door to get out, "whoever the fuck he is, I hope he's tactful."

Their knock at the door was answered by a tall, slender, blonde who appeared to be about twenty-five. She wore dirty jeans and a thin white T-shirt under a black leather vest. She was bra-less and well endowed, barefoot with a nice, easy smile.

"I'm Cheryl," she said. "Papa Man is expecting the heat, and you guys seem to fit the bill. Am I right?"

Rizzo chuckled. "Well, I'm Detective Sergeant Rizzo, and this here is Detective McQueen and Officer Jackson. But I don't know if we generate much heat, Cheryl."

She pressed her lips tightly together and waved an index finger at Rizzo.

"Shame on you guys," she said. "Two white males and you're detectives, one black female, and she's just an 'officer.'" She turned to Priscilla and smiled. "What was it, honey? Sexism or racism got them promoted over you?"

Priscilla smiled. "Both, sister. Both."

They followed Cheryl into the foyer, an uninhabited living room in pleasant disarray to their right, an open staircase rising before them. To their left, a doorway, the door ajar, led to the basement stairs. The odor of cigarettes and burning marijuana wafted up the steps into the foyer, and the heavy bass of an elaborate sound system pounded from below. Cheryl smiled.

"We party on Wednesday nights," she said, her eyes twinkling. "And any other night when it's raining. If you can't ride, you party. We keep it simple."

She turned and led them up the exposed main stairway to the second floor, then knocked on a closed door. When they heard "Come in," Cheryl led them into the room. It appeared to be what probably had once been the master bedroom of the residence, a spacious room with two narrow floor-to-ceiling windows looking out across some backyards.

Leather chairs and two broad, black leather sofas dominated the room. Against one wall, behind red velvet ropes that hung from gold-plated posts, stood the bent frame of a battered and broken royal blue customized Harley-Davidson motorcycle. A black, World War II–era German Army helmet sat atop the twisted, torn padded seat. The name "Jose" was stenciled onto a white piece of poster board taped to the wall above the cycle. A slight odor of gasoline hung in the air. The three cops looked at the display, surprised to see the carcass of an eight-hundred-pound Harley in this second-floor room.

"All that remains in earthly goods from our departed brother, Jose the Cuban," they heard from their left.

Turning, their eyes fell on Papa Man, a sight familiar only to Priscilla.

He sat spread-legged on a black leather love seat at the rear corner of the room. He appeared to be about sixty, although Rizzo felt with allowances for lifestyle, he could very well be in his early or midfifties. He was a huge man, over six feet tall, and carried a paunch that brought him to over two hundred and sixty pounds. He was dressed in black jeans and a black riding jacket over a bare chest and bloated, hairy stomach. He held a bottle of Budweiser in one hand. His black hair was grizzled and unkempt, but oddly not unpleasant-looking, and his face carried the graying shadow of a day's growth of beard. He smiled at them and rose from his seat.

"It's a tradition of ours. Whenever an Angel dies on his bike, we set the wreck up here. It stays until the next guy goes down. Jose there, he's been dead for three months. We had a good run this spring." He smiled at them, wolflike. "But hell, it's the summer now. I figure we should be moving old Jose out in about a week or two."

He turned to Cheryl. "Go find Mama Man and send her up here, honey, and bring our guests beers. But not this piss"—he waved the long-neck bottle of Bud—"the Sam Adams Summer Ale. New York's finest deserve our best stuff."

Cheryl smiled and left the room, closing the door behind her. They all shook hands, Priscilla kissing Papa lightly on his lips, then got arranged in their seating. The boom-boom of the bass from the basement vibrated the floor beneath their feet and the chair cushions they sat on.

"Please, Officers," Papa said, "before you begin, I ask that you wait for my lovely bride to join us. There are those who will say—outside of my presence, of course—that she's the brains and I'm just the brawn of this operation." He flashed the wolflike grin again. "They may be right."

They sat in silence for a few minutes, McQueen fidgeting nervously on the couch, Rizzo scanning the room and its eclectic and not uninteresting contents. The twisted motorcycle, oil seeping from its broken motor, sat like a specter beside them.

Mama Man entered the room, followed by Cheryl carrying a cooler full of Summer Ale. Mama greeted the three cops with a smile, shook their hands, then went to the love seat and sat beside Papa. She was dressed in a fashion similar to his, but with a black vest like Cheryl's over a red T-shirt. A large black button with white lettering pinned to her vest read "My Other Toy Has a Dick." Her brown hair was tied back behind her head in a casual knot. She seemed about thirty, fairly trim, only a hint of a midriff beer belly. She wore no makeup and was not unattractive.

Cheryl set the cooler down in front of the couch where Rizzo and McQueen were seated. She knelt on the floor next to Mike's left knee and smiled up at him, opening a beer and holding it out to him.

"You're the cutest pig I've ever seen," she said, her eyes running across his face and body. She turned to Priscilla. "Is he yours?" she asked.

Priscilla laughed.

"Not at all, girl, not at all."

Cheryl turned to Papa.

"Can I have him, Papa?" she asked.

The man smiled. "Well, I don't know." He looked at McQueen, addressing him directly. "Would you be interested in young Miss Cheryl, Detective McQueen? I can assure you, her charms and talents are quite considerable."

McQueen felt his stomach tighten and his ears redden. He glanced at Joe, who was staring fixedly at what appeared to be an actual stuffed alley cat sitting on a small table next to Papa's seat, its paw raised, claws extended and teeth bared. Priscilla, Mike saw, wore a small, amused smile, merely raising her eyebrows at him in a questioning manner as their eyes met.

Mike cleared his throat before responding. He felt Cheryl's hand fall gently on his leg, above his left knee.

"I'm working tonight, Papa," he said, his voice sounding strained, even to his own ears. "I don't think I can."

Papa frowned. "Well, Cheryl, there you have it. I'm sorry, but we have here a man convinced of his own nobility, blind to the middle-class bullshit he drowns in. Go on, Cheryl, go find a more agreeable amusement. I suggest you start in the basement."

She stood and smiled sadly at Mike, then turned to Papa. "Will you need anything else?"

"No, thank you, Cheryl. Go on."

She nodded pleasantly at Rizzo and Priscilla, then turned and walked from the room with a bounce in her step that tossed her not-quite-clean hair jauntily around her head. She closed the door behind her.

"Gentlemen," Papa Man said, with a slight nod to Priscilla, "I have a few items of business to attend to tonight, you being only one of them. So let's get started. I've been told by my associates in Brooklyn that Priscilla here is good people, and I remember her to be so. I assume she will tell me the same about you—with the understanding, of course, that you are all three pigs, and the scope of your trustworthiness can only be so broad. I accept that. I've also been told by Brooklyn that you need access to The Dutchmen. Access that you believe I can arrange for you."

Rizzo nodded. "That's correct. Can you? Arrange it, I mean?"

Now it was Mama who smiled and spoke as she leaned forward in her seat.

"Papa can do anything he wants, Detective Rizzo. The Dutchmen are evil and sick people, and periodically, Papa finds it necessary to remind them whose city this is. That's why he agreed to this meeting in the first place. If you have an even remotely reasonable request, Papa will grant it. Forcing those savages to meet with you will reinforce his supremacy." Now her smile broadened and she sat back in her seat, lifting a beer bottle to her mouth as she spoke.

"And it's so much more civilized than throwing one of them off a roof, don't you think?"

Now Papa Man spoke, his eyes moving from Rizzo to McQueen. "Can you see, gentlemen, why I've married this woman? She uncomplicates my life."

He took a long pull on his Budweiser.

"So," he said, wiping the back of his hand across his mouth. "What brings you here? What's your beef with our friend, The Surgeon?"

"No beef, Papa. No beef at all. Let me tell you the situation," Rizzo said.

When he had finished, Papa Man sighed and looked at Mama. She smiled and shook her head.

"This is about some runaway rich kid?" he asked. "That's the problem? Hell, I got three of 'em right here, in the basement, probably with their asses up in the air right now. Why don't you take one of them and forget about The Dutchmen?"

Rizzo shook his head. "I'm not after them, Papa. I'm after her."

Papa compressed his lips and ran a hand through his hair. He sipped at his beer, then spoke.

"Detective, you're jaywalking a dark boulevard."

Rizzo frowned. "What does that mean, Papa, I'm not following you."

"This is nothing but an ego thing with you," Papa answered. "It's like when I'm riding in the night. I'm tearing down some broad street somewhere, and some citizen, he's jaywalking across the road, in the dark, his head up his ass. He's all wrapped up in his own history, full of his own memories, making his plans, the center of his universe. He can't conceive of being nothing but an unseen object on somebody's road, like some scrap of paper or a grain of sand. No, he believes he's so important, so special, that everybody must see him, must know who he is. He can never get it that in a split second, him and his memories and his plans can all be gone, just like that. Erased from the slate. That's ego. That's what this is for you, Detective Rizzo, ego. Find the big shot's daughter, and you'll be a big shot, too."

Joe shook his head slowly and smiled a smile dark enough to cause Mike's stomach to tighten again and Priscilla to unconsciously slide herself closer to the edge of her seat.

"Do me a favor, Papa Man," he said softly. "Save the two-dollar philosophy for the tribe. Just help us save this kid's life, okay?"

Papa Man held Joe's gaze. The room was very still, and Mike saw an unhealthy glow of anticipation in Mama's eyes as she leered and smiled back and forth between Rizzo and Papa.

"So," Papa said at last. "You're asking for an act of Christian charity, is that it?"

"Okay," Joe said.

Papa nodded and spoke with hard eyes. "I'm a good Christian, Detective. I know that Jesus expects His flock to be flawed and to exhibit human weaknesses: I try never to disappoint Him. As a good Christian, I know that acts of generosity and compassion have their rewards in the next life. What I would like to know from you is, can I perhaps expect some less theoretical reward, something, say, in this life?"

Rizzo remained silent. McQueen saw the glint in his partner's eye and spoke before Joe could respond.

"What do you need, Papa? If it's doable, we'll do it."

Papa turned to Mike. He began to smile and appeared to relax somewhat. Mike noticed a flicker of disappointment in Mama's eyes.

"Occasionally, a friend or colleague, even a brother Angel, may have a problem over in Brooklyn. If that should happen, I would like to know that you and your partner here, as well as Priscilla, can look into it for us. Maybe clear up any misunderstanding the arresting officer might have been working under."

Mike turned to Rizzo. "Joe?" he asked.

Rizzo considered it, then stood and smiled slowly. He crossed the room to Papa, who also stood. They shook hands as Joe said, "It's a deal. Your people get jammed-up in Brooklyn, call me. If I can work it out where everybody is happy, I will."

"Good," Papa said. "Now, if you'll excuse me, I need to call The Surgeon. On a rainy night like this, he should be available. You'll get your sit-down, and if he has the girl, he'll give her up. The price will be his to name. You meet it or not, that's up to you. Satisfactory?"

"Yes," Joe answered.

Papa nodded and left the room. Fifteen minutes later, he returned. He reached into the cooler and took out two Sam Adams. Using an opener that dangled from his leather jacket, he opened them both, then handed one to Mama. He drank from his and smiled at Rizzo.

"Tomorrow night," he said. "Nine o'clock at The Dutchmen's joint in Coney Island. Just you and your partner." He turned to Priscilla with a sad smile. "I'm sorry, but The Surgeon is old world. He said no women at a sit-down. It's like Mama said before, they're nothing but savages."

"Did he say anything about the girl? Does he know who we're looking for? Is she there?" Mike answered.

Papa turned to him. "He claimed the name you told me meant nothing to him, but there are fifty people in my basement tonight, and I may know twenty of their names. Among ourselves, we don't use labels, names, titles, that shit. He did say there was some rich kid riding with them lately. She actually bought one of his guys a custom Harley, went for about twenty-two thousand. Bought it cash, on the spot. Could that be her?"

"No," Mike answered after a moment's reflection. "I can't see how. This kid's trust fund is tied tighter than Fort Knox until she's—what'd the mother say, Joe—twenty-one, twenty-five?"

"Twenty-five," Joe said.

Papa shrugged. "Well, then, it's some other muff. You'd be surprised at how many escapees from plastic land we've collected over the years."

They exchanged parting handshakes, and Papa Man escorted them downstairs to the front door. Upon entering the foyer, they were greeted by the sight of Cheryl, laughing and running naked through the living room, two drunken Angels chasing her with almost childlike abandon. Papa smiled at Rizzo, his wolflike aura accentuated by the dim lighting of the foyer.

"Lock up your daughters, Detective, if you've got any," he said in a happy hiss to Rizzo. "There are Hell's Angels all around you!"

# Chapter Fourteen

IT WAS THURSDAY NIGHT at eight-fifty when Rizzo turned the Impala onto the blighted, dismal block of West Twenty-fifth Street, just off Neptune Avenue in the Coney Island section of Brooklyn. The rain of the previous day and night had passed, leaving the streets shrouded in a steamy, humid mass of air that hung like a fog.

As on the previous night, they had little trouble locating their destination—a rambling old Victorian-style house, once the crowning jewel of the formerly magnificent block in the storied playland neighborhood. The structure stood in darkened disarray, surrounded by dozens of glistening, evil-looking Harleys bearing custom paint schemes and garish colors that seemed to mock their blighted surroundings.

They climbed the front steps to the covered porch. Sounds of music and loud, intoxicated voices reached them from somewhere behind the house where members of The Dutchmen were gathered. Rizzo reached out a hand and knocked solidly on the front door.

A few moments passed before the huge, heavy wooden door swung inward and open, groaning on rusted hinges. A squat, muscular man appeared in the doorway and eyed them with unconcealed distaste. He stood five feet seven inches tall, broad through the chest with heavy, exposed muscular arms. He wore a red leather riding vest over a bare, hairless chest, and his head was shaven. Dirty blue jeans met beaten black leather boots. From his exposed, pierced left nipple, a silver chain dangled, holding a small, black swastika.

Rizzo and McQueen looked into his face. They noted the pale, bloodless stub of scar tissue where his left earlobe had once been. On his forehead, between the ends of his black brows, was a red and black tattoo, an
inch long and half as high. It was a vampire bat, and it glared back at
them with equal malice.

McQueen felt a slight shiver begin to develop in his right leg. The
muscles seemed to twitch as if electrified: he pressed his foot harder
onto the wooden planking of the porch, and the twitch subsided. He felt
his ears begin to redden with embarrassment but quickly realized that
he, and he alone, was aware of his fear.

Rizzo smiled coldly at the man. "Good evening," he said pleasantly.

The man moved his eyes slowly from one to the other of the detectives. The eyes were black and flat, seemingly without moisture. When
he spoke, it was in a cigarette-mauled rasp, barely loud enough to be
heard despite his close proximity.

"You the cops here to see The Surgeon?"

"Yes, we are," Joe said, allowing a pleasant lilt to brush at his voice.

The man's deep scowl softened to a frown. "Show me some tin," he
said.

They produced their shields and IDs and held them at the man's eye
level. He glanced at them without interest or comment, and McQueen
followed Joe's lead in slipping his case back into the front left pocket of
his pants.

"Are you both carryin'?" the man asked.

"Of course," Rizzo said.

Now the frown turned to what served the man as a smile.

"You got to leave the hardware with me if you want to see the man."

Rizzo smiled broadly. "Now you know *that's* not happenin', don't
you, son?"

"I ain't your son."

Rizzo let his eyes harden. "Yeah, well, we can't be sure about that,
can we? Papa Man already gave me all the rules I need, *son*. We're here
to see The Surgeon, not you."

The man seemed to consider Rizzo's words and tone. Then, slowly,
he turned and started to walk deeper into the house.

"Close the fuckin' door behind you," he said.

They followed him through the foyer to a doorway leading to the basement steps. Once downstairs, they found themselves in a large room with chairs and sofas and small tables arranged loosely around a large projection television set. There was no one in the room. They followed the man to a rear door and waited as he knocked. Hanging in a golden picture frame on the door's outer surface was what both detectives recognized as an official police department crime scene photograph. It showed a young man's face in a tight, close-up color print. The man was clearly dead, one eye fixed open, the other lost in a pool of bloody tissue. His mouth was open, and what appeared to be human male genitals hung from it. Blood had trickled out onto his chin.

The significance of the photo was not lost on either of them: enter this room and you were pledging silence. If you betrayed The Dutchmen, the traditional mob-style murder and mutilation decreed for stoolies would be your fate.

"Come in," they heard from behind the door. The voice was not unpleasant.

The Surgeon sat behind a surprisingly neat desk, a small fluorescent lamp casting a warm glow across its surface. The room was a rather standard home office arrangement, showing signs of also being used, on occasion, as a temporary storage area for the household items most families tend to accumulate.

The Surgeon himself appeared to be in his late forties, and when he rose to greet them, he stood nearly six feet. A thin man, but well-muscled, dressed casually in an almost antiseptic imitation of a biker outlaw. His clothing was clean, as were his hands, and the brown hair was long but trimmed and shone under the bright lighting of the room.

They shook hands, and he gestured them to take seats opposite his desk. Then, from his own seat, he raised his eyes to the man who had brought them in.

"Thank you, Bats," he said. "That will be all."

The man glared from Rizzo to McQueen. He shook his head slightly.

"I never thought I'd see two pigs walk in here without a warrant in their hands," he said in low, gravelly tones. "And foreign pigs at that."

The Surgeon laughed. "Well, Bats, the world is constantly changing. I suggest you try to change along with it."

The man left the room, closing the door behind him. The Surgeon leaned forward on his desk, interlocking his fingers and resting his weight on his forearms. They noticed the same bloodless ear stub, only his showed on both ears.

"Can I get you anything, gentlemen? Beer? A drink? Some fresh pussy?"

Rizzo shook his head. "No thanks," he said.

The man looked to Mike. "I'm good," Mike said.

"So," Rizzo began, crossing his legs and reaching for his cigarettes. "I'm Detective Sergeant Joe Rizzo; this is Detective Mike McQueen. What should we call you?"

He smiled. "You told me who you are, Detective, but not what I should call you. Why don't you do that first? Set the tone, if you will."

Joe thought for a moment. "Okay," he said. "I'm Joe; he's Mike." He paused again. "Who are you?"

"I am Edmund Zieling Haas. But you can call me Eddie."

Rizzo leaned forward and they reshook hands. Mike did the same.

"Mind if I smoke?" Rizzo asked, a Chesterfield in his hand.

"Not at all. Here." Eddie reached into his desk drawer and produced a large, heavy, ornate crystal ashtray. He placed it before Joe.

"That's leaded Austrian crystal, Joe. From Tiffany's."

Joe glanced at it. "Yeah," he said, lighting the cigarette. "I figured."

"Now, Joe," Eddie said, "before we begin our business, is an apology owed for anything Bats may have done or said? Did you take offense at him?"

"No, Eddie," Joe said with a wave of his hand. "He's an offensive little prick, but no offense was taken."

Eddie smiled. "Good. Bats is very loyal to me. I've ridden with him for almost fifteen years, since he was only sixteen. He's my personal security man, very protective. I make some allowances for his antisocial personality."

Joe smiled. "Antisocial? Are you kiddin'?"

Eddie laughed aloud. "Antisocial by *my* standards, Joe, not the citizens'."

"Oh. Okay, then."

"So, Joe, Papa Man has requested I cooperate with you, and as long as it costs me nothing and I can, in fact, gain from it, I'm fully prepared to do just that. Papa tells me some corporate puppet master has misplaced his daughter, and you believe she rides with The Dutchmen. I have some questions."

Joe nodded. "I figured you might. Ask them."

"Do you intend to arrest this girl for some supposed crime?"

"No."

"Do you intend to arrest any of my riders for their possible involvement with or use and/or misuse of this young lady?"

"No."

"You guarantee that?"

Joe shook his head. "No," he said. "You asked if I intended to arrest. I can guarantee you I won't be arresting *her*. But if one of your guys carved her face up or threw her under a bus, I *will* lock him up. But as of now, with what I know, I have no intentions of arresting anyone."

The Surgeon pondered that for a moment, then nodded.

"Alright, then. Next question: What do The Dutchmen get for our civic-minded cooperation?"

"What do you want?"

The man sat back in his chair and looked at them from across the desk. His eyes fell on Mike and remained there.

"You *can* speak, right?" he asked with an unpleasant smile.

Mike let a moment pass before responding.

"When I have something to say to you, I'll say it."

Eddie nodded, and the smile became passive. "Good," he said. He turned back to Rizzo.

"Now, Joe, you asked what I want. Well, that depends. This valuable little bit of cooze may not even be here. Why don't we see if I've got anything to sell before we decide what you'll pay?"

"Show him, Mike," Joe said.

McQueen slipped Rosanne's photo from his jacket pocket. His hand brushed against the reassuring presence of the silenced Motorola also tucked in the pocket.

Eddie looked briefly at the photo and smiled. He tossed it gently back across the desk to land in front of Mike. Then he leaned over and pressed a button on the telephone.

"Bats?" he said.

"Yeah, Boss?" they heard through the speaker of the intercom.

"Go find Chick and bring him to me."

"Okay, Boss."

He now turned his attention back to Rizzo.

"She's not here," he said. "You're about a week or two behind her. But not to worry. The information I'm selling is good. You should be able to find her in a day, two at the most, if you're half as good a detective as I know you to be."

Rizzo smiled. "And how do you know how good I am, Eddie? Until a few days ago, we never heard of each other."

He nodded. "We're not active in Bensonhurst. By prior arrangement with a local entrepreneur named Louie 'The Chink' Quattropa." Haas smiled pleasantly and resumed, this time in an exaggerated, singsong tone.

"Do you know the man?"

Rizzo kept his face and tone neutral. His peripheral vision caught Mike's quick glance. "Yeah, he runs what's left of the Brooklyn Italian mob. Actually, he lives in Bay Ridge."

"But he's based in Bensonhurst," Eddie said.

"Okay," Joe answered with a shrug.

"But," Eddie said, waving a hand in the air, "all that aside, to answer your question, I know you're good because Papa Man told me the girl you're looking for is some big shot's kid. They don't send the assholes out to find the big shot's kid. They send the assholes to look for Joe Citizen's kids. So you must be good." He smiled and looked at Mike. "Even Harpo, here, must be pretty good. He just doesn't talk much, that's all."

"What information are you sellin', Eddie?" Joe asked.

Eddie stayed locked on Mike's eyes for a moment longer, watching as their blue grew colder under his gaze. He smiled before looking away and back to Joe.

"I can put you on to her. And maybe to bigger things than her if you're interested. But let's stick to her for now. And, of course, me. Let's stick to me . . . and my price."

"Tell me," Joe said.

"The previously mentioned Chink. I need to get a message through to him. I can do it on my own if I have to, but I think it would hear heavier coming from you, a respected member of one of the world's foremost police departments. You deliver my message, then you tell me his response."

"What makes you think I can deliver messages to The Chink?" Rizzo asked, again in a flat tone.

Eddie chuckled. "Well, Joe, let me be frank. I've got a baby sister who lives in Manhattan a couple of blocks from Police Plaza. She runs a little business out of her apartment. Spends a lot of time with her legs open—sometimes with a cop between them. Even asks a question or two for her dear brother. It works out well for both of us."

"So?" Rizzo asked.

"So, I don't take orders from Papa Man. When he called last night, I said okay because I figured maybe some Bensonhurst cop could serve my needs with The Chink. After I spoke to Papa last night, I called my dear sis. She made a few calls this morning, and guess what she told me?"

"What'd she tell you, Eddie?" Rizzo asked, his eyes hardening.

"Well, it seems like the gods have smiled on me. They have rendered unto me that which is mine: a pipeline to Quattropa. The gossip is you and The Chink have bartered before."

Eddie saw the anger rise in Rizzo's eyes. He thrust out a hand, palm outward.

"Of course, it's just rumor," he said pleasantly. "I can sympathize. You should hear some of the horrible mistruths spoken about *me*."

Rizzo forced the tension from his facial expression.

"I guess that explains your access to the C.S.U. photo nailed to the door," he said. "A little gratuity for your kid sister."

Eddie smiled. "Exactly, Joe. Now, what about my message?"

"The message being . . . ?"

Eddie sighed. "Couple of my riders had an unfortunate misunderstanding out in Canarsie about a week ago. By the way, we are off-the-record here, right, Joe?"

"Absolutely."

"With, of course, the usual exceptions, I assume?" Eddie smiled.

Joe nodded. "Right: murder, future crime, terrorist shit, you know the deal."

Eddie nodded. "Well, this misunderstanding involved some vegetable seller out on Rockaway Parkway. My people were offering him a little business insurance, and at a very reasonable premium. But the guy laughed at them and told them to fuck off. Unfortunately, just a few days later, the business suffered a fairly serious setback."

"And the problem?" Joe asked.

"Well," Eddie said cheerfully, "this stupid fucking immigrant fruit seller didn't mention that he was already fully insured by the good-hands people of the Saverese family. You know Frankie Saverese?"

"I know the name. Wise-guy out of Mill Basin and Canarsie."

"Yes, indeed. And first cousin to The Chink."

Joe shrugged. "So your people stepped on their dicks and pissed off two seriously made guys. My advice to you is, forget the message and just don't stand next to them for a while. Chances are, in a few weeks, you'll have a couple of spare motorcycles around here."

Eddie laughed. "My first reaction exactly, Joe. Great minds *do* think alike. Do you ride, Joe? A bike I mean."

"No, I never have."

He shook his head. "That's too bad. You've got the balls for it. But anyway, your suggestion, while a good one, won't fly here."

"Why not?"

"This wasn't our first offense. Last year, despite our formal arrangement with The Chink, a couple of my guys ventured into Bensonhurst with an ill-thought-out stolen-auto scheme. The Chink was not pleased, and you know what? I never saw either of those two boys again. It was a shame, too, they were two of my better earners. But you see my position?"

Joe ground out his cigarette in the crystal ashtray and reached again for his pack and lighter.

He smiled as he lit another Chesterfield.

"Oh, yeah, Eddie, I see your position. You figure this time Quattropa sends the troops out for you personally."

Eddie nodded, a broad grin on his face. "Exactly. See, I knew you were a sharp cop, Joe. Now, believe me, if he wants a fight, he can have one. He's barely one step ahead of the feds as it is, all those old guineas are. A fight with me will just speed up his indictment. This thing in Canarsie, it was just a mistake, pure and simple. The Bensonhurst thing, that was different, my guys fucked up. They went independent, behind my back, forgot they were borderline morons who need my brains the way men like you and I need oxygen. With them, whatever The Chink did or didn't do he had the right. But this, this situation in Canarsie, this is different."

Rizzo dragged on his cigarette and thought for a moment.

"So, I go to The Chink, call him off, tell him you regret the mistake and you'll take care of it in-house. So what does he get?"

"Discussing that would compromise your integrity as a sworn officer of the law, Joe," Eddie said with a grin. "Just get him to agree to hear me out. I'll reach out to him with my peace offering, and he'll be happy at the end of the day. Plus, my two guys will make it right with the immigrant in Canarsie, and The Chink can take the credit. Or Saverese can, however they choose to handle it."

"And you figure I can do all this?" Joe asked.

He nodded. "Joe, I've had dealings with the police on three continents: in my native Netherlands, my adopted and beloved home here in the States, and on those occasions when I've vacationed down in sunny, historic, and fertile South America. I know what cops can and can't do. You can do this."

Joe pursed his lips and glanced at Mike. The younger detective's face was expressionless, and Joe was pleased to see it. They both knew how close they were to Rosanne; they could sense it. The Surgeon could put them on to her, perhaps even deliver her himself. All that was required was a short visit to the Starlight Lounge, the small bar on Bay Ridge Avenue where Louie "The Chink" Quattropa held court. The Starlight, located squarely in that gray area between "legal" and "illegal," "right" and "wrong," now held the key to Rosanne Daily's immediate fate.

"And I get the girl?" Joe asked in a low voice.

Eddie nodded. "I give you the info you need tonight, you grab her tomorrow or the next day, whenever. Only after you actually get her do you have to go talk to The Chink."

Joe smiled and sat back in his seat. "So, you'll take my word on this, Eddie? We got ourselves a special little bond going here?"

Now a knock sounded, and Eddie glanced at the door, then back to Rizzo, his eyes hardening.

"You know exactly what we have here, Joe," he said, his voice a hiss. "We've got business. I give you the girl and you pay for her with The Chink."

He glanced back to the door as a second knock sounded.

"Come in," he said, then turned back to Rizzo, lowering his voice as two men entered the room.

"You try to fuck me, Joe, you better hope Quattropa chills me. And soon."

Rizzo smiled coldly. "You seem a little tense, Eddie," he said casually, turning to face the two men as they crossed the room. "Quattropa's been known to have that effect on a man."

Bats walked slowly behind the desk and stood beside Eddie, facing the detectives. The man he had led in took a seat to Mike's left after Eddie had gestured for him to do so.

"Show him the picture," Eddie said to McQueen, with a tilt of his head to the seated newcomer.

Mike turned his gaze to the man. He appeared short, five-six at best, and very fat. His flesh bulged obscenely against the thin material of his graying white T-shirt. His dirty jeans were open at the waist, partially secured with a heavy metal chain almost obscured by the overhang of his belly. His face, pockmarked and burned dark by the sun and wind, was equally obscured by a wild, matted red beard. It was difficult to determine where the beard ended and the tangled, dirty mane of head hair began. A caveman, the bartender at McDougal's had said in describing him.

McQueen slipped the photo of Rosanne along the desk's edge. He let it lay there under the dull gaze of the man.

His eyes flickered as he looked at the photo.

"Chicks," he said, an eerie falsetto pitch to his voice. Mike caught the strong scent of alcohol on the man's breath and the sickly sweet odor of burned marijuana clinging to his clothing.

Eddie smiled. "Gentlemen," he said to Rizzo and McQueen. "As you can see already, Chick here is not the brightest member of my choir. And on top of it, he's drunk. If you intend to get anything from him, I suggest you let me handle this."

Rizzo, a slow anger still burning him from Eddie's barely veiled threat of a moment ago, answered for them.

"Be my guest," he said softly to Eddie. "I'm a cop, not a fuckin' anthropologist."

The Surgeon laughed, genuinely amused. "Joe," he said, "you really must take up riding. You're hung for it."

He turned to the man.

"Chick," he said in a kind but firm tone. "I want you to answer my questions. Simply and to the point. Don't explain anything, just answer. Do you understand?"

Chick looked into The Surgeon's eyes, then glanced nervously to each detective.

"Did I fuck up, Chirurg?" he asked, using the Dutch word for surgeon, fear pushing through the alcoholic slur.

"No, Chick, you didn't. Just answer my questions."

The man relaxed a bit and smiled. "Okay, Boss. Shoot."

"Chick, do you see that picture?"

"Yeah."

"Who is it?"

"That's my ex-girl. Chicks."

"Is that what everyone called her? Chicks?"

He nodded. "Yeah, Chicks, 'cause she didn't have no real name, and she was mine, so the guys, they said she was Chick's, sos that's what we called her: Chicks."

Rizzo shook his head and looked to McQueen. "This kid's got more aliases than Lucky Luciano," he said bitterly.

The Surgeon chuckled at the remark, then turned back to Chick.

"Where did you find her?" he asked.

Chick shrugged. "Out at the Bow-Wow, the hamburger joint on Cross Bay Boulevard. In Queens."

"When?"

He thought for a moment, squinting with the effort. McQueen noticed beads of sweat forming on the man's brow despite the cool airconditioned breeze moving gently through the room.

"I dunno. A couple a months ago, maybe. Out at the Bow-Wow."

The Surgeon nodded patiently. "Yes, Chick, the Bow-Wow. We got that part. She's the one bought you that soft-tail custom Harley you're wheeling, right?"

Chick's face beamed. "Yeah," he said happily. "She's the one."

"Tell these two cops how that happened, Chick."

The man looked nervously at Rizzo and McQueen. His eyes then darted back to The Surgeon. He began to perspire more profusely.

"What?" he said dully.

Eddie sighed. "It's okay, Chick. Just tell them."

He cleared his throat and glanced at Bats who nodded discreetly to him. "Okay," he said. "If that's what you say."

"That's what I say," The Surgeon said softly.

"Well, she had a sack fulla money. Hundreds and fifties and a few five-hundred-dollar bills. I never seen one before I seen those, goddamned. I told her I been wantin' a custom soft-tail from that shop over in Jersey. She said, okay, let's go get one. So I took her, and she gave the guy the dough right on the spot. He put it all under a light he had, said it was good, not counterfeit. That was a cool light."

"What happened to her, Chick? How come she's not here any-more?"

Chick frowned and looked sheepishly down at the floor.

"You know why, Boss," he said.

Eddie smiled benignly and glanced up at the amused face of Bats.

"Yes, Chick, I do. But these cops don't. Tell them."

"Well," he said, scratching nervously at his matted hair. "I was back out at the Bow-Wow a couple a weeks after I got the new bike. Mother-fucker has a hundred and fifty horses with Screamin' Eagle heads and cam. I was gonna tear up some dudes on Cross Bay."

"And how'd it all turn out, Chick? Tell them."

The man grinned sheepishly, apparently taking bizarre pride in demonstrating his ineptness to the strangers.

"I lost the bitch. There was a guy there with a Jap bike looked like a pig. But he had a slit with him lit my eyes up. She had a ass like a peach, I tell ya. We got to talkin', me and him, and we bet the slits on the bikes." Here he frowned, regret briefly flickering in his eyes. "I thought I could blow him down, Boss, with that new ride I had."

"Yes, Chick. We figured you thought that. But what actually hap-pened?"

He slammed a suddenly balled fist into his thigh.

"I missed a fuckin' shift! Missed a fuckin' shift and blew it! God-damn stupid fuck, I missed a shift."

Rizzo leaned to his left, almost touching McQueen's body.

"You lost her?" he asked. "You lost her on a bet? What the fuck does that even mean?"

Chick looked puzzled. He turned to The Surgeon with questioning eyes.

Eddie smiled coldly, clearly enjoying himself, and made pointed eye contact not with Rizzo, but McQueen.

"Tell him what it means, Chick," he said.

Chick turned back to Rizzo, speaking very slowly, as if to a child.

"It means I lost her. It means she had to go off with the guy. He won her, and now he's got two bitches. And me, I'm back to sloppy seconds and jerkin' off."

They sat in silence for a moment. Then an angry McQueen spoke directly into The Surgeon's eyes.

"Ask this moron who the guy was," he said to Eddie.

Eddie's face lit with amusement. "Why, Harpo, it's good to hear from you. I knew you were in there somewhere." He turned to Chick. "You heard the man. Who was the guy you lost her to?"

Chick, seemingly unfazed by the young cop's harsh words, shrugged.

"Some guy rides with The Others. From Staten Island. He said his name was Cake."

"Thank you, Chick," Eddie said. "You can go now. I'll tell them the rest."

Chick stood, eager to leave. "Okay, Boss. Thanks. I'll catch you later." He turned and walked unsteadily to the door, exiting the room with obvious relief and closing the door gently behind him.

After he had gone, Bats circled the desk and sat in the vacant chair. The Surgeon smiled coolly at his visitors.

"Ready for that drink yet, gentlemen?" he asked.

"No," Rizzo answered for both of them. "Let's wrap this up. You said you'd tell us the rest. So tell us."

Still smiling, The Surgeon reached into a desk drawer and removed a bottle of cognac.

"Well," he said, "do you mind if I have one?"

"Go ahead," Joe answered.

They watched as the man uncorked the bottle, raised it to his lips, and took a long swallow. Then he sat the open bottle down on the desk and turned his attention back to the detectives. He made no offer of cognac to the still present, silent Bats.

"Where shall I begin?" he asked, a light, conversational tone injected facetiously into his voice.

"With the money," Joe responded. "Where did this kid get enough cash to buy that clown a bike?"

The Surgeon laughed. "Ah, Joe, you see, I was right. Great minds do think alike. That's exactly the question I asked when I first found out about Chick's good fortune."

"Who did you ask?"

"Why, Joe, I asked her, of course. Do you not fully realize that Chick is a bit intellectually challenged? A moron, I believe Harpo here called him." He smiled coolly at McQueen, who answered the smile with hard eyes.

"What did she tell you?" Rizzo asked.

"She said she stole it. From her father. It seems he'd been prying into her life lately. She was very upset about that; although what a modest young lady like Chicks could possibly have done of an embarrassing nature is beyond me. She said she waited until he had gone off to corporate land, then she went into his den. She had a key to his desk and the combination to his wall safe, apparently from nosing around the office during her formative years."

Here he paused and took a second pull from the cognac bottle.

Rizzo leaned forward and spoke. "So she was still livin' at home at the time?" he asked.

"Yes. In fact, I believe she mentioned that it was partially why she had run off. She took about a hundred thousand in cash. By the time she started running with Chick, most of it was gone, or so she claimed. As a matter of fact, he rode her over there, to her house, to try and get more, but the combination on the safe had been changed."

"She told you this?" McQueen asked.

Eddie turned to Mike. "Oh, she told me lots of stuff. She told me her father was some kind of crook, and she had proof. She said if he ever tried to put her away, she'd use it against him. I wasn't sure if I believed her till now. She was really flying, all hyper and excited, she was so happy I figured she had forgotten she was going to die someday. I asked her if daddy knew about this proof she had and she said absolutely not. Just about the money she stole. All I was really interested in was whether or not there was any more cash lying around the house. She said there wasn't, so I dropped it. I considered the possibility of selling her and her evidence back to the old man, but I was busy at the time and next I heard, Chick had lost her. She was totally broke by then anyway, so it didn't matter much."

"Where's this evidence?" Rizzo asked.

He smiled at the two detectives. "Ah, yes, I thought you might ask. Remember, gentlemen, I told you before that I could give you the girl and maybe more if you wanted it? Well, that's it. The old man sent you after his money. It's the reason you really came. The reason I now know she was telling the truth about the old man being crooked."

Rizzo frowned at him. "What? What do you mean?"

Now The Surgeon's eyes went flat, the smile left his face. "Don't confuse me for a fool, Joe. Papa Man has friends, I have friends, some of them cops. He knows you been lookin' for this kid full-time. Cops don't do that, so you guys are working a contract. I know her father is a wheel, big-shot politician, and he couldn't give a goddamned about his daughter. She told me that, and on that I believed her. Hell, you can't even blame the guy: we specialize in dysfunctional females around here, and she was this year's trophy winner. Her old man had threatened to lock her away somewhere and soon. See, she knew he was a crook and she figured if she could prove it, he'd have to leave her alone. The old man tried to hijack her off to some nuthouse once before, but somehow her shrink stopped it. Chicks figured she needed protection against her old man. So what does he do? He sends you two looking for her. I figure he *does* know she's got something to hurt him with. I guess I'm sitting here with the next police commissioner and his right-hand man, Joe, and I want you to know I'll always feel free to call on you in the future should I ever need a favor or two. You have to be in on it. Daily would never have gotten straight cops involved. See, I'll know that you found whatever she's got, and I'll know it magically disappeared. And you, well, you'll never know just what I can and cannot prove."

He looked from McQueen to Rizzo and his cold smile returned.

"So you see, gentlemen, you're working for two coldhearted scumbag criminals now: William Fuckin' Daily and me, The Surgeon." He leaned forward across the desk and lowered his voice to an almost pure hiss. McQueen felt the hairs on the back of his neck begin to stir at the sound.

"If you've got time, why don't I send for my scalpel? We can initiate both of you right now. Right here. It'll only take a few minutes."

# CHAPTER FIFTEEN

RIZZO AND MCQUEEN SAT SIDE BY SIDE at the end of the long, battered bar, hunched over their beers. The tavern on Surf Avenue stood diagonally across from the minor league ball field that was home to the Brooklyn Cyclones, and it was nearly deserted. The person closest to them was the disinterested bartender thirty feet away, leaning against the back bar and leafing idly through a *Daily News*.

"So," Rizzo said, "the Surgeon knew it was Rosanne we were looking for as soon as he got the call from Papa Man. And now we know what the problem has been from the start. The old man is crooked."

McQueen nodded and drank from his beer, trying to wash the taste of The Dutchmen from his mouth. "Yeah," he said drily. "So much for my abuse theory."

Joe smiled. "Hey, it looked good to me, too. And in a way, we were right. It is abuse. Maybe not quite like we thought, but abuse just the same."

Rizzo sighed. "That son of a bitch Surgeon may be a wacko, but he's no dummy."

McQueen dropped his eyes to his beer. "You mean the Quattropa business?"

Rizzo nodded, his right hand fingering the pack of Chesterfields in his jacket pocket. "Friggin' no smokin' laws," he mumbled. Then, in a stronger voice, he said, "Yeah, the Quattropa business. That slimy little prick took the call from Papa Man, sized the situation, and got on the horn to his whore sister. God knows how many Plaza bosses she's ban-gin' gratis to pay for her protection and his inside info."

McQueen sipped at his beer. "What a set of parents those two must have had."

Rizzo laughed bitterly. "You think?" he asked.

They sat silently and drank. After a while, McQueen spoke up. "So, Joe, how are you going to play this out? Even if you can somehow get an audience with The Chink, would it be smart to do it? If DeMayo gets wind of it, how's it going to look to him?"

Rizzo shrugged casually. "What's the fuckin' difference? It doesn't matter what I do. I.A. figures me dirty, that hard-on Surgeon figures me dirty . . . fuck it. They can't prove what never happened. As far as get-ting in to see The Chink, I can do that easy enough. We've crossed paths dozens of times over the years. Hell, Quattropa helped me put more street skells away than any cop ever did. I can handle it with Quattropa. If The Surgeon's info pans out, I'll deliver the message. Maybe we'll get lucky and The Chink will just blow me off and still whack that psycho. We'll see."

They sat quietly, Rizzo waving for two more beers. Then once more McQueen broke the silence.

"What now, Joe?" Mike asked.

"Well, we finish our beers and go home, make a couple of calls, then call it a night. Then, at some point, we go see this priest at Saint Ephrem's and see if The Surgeon was telling us the truth."

"You think maybe he was lying? Why?"

Rizzo shrugged. "Who knows? The guy is the most genuine so-ciopath I've ever met, and I've met a few, believe me. But if he really does think we're crooked and he'll be able to extort us later on, he probably was telling us straight. He wants us to succeed. That's why he's aiming us at this priest."

"So The Surgeon was telling us the truth about Chick riding her over to the church so she could give this evidence to the priest? And what do you think he did with it?"

"I guess he put it under his bed or something. I don't know. But he promised her he'd hold it and respect her privacy. According to The Sur-geon, the only two people Rosanne trusted were Dr. Rogers and this

Father Charles. She was right about Rogers: he stood up to her father and he stonewalled us. The good doctor probably figured we were working for the old man, after that money, same as The Surgeon did. Rogers never once mentioned any of this other stuff, but looking back, I can see he knew about it. He wanted us to find *her,* but nothing else. God only knows if Rogers or anybody else knows about this proof she claims to have."

"So," Mike said, "now we know who 'FC' is—Father Charles. Do you think he'll give us whatever Rosanne left with him?"

Joe shook his head. "Who knows? It never occurred to The Surgeon that Daily didn't know about this so-called evidence and that we were just two cops doing our jobs. To him, we were just hired guns, bought and paid for. Let's see if we can convince this priest that we're legit."

McQueen hesitated as the silence grew around them. At last, he spoke.

"Are we, Joe? Legit?"

Rizzo drank from his beer bottle, then turned to Mike.

"You familiar with the Alamo, Mike?" he asked, his voice soft.

Puzzled, McQueen frowned. "In Texas?"

Joe nodded. "Yeah, in Texas. When I was a kid, the Alamo was a big thing where I lived in Nebraska. We used to play Alamo all the time, and every kid wanted to be David Crockett or Jim Bowie. The consolation prize was William Travis, the commanding officer during the battle. We always tried to make this Puerto Rican kid Santa Ana, but even he wanted to be Crockett."

"Where's this going, Joe?"

"Well, when we played, I always wanted to be James Butler Bonham. You ever hear of him?"

"No," McQueen answered.

Joe nodded. "The other kids hadn't either. They said, 'Okay, Joe's Bonham,' then argued over being Crockett or Bowie. And that was fine by me. See, my old man was a big American history buff. He was real interested in the story of the Alamo, even took me, my mother, and sister down there one time to San Antonio to visit the place. That was about a year or two before he died. They got a street named after Bonham down there."

"And?" Mike asked.

"Well, kid, lately we've been talking about right and wrong and what is and what isn't, and it looks like we've got us a situation here. We know where Rosanne is, on Staten Island. We've got the exact location and name of the guy she's with. We ride out there and pick her up and that's the end of it. Or, we go see this priest, take a look at what he's got, and if we see any evidence of a crime, a corrupt city councilman, we go straight to the feds with it. We can't trust the Brooklyn D.A.'s office, they're too political. We certainly can't trust the police department, not with Inspector Manning pulling the strings on this whole thing. We've got a choice: ignore it, or act on it. Or we can just ditch it. Burn it, whatever. Daily can't possibly know it exists. He would never have sent cops looking for her if he did. No, he figures it's just the money, and he knows with her being bipolar, she'd have blown most of it by the time we find her." Rizzo paused and ran a hand through his hair. When he spoke, it was in a flat, unhappy tone.

"And then of course," he said, "there's always option four."

"Which is?"

"Take it to Daily. Deliver Rosanne to Dr. Rogers and this evidence to Councilman Daily. That's what Daily himself would do. That's what Papa Man would do. That's what The Surgeon would do."

They sat in silence for a moment, then Joe spoke.

"But getting back to James Butler Bonham. See, he was a lieutenant in the Texian Army. That's Texian, not Texan. Half of them were Mexicans. Anyway, Colonel Travis sent Bonham out of the Alamo a few times during the actual siege. He would ride through Mexican lines to deliver messages and try to bring back help. Then he'd ride back through the lines and reenter the Alamo. A few days before the place was overrun and everybody got killed, Bonham was sent to this small town called Goliad to bring back help. But when he gets there, guess what? There is no help, there is no volunteer army. So he changes horses, mounts up, and heads back to San Antonio.

"When he gets back from Goliad, Bonham's on high ground, looking down at the mission yard. He sees that the enemy has closed in, the noose around the Alamo even tighter. By then, the Texians couldn't surrender because General Santa Ana already told them he was going to massacre the entire garrison. No quarter would be offered, and eventually he made good on that promise.

"So, what should Bonham do? He's a young guy, maybe twenty-eight, he's got a lot of years ahead of him. See, Mike, it's one of those things: what's right, what's wrong—who knows?"

McQueen scratched at his chin. "So, what *did* he do?"

Rizzo smiled sadly and drank more beer, then answered.

"He spurred his horse and rode through the lines one last time, back into the Alamo. Then he gave Travis the bad news: they were on their own, no help was coming. Later, he died along with the rest of them." After a moment, Joe spoke again.

"See, Mike, that's what I mean. Some people would say what Bonham did was the right thing, some would say it was the wrong thing. Me, I'd probably say it just *was*, Mike. It just was."

"What are you really trying to tell me here, Joe?" Mike asked.

"Well, Mike, we've got a little clearer choice to make here. We have 'legal' and 'illegal,' like I explained before. Me, I've got twenty-six years in. If I piss off Manning or Daily or the mayor or the freakin' Pope, I just say, 'So long, fellas,' and I put in my papers. My house is paid off, my kids can just borrow a few more bucks for their tuition. It's time for me to go, anyway. But you, it's different for you. You've got what? Twelve, thirteen more years minimum to a pension? On this one, Mike, you've got to make the call."

McQueen sat back on his bar stool, his eyes wide.

"Are you kidding me, Joe? You're putting this on me?"

Rizzo nodded. "It's got to be your call, Mike. The stakes are too high. You get enough bosses trying to hurt you on this job, they can usually figure out a way to get you indicted, eventually. Especially if the politicians and the D.A.'s office share the same hard-on with them. You ignore Rosanne's evidence, you're out of danger. You give it to Daily, you probably go over to the Plaza and help Manning plan the Saint Patrick's Day parade, then have lunch with the mayor. You go to the feds with it, you may have to face Santa Ana's army."

McQueen shook his head. "This is fucked up, Joe," he said. "What happens to your idea of touching Daily to get I.A. off you? How does all this play into that?"

Rizzo shrugged. "I don't know. You can't have your cake and eat it, too, whatever the hell that means. But it's about time I get out. This I.A. thing soured me pretty good. The other day my youngest, Carol, tells me she wants to be a cop. I'll break one of her kneecaps before I see her tied up in all this shit."

Now McQueen sighed sadly. "This sucks," he said softly.

Rizzo drew a long, deep swallow from his beer bottle. He placed it back on the bar top, empty, and waved at the bartender for another round. Then he turned to face McQueen.

"Take some time, Mike. Think it over. I believe you know how I feel about it, but you let me know and I'll go along with whatever you decide." Now he smiled, a rare softness in his eyes suddenly apparent to McQueen.

"You let me know, Mike," he said softly. "Do we stay in Goliad, safe and warm? Or do we return to the Alamo?

"You tell me."

# CHAPTER SIXTEEN

THE FOLLOWING MORNING, Rizzo sped the Chevrolet toward the Bedford-Stuyvesant home of Priscilla Jackson, the rising sun behind them glaring harshly in the rearview mirror. McQueen sat silently beside him, leafing through the lengthy, detailed notes he had compiled throughout the investigation.

Rizzo lit a cigarette and opened the driver's side window. He spoke above the sound of the rushing wind pouring into the car's interior.

"I spoke to Dr. Rogers last night after I got home," he said. "He'll be at the hospital twenty minutes after we call him. He admitted knowing about Father Charles. In fact, they'd been conferring with one another, trying to straighten her out. Rosanne used to see the guy at the rectory two or three times a week. She saw him more than she did Rogers. The doc didn't tell us about Father Charles because he knew the priest hadn't seen her recently and had no idea where she could be. He saw no reason to violate his professional ethics for something he figured wouldn't help us. Typical civilian, doctor or no doctor. He's gonna decide what's important to us." Joe shook his head. "They just don't get it."

McQueen looked up from his notes. "Did he indicate that he knew Father Charles had something of Rosanne's? Does he know about that angle?"

Joe shrugged. "I'm not sure. I can't say. Rogers *probably* knows the old man's a crook and he *probably* knows that her father has no clue that Rosanne's on to him. Whether or not he's aware of this evidence, I have no idea. He's still playing his doctor-patient card pretty close to the vest. But the important thing is he'll be there to admit Rosanne when we get her to Gracie Square. What arrangements did you make with the One-Two-Three?"

Rizzo was referring to the One Hundred Twenty-third Precinct on Staten Island.

McQueen closed his notepad and slipped it into his jacket pocket. He turned to Joe and nodded.

"I spoke to the gang liaison officer last night," he said. "He's off today but he told me to see this guy Downing at the squad this morning. He'll get a sector car and ride out with us, but he said there shouldn't be any trouble. Apparently, this gang, The Others, they're pretty lightweight. The guy who founded it is some ex–Madison Avenue advertising whiz kid who made a few million bucks, then had a midlife crisis. He bought some broken-down old house in the middle of nowhere and started this motorcycle gang. Most of the riders in the gang are just recycled citizens like him. According to the One-Two-Three, the precinct gets a couple of calls a month about The Others, mostly noise complaints or racing stuff, an occasional dis-con in a bar somewhere. But they're mostly harmless."

Joe nodded contently. "Good. I've had enough psycho bikers for a while. We'll stop at the precinct, pick up Downing, and head for The Others. If we're lucky, they'll all still be asleep and we can catch her in bed."

The shrill ringing of a cell phone sounded.

"That's mine," Rizzo said, dropping his right hand from the steering wheel and reaching into his jacket pocket.

"Hello?" he said.

"Joe? It's me."

Rizzo frowned. "Jen? Everything all right?" he asked.

"Well, yes. No. I don't know."

"Where are you? What's going on?"

Jennifer Rizzo sighed heavily. "I'm at work. In my classroom. I just had a visitor."

"Who?"

There was a pause. "Ralph DeMayo," she said softly.

"Tell me," Joe said.

"He knew my schedule, Joe. He knew that on Friday in my summer school programs I have a morning prep period. How did he know that?" she asked.

"A phone call, Jen, a simple phone call," he said impatiently. "He's not a goddamned mystic. Relax and tell me what he wanted."

"Well, it was financial, mostly. He asked me about the girls' tuition. Marie's at Cornell, mostly."

"What did you say?"

"I told him the truth. About the loans we have, the loans the girls have, I even told him about the money my mother gave us, when she sold her house."

Rizzo thought for a moment, glancing over at Mike. "Good," he said. "Like I told you, we have nothin' to hide. Let him knock himself out. Did he ask you to sign anything? A statement, a financial disclosure release, anything like that?"

"No," she said. Rizzo heard the tension in her tone. He softened his own when he spoke again. "Okay, honey," he said. "Remember, if they ever do ask you to sign anything, you tell them you'll only do it with me present. Okay?"

"Yes, Joe. I remember," she said flatly.

"How was he?" Rizzo asked. "Did he behave himself?"

"He was a perfect gentleman. Very kind."

Rizzo chuckled bitterly. "Yeah," he said. "That's Ralph. But if you shook his hand, you might wanna count your fingers."

"This is not a joke, Joe," she answered, anger touching her voice. "Having police come to the school, checking in at the administration office. It's frightening and it's embarrassing. The school secretary thought you'd been shot. Haven't we had enough, Joe? Isn't it time? You said—"

"Yes, Jen," he interrupted. "I know what I said. Soon. I promise." He glanced again at McQueen, by now staring at him, a question in his eyes.

"Maybe even sooner than I figured," he said.

When Rizzo closed the phone, he turned again to his young partner. He summarized the phone call. They drove in silence.

*  *  *

WITH PRISCILLA in the backseat, Rizzo pointed the Chevrolet west toward the Verrazano Bridge, which would carry them into Staten Island. He spoke without turning his head as he drove, occasionally making eye contact with her in the rearview mirror.

"Thanks again for coming along, Priscilla," he said. "We can use a female cop to pat her down, make sure she's not armed and maybe keep her calm. You know, soothe her a little."

Priscilla shrugged. "Hey, no problem, Joe, I like this detective stuff. No uniform and lots of free time."

Rizzo chuckled. "Yeah, it's a real racket. But you know, Cil, I gotta tell you: you're too sharp a cop to be ticketing French poodles for pooper-scooper violations up on Fifth Avenue."

She spoke with a twisted face. "How'd you know about that? Mike tell you that story?"

Rizzo put a serious tone into his voice. "Cil, when this is over, I owe you. You set us up with the Angels and got us in to see that scumbag Surgeon. Without that, we're nowhere."

Priscilla shrugged. "Glad to help, Joe. No biggie."

Rizzo shook his head. "Wrong. Biggie. I'm gonna talk to The Swede, my boss at the Six-Two. I want you to transfer over."

Now she laughed, genuinely amused. "Yeah, Joe, that's what I wanna do. Leave Manhattan for friggin' Bensonhurst."

"I can help you in Brooklyn, Cil."

Again she laughed. "And I'd surely need the help, Joe. Good Lord, think about it. Mike tells me you're a big baseball fan, right? Well, picture this: the big game, bases loaded, Priscilla Jackson is up to bat, Bensonhurst is pitching. Female: Strike one! Black: Strike two! Lesbian: Strike fuckin' three, and I'm out on my pretty little butt. No thanks, brother, I think I'll stay in the silk stocking district with the sophista-cats. They bust their rich humps to show me how cool they are with the PC bullshit. Why, they just loves their black mammies!"

Both Rizzo and McQueen laughed.

"I told you not to fuck with her, Joe," Mike said pleasantly.

Rizzo shook his head and found Priscilla's eyes in the mirror.

"Don't you worry about the neighborhood, Cil. I'll hang a cannoli around your neck and tell everybody you're my cousin from Sicily. And lesbians are cool nowadays, don't you read *People* magazine? Besides, I'm talking gold here, not black, white, green, or purple. Gold. You come to the Six-Two, I hook you up with some of my—our, me and Mike's—cases. Then we stat you on the precinct reports to the Plaza. I have friends, Cil, influential friends, in the department."

McQueen raised his eyebrows in mock disbelief. "Friends, Joe? Say it ain't so, buddy. Please."

Rizzo smiled. "Well, not friends exactly. But a bunch of guys who owe me. One big shot that owes is worth twenty friends with nothin' but their joints in their hands, believe me. Cil, if I get your name on some paperwork, that's all the justification they would need to square me a favor. I can get you a gold shield, and I know you well enough to know you should have one. Think about it. Let me know. That's all I'm saying."

Mike turned in his seat and looked into his old partner's face. "The man's magic, Cil," he said. "I'd listen to him if I were you. Just think about it."

Priscilla sat back in her seat and sighed.

"What good is being a cop if you got to think about something?" she said, a tight smile on her face. "Can't we just go get some donuts?"

THE ONE Hundred Twenty-third Precinct was housed in an old, limestone and steel building in the Saint George section, on the south side of Richmond Terrace. The front of the building overlooked the dour waters of the Kill Van Kull and the industrialized waterfront of Bayonne, New Jersey. Detective Jim Downing smiled as he shook their hands.

"Welcome to the boonies," he said. "I was told you needed a hand with The Others."

Rizzo nodded as he took a seat at a desk in the small second-floor squad room opposite Downing. "Yeah, that's right. We've got a warrant to pick up a young girl that's been riding with them. She has some mental problems and we need to get her to the hospital."

Downing frowned. "So this is a mental hygiene case? And Brooklyn can spare three cops for it? Maybe Staten Island isn't the boonies after all."

Rizzo laughed and waved a hand. "It's a long story, Jim. She's some big shot's kid."

Downing nodded, his eyebrows raising. "I got it," he said. "None of my business, anyway. Stay here, I'll run downstairs and have them radio the sector car to meet us a few blocks from the location, then I'll come back and we'll leave. I might as well ride with you, I can hitch back with the sector. Where are you taking this kid?"

"Into the city, Gracie Square Psych ER."

Again Downing frowned. He knew procedure: a mental hygiene warrant was executed by delivering the respondent to a sitting judge in the county of apprehension or county of original jurisdiction. But he stood slowly without comment.

"I'll be back in a minute" was all he said before leaving them.

Rizzo smiled when the man had left the room. He leaned in toward Mike and Priscilla and said in a low voice, "Now, that's a good cop. He knows *exactly* what he doesn't want to know."

THE HOUSE stood desolate on the north side of the road, not another structure in sight for three hundred yards in any direction. Like the precinct, it stood on Richmond Terrace, the winding, snakelike thoroughfare that traversed the entire northern edge of the New York City county of Richmond, also known as Staten Island.

The two-story wooden-frame structure nestled in among the tangled, overgrown vegetation surrounding it and running down to the banks of the water's edge where the Kill Van Kull spilled its murky contents into the equally dismal, meandering Arthur Kill. Despite being less than ten miles from the precinct, the ride along the narrow, twisted, and often potholed and crumbling Terrace had taken them more than thirty minutes.

Rizzo swung the Chevy off the roadway and onto the graveled expanse to the right of the house, the blue-and-white sector car following behind him. A dozen motorcycles sat randomly scattered before them. At the rear of the property stood a makeshift kennel, a chain-link fence surrounding the large shedlike structure. From the far side of the house, the thunderous roar of a half dozen Harleys coming to sudden life drew the gazes of the cops. The bikes appeared from behind the house and turned right onto Richmond Terrace, accelerating quickly away. Three huge mongrel dogs, aroused by the approach of the police vehicles, trotted up to the fence and began to growl in low, threatening tones as the cops climbed from their cars.

In a bedroom within the house, Rosanne Daily blinked her eyes open, unsure of just what had awoken her. Had it been the slight light that filtered through her eyelids and touched her retinas, or the angry rumblings of the huge Harley-Davidson engines as they had growled to life just outside the window?

She rolled onto her back and steadied her head with trembling fingers. The bed seemed to turn slowly beneath her, and she pressed her thin body deeper into the bare, soiled mattress she had slept on. Her blond hair, cut almost boyishly short, was dank and matted with perspiration. A sickly sweet odor rose from her armpits and bit at her nose. Bile rose in her throat, but the equally bitter remnants of the previous night's gin and cigarettes lingering in her mouth chased it back down into her churning stomach. Her temples throbbed heavily with each heartbeat.

Rosanne heard the motorcycles crack with sudden acceleration, rattling the spiderwebbed, glass panes in the window behind her. The red digital of the clock radio next to the bed, blurry in her vision, read 10:45. The faint daylight leaking into the small bedroom told her it was a.m., not p.m.

She closed her eyes and found herself sobbing silently as reality slowly reentered her consciousness.

Another of her unwanted days was beginning. She squeezed her eyes tightly closed and willed herself back into a fitful, shallow sleep.

Outside, a lone biker, investigating the dogs' reactions, appeared from around the side of the kennel. He looked across to the six cops watching him and smiled. Wiping his hands on an oil-stained rag, he crossed the yard and stopped in front of Rizzo.

"You need somethin'?" he asked in neutral tones.

McQueen produced the picture of Rosanne and held it out to the man. He appeared to be in his late thirties, scruffy but not filthy. He wore jeans, black leather boots, and a faded Jets football jersey with the sleeves cut off. His arms were sinewy and powerful-looking.

"We need *her*," McQueen said.

The man looked at the photo and sighed. He stuffed the rag into a back pocket and nodded slowly.

"I figured somebody was looking for the bitch," he said. "Either that, or she's paranoid on top of the rest of her problems."

"You got a guy named 'Cake' here?" Rizzo asked.

The man seemed surprised. "Yeah," he said. "That's me. Why?"

"We heard the name," Rizzo said. "Is she with you?"

Cake shrugged. "Last I know she is, but that was a few days ago. I've been kind of avoiding her lately." He smiled and looked from man to man and then back to Rizzo.

"I don't mind a little funky pussy once in a while, but man, this one was startin' to peel the paint off my helmet. If you know what I mean."

His smile turned evil as he swung his eyes to Priscilla.

"No offense, sis-tah," he said sarcastically.

Priscilla held his eyes with her gaze but remained silent.

"Is she here?" McQueen asked, keeping his voice flat.

Cake turned from Priscilla and nodded. "Sure. She's upstairs, sleeping off a quart of Beefeaters. What did she do?"

Rizzo produced the warrant from his pocket.

"Nothing," he said. "She's sick, she's going to the hospital."

The man scrunched up his forehead and glanced at the papers Rizzo held out. "Sick? What do you mean, 'sick'? I been fuckin' this bitch, what's she got? Can I catch it?"

Now Priscilla responded. "Relax, bro-thah, it ain't HIV. She's bipolar, that's all. Mental stuff. I can tell from just looking at you what a good job your momma did on your psyche."

Cake smiled without humor. "Well, that's real good, Lady Po-lice. That's very funny. But this here is private property. So go get her and then fuck off."

"Show me," Joe said, stepping toward the house.

THE BEDROOM stood on the top floor at the rear of the house. It was a small room, barely large enough for the double bed that sat in the right rear corner against the back and side walls. The only other piece of furniture was a small night table that stood beneath a single window next to the bed.

McQueen and Rizzo peered into the semidarkness of the room. The blinds were drawn closed, and someone had taped large, square pieces of cardboard partially across the front of the window recess. Weak sunlight showed through gaps. A vile, bitter odor touched them from within the room. A small figure lay at the center of the bed in a fetal position beneath soiled sheets. The sound of a troubled, nasal snore was barely audible.

"She's been like this for a bunch of days," Cake said to them. "She only comes out to get more booze or hit the head. I can't remember the last time she took a shower. I mean, this ain't exactly the Miss America training camp, but at least the broads here hose down every couple of days." Now he shook his head. "Funny thing is, not too long ago she was the life of the party, dancing on the picnic tables out back, butt-ass naked, a joint in one hand and a bottle of gin in the other. Now look at her. Go figure."

Rizzo turned to face the man. "Okay, Cake, thanks for your cooperation. What were you doing when we got here?"

Cake furrowed his brow. "When you got here? I was feeding the dogs when you got here."

Rizzo nodded. "Good. Go feed the dogs. We'll handle Rosanne."

"Who?" he asked.

McQueen pointed into the room. "Her. Rosanne. That's her name."

The man nodded. "Oh," he said. "She told me her name was Chicks. After the guy I won her from."

He turned and walked away, squeezing past the other cops and toward the staircase.

"Don't forget to clean up the dog shit," Priscilla said with an exaggerated smile as he passed her.

Rizzo took a breath. "Okay, Mike," he said. "It's showtime."

The three cops entered the room, and Rizzo switched on the small light atop the night table. The twenty-five-watt bulb threw an anemic glow about the room, a semicircle of light falling across the face and shoulders of the sleeping Rosanne Daily.

Rizzo looked down at the drawn and pale, expressionless profile of the young girl, trying to erase thoughts of his own daughters from his mind. The remnants of a slight teenage acne dotted her cheek, and her lashes, thick and full, fluttered slightly under the invading light of the lamp. Her breathing began to quicken, and suddenly her eyes opened wide, showing an immediate and compelling fear. Rizzo reached out and touched her shoulder gently, prepared to restrain her if she bolted upright and attempted to flee.

"Rosanne," he said soothingly, looking into the red-rimmed green of her large, pretty eyes. "It's okay, Rosanne. Don't be frightened."

Her eyes darted from Rizzo to McQueen and back again. Then they closed tightly, and a second later, the first tear of her day squeezed out from under the left eyelid and across her cheek. Rizzo noticed the web-like wandering tracks previous tears had left on the dusty, dirty skin of her face. Again he patted reassuringly at the bare shoulder beneath the sheet.

"It's okay, honey. Really. We're here to help. We're here to make things better for you," he said, his voice barely a whisper.

Instinctively, and without communication, both detectives squatted beside the bed, making themselves smaller, less looming before her. When her eyes reopened, they were listless and dull. Her first rush of fear and feeling was gone now, replaced instantly by a void and vacuum of emotion.

"My father sent you," she said in a hoarse, cracking whisper. "To bring me back. So he can lock me away like a lunatic." Her eyes moved slowly from one to the other of their faces. A false, empty smile flitted across her mouth, but it couldn't take firm hold there.

Priscilla pushed passed Rizzo to the bedside and laid a gentle hand on Rosanne's head.

"I don't care," the girl said, her eyes closing once more. "It doesn't matter."

Now Priscilla spoke as softly and clearly as she could. Emotions jumped wildly in her throat, and she was unsure how she might sound if not careful.

"Everyone is worried about you, Rosanne. We just need to get you away from these people," she said.

Rosanne's eyes opened slowly, the dullness still dominating them, chasing their green beauty away.

"He doesn't care," she said flatly. "You all know that. And my mother's so afraid of him, she just wishes I'd die. That would be best for everyone, if I would just die."

Rizzo and McQueen exchanged looks. Rizzo patted her shoulder gently. "That's not true, Rosanne. Dr. Rogers is waiting for you. And we can have Father Charles come and see you. You can trust us, Rosanne. I swear. We just want to help you."

Now she looked at Rizzo with open distaste.

"You're a liar. Just like *him*. And you'll never get what he really sent you after. The money is all gone. So fuck him. And fuck you, too."

Rosanne closed her eyes firmly and compressed her thin body into an even tighter ball beneath the sheet. As Rizzo and McQueen stood, Priscilla squatted next to the bed. She stroked Rosanne's head gently.

"Step out of the room, gentleman," she said in a whisper. "I'll get her dressed."

She turned and looked over her shoulder and up into Rizzo's face.

"We need to get this child out of this hellhole. We need to get her to the hospital."

She dropped her gaze back to the young girl's tormented features.

"Now," she said softly.

# CHAPTER SEVENTEEN

THE THREE COPS FOLLOWED DR. ROGERS into the small consultation room just outside the electronic doors of the hospital's psychiatric ward. Rogers closed the door behind them and they took seats around a small, round table.

"Well, she's resting comfortably," Rogers said, a small smile on his face. "We've got her cleaned up and sedated, and she and I had a very productive talk. You may have found her at exactly the right moment: she *truly* seems receptive to treatment, more receptive than ever before. I think she honestly believes that she can get well, and that kind of attitude has been shown to make a significant difference in cases like this. We'll be starting her on psychotropics as soon as possible."

Now his smile broadened and touched at his eyes. "I'm actually very optimistic."

"That's good to hear, Doc," Rizzo said with a smile of his own.

Rogers cleared his throat. "Of course," he said, holding up a precautionary hand, "we need to detox first—there's been considerable alcohol and substance abuse at play of late. I've arranged for a full medical and gynecological examination and God only knows what we'll find. But, in general, I'm quite optimistic."

"We know you'll do your best, Doctor," McQueen said.

Rogers nodded. "Be assured of that, Detective. And let me say this . . ." He paused here and looked from one to the other, his face somber. "If I've misjudged your motives in any way, if I've seemed . . . defensive, I apologize. My concern was only for Rosanne and what was in her best interest. I hope you can understand that."

Rizzo smiled. "What exactly are we saying here, Doctor?" he asked in a light tone.

Rogers hesitated, then returned the smile. "Well, Detective, I'll maintain my doctor-patient confidentiality, and you maintain your policeman's enigma. Whatever your motives, Rosanne is safe now. That can only be a good thing."

They rose and shook hands and Joe said, "Well, good luck, Doc. We'll check in periodically to see how she's doing. If you need anything, call. We'll do what we can."

"I believe you will, Detective Rizzo," Rogers replied.

Joe turned to his partner. "Mike, you get the warrant lodged by the admitting desk, I'll go get the car and bring it around to the main entrance and meet you downstairs."

"I'll ride down with you, Joe," Priscilla said. "I've got to get going. I'm supposed to meet Karen for a late lunch."

"Will you be notifying Rosanne's parents?" Rogers asked of Rizzo.

Joe paused at the doorway and turned to smile broadly at him.

"Oh, you bet, Doc. We'll take care of that." He turned and left the room, Priscilla following.

Rogers looked at Mike. "Your partner is a very interesting man. His first impression does not quite do him justice."

McQueen laughed. "No, that it does not," he said.

"Come, I'll walk you out to the desk and speed up that paperwork for you."

When their business was done, Rogers walked with McQueen to the elevator banks. He faced the young detective and took hold of his hand in a warm firm handshake.

"Again, I must thank you. It's incredible that you were able to find her, truly a remarkable piece of police work. You should be very proud of yourselves, you've done a marvelous thing for this poor young tormented soul. God bless you for it."

McQueen shook the hand and smiled. He thought suddenly of Ted, the black beat cop who had treated young Priscilla with kindness and ice cream.

He smiled with his answer.

"Well, you know, Doctor, I'm a cop. It's what I do," he said.

As he stepped into the arriving elevator, he heard the doctor speak to him one final time.

"Oh, and Detective McQueen—I almost forgot. Rosanne told me I should thank you on her behalf." He smiled sheepishly and spoke just as the doors began to close between them.

"I believe her exact words were, 'Tell those three cops thanks—and tell them they don't suck too much.'"

MCQUEEN FOUND Rizzo waiting in the Impala's front passenger seat, the car idling quietly outside the hospital's main entrance. He climbed in behind the wheel and watched as Rizzo punched at the cell phone he held.

"Priscilla said 'So long.' She had a date," he said as he dialed.

"D'Antonio," Joe heard through the earpiece.

"Vince," he said, winking at McQueen as Mike pulled on his shoulder harness and buckled in, "It's me, Joe."

"Hello, Joe, what's up?"

"We got her, Vince. It's over. Just checked her into Gracie Square. Her shrink is handling all the details."

There was a pause. "That's great, Joe, I knew you were getting close. But you got her? Just like that, out of the blue?"

"Not exactly, Vince, but we were a little too busy to check in with you on every little thing. We had to move fast when we got her last location. It would all be in the DD-fives, if you had any."

D'Antonio's voice was flat when he responded. "Is she okay?"

"Well, she's got some miles on her, Boss, and a few scratches and dings on her fenders, but all in all, yeah, she's okay."

"Thank God. Great work, Joe, tell Mike for me, great work. I knew you were good, but damn, this is unbelievable. Does her old man know yet? Is he at the hospital?"

"Funny thing about that, Vince," Joe said, his eyes twinkling at Mike.

"I couldn't find his phone number. Imagine that? All these notes and numbers, cells, faxes, home lines, and I can't find his number. Why don't you call him for me, tell him his daughter is fine. I'm sure it'll make his day."

"Okay, Joe, I will." Now there was a pause, and Rizzo raised his eyebrows and gestured with his free hand in a come-on-and-tell-me fashion.

"What about her stuff, Joe? You know, personal belongings, things like that," D'Antonio said in the same flat tone.

"Oh, yeah, we got all that," Joe said. "But you know, Vince, Rosanne changed locations sort of spur of the moment, so basically all she had was the clothes on her back and some odds 'n ends. Nothing significant. Tell the old man I'll be glad to call the hospital and tell them to release it all to him. You know, when he rushes over there to visit her."

"I'll tell him, Joe," D'Antonio said drily. "But you know, Daily was pretty adamant. He's called me about a dozen times. It seems she may have left with something of value and he's anxious to get it back."

Rizzo laughed. "I bet he is, Boss. But I can't help him. The kid was empty-handed and broke when we found her. No family heirlooms that I could see."

"Alright, Joe, come on in and give me a full report."

Rizzo shook his head, his eyes narrowing. "Can't do that, Vince. Not just yet."

There was another pause, longer than the previous one. "And why is that, Joe?"

"Well, we got a few loose ends to tie up. People to see, places to go. You know, loose ends."

Now the lieutenant's voice took on a harder edge.

"Loose ends? What kind of loose ends can there be? She's found, she's in the hospital with her doctor, and I'm notifying the family. What loose ends?"

"Well, for one thing, I need to drop by the Starlight Lounge and get an audience with Louie Quattropa. We owe out some favors, Boss, and we need to square them. Now, do you want to hear about any more loose ends, or do you want to say 'Have a nice day, Joe, I'll see you when I see you?' "

A sigh came through the line.

"Have a nice day, Joe," D'Antonio said.

"And?" Joe pressed, a smile in his voice.

"And, you scumbag, I'll see you when I see you," the lieutenant answered, without malice in his tone.

"Okay, Vince, thanks. Bye."

Rizzo turned to Mike and said, "Let's get to Brooklyn. Saint Ephrem's rectory is on Seventy-fifth and Fort Hamilton. Let's go."

McQueen pulled the car away, and Rizzo filled him in on his conversation with D'Antonio as they drove.

"Do you think he knows about the cash Rosanne took?" Mike asked.

Rizzo shook his head. "I doubt it. D'Antonio's too smart to ask a lot of questions. He knows she had something the father wants, and he doesn't particularly care what it is. But I don't know for sure. Maybe he's in on it, maybe he isn't. It doesn't matter though, we've got bigger problems than just a squad boss. Let's see how it all plays out."

He pulled a Chesterfield from his pocket and lit it, blowing smoke out the open window. Then he turned to Mike's profile.

"You decide how you wanna go with this yet?" he asked in a neutral voice.

McQueen turned to face him, a small smile on his lips.

"First let's see what we're dealing with, Joe." Then after a moment, he said, "I guess I'm still thinking about it."

Joe nodded and leaned forward, switching on the car's radio.

"Okay," he said. "You think it over." He smiled and took a long drag on his cigarette.

"Let me know," he said casually.

# CHAPTER EIGHTEEN

"THANKS FOR SEEING US, Father," Joe said as he and Mike took seats before the neat, sparsely arranged desk of Father Charles Rivard, one of three priests serving Saint Ephrem's parish in the heart of Bay Ridge.

Rivard smiled. He was fifty-nine years old and still carried the easy, fluid movements of a former star running back from Georgetown University. He looked across his desk with clear, sharp gray eyes and casually waved his hand.

"Well, Detective," he said, "in all honesty, I'm generally not very busy at this hour on a Friday afternoon. Particularly during the summer months." He paused here and let the smile fade slowly from his lips. "But," he continued, "do tell me. How is that poor child doing? I can only imagine what she's been through these past weeks."

Rizzo removed his notepad from the inner pocket of his jacket. He flipped it open and looked up at the priest.

"I've got her information here, Father, if you need it. Phone number for the hospital, visiting arrangements, her doctor's number. I'll give it all to you and you can speak directly to the doctor. He can tell you more than I know. She seemed okay, I mean, considering. According to Dr. Rogers, she wants to get better, she's 'more receptive to trying' were his words. I guess time will tell."

Father Charles nodded. "Yes, it will. I've been praying for Rosanne to be found; now I'll pray for her to get well."

"We all will," Joe said, his head nodding. He glanced at McQueen. "Won't we, Mike?" he asked.

McQueen nodded as well. "Yes," he said.

"Now," Father Charles said, "how, specifically, can I help you?"

"Father," Joe began. "It's our understanding that you were counseling Rosanne *and* conferring with Dr. Rogers. Is that so?"

He nodded. "Yes. How did you know that?"

"It came up during the course of our investigation," Joe said with a shrug.

The priest smiled. "I see," he said. "So I no longer have to pretend to need Dr. Rogers's phone number? That's a relief. I'm not very good at deceiving people. Certainly not two detectives."

Rizzo returned the smile. "Well, relax, Father. We already know you're a legit guy, very concerned for Rosanne's welfare. Finding that out was pretty easy, actually. Now we come to the hard part."

Rivard looked from one to the other of their faces. He leaned forward slightly, resting his forearms on the desktop and folding his hands.

"And that would be?" he asked evenly.

"She gave you something to keep for her. We need to see it. Actually, we need to take it with us."

Rivard sat back in his seat.

"How did you find out about that?" he asked. "Did Rosanne tell you?"

Rizzo nodded. "Yes," he lied. "How else would we know?"

Rivard remained silent for a moment. "I can't imagine. But then, I'm not a policeman."

Now it was Rizzo who leaned forward. "Father," he said, his voice low and even. "We found her with some motorcycle gang, a real bad bunch called The Dutchmen. That's how she brought that stuff over here in the first place, on the back of a Dutchman's Harley."

Rivard held Rizzo's gaze. "How is that relevant?"

Rizzo sat back and smiled sadly. "Oh, it's relevant alright. Do you have any idea what you've been safeguarding?"

Rivard shook his head. "No."

"You never looked at it, not even once?" Rizzo asked. "That's kind of amazing, Father. Weren't you curious?"

"Detective Rizzo," Rivard said, his voice hardening, "Rosanne gave me that 'stuff,' as you refer to it, in confidence. She asked that I hold it for her. It's a shoe box and she assured me it held no contraband. Despite her history, despite her illness, I've never known her to lie to me, nor I to her. It was the basis of our relationship, the trust that I and Dr. Rogers hoped would help steer her to stability. So I'll say it again: I did not look inside that box."

Now McQueen spoke up.

"Father, please, I think you may have misinterpreted my partner's comment and questions."

"I think not, Detective."

Rizzo smiled. "No, Father, you didn't misinterpret anything. I was skeptical. I apologize, but I get paid for my skepticism."

"And are you still, Detective Rizzo? Or do you now choose to accept my statement?"

Rizzo nodded. "Absolutely," he said.

"Good. Now once again, how is it that I may help you?"

"We need that box, Father," Rizzo said in blunt tones. "And we need it now."

Rivard shook his head. "Impossible. Perhaps after I speak to Rosanne, if she's able to make a rational choice and it's her wish that it be turned over to you—"

"No good, Father," Rizzo interjected. "That's days, maybe weeks from now. She's in detox, sedated, and soon she'll be under heavy psychotropics. We need that box now, today."

"Why? What can the urgency be?"

Rizzo smiled. "I'm glad you asked. The urgency is twofold. One, we think something she left with you may be tied to why Rosanne ran away from her home, why she got herself all entangled with these motorcycle characters. If that's the case, it may be something that will help Dr. Rogers, maybe even help you, to help her."

Rivard looked unconvinced.

"And the second reason?"

Rizzo let his smile fade.

"They want it, Father. The Dutchmen. You want to know a little something about them, Father? They cut off one another's earlobes to initiate themselves into the gang. They run drugs, guns, and extortion rings. They eat priests for breakfast. Once they realize she ran off without leaving that stuff behind, the cretin who drove her here will figure out exactly what's in the box she left with you. And next thing you know, you've got Genghis Khan banging on the church door."

Rizzo paused and glanced at McQueen. The young detective's face was without expression, Rizzo's series of lies landing on his ears with no visible effect. Rizzo was pleased by the sight.

Rivard thought for a moment, then spoke.

"Did she lie to me, Detective Rizzo? *Is* there contraband in that box?"

"No, Father. She didn't lie to you. There's evidence in that box, evidence of crimes committed by The Dutchmen, and maybe someone else. But we have no reason to believe there's anything illegal per se."

They saw the relief on Rivard's face, and it further confirmed his sincerity. Then they watched as apprehension slipped into his eyes.

"Is Rosanne in danger, Detective? I mean, physical danger from these thugs?"

Rizzo shook his head. "No. They just want that box. Whoever has possession is the one in danger. And the people around that person, too. It wouldn't be beyond The Dutchmen to come after you through some other priest or maybe one of your parishioners. Even, God forbid, a nun. They grab somebody and then swap them for the box."

"Good Lord," Rivard said.

Rizzo leaned over the front edge of the desk and spoke in low, earnest tones.

"Father," he said, "I can waste a couple of days and get a court order for the box by Monday. Then you'll have to turn it over. And until then, I can assign a radio car to park outside the church twenty-four seven to keep The Dutchmen at bay. But I can't protect every nun in the city, or every priest. And certainly not all of your parishioners. If you give us the box now, I guarantee you, in an hour, The Dutchmen will know we've got it. We have an inside contact with a rival gang, the Hell's Angels. They'll be glad to send the bad news over to The Dutchmen, believe me. Then you're out of it, and so's the church."

Rivard paled, a slight perspiration breaking across his brow.

"Perhaps I should call the bishop or maybe Dr. Rogers . . ."

Rizzo stood suddenly and leaned forward, his clenched fists resting on the desktop. He bent his head to Rivard's face.

"You don't need a bishop, Father, and you sure as hell don't need a psychiatrist.

"The only people who can help you now, Father, are cops." Rizzo paused and allowed a small smile to tug at his lips, bringing a soft, sincere aura to his face.

"And that's what *we* are, Father. Cops."

WHEN THEY returned to the Impala, parked just around the corner from the rectory on Fort Hamilton Parkway, McQueen turned from the driver's seat and looked at Rizzo.

"Man, you are *so* going to hell," he said to Joe.

Rizzo smiled and examined the small, battered box that he held on his lap.

"Yeah, well, if that's true, it's been true for a long time," he said with a tight smile. "You think that's the first priest I ever lied to? I wish."

"Why, Joe?" McQueen asked. "Why not just tell him the truth?"

Rizzo shook his head. "Thirty seconds after I met the guy, I knew the truth wouldn't fly. He'd never violate Rosanne's trust, no way. So I tell him that she wants us to have whatever's in the box and as long as he has it, the people around him are in serious danger. He probably wouldn't have given it up if he thought it was just *his* neck sticking out, but, I gotta tell you, that 'save the nuns' stuff, that was pure fuckin' genius, if I say so myself. He had to go for it after that."

McQueen shook his head. "Straight to hell, Joe. Nonstop."

Rizzo laughed. "Yeah, well, I can hang out there with all the other cops." He shook the box gently and a slight rattling sounded.

They recognized it as soon as Rivard presented it to them. A shoe box, similar to the ones strewn across the floor of Rosanne's closet and identical to the one McQueen found her diary in. It was even tied closed with the same red ribbon.

"Well?" he asked Rizzo.

Rizzo shrugged. "Yeah, now's as good a time as any."

He untied the ribbon and pulled off the cover.

They both looked in, Mike leaning across from the driver's seat. The box held three objects, the most prominent a stack of currency tightly wrapped in a rubber band. A black diary, identical to the one they had removed from Rosanne's room, lay beneath the money. Next to that was a battered Tally-Ho playing card box, sealed with cellophane tape.

Rizzo took the stack of bills from the shoe box and slipped off the rubber band. He quickly counted the money.

"Jesus," he said softly. "Thirty-two thousand bucks." He replaced the rubber band and tossed the cash back into the box. "Must be all that's left from the hundred grand Rosanne told The Surgeon she took from her old man's safe."

Mike shook his head slowly. "Thirty-two in the box and twenty-two she blew on that idiot's new Harley. I wonder what she did with the other forty-six thousand?"

Joe lit a cigarette and blew smoke at the dashboard. "I'd be more interested in knowing why Daily had a hundred grand in his wall safe," he said.

Mike reached over and took the diary in his hand. Opening it, he said, "Starts just about where the other one left off."

He flipped to the last entry. "Ends when she ran away."

Rizzo glanced at the book. "Well, if that's her proof, she's as delusional as she is bipolar. Nothing in there is more than hearsay, legally— and the cash, that's so circumstantial it's almost useless."

Rizzo eyed the last object, the playing card box. Reaching in, he smiled as he heard a rattle from within.

"No cards in here, Mike," he said, opening the box and looking in. Slowly, he inserted two fingers and pulled out a small object. "Bingo," he said, a tight smile on his face.

Mike looked into the outstretched palm of his partner.

McQueen and Rizzo's eyes met, separated by less than two feet in the confines of the car.

"I guess we go buy a tape player now, right, Joe?" he asked.

Rizzo smiled as he began to place the items back into the shoe box.

"No," he said, securing the box top carefully. "We go to my house. That's a Panasonic microcassette, the same kind my daughter uses at school. They're voice activated, she tapes her lab classes and uses them as notes. The med students even tape lectures and classes for each other if one of them can't attend. Marie has a bunch of these things and at least two or three recorders. We'll borrow one, if she's home. If not, I'll just grab one out of her room."

McQueen smiled as he scanned the car's mirrors and slowly pulled out into traffic on Fort Hamilton Parkway.

"Okay, Joe," he said. "Maybe we'll get lucky and stumble across *her* diary."

Rizzo blew cigarette smoke through his lips and threw the crumpled red ribbon he held at McQueen's head.

"Just drive the car, wise-ass. Just drive the car."

THE TWO men sat opposite each other, across the cluttered, gunmetal gray desk in Rizzo's basement home office. The room, McQueen had noted, was not unlike that of The Surgeon's, except where Rizzo's was typically unkempt, The Surgeon's basement had an almost obsessive order to it.

Now Rizzo reached over and pressed the "stop" button of the recorder, and the tape switched off into silence.

"And that," he said, reaching for his cigarette pack, "was the Honorable Alexander Simpson and Jason Miller, Brooklyn's newest judges, live, on tape, shelling out fifty thousand dollars apiece. They pay their bribes, then get the party's endorsement for fourteen-year terms as Supreme Court justices in the county of Kings."

McQueen shook his head. "County of Crooks, more accurately."

Rizzo sighed. "Well, only some judges, not all of them. But that other shit they were talking about, the suppliers and service providers, those are citywide contracts Daily's selling. Everything from private sanitation to hospital supplies. Unbelievable: day-care centers, homeless shelters, drug programs, this guy had the whole city up for sale. And anybody who wanted the party's endorsement, anybody who wanted to get anywhere in Brooklyn politics, had to go to this guy and cut a deal. And there's Daily, taping it all."

"Why, Joe? Why tape it?"

Rizzo shook his head. "That's not the question, Mike. The question is, how did Rosanne get her little hands on it? And if Daily knew it was missing, how could he not figure she had it? And if he suspected she took it, how could he be stupid enough to use cops to track her down?"

Joe shook his head. "It makes perfect sense for him to tape his crooked deals. He figured if anyone ever did give him up, if the feds ever did get wise to him, he could negotiate. If they grabbed him, he'd say, 'Hey, I'm just one guy. I can give you contractors, district attorneys, judges, city council members, state assemblymen, I can make you a star, the next Rudy Giuliani.' He must have a pile of these tapes stashed away someplace. There isn't a United States attorney in the country who wouldn't cut a deal for that. *That's* why he taped it. That and maybe to squeeze a few of these scumbags if they tried to push him around some time in the future." Joe grinned broadly. "He just never figured Rosanne would get her hands on it. I'd like to see him try to fuck with her while she was holding this little chestnut."

McQueen reached out and hit the "eject" button on the player. Idly, he turned the tape over in his hand, reading the date inscribed on the small label in Rosanne's childish hand.

"Remember when we met with him, Joe?" McQueen asked. "You guys started sucking on those cigars? When Daily noticed the smoke was bothering me, he reached under his desk and switched on a smoke eater. He said he used it when he met there on political matters."

Rizzo nodded. "Yeah, I remember. He must have had two switches down there, one for smoke and one for tapes. A regular Tricky-Fuckin'-Dick, he is."

They sat in silence for a moment, each with their own thoughts. Then Joe spoke up.

"Ironic, ain't it?" he said with a smile. "Daily made this tape for insurance. So he'd have something to bargain with if he ever got jammed up. So what happens? His daughter grabs the tape for the same reason. Insurance against him. So the very thing he figured would protect him jumps up and bites him on the ass."

Mike shook his head. "This doesn't make any sense, Joe. The money, the hundred grand, he probably figured that would be mostly gone. And even if it wasn't, he could always deny it was his. Who would believe Rosanne? No, that money wouldn't prove a thing, even if she still had it all. But this tape. That's something else. And wherever he's got the rest of them, if there are any more, the feds would eventually find them. Hell, his lawyer would probably hand them over, cut a deal, like you said. But he couldn't afford to let this first one get loose. It just doesn't make sense."

Rizzo, secure in the knowledge that they were the only two in the house, lit a Chesterfield. As he did, he picked up Rosanne's newly found diary.

"Let me see that tape," he said. Glancing at the date on the cassette, he flipped open the diary. As he smoked, he slowly thumbed through the book.

When he came to the diary entry made on the date of the tape, he stopped. Reading the broad, florid strokes of Rosanne's now familiar handwriting, Joe smiled slowly and looked up into his partner's eyes.

"It makes sense now, Mike," he said. "This kid may be screwy, but she sure as hell isn't stupid."

"Why?" Mike asked. "You find something?"

Rizzo nodded and pulled deeply on his cigarette. "Yeah, it's right in here. That's why she took this diary with her. She couldn't afford to have the old man find *this* one. And that's why she tore a page out of the diary we found in her room. It must have mentioned her knowing Daily was a crook."

McQueen leaned across the desk and looked at the page.

"What is it?" he asked.

"This tape is just a copy. Rosanne left the original tape right where she found it. Seems that the night these two characters stopped by Daily's house to pay their way to judicial respectability was the night of the Democratic Club's annual dinner dance. They were all getting together to celebrate the legacy of Franklin Roosevelt and John F. Kennedy and pat each other on the back. So Rosanne waited for them to leave, then went into her father's office. She had a key to the desk, remember? And the combination to the wall safe. That's what she told The Surgeon. Well, Daily had no time that night to secure the tape in whatever bank box he uses, so he tossed it into the wall safe along with the cash they had just handed him. Now, little Rosanne cracks the safe, grabs the money and the tape. She unlocks his desk, takes out a blank cassette, and uses his own machine to copy the original, which she then puts back into the safe.

"After that, she packed a bag and headed off with the gorilla to

Dutchmen country. And somewhere along the line, she dropped the stuff off to Father Charles."

McQueen nodded. "So the old man figured she just took the cash."

"Yeah," Rizzo said, crushing out his Chesterfield in a coaster on the desk. "There was probably lots of stuff in that safe. He saw it hadn't been disturbed, figured the kid was just a crazy pain-in-the-ass anyway, not a real threat, and he figured he would confront her for the dough. But when she disappeared, he had to deal with his wife and his political image, which both demanded he play the concerned daddy and look for the kid." Rizzo leaned back and smiled. "A real prick, this guy, wouldn't you say?"

Mike laughed without humor. "Is there any politician who isn't?" he asked.

Rizzo's laugh was genuine. "Not these days, Mike, not these days."

After a long, thoughtful silence, McQueen spoke up. "So you figure this is definitely federal, Joe?" he asked.

"Absolutely," Rizzo said, lighting another Chesterfield. "We can't trust the department on this, half the inspectors at the Plaza probably owe their jobs to this guy, either directly or indirectly. The D.A.'s office is no better. They probably bought their jobs, too. The county D.A.'s are elected, but whoever the bosses pick for the Democratic nominations always win the election, same as with the judges, especially in Brooklyn. If we run with this ball, we go straight to the feds, right over to the U.S. Attorneys Office on Cadman Plaza."

McQueen expelled air from his lungs. "What a fucking mess," he said. "And me right in the middle of it. I always tried to stay clean, Joe, avoid problems. Now look at this shit."

Rizzo dragged on his cigarette and blew smoke off to the side, away from McQueen. When he spoke, he kept his voice gentle.

"Look, Mike," he said. "I'm not going to lie to you. We do this, even if we can figure a way to do it indirectly, the brass may know it was us, or at the very least strongly suspect that it was us. You better know that going in, before you decide how we play this."

"I know," McQueen said, his voice somber with an almost painful sadness. "All that keeping my nose clean, Joe, out the window. My career is done, here. Done."

Rizzo smiled. "Kid," he said, "do you really believe that you've kept your nose clean? 'Cause if you had, and if you continued to, the bosses couldn't touch you. But let's reflect here for a moment, Mike, on this clean nose of yours. See, there are too many rules, too many gray areas on this job and in this society and in this life, for anyone—anyone—to keep a clean nose. Especially a cop."

McQueen raised his eyes to Rizzo's and listened. Then Rizzo explained.

He explained how, in the eleven short months they had worked together out of Mike's seven-year career, McQueen had lied about Peter Flain's death in the toilet of the Keyboard Bar, dated the victim in an active criminal investigation, dined at a precinct restaurant at a reduced price and then later provided a private escort for the restaurant's owner.

Joe reminded Mike how they had overlooked the underage drinking and probable police corruption at McDougal's bar, submitted exaggerated overtime bills throughout the investigation, ignored evidence of crimes by the Hell's Angels and The Dutchmen, and even agreed to facilitate a criminal communication between The Dutchmen and the local mob leader Louie Quattropa.

"And that's just what you've done with me, Mister Clean Nose, and mostly just recent stuff," Rizzo said with a smile. "I'm gonna take a guess here. At some point, you were rolling along in your blue-and-white, protecting the good citizens of Greenwich Village, and you spot a car going by and it looks wrong. You can't say exactly why, but you're a cop, and the car looks wrong. So you run the plate and it comes back clean. But by that time, you've been riding behind the car for a while, and you notice the guys inside are starting to get antsy, real antsy. They're turning and looking over their shoulders, fidgeting around. Now you *know* the car is wrong. So you hit the lights and pull them over. Ten minutes later, you got yourself a gun collar."

McQueen shrugged. "Okay, something like that may have happened."

Rizzo laughed. "Yeah, I bet it did. Now let me take a stab here, just another wild guess at how your arrest report read. Let's see, maybe something like, 'At time and place of occurrence, did observe blue Ford fail to stop for stop sign on Blipity-Blip Street. During routine traffic stop, arresting officer did see the butt of a weapon protruding from beneath front seat. In fear for personal safety, did conduct search of vehicle and recovered illegal handgun, etc., etc., etc.' How 'bout it? That close enough?"

McQueen grinned. "Pretty close."

Rizzo nodded. "Damn right. But what really happened was you stopped that car for no legally permissible reason, you stopped it because you're a cop and it looked 'wrong,' and then you searched them and found that gun. Good job, helped keep all the civil libertarians down on West Fourth Street safe and free to go to the ban-the-bomb rally. Good work, but pretty shitty from a constitutional point of view, and perjury to boot."

McQueen shrugged. "So, okay. Every cop knows the protruding gun butt story, same as the burned-out taillight and smell of marijuana stories. What's that got to do with all this we're dealing with now?"

"Everything, Mike. You have a decision to make, kid. A big one. Don't make it under the mistaken impression that you're clean, that you'll stay clean in the future. We break five rules a day, Mike. The only cops who don't are the ones not doing their jobs to the slightest degree, the guys who ride around for their whole shift and see, hear, and smell no evil. The slackers, the deadbeats. To do this job right, you gotta break some rules. Period. And if some boss has a hard-on for you and wants to hurt you, he can. The only thing that keeps it in check is that the bosses do the same thing, the real bosses, anyway. They have to break the same rules. But if you get the Plaza on your ass, those bosses aren't even real cops anymore, just stuffed-suit politicians, no different or better than Daily and his asshole buddies."

McQueen slumped in his seat. When he finally spoke, it was softly.

"Joe, what are you saying? You want to let this guy walk away from this? Let him off the hook?"

Rizzo shook his head. "No, Mike. Remember me? James Butler Bonham, at the friggin' Alamo. I say nail the prick. But I'm twenty years ahead of you. We hit a wall, I'm out of here with my pension in my pocket. That's why it's got to be your decision. Whatever it is I'll live with it, but *you* have to make this call."

After a few moments passed in silence, Rizzo spoke again. He kept his voice gentle and even, allowing kindness into it.

"Mike, I know how you feel. Listen, I've been very careful over the years, very careful. All the guys I've worked with, the ones I've worked *for*, they all knew I'd look the other way when necessary. I've nursed that image and it's served me well. I always fit in, and they always left me alone, left me to do my job my way. I've seen cases of corruption, I've seen the brutality situations, and I've looked the other way. That's one reason D'Antonio gave us this case, because he knew if there was something wrong about it, you were too green to bump heads on it and I'd just take the pragmatic view, just find Rosanne and walk away. They feel safe with me, and that's fine. But I've always had my own standards, Mike, and this one is over my line. I don't want to ignore it. Unless, of course, *you* have to, in which case I'll understand. Believe me."

Joe paused and stubbed out his cigarette. He reached for a fresh one and tapped its unfiltered end against his thumbnail, then spoke again, even more softly, as he lit it.

"This is what I think you—we—should do. I'll call D'Antonio tonight. I'll tell him we've still got some loose ends to take care of but I'll handle them myself. We take two weeks leave. You get into that little black hot rod of yours and go see Ma and Pa McQueen down in Virginia. When you come back, you tell me how you want to handle the tape."

McQueen raised his eyes to Rizzo's.

"And the thirty-two thousand," he said.

Rizzo shook his head. "No, kid," he said softly. "Forget about that. I'll handle that. The less you have to do with it, the better."

McQueen felt color coming to his face as his heart rate increased.

"How, Joe?" he asked, his voice hard-edged. "How're you going to handle it? A visit to the Cornell bursar's office, maybe?"

Rizzo smiled. "I won't take any offense to that, kid, 'cause I know you're right to say it. But you're gonna haveta trust me here, Mike. Trust me, or take this here box and go to whoever you figure you *can* trust with it. And good luck."

McQueen's mind reeled and he felt perspiration breaking out on his forehead. After a few moments passed in tense silence, he spoke in soft, resigned tones.

"What's the plan, Joe?" he asked simply.

Rizzo smiled, a rare gentleness touching his eyes. "Okay, Mike. You earned an explanation, but it might be better if you can say you didn't know, you were in Virginia and . . ."

"You have to tell me, Joe," Mike said with finality.

Rizzo sighed sadly as his smile faded. "Alright, Mike. I was young and stupid once. I guess you got the same right."

After a moment, he continued. "That cash doesn't prove shit. By itself, it's useless. Daily could deny he ever saw it, deny it was ever in his safe. Rosanne is a drug-using, drunken, bipolar teenager with a proven hatred and resentment for her father. She couldn't convince anybody of anything. Hell, she probably doesn't even know if there's any cash left."

Rizzo paused and crushed out his cigarette. He leaned back in his seat, and this time his smile was one of satisfaction.

"But the tape, Mike. That nails him real good. In his own voice, his and those two assholes who bought their judgeships that night in his den. It's the tape that would have to go to the feds, Mike, the tape. If that's what you decide we should do when you get back to New York."

"And the money? Where does that go?" McQueen asked.

Rizzo shrugged. "I'm thinkin' it goes to Manning. Remember his call to you, Mike? He said if everybody was happy at the end of this, we'd get taken care of. I want that prick DeMayo off my back and I want out of this job with the fattest pension I can get. You wanna go to the Plaza. That money buys it for both of us. I give the dough to Manning, he gives it back to Daily. All of us know the money *implies* Daily is crooked, but we also know it doesn't *prove* nothin'. Daily doesn't want its existence known, not just before his reelection campaign, that's for sure. Think about it, Mike. It's perfect. And what am I really doing anyway? I'm handing over cash recovered in an investigation to a superior officer who expressed an interest and involvement in that investigation. An investigation, I might add, that's been outside normal channels since day one."

Rizzo reached for a third Chesterfield. "It's perfect, Mike. Everybody wins." He lit the cigarette and snapped the Zippo closed sharply.

"Except for Daily," he said softly. "Eventually he loses. He loses if we get that tape into the right hands." He sat silently for a moment before continuing.

"It's your call, Mike. You go see the folks in Virginia." Rizzo pulled on the Chesterfield. McQueen saw its tip burn a deep, bright orange.

"Then," Rizzo said softly, "when you come back, you let me know."

# CHAPTER NINETEEN

RIZZO REACHED ACROSS THE SMALL TABLE and lifted his glass, touching it gently to an identical glass held by Louis "The Chink" Quattropa. It was the next day, early Saturday afternoon.

"*Salute,*" he said.

"*Salud,*" Quattropa answered as they both downed clear, thick shots of Sambuca in single swallows.

Quattropa's oddly colored tawny skin and almond-shaped eyes, the features that had earned him the nickname Chink, were now shadowed in the dim lighting at the rear of the Starlight Lounge. He leaned across the table as he spoke.

"So," he said in a deep, raspy tone, "what brings you to see me, Sergeant Rizzo? Is somebody double-parked outside? You want me to get them to move?"

The two men standing behind Quattropa, their hands clasped above their groins, laughed dutifully. Rizzo smiled.

"No, Louie, not today. But thanks for seeing me. It's appreciated. I'm sorry to take away from your Saturday afternoon."

Quattropa waved a hand and then turned slightly in his seat, calling for two more drinks. "It's nothing, Joe, don't worry about it. What do you need? You can speak freely. We swept for bugs an hour ago."

"Well, I really don't need anything, Louie. I'm just here to deliver a message to you."

Quattropa frowned. "A message? Since when is Joe Rizzo a messenger boy? This must be good."

They waited while a nervous-looking bartender hurried to the table, poured the fresh drinks, placed the bottle down, and retreated to his haven behind the bar.

"I owe out a favor. This is my payback."

"Really?" Quattropa said, his eyebrows raised. "Who you owe?"

Rizzo rotated his glass slowly between his fingers and watched as its clear liquid caught rays from the dim light, tossing them around the glass.

"Some guy they call The Surgeon," he said, raising his eyes to meet the cold black of Quattropa's. "You know him?"

Quattropa's face was impassive. Then, slowly turning his head to the right, he spat hard at the floor.

"That's for that animal," he said coldly. "I'm sixty-eight years old, in a tough business my whole life. Since I was nine years old, Joe, that's a long fuckin' time. I only met maybe two or three men in all those years I had a true hatred for. Not a business problem, a hatred. This asshole—this guy Haas—he makes the list. I don't want no message from him. You tell him that for me—if he's still breathin' when you find him, that is."

Rizzo shrugged and sipped at his Sambuca. "Louie, I gotta tell you I'm not real fond of the guy myself. But I made a deal to carry his message and tell him when it was delivered. After that, I'm done with it. I just need you to hear me out."

Quattropa seemed to ponder it. Then, after a moment, he turned to the man standing behind his right shoulder. "*Questo poliziotto è bravo, mi sembra che ci conziene ascoltarlo,*" he said.

"*Cone credi sia meglio, Lu,*" the man answered.

Rizzo smiled. "I'm glad you think I'm alright, Louie, and I'm grateful that you'll hear me out."

Quattropa smiled. "I forgot, Joe, you speak the language." He paused for a moment, allowing the smile to pass from his face. "So, say what you came to say."

Rizzo drained his glass and set it down on the table. He placed a hand over it as Quattropa started to reach for the bottle.

"No, thanks, Louie, no more." He shook a cigarette loose from its pack and placed it between his lips.

"Haas once had a problem with you in Bensonhurst. You corrected it, and the problem went away. He understands that and knows you had a right to act. Now, he's got another problem with you, this time in Canarsie."

Quattropa smiled evilly, sipping at his Sambuca and speaking from around the rim of the small glass.

"This here is gonna be my last problem with this prick, Joe, I got a feeling."

Rizzo smiled. "I think he suspects that. That's why he wanted me to come see you."

Now Quattropa frowned. "Joe," he said, "with all due respect, I gotta ask you something. I mean no insult, it's a rough question, but it needs askin' and answerin'."

Rizzo nodded. "I'll save you the trouble, Louie. You don't have to ask. No. I'm not on his payroll. I'm here because he gave me information that played out and helped me find a runaway kid. This was his price for that info."

Quattropa pondered it, then after a moment, smiled again. "Okay, Joe. That's good to hear."

Rizzo nodded again. "Okay," he said.

"So, Joe, tell me what this animal has to say."

"He said the Canarsie thing was a misunderstanding, a failure of communication between his guys and the fruit seller. He says he'll make it all right and you decide who gets the credit. He says it won't happen again. He says you should allow him to reach out to you and he'll make it good for you. He says you'll be happy with his offer."

"What's his offer, Joe?" Quattropa asked, interest beginning to stir in his eyes.

This greedy old bastard, Joe thought, as he smiled at the man. "He couldn't tell me that, Louie. He said he'll only tell you, and you'd be happy with it. That's all I know."

Quattropa let twenty seconds of silence pass before speaking. When he did, it was in a curt, clipped tone that told Rizzo the meeting was now over.

"Okay, Joe, I'll hear him out. Tell him to reach out. I'll listen." Rizzo stood, extending a hand to Quattropa. They shook.

"Thanks for the Sambuca, Louie. I'll tell The Surgeon."

Quattropa smiled. "You better tell him quick, Joe. I hear a clock tickin' in my ear."

Rizzo released the hand and pushed his chair back to its place at the table.

"One more thing, Louie, if you don't mind," Rizzo said, injecting a fallacious respect into his tone.

"Yeah, Joe?" Quattropa asked with little interest.

"Officially, if anyone should ever ask, I came here to see you 'bout some stolen cars. Seems like somebody's been boosting Lexuses over in my precinct. So if it ever comes up, I came here to ask you about it. Bein' as how you run a few body fender shops and all."

The Chink smiled, a knowing glint forming in his black eyes. "Funny you should bring it up, Joe," he said. "Somebody has been askin' about you."

"Oh? Who's that?"

Quattropa shrugged. "Some flunky asshole cop named DeMayo. Came in a couple a weeks ago."

"Tell me," Joe said.

"Not much to tell. He was hummin' that same old tune about your ex. What's his name? Morelli?"

"Yeah," Joe said. "Morelli."

"This guy DeMayo, he's convinced me and Morelli had some kind of arrangement. But I'm sure you know all about what DeMayo figures."

Quattropa shrugged again. "Anyway, I told him he was beatin' a dead horse. That guy that got whacked, hell, I never even hearda the fuckin' guy let alone put out a hit on him."

"Word is, Louie, that guy was working for you when he turned up dead."

Another shrug. "Lotsa guys work for me, Joe, and twice as many say they do. Helps 'em get laid in certain circles, I guess." Here he chuckled and reached for the Sambuca.

"Sos I told this guinea prick cop, this DeMayo, to fuck off. Told him I never once spoke to you *or* Morelli except on police bullshit. I told him next time he comes in here and gets in my face he better have a warrant in his fuckin' hand. Next time I see him, he's gonna find out I ain't so old I can't smack some punk-ass cop, pay the fine, and then go eat dinner."

He smiled up into Rizzo's face. "You should keep that in mind, too, Joe."

Rizzo nodded. "I will, Louie. Thanks for the info."

Quattropa sipped his Sambuca. "No problem, Guiseppe," he said, his eyes darkly lifeless.

"Now, Louie, if you'll excuse me, I gotta go see a priest I know." Then after a moment, he spoke one final time in a low, somber voice.

"Whatever happened between you and Morelli was between you two. I don't ever wanna know about it."

Quattropa smiled indifferently.

"Okay, Joe," he said. "The world can always use another fuckin' virgin."

Rizzo turned and strode out of the bar, into the bright sunlight of the street. Drawing clean air into his lungs, he tossed the Chesterfield into the gutter and headed for his Camry, parked a half block away.

WHILE RIZZO buckled himself into the driver's seat of the Camry, McQueen took a table seat at a midtown restaurant. The two detectives had essentially gone incommunicado, agreeing to respond only to each other's calls, and only on their own cell phones after caller ID verification. They both thought it best to remain isolated from Lieutenant D'Antonio and other police personnel until after Rizzo played out his hand and they decided on a final course of action.

"Remember," Rizzo had said. "Manning made it clear: make Daily happy on this and he would take care of us. You really shouldn't speak to anybody just yet. Not until we know where we're going with this. Let me handle things for now. Just go visit your parents."

McQueen heard Rizzo's words echo in his ears as he reached across the table and shook hands with Assistant District Attorney Darrel Jordan.

"Thanks for coming, Darrel," Mike said.

Jordan shrugged. "No problem, Mike. You said it was important, and you sounded stressed. Besides," he said, allowing himself a wide grin, "this is an expensive place, and I gotta assume lunch is on you."

Mike returned the smile. "You bet," he said, hailing a waiter.

They ordered cocktails and lunch at the same time, then made small talk until the drinks arrived.

"So," Jordan said, raising his vodka in a gesture of toast to Mike. "Why don't you tell me what's going on?"

McQueen returned the gesture, then took a huge swallow of his Manhattan.

"Darrel, you and I go back a little ways. We've won some cases together, put some bad guys away. And you know, we may have bent a rule here and there, to make a case stick. But we always trusted one another."

Jordan smiled again. "Mike, we both know how it is. Nothing firms up a case like a little retaliatory perjury. The bad guy lies a lot, we lie a little, and the chips fall where they may. It's a beautiful system."

Mike nodded. "So we trust each other, right? I need to go completely off the record here. Okay?"

Jordan looked puzzled. "Sure, Mike. What's the problem?"

McQueen explained, briefly, and without drama, the whole story, from when he and Rizzo had first caught Rosanne's case, through the phone calls from Manning and DeMayo, to the playing of the tape in Joe's basement. When he finished, they waited while the server placed their food before them. Once he left, Jordan leaned forward in his seat.

"I've heard the rumors about Daily, Mike. About judgeships for sale in Brooklyn, some complacency on the part of the Brooklyn D.A.'s office. It's actually common knowledge among political circles. The rest of it, the stuff about the city contracts, that's news to me. But it certainly makes sense; corruption doesn't exist in a bubble, it tends to spread itself out."

"What about the rest of the city, Dar?" Mike asked. "Is the bench up for sale all over?"

Jordan shook his head. "I'd say no. Like I told you, I heard the rumors about Brooklyn, but not about any other borough. As far as I know, the rest of it's as legit as politics get, which might not be saying a whole lot. See, Mike, I'm a star, NBA MVP, good-looking, black, smart—shit, I'm a fucking celebrity. I've got a bunch of white, tired old fool politicians kissing my ass everywhere I go. They can't wait to make me a judge, and I don't even have to talk to them, let alone pay anybody off. I'm visible proof that they're all broad-minded, unbiased, righteous motherfuckers. And for the most part, they make my skin crawl."

Mike poked absently at his food.

"What about Daily, Darrel?" he asked. "You ever meet him?"

Jordan cut a piece of veal and raised it to his mouth.

"Yeah," he said, chewing slowly. "At a couple of political functions I had to attend so they could show me off, get me to sign autographs for their spastic kids who think they can play ball. I've met him."

"What was your take?" McQueen asked.

Jordan laughed.

"Well, Mike, I think he'da been a hell of a lot more comfortable seein' me around if I was serving hors d'oeuvres on one of those little trays. That's my take on him."

They ate in silence for a few moments. Then Darrel spoke, his voice somber.

"My friend, you're in grave danger of making some very powerful, petty-minded, vindictive enemies. You better think this all the way through, brother."

Mike nodded. "I intend to, believe me. But let me ask you something: If it were you, what would you do?"

Jordan thought for a moment and put down his knife and fork. He then interlaced his fingers and leaned toward Mike.

"Honestly . . . if it were me . . . I'd go to the feds. And then I'd call an old friend of mine, publicist with the NBA, and have him get me on a few local Sunday-morning talk shows. Maybe some late-night stuff, too. Then I'd tell everybody what a hero I was, and all these cockroach politicians would start runnin' from the light. They'd turn on Daily like the pack of jackals they really are. That's what I'd do."

McQueen drained his Manhattan glass and waved to the waiter for a second round. Then he turned back to Jordan.

"Okay," he said. "Now what do you think *I* should do?"

Jordan thought for a full twenty seconds. Then he sighed and picked up his utensils, turning back to the veal on his plate.

"If I were you, I'd hand that tape back to Daily, tell him I hadn't listened to it, take my promotion and run to the Plaza. Then I'd get religious and spend the rest of my career trying to atone for it all. That's what I'd do—if *I* were you."

# CHAPTER TWENTY

JOE RIZZO SAT IN THE KITCHEN of his Bay Ridge home, sipping coffee and allowing his eyes to smile across the table at Jennifer.

"It's the smart thing for him to do, Jen," he said. "Hell, it may be the only thing he *can* do."

It was just after ten on Sunday morning, and they had the house to themselves. Marie was at a weeklong medical seminar in Baltimore and Jessica and Carol had gone to the ten o'clock mass at Saint Bernadette's.

Jennifer Rizzo returned her husband's smile with a tight, sad frown.

"Really, Joe?" she asked. "Do you really think he'll want to give Daily the tape?"

Rizzo nodded. "I told you, Jen, the kid is ambitious. Not *bad* ambitious, but ambitious just the same. He wants to move up, wants to work a special squad in the city, maybe even at the Plaza. And you know, I can't blame him. The department and the politicians taught this kid well. This is the perfect opportunity for him. He's a good cop, real good, smart and tough, and he cares about people. He had a great record for, what?, six years? And where'd it get him? He was still on patrol in a blue-and-white. Then he locks up a guy, and, bingo!, detective shield three weeks later. And why? 'Cause he earned it? 'Cause they thought he'd make a good detective? Of course not. They gave him the shield because he saved the mayor's daughter's roommate's ass, that's why. Yeah, they taught him well. Save Jane Citizen from a rape and maybe you'll make some overtime down at central booking. But lock up a guy who attacks some big shot and, well, then it really pays off. That's how it works, Jen. You know it, I know it, and Mike knows it."

"But Joe, there must be other options."

Rizzo chuckled. "Oh, yeah, Jen, there are. Always lots of options on this job. I talked to Mike about them. We can toss the tape, burn it. Mike goes on with his career, tests up to sergeant. Maybe Daily even does the right thing and brushes some crumbs off the table to us, for finding his daughter. Maybe Mike gets to go to the Plaza, moves on, tests up further, maybe to captain. With the wheels greased a little, he always gets a good assignment somewhere. Me, I'll stay put, happy and ignorant, and with I.A. still on my ass."

He paused and put an unlit cigarette in his mouth, then continued.

"Problem with that is Daily would never know what Rosanne might have told us about him. He probably figured the kid knows he's a crook, he just doesn't know she can prove it. He'll always have suspicions about me and Mike, and he could never fully relax. If, on the other hand, we deliver the tape to Daily, we put him at ease. He'll know me and Mike are no better than he is, and that'll comfort him, confirm his view of things. Mike gets paid off big-time, and so do I. Then we all live happily ever after. Especially those pompous, crooked judges handing out jail sentences to street kids for robbing sneakers while the politicians are stealing the entire courthouse. The bribes from the contractors keep flowing, and the city contracts keep making them richer. Yeah, we give Daily the tape back and we all live happily ever after."

Jennifer reached across the table and gently took the Chesterfield from Joe's mouth. She placed it down on the table and raised her eyes to his.

"That's it?" she asked. "Those are the choices?"

Joe shrugged. "Far as I can see. Except, of course, for the right choice: give everything to the feds. They'll start dropping subpoenas all over the city like confetti. Indictments will follow, and one by one, these spineless hypocrites will be lining up to cut deals, give each other up for immunity or reduced sentences. It'll be like shooting fish in a barrel for any U.S. attorney. Me and Mike lay low until Daily gets locked up. Then we watch our backs and go about our business. I put in my papers and both of us stay in the Six-Two. Hope for the best. Mike, well, I don't know. He'd have enemies everywhere."

Jennifer drank deeply from her coffee cup. Then, setting it down, she spoke softly.

"I'm beginning to see Mike's point, Joe. If he does decide to go bad on this one."

Rizzo nodded. "That's why I had to leave it up to him. It's got to be his call. Me, I can bail out. I'd miss the job, and we'd have to tighten our belts on my pension. But you've still got a few years left teaching, and we'd manage. And when you retire, we sell the house and by then move in with our rich doctor-daughter."

She smiled. "I can't see that happening, Joe. But I see your point. It does have to be Mike's call."

They sat in silence for a while, Jennifer sipping her coffee, Joe eyeing the still idle Chesterfield on the table before him. Then Jennifer looked up, a gleam in her eye.

"You know, Joe," she said, leaning forward slightly. "This doesn't sound quite like you—the crafty Joe Rizzo caught between a rock and a hard place. Are you telling me everything?"

Rizzo smiled, reached for the cigarette, and stood up. Digging the lighter from his pocket, he turned and headed for the side door and his smoking sanctuary beside the garage.

He stopped at the doorway and winked at her.

"Well, we'll see, hon. The next few days could change things. When Mike gets back to New York, I'll hear him out. Then, we'll see."

TWO DAYS later, Joe Rizzo parked his Camry at the corner of Chambers and Centre Streets in lower Manhattan and tossed his NYPD plaque on the dashboard. He took the plastic shopping bag from the passenger seat and glanced at his wristwatch: nine-twenty.

He crossed Chambers and strolled slowly passed City Hall and its parklike surroundings. When he reached the concrete security barriers and blue-and-white NYPD radio car guarding the hall's east access, he angled across the off-ramp of the Brooklyn Bridge, climbing the steps to its lower promenade. Eyeing an empty bench, Joe sat in the bright sunlight watching as the morning crowd of workers and joggers, bicyclists and dog walkers went about their Tuesday-morning routines.

The bench Rizzo occupied at the foot of the bridge was only a short walk from the square, craggy building known as One Police Plaza.

After some ten or twelve minutes, a shadow fell upon him. He raised his eyes to the ruddy face of Inspector David Manning.

"Rizzo?" the man asked.

Joe smiled and indicated the seat next to him on the bench.

"Yes, sir," he said, a pleasant smile on his face.

Manning sat. He adjusted his suit jacket and extended a hand to Joe. "Well, it's nice to meet you at last, Joe," he said in a cordial tone. "Although why you insisted on meeting here, and not in my office, eludes me."

Rizzo chuckled. "Well, Inspector, it's like I said when I called. I'm gonna clear up a few things. That'll be one of them."

"Alright," Manning said. "What's on your mind?"

Rizzo bent and picked up the grocery bag from the ground near his feet. He offered it to Manning. "I've got somethin' here for your pal, Councilman Daily."

Manning dropped his gaze to the bag, then raised his eyes to Rizzo.

"What makes you think he's a pal?" he asked.

Rizzo smiled. "Associate, then. Okay? Here, take it."

Manning glanced around, his eyes suddenly narrowing and fearful.

"Relax, Inspector," Rizzo said. "If this was a setup, I woulda come to your office. We're sittin' outside with traffic all around us, cars coming over the bridge, the wind blowin' and a jackhammer poundin' half a block away—there ain't a wire in the world could pick us up if you keep your voice down. Go ahead," Rizzo urged. "Pat me down."

Manning scanned Rizzo's face, then seemed to relax. "Why don't you just put it down, Joe? The bag, I mean. Here, on the bench."

Rizzo complied, placing it between them on the bench. The strong summer breeze coming off the East River stirred the thin plastic bag.

"There," Joe said with a smile.

"So what's in it?" Manning asked.

"It's a shoe box I came across while I was lookin' for Rosanne Daily. It's got her diary in it. And the cash."

"Cash?" the inspector asked, his voice neutral.

Joe smiled. "Yeah, Boss. Cash. All that was left from what she took outta Daily's safe the night she disappeared."

Manning's eyes fell to the bag. He slowly opened it and slipped the box top off. Looking inside, he spoke without lifting his gaze.

"How much is here?" he asked.

"Twenty thousand. Every nickel she had," Rizzo said, his voice casual, his eyes fixed on the man's profile.

Manning looked up, his eyes hard. "Twenty thousand dollars, eh?" he asked.

Rizzo nodded. "Yeah," he said. "There was more at one time. Probably a lot more. The kid dropped twenty-two grand on a custom Harley-Davidson for some cretin she was fuckin'. God knows how much more she pissed away over the weeks."

Manning frowned and glanced again at the tightly packed hundred-dollar bills. "What makes you think she took the money from Daily's safe?" he asked as he looked back to Rizzo.

Rizzo shrugged. "That's what the motorcycle cretin told me she said when she bought him the bike."

Manning sighed. "So, now you and McQueen think what? You seeing bogeymen, Joe?"

Rizzo shook his head. "McQueen don't think a fuckin' thing. He don't even know this money exists. I made sure of that."

"And why is that, Joe?" Manning asked. Rizzo detected a slight relaxation in the man's tone and smiled. Rizzo knew Manning was growing more comfortable with what he now perceived as just another cop doing business. A familiar element for him.

"Because as sharp as he is, he's still a kid. Kids are too unpredictable. And I'm too old for surprises. I got a feelin', Inspector, you ain't going to surprise me."

Manning leaned back into the bench and sighed again. After a moment, he spoke in a soft, low tone. A city bus rumbled and thundered along Centre Street just to their right.

"Make your pitch, Rizzo," he said.

Rizzo smiled. "Okay, here it is. Daily has an election comin'. It could be a little embarrassing, this missing daughter episode. Especially if the money thing gets out. Some reporter starts poking around Rosanne's recent past, God knows what shit hits the fan."

"There are any number of explanations for that money, Joe . . ." Manning said, his voice hardening.

"Yeah, I know. Like Watergate and Iran-Contra and Whitewater and all the other bullshit explanations. That isn't the point. The point is, does Daily wanna get into all that? When it could all just be avoided?"

Manning fingered the plastic bag, then ran a hand through his hair. "And how could it be avoided, Joe? In your opinion."

Rizzo laughed. "Okay. I can do that. Offer an opinion, sort of."

They sat in silence for a moment as a young mother, baby stroller before her, jogged past them onto the pedestrian walkway toward Brooklyn, a half mile away. Then Rizzo turned back to Manning.

"My opinion is this: You take that money to Daily. You tell him, as far as I'm concerned, it's his dough, and how it came to be in his safe with the rest of the money the kid blew is none a my business. You tell him it's my pleasure to help him out. So he gets reelected. I'm just happy to help foster good government for our fine city."

Manning smiled. "Very noble, Joe. I'm sure he'll be appreciative."

Rizzo laughed. "Yeah, well, I figured. Matter a fact, I even got an idea how he could show me just how very appreciative he is. You, too, as a matter of fact."

Manning frowned. "Me? What makes you think—"

"Let's just cut the shit, okay, Boss? I've had enough fresh air and sunshine for today. I'd like to get off this fuckin' bridge before some rag-head decides to fly a plane into it."

Manning casually knotted the bag's handles closed.

"Spit it out, then, Rizzo," he said.

Joe smiled. "I'm not greedy, Boss. I just want what you offered McQueen during that phone conversation. I don't want any of it slipping your mind. I want that prick, DeMayo, off my back. I want my I.A.D. file closed and shit-canned. And I want McQueen transferred to the Plaza. Someplace he can't hurt himself. Policy and Planning, maybe. Something like that. He's a college boy, NYU no less, and he dresses nice. He'll fit right in."

"Anything else?"

"Yeah, Inspector. Terrorist Task Force. You hook me up to it. Unofficially official. But I stay at the Six-Two lockin' up skells as usual for six more months. During that time, on my way home every night, maybe I swing by the Brooklyn side of the Verrazano Bridge, make sure it's all secure, no Jihadists around. You pay me overtime, process it through the Homeland Security federal grant money. Nobody at the Six-Two ever knows about it. I want my final average salary jacked up about twenty-five grand. Then in six months, I retire. With years on the job plus my military credit, I get out at over sixty percent of my salary. Sixty percent of that twenty-five overtime is fifteen thousand dollars a year on top of my regular forty-nine, fifty grand pension. For the rest of my life."

Rizzo smiled and reached for his cigarettes. "Chump change by Daily's standards. He'll be amused by the simple needs of the workin' class." Now Joe lit a Chesterfield.

"Deal?" he asked, blowing smoke at Manning.

"That's it?" Manning asked. "Nothing more?"

Rizzo smiled. "No," he said. "Just be sure to tell the good councilman how I sympathize with his predicament. What some people might assume about all that loose cash, I mean. After all, I've been living under some false assumptions myself lately. I know how frustrating it can be."

Manning stood, brushing his pants and straightening his suit jacket.

"Just suppose, Joe," he said in conversational tones, "I—we, Daily and I—were to tell you to go fuck yourself? What then?"

Rizzo stood slowly and stepped close to Manning. The inspector held his ground. Rizzo leaned his face to mere inches from Manning's.

"Well, Boss," he said, his voice an evil hiss, "why don't you just try it and find out?"

Manning held Rizzo's eyes. In a moment, he responded in a soft, cautious tone.

"I'll be in touch, Joe," he said, taking the bag into his grasp. Then he turned and walked off toward Police Plaza.

Rizzo walked slowly back to his Camry and climbed in. He took his NYPD plaque from the dash and placed it in the glove box.

Then he reached into his pocket and removed a legal-sized white envelope thick with bills. Smiling, he recalled McQueen's remark about the Cornell bursar.

He tossed the twelve thousand into the glove box and drove slowly back to Brooklyn.

RIZZO SPENT the next few days busying himself around the house on projects he had long promised Jennifer he would attend to. On Friday morning, as the first of his and McQueen's two weeks leave drew to a close, he was preparing to paint his den. Jennifer and the girls were out and he had the house to himself.

Just as he was about to open the paint can, the bedroom phone sounded. Sighing, he crossed the hall and went to answer it.

"Hello?" he said.

"Joe? Is that you?"

Rizzo frowned. "Yeah." He paused. "Who's this?"

"Ralph. Ralph DeMayo, Joe. How the hell are you?"

Rizzo dropped onto the edge of the bed. His eyes narrowed as he spoke.

"What do you want, DeMayo?" he asked.

DeMayo's chuckle came through the line. "Relax, Joe. You sound a little tense."

"When a lightweight like you can tense me up, DeMayo, I'll turn in my papers. What do you want?"

"Well, Joe, I just want to share my good news with you. You know, I been with I.A.D. for three years. Three fuckin' years in this leper colony. I've had a transfer request in for two years now."

Rizzo laughed. "Transfer?" he said. "To where: the fuckin' Gestapo?"

DeMayo returned the laugh. "Naw, nothing that work-intense. No, I always figured I belonged on Mayoral Security Detail, Joe. You know, with the rising stars, hobnobbin' with the big shots and all those Brazil waxed administrative assistant broads they got working around City Hall."

"You got some kinda point here, Ralph?" Rizzo asked.

"Yeah, Joe, yeah, I do. See, funny thing. Out of the blue, I get a call from Inspector Polanski. He's the security detail commander over at City Hall. Seems my transfer request just landed on his desk. Magiclike. Polanski was impressed, figured me for just the guy to come on board guarding our beloved mayor at all the cocktail parties. I start in two weeks."

Rizzo sat up straighter. He kept his voice casual.

"Two weeks, eh, Ralph?" he said. "Doesn't leave much time to clear off your desk."

"No, Joe, it sure don't. And I would hate to leave a lotta loose ends laying around for the next guy. It's like my work ethic, you know? So what I'm doing is, I'm weeding through a lot of pending stuff. Seeing what I can put to bed."

"Really?" Joe asked.

"Yeah. Like for instance, I was just looking over your file, yesterday, and I think I've covered all the bases there, Joe. I really do. I even talked to The Chink about the whole thing. And you know, Joe, I don't think there's anywhere else to go with it."

"Is that right, Ralph."

Rizzo could almost see DeMayo's crooked smile. "Yeah, Joe, that's right. So, what I did was, I wrote my final report and marked your jacket 'unfounded.' I sent it up to the captain, and he signed off on it. I want you to know you're all righteous again, Joe. Sorry for any sweat I wrung out of you. Nothing personal, you understand. Just doing my job."

Rizzo let air out through his lips. "Good-bye, Ralph. Plant a nice big wet one on the mayor's ass for me."

He hung up the phone on DeMayo's laugh.

# CHAPTER TWENTY-ONE

### *August*

JENNIFER RIZZO SMILED as she opened her front door.

"Hello, Mike," she said, ushering McQueen into the foyer. "Welcome back. How are your parents?"

"Fine, thanks. They're really happy down there," Mike answered. "Very relaxing atmosphere."

"Well," Jennifer said, noting the dark circles and stress lines the young detective's eyes swam in, "that's wonderful. Right this way, Joe's expecting you. He's down in the basement, probably smoking and running that ridiculous fan he thinks he fools me with."

McQueen laughed perfunctorily. "Yeah, well . . ." he said, following Jennifer to the heavy wooden door that led to the basement.

Jennifer swung the door inward and leaned slightly over the staircase. She shook her head as the faint odor of burning tobacco touched her nostrils.

"Joe," she called. "Mike is here."

Rizzo's voice resounded from deep in the basement. "Okay, send him down."

Jennifer stepped aside as Mike moved past her. "I'm going out, Joe," she said. "I need to get to Sears. I'll see you later. And put out the damn cigarette."

"Okay, Jen," Rizzo responded.

She sighed and began to close the door. As Mike descended the steps, she spoke softly to his back.

"You guys will have the house to yourselves, Mike," she said. "There's no one else home."

McQueen made his way to Joe's small basement office. They greeted each other warmly, genuinely glad to see each other. For McQueen, the sight of the older cop, calm and confident-looking, was comforting. He sat opposite Joe at the cluttered metal desk, the soft whirling of the desk fan and slight hum of the fluorescent lights a soothing backdrop.

Rizzo sat down behind the desk, reflecting on the dark circles beneath his young partner's eyes. He smiled at Mike as he spoke.

"You look beat, kid. Rough two weeks down on the Bayou?"

McQueen returned a smile weakly and shrugged.

"I've had easier weeks, Joe," he said.

Rizzo laughed. "Yeah, Mike, I guess you have."

Some moments of silence passed as Rizzo waited for Mike to speak.

"What'd you do with the cash, Joe?" he asked at last.

Rizzo shrugged. "What do you think? I gave it to Manning. I told him you never saw it, didn't know shit about it. So if it ever does come up, Mike, just play dumb. You never saw it, period. Then I reminded him about that phone call he made to you. Just to sort of jar his memory a bit."

McQueen leaned forward. "What'd he say?"

"Well, you know, in this business it's usually more about what somebody *does* than about what they say. He didn't say much of anything. But here's what he *did*."

Rizzo went on to tell Mike about the call from DeMayo and the closing of Joe's case. When he was done, he saw Mike smile. Some of the tension ran out from the young cop's face.

"So he went for it," McQueen said.

"Yep," Joe responded happily. "He went for it. Along with a few other things." Here Joe explained his arrangement to pad his salary with phantom overtime hours and then, in six months, put in his retirement papers.

"That's great, Joe. I'm really happy for you."

Rizzo nodded. "Well, thanks, Mike. But the deal ain't done until you cross over the river. To the Plaza. Just like you wanted."

Rizzo recapped further details of his conversation with Inspector Manning.

"Figure a month or so. Tops. They'll want it all in bed before the No-vember election. Congratulations, Mike. You're on your way."

This time McQueen's smile was bittersweet. "Yeah, Joe," he said. "On my way. But to where? I think that's the next question."

Rizzo shook a cigarette loose from its pack, raised it to his lips, and struck the Zippo. "*One* of the questions, Mike," he said as he lit the Chesterfield. "But not the next one. The next question is: What did you decide? About the tape, I mean. What are we going to do with this prick Daily."

McQueen nodded. "Yeah, Joe, well, I have made a decision," he said.

"Did you talk it over with anybody first?" he said.

McQueen nodded. "A friend."

Rizzo frowned slightly. "Well, okay," he said in a neutral tone. They sat in silence for a moment. Then McQueen sighed.

"You know, Joe, it was politics that got me my detective shield in the first place."

Rizzo nodded. "I know," he said in the same neutral tone.

"A politician. The friggin' mayor himself. That's the way things work."

Again Rizzo nodded. "I know that, too. I've known it for a long time. I watched my grandfather turn just from being a good cop to being a good politician. He rose to chief of detectives in Brooklyn and retired as deputy inspector. When I came on the job, he had enough friends in the department still owed him favors and he got me *my* gold shield."

He saw the look on McQueen's face and smiled. "Yeah, kid, what'd ya think—it was my talent and personality? It was a hook, just like everybody else."

Rizzo leaned across the desk and softened his tones when once again he spoke.

"You know, Mike," he said. "We all wind up where we belong in this life. I don't know how it works out, but it does. Everybody, and not just cops, winds up right where they belong. So if you belonged in the Six-Two, that's where you'da wound up. If it's the Plaza where you belonged, then that's what it will be. In the meantime, guys like you and me, we just wander through people's lives looking for things they wish never existed in the first place. That's what we do. And on the way, we just have to be who we are. The rest will work itself out."

After a moment had passed, Rizzo spoke again, softly.

"So, tell me, Mike. Who are you?"

Mike sat silent for a moment. He sighed before speaking, and Rizzo could feel the burden on the young man's shoulders. Yet he remained silent, and waited.

"There was this kid once," Mike said, his eyes hooded and tired-looking. "Hispanic, maybe nineteen. I was riding a sector car in the Village back then, me and a guy named Bobby Noe. We partnered for about two years. Well, we knew this kid was dealing a little grass to the preppies from Jersey and Long Island, down by the Café Wha? but we looked the other way. After all, we were in the Village and you had to prioritize. So one day, Noe hears that the kid started moving H and some crack. We check him out, and sure enough, he's holding ten bags of heroin and twenty vials of crack, not to mention a sack full of grass. We arrest him and he gets an attitude with us, mouths off a little, so Noe, who never had much patience, gives him a little smack. Just to shut him up. So we're heading for the house, I'm in the backseat with the kid, Noe is driving. And all of a sudden, the kid turns on me. 'This is bullshit, man,' he says. 'Bullshit.' So I say to him, 'Hector,' I just remembered his name was Hector. I say, 'Hector, how do you figure it's bullshit? You're dealing heroin on the street, scaring all the tourists, where's the part that's bullshit?'"

Rizzo smiled. "And his answer was . . . ?"

McQueen chuckled, a sad, unhappy sound. "His answer was, 'Why don't you pretend like I'm some hooked-up white rich kid from NYU, then you'd drive me home and daddy'd grease your palm for you.'"

Rizzo nodded. "Kid wasn't too far off base. Bet that's happened a few times."

McQueen spoke again, leaning forward in his chair. Rizzo saw a new animation in his partner's eyes, strong enough to push away the fatigue.

"Yeah, Joe," he said. "But at the time, the kid really pissed me off. Who did he think I was, some two-dollar hooker? Now, though, now I get his point. There's so much crap in the water you can't see anymore. It's like some giant polluted lake nothing can survive in."

A few seconds of silence passed, the two cops gazing at each other

over the cluttered desk. The fan and faint hum from the overhead fluorescents was the only sound they could hear.

"That's why we have to go to the feds, Joe. Because of that kid. Because of all the people like that kid. If we don't go to the feds with that
tape, we could never lock up another soul. Not ever. No matter what they
did."

Rizzo sat back in his seat. He felt his jaw muscles relaxing. He smiled
at Mike.

"You sure, kid? Hundred percent?"

McQueen nodded, smiling sadly. "Hundred percent. We'll take it in
as soon as you think the time is right."

Rizzo grinned. "So, we're riding out from Goliad and back into the
Alamo? Like a couple of crazy heroes?"

"I guess so, Joe. You always wanted to be that guy—what was his
name?"

"Bonham. James Butler Bonham. That's right, Mike. I always wanted
to be him. But you got to remember, that was just a game, and I was just
a kid. As a kid, Bonham going back in made sense. As an adult, I always
sort of wondered: What was the guy thinking about? What we got here
is no game, and neither one of us are kids. If I wanted to be a fuckin'
hero, I'da been a fireman."

McQueen looked puzzled. "I'm not following you, Joe. What are you
saying?"

"Well, Mike, you remember when we first caught this case? Back
when The Swede made his pitch? We knew it was political, we knew it
smelled bad, remember? And we decided to take it on anyway? I told
you something then. Do you remember?"

McQueen shook his head. "No, Joe, I don't think so. What?"

"I told you I wouldn't let us get hurt on this. I assured you of that, as
I recall."

"And?"

"If we go to the feds with this, we will get hurt. You more than me. We
go to the feds with this, your career is dead in the water. Some hard-on at
the Plaza can let six months, a year go by, then set you up on something,
get you jammed up real good. Indicted maybe. Who the fuck knows?"

281

McQueen felt his cheeks flushing red. "So what? We knew that all along, we've discussed it ten times, at least. How come all of a sudden you're having reservations? Were you hoping I'd be the one to cave on this, I'd want to play it safe? Get you off the hook with I.A.D. and you could tell yourself it was my idea and you just went along for my sake? Is that supposed to ease your conscience? What's going on here, Joe?"

Rizzo laughed and held his hands palms out toward McQueen.

"Relax, Partner, relax. Hear me out. Trust me a few minutes more, okay? You can start preparing your apology while I explain it. It'll save you some time when I'm done."

McQueen's face was grim, his jaw set. "I'm listening," he said.

"When we first got the tape from Father Charles and listened to it, the idea started to come to me. You see, there were *two* legit priests we ran into on this case. Remember Jovino? Father Tillio Jovino down at the Non-Combat Zone runaway shelter in Red Hook?"

McQueen's face puzzled over. "You mean the guy who extorted the donations from us?"

"That priest, yeah. Well, I went to see him last week right after I left The Chink at the Starlight. I told Jovino there was a slight chance I would be comin' across some evidence in the near future, evidence against Daily, from Rosanne. I explained to the good Father that if I did, I had a problem. I didn't get real specific. But I told him, I figured with him running that shelter, it wouldn't be unreasonable for anyone to believe that Rosanne's little goody bag could fall into his hands. And if it did, he'd be obligated to turn it over to the proper authorities. Funny thing was, his eyes lit up when I told him about it. Now, don't get me wrong, I'm not suggestin' the good Father is looking for any un-Christianlike revenge, but it seems he's come across Daily a time or two in the past. Like the time when Jovino was trying to get some money for his shelter. It seems Councilman Daily got wind of it, and suddenly, this private, for-profit agency submits a proposal for a similar shelter, funded entirely by the city, and at roughly twice the amount Tillio Jovino would ever need. He figured Daily was in for a kickback so he started up enough of a stink that Daily got cautious. Jovino had this newspaperman friend, an editor at the *Times* that served with Jovino in Vietnam. So the guy called the good councilman. Next sound they heard was the council vote authorizing a contribution to Jovino's operation. The whole episode left a bad taste in the priest's mouth, and he's been bothered by it ever since. He felt he should have done more to try and redeem Daily's soul. Or at least kick his ass, as Jovino phrased it. Well, he said he'd help us. He even said he'd visit Rosanne at Gracie Square and offer her a little spiritual guidance. Not to mention establishing a direct link between them, and a priest-confessor relationship to boot."

Rizzo crushed out his cigarette.

"Rosanne is so screwed up, she probably won't even remember what she did with any of this stuff. We're clear on the box we got from Father Charles and handed over to Manning. I read the second diary and tore out the page implicating Daily. Remember the first diary we found in her room? With that page torn out? We wondered what she needed to hide from her parents considering all the other shit in there. Well, that was it. She made reference to him being a crook in that first diary, and she couldn't let him find out she was on to him. So she tore it out. And when she started her next diary, she made damn sure to take it with her when she left."

Rizzo held up a hand to cut Mike off as the young cop tried to speak.

"Wait," he said to McQueen. "Let me finish. Six months from now, if you still want to, we could take the tape to Jovino. He takes it to the feds, says he found it in some old stuff some kid left behind at his shelter. Remember, Mike, we filed no official DD-fives on this investigation: there's no link between us and Jovino. So after the feds get the tape, the shit hits the fan. All of Daily's pals run for cover, especially his buddies at the Plaza. If some of them begin to suspect it was us behind it, they'll figure it was more me than you. And I'll be retired by then. Plus Daily's Plaza flunkies already squashed the I.A.D. case on me. None of them will wanna have to explain that, it would expose them too much. They'll be all too happy to avoid tracing anything back to us, and let it all rest in peace. Most of them are too stupid to imagine this story could be anything *but* the truth. Once Daily gets jammed up, he's on his own. Everybody runs for cover and tries to save their own ass. Even Rosanne won't have to fear him anymore. He'll be history. Him and half the crooked politicians in the city."

Now Rizzo smiled and softened his voice.

"It's perfect, Mike. We're even covered with that psycho, The Surgeon. If he ever tries to squeeze us over the box he told us about, we'll tell him fuck off. I personally turned that box over to a supervising police inspector."

McQueen smiled grimly. "To save himself, Manning would have to say he gave the box to Daily, the father and legal guardian of an incompetent person."

Rizzo nodded. "There would be no reason for him to deny it. We could easily prove he was pulling the strings on the Rosanne investigation. Hell, he set it up with D'Antonio. And up to then, nothing he did was illegal. Irregular, maybe, but not illegal. Any lawyer with a brain would tell him to admit he took the box from me, recovered property from an investigation, and returned it to the kid's father."

They sat in silence for a few moments, McQueen digesting it all, running Joe's words through his mind. Then he leaned forward in his seat, a frown on his lips. When he spoke, anger tugged at his words, exasperation in his tone.

"You had this figured out all along, and you didn't tell me? Do you have any idea what I've been going through the last couple of weeks? Any idea? I swear to Christ, Joe, I feel like punching your fucking lights out!"

Rizzo chuckled. "And you probably could, too, Mike. But afterward, you'd know you'd been in a fight, I can guarantee you that."

They sat in silence while Mike cooled down. When he spoke again, it was in a calmer, conversational tone. Rizzo noted the relief in the young man's voice and body language. It made him feel good.

"You could have saved me a lot of grief here, Joe, if you'd have let me in on your little plan."

Rizzo nodded. "Sure I could have, kid. But then you'd never know. You'd never know how you would have played it. You'd never know just what kind of a cop you really are."

McQueen smiled grimly and looked deeply into Rizzo's eyes.

"And you, Joe," he said softly. "You'd never know what kind of a cop I was, either, would you?"

Rizzo compressed his lips and nodded. "That's right, Mike. But I know now. We both know now. See, I *had* to see what you would do. At your age, it's good you want to be noble—it shows character. And character doesn't change, only circumstances change. So, when you get older, when you're my age and you been fighting off mortgages and doctor bills and tuition—not to mention crooked bosses and lying citizens—you'll adjust to it. We can joust windmills, Mike, and lose, or we can fight dirty and maybe win once in a while. That's what this is, a dirty fight. We sneak the ball into their court and we walk away. It's the best we can do."

Rizzo paused for a moment before continuing.

"This is a perfect example of what I'm sayin'. This whole Rosanne business. Look at what we've done here, Mike. We saved that poor girl's life. We got me out from under a bum rap with those I.A.D. vultures. And we're getting you the job you deserve, a job you'd never have gotten on merit alone." He nodded his head as he spoke again.

"Did we break any rules?" he asked softly. "Cut any corners? Sure. But Mike," he said, leaning forward slightly and lowering his voice. "That's how it's done. It is what it is."

After a moment or two, Mike raised his eyes to Rizzo's.

"One thing, Joe," he asked quietly.

"Yeah?"

"When you started telling me all this, you said something. Something you need to explain."

"Oh, yeah, Mike? What's that?"

"You said, 'In six months, if you still want to, we turn the tape over to Jovino.' What do you mean, if I still want to?"

"Like I said, Mike. Circumstances change. Six months from now you'll be over at the Plaza in a nice sharp suit, dictating memos to some secretary ain't wearin' no panties. You might want to rethink things. That's all I was sayin'."

McQueen shook his head. "You also said now you know—*we* know— what kind of cop I am. What about that?"

Rizzo reached for another cigarette. "Yeah, Mike," he said softly. "We know what kind of a cop you are going *into* the Plaza. We still have to see what kind of a cop you'll be after you've been there awhile." He paused and lit the cigarette. "See, Mike, it never really ends. The test, I mean. It grinds a lotta guys down." He paused again. "So, we'll see. In six months, you call me. And we'll see."

They sat silently for a few moments, a sadness settling on McQueen. His eyes fell to the crumpled pack of Chesterfields lying beside the whirling fan next to Rizzo.

"I haven't had a smoke since I was a freshman in college," he said.

Rizzo smiled and tossed the pack to McQueen. He produced his lighter and struck a flame.

"One won't hurt," he said.

McQueen placed a cigarette between his lips and leaned over the desk to accept Joe's light. He pulled tentatively on it and sat back in his chair, expelling smoke slowly.

They sat and smoked without speaking. After a few moments, Mike broke the silence.

"You know, Joe," he said. "This stuff is universal."

Rizzo squinted. "What stuff?"

"All this political bullshit. I was talking to my dad last week. When I first got down there. I guess he suspected something was bothering me. Something from the job." He looked up from the burning cigarette in his hand. His steely blue eyes met Joe's.

"You know what he said?" he asked softly.

Rizzo shrugged. "No, Mike, I guess I don't."

"He said he and my mother had met some U.S. senator. Some guy from the county they live in. My parents have been helping out with some local union stuff down there, and this senator is a big supporter of labor. And vice versa."

Rizzo laughed. "Let me guess the rest," he said happily. "Your old man said something like, 'So, Mikey, if you need a favor sometime, maybe ol' Senator Beauregard B. Blowhard can help.'"

Now McQueen laughed. "Something like that," he said, shaking his head slowly.

"Well," Joe said, "I'd keep that in mind, I was you. If this Daily thing ever gets hot, that senator could maybe be a cool breeze."

Again they sat in silence, and again it was McQueen who spoke first.

"One more thing, Joe," he said, his voice soft. "I gotta ask you one more thing."

Rizzo nodded. "Sure, Mike. Ask."

"Morelli. I just don't get it. I know you're no angel, Joe. I know you'll bend a rule, play outside the lines sometimes. But you're not a fool. This whole mess with Daily could have been played out a lot differently if you weren't in that I.A.D. jam-up he got you into. Why'd you carry him so long, Joe? Why do you owe him?"

Rizzo sighed and sat back slowly in his chair. He laced his fingers together and laid his hands across his stomach.

After a moment, he spoke. His voice was soft, almost wistful. McQueen had never heard the tone from the older cop before.

"Couple more weeks, Mike," he said, "will be one full year we're workin' together."

McQueen smiled. "Happy anniversary," he said lightly.

Rizzo's answering smile only touched at his lips, then disappeared.

"Not very long, really. I've worked with guys a lot longer than that," Joe said. "A lot longer."

McQueen sat silently. After a moment, Rizzo sighed heavily.

"What the hell," he said. "All these friggin' priests running through this case, I guess I got confession on my mind."

He reached to the ashtray and took up his cigarette, crushing it out gently as he continued.

"I never told anybody this, Mike. It was never nobody's business."

McQueen felt a slight discomfort. The sudden vulnerability he sensed in Rizzo was unsettling, almost frightening, and he wondered how he had provoked it with his question.

"Look, Joe," he said, "if you'd rather . . ."

Rizzo raised a hand. "No, Mike. It's okay. I want you to know." After a slight pause, he continued.

"We're different generations, Mike, and maybe this'll sound lightweight to you. But believe me, it's heavy with me. See, my whole life is my family. Jennifer and the girls. So many guys let the job destroy their families. Too many. But over the years, Jennifer has been my oasis. No matter what the job brought, no matter what I saw or what I did or felt, at the end of the day, I had my family. My Jennifer. My girls. My little house and my peace of mind. It's what's kept me sane. It's what's kept me going."

McQueen nodded. "Okay," he said. "I can understand that."

Rizzo slipped yet another Chesterfield from the pack. He lit it slowly and inhaled deeply. Then, smoke tumbling from his lips, he continued.

"I almost threw it all away, Mike. About twenty years ago. Marie was very young, my middle girl Jessica about a year old. Carol wasn't born yet."

He shook his head, remembering. "I think it was that screwy comedian, that guy Robin Williams said, 'God gave man a brain and a penis, but only enough blood to run one at a time.'"

McQueen laughed. "True enough," he said.

Rizzo's smile was tinged with sadness. "Yeah," he said.

After a moment, he continued. "Well, anyway, I was in uniform back then, workin' with Morelli. He was a very different guy then, a completely different person. Good father, good husband. Great friggin' cop: brains, balls, compassion. I learned a lot from him."

"So," McQueen asked tentatively. "What happened?"

Rizzo dragged again on his Chesterfield. "Well, back in those days, Brooklyn was a lot different, too. A lot worse. 'Specially the precinct we were working. Me and Morelli were very active, lots of arrests, lots of action. We spent half our time at the emergency room over at Kings County Hospital. Stabbing victims, accidents, gunshots—everything. Place was like a fuckin' M.A.S.H. unit back then. Best trauma and gunshot ER in the borough, maybe the whole city. If a cop got shot two blocks from some hospital and five miles from KCH, they would throw the guy in back of a radio car and rush him over to KCH."

Rizzo's head shook unconsciously and McQueen saw a long-forgotten memory flitter through Joe's eyes. After a moment, Rizzo continued.

"There was this nurse working there," he said softly. "Cathy. Cathy Andersen." He paused for a while and smiled, some of the old familiar Rizzo returning to Mike's eye. "You know, Mike, I looked a lot different then. Forty pounds lighter, all my fuckin' hair on my head 'stead of sproutin' on my back. I was a good-looking cop, Mike, in my blue uniform. You know how it is, you been there."

Mike smiled. "Yes," he said. "I've been there."

"Well," Joe continued, "one thing led to another. She was single, year or two younger than me. We got involved."

McQueen shrugged. "Okay," he said. "Shit happens. But what's it got to do with Morelli?"

"Yeah, well, I'm getting to that. See, Mike, at first, I was just bangin' her. Cathy, I mean. I had some headaches at home. Two young kids, a mortgage, a wife all frustrated 'cause she had to put her career on hold. Plus, the job. All that shit. And Cathy was like . . . I don't know, like that oasis I was talking about. Anyway, after a while, I started to think I was in love with her. She loved me. I seriously started to consider walking away from Jen and the girls. Cathy was such a sweet kid, Mike. She never broke my balls to leave Jen, never showed up at the precinct screaming or makin' a scene like some of the other guys' goomadas. Nothing like that. I was crazy for her then. But, now, looking back, I see it was more like I told you with Amy. An infatuation. If I was single, if I was never with Jen, yeah, maybe Cathy and I woulda been good together. I guess I'll never know."

Here he leaned forward in his seat. His eyes implored McQueen, and the young cop felt ill-at-ease, awkward. He wished he had never asked about any of this.

"But believe me, Mike," Rizzo said. "I *do* know with Jen. She's my life. I love her in a way I hope you'll love someone someday. Morelli, he was on my ass from day one. He begged me to drop Cathy. He even refused to cover me. You know, after a tour I'd want to tell Jen I was havin' a few beers with Johnny, be home late, stuff like that. But Johnny wouldn't do it."

"So," McQueen asked, "what finally happened?"

Rizzo smiled, his eyes softening. "Johnny Morelli saved my life," he said softly. "He went direct to Cathy and talked to her. He told her what I had at home, two babies, a great wife, a future. He asked her if she really loved me. When she said yes, he told her to show how much. Break it off. Send me back to my future."

Rizzo's brown eyes hooded slightly as he concluded.

"And she did. Cut me off, cold and final. I was furious with Johnny. The guys had to pull us off each other in the precinct ready room. That afternoon I went to the shift commander. Next day, I was riding with a new partner."

Rizzo's sad face glistened under the fluorescent.

"Broke Johnny's heart," he said. "But he took it. He took it because he knew he did the right thing for *me*. That's all that mattered to him. That's the kind of friend Johnny Morelli was. That's the kind of man he was. Until this fuckin' job ate his heart and spit him into the gutter."

Now Rizzo shook his head bitterly. "And when it was my turn to help him, what'd I do?"

McQueen saw color coming into Rizzo's face.

"I fucked it up. That's what I did," he said softly. "I thought I was doing the right thing. But I fucked it up."

They sat in silence. Mike leaned forward and crushed out his cigarette among the ashes and butts in the ashtray. He searched for words, but could find none. He felt his emotions, so tested over the last weeks, welling uncomfortably in his chest. He sought casualness and a light tone when at last he spoke.

"Well, Joe," he said. "You have to admit one thing, Partner, with this Daily thing, despite all the bullshit, there is a 'right' and we *are* doing it."

Rizzo laughed joylessly and pushed back deeper into his seat. He took a deep breath and let it out slowly, then shook his head.

"Well, Mike, I wouldn't put it quite like that," he said.

Smiling, he leaned across the desk and looked deeply into the eyes of his young partner as he spoke.

"All things considered, the way we're gonna handle this isn't right, and it isn't wrong.

"It just *is*, Partner.

"It just is. . . ."